DATE			

THE CRITICAL WAY IN RELIGION

Testing and Questing

Duncan Howlett

Prometheus Books
1203 Kensington Avenue
Buffalo, New York 14215

Books by Duncan Howlett

Man Against the Church: The Struggle to Free Man's Religious Spirit
The Essenes and Christianity: An Interpretation of the Dead Sea Scrolls
The Fourth American Faith
No Greater Love: The James Reeb Story

Published by Prometheus Books
1203 Kensington Avenue, Buffalo, New York 14215

Library of Congress Catalog Number: 80-7460
ISBN 0-87975-133-9
Printed in the United States of America

To Our Children
Margaret
Albert
Richard
Carolyn

to their children

and their children's children

Contents

Part IV
The Critical Way

Preface

This book outlines a religious tradition that has been evolving for at least twenty-five centuries and probably much longer. Many think it secular; some think it antireligious. Yet it is deeply religious and it is the religious outlook of millions today. The formal allegiance of these people may be Christian, Buddhist, or any other, but they share a common commitment to the way of inquiry, criticism, and imagination in religion. They believe profoundly in testing and speculating in every aspect of thought and experience, religion not excepted. This tradition has no name of its own. I have called it the "Critical Way in Religion" and have contrasted it with the "Ecclesiastical Way" with which it has been in conflict from the beginning.

The exposition that follows is the result of a lifelong effort on my part to identify the critical way in religion, to trace its development, to state its principles, and to test their validity. Part I deals with our human fallibility, the aspect of experience that requires us to be careful in all things, religion included, lest we fall into error.

Part II is historical. It relates in as brief a compass as possible the origin and development of the critical tradition and of its interaction with organized religion and with the culture of which, in the West, it has been so much a part.

Part III deals with the beliefs and principles of the ecclesiastical way in religion that stand in opposition to those of the critical way. Part IV states the basic principles of the critical way. Each of the four parts of the book can stand as a separate unit, yet all four are closely interrelated and interdependent.

The many references required by a book like this are set forth in detail in the Notes which appear as a unit following the text. My indebtedness to the world of scholarship is evident there.

In a different sense, I have called on two earlier books of my own, *The Essenes and Christianity* (New York: Harper and Brothers, 1957), and *The Fourth American Faith* (New York: Harper & Row, 1964). Neither needs to be read in order to follow the argument developed here, although both, *The Fourth American Faith* in particular, develop in some detail points that are basic to an understanding of the critical way.

As with all writers in fields like religion, history, and culture, my indebtedness to friends and acquaintances, over and beyond that to the world of scholarship, is very great. There are, however, a few individuals deserving of particular mention. They are:

Melvin Arnold, former President of Harper & Row and editor of their Torchbook series, who launched me on the writing of this book and whose unfailing encouragement kept me going until it was finished;

Roland Bainton, scholar, unsparing critic, and longtime friend, who was of the greatest help to me, in particular in the historical sections of the book;

Julius Seelye Bixler, teacher, counselor, and friend under whom, more than forty years ago, this project may be said to have begun, as an honors thesis at the Harvard Divinity School;

Martin E. Marty, mainline churchman, author, historian, and acute observer of the religious scene, who encouraged the publication of *The Fourth American Faith* and the present work even more.

Special recognition is due Polly Lutte of Fryeburg, Maine, who faithfully typed and retyped countless pages as the manuscript went through several revisions. To the many others who helped along the way, my colleagues in organized religion and in education, fellow-workers in various causes, and members of my family: to all these and for all these I give thanks that can never be adequately expressed. Finally, to Carolyn, wife, companion, counsellor, and friend, in this as in all things, ever growing, ever deepening gratitude.

PART I

Divine Truth and Human Error

The yearning to know the truth is as old as human thought. No less ancient is the knowledge that we can be tragically mistaken even when we are very sure we are right. From the earliest times religion has resolved this problem in some of the more basic areas of life through the idea of divine intervention. God or the gods were assumed to know what mere humans could not know. Thus, divine knowledge, revealed to humanity, could be regarded as certain. The methods by which God or the gods were said to have communicated with humanity were many. But the end result was the same—knowledge where there had been ignorance, certainty where there had been uncertainty, truth where there had been error, and agreement where there had been argument without end.

"Revelation" is the word most commonly used to designate truth made available by divine intervention. The history of religions offers innumerable instances of such interventions in ancient and modern times, among primitive and sophisticated peoples alike. Sometimes the claim is very explicit, as when Isaiah told of seeing the Lord sitting upon his throne in the temple and heard him say, "Go and say this to the people . . ." or when the Book of Mormon declares itself to be "An Account Written by the Hand of Mormon upon Plates Taken from the Plates Nephi," and asserts further that it was "written by way of commandment and also by the spirit of prophecy and revelation." Not all claims of divine revelation are so directly made, but, in effect, all such statements claim special status and indubitable certainty because of their divine origin.

Even in ancient times, however, people openly questioned the supposed certainties of the religions. Socrates, we recall, feeling very uncertain about the answers to fundamental questions current in Greek culture in the fifth century B.C., went around questioning all the wise men of his native Athens and eventually was executed for his impertinence. By the late fourth and early third century B.C., Pyrrho of Elia in southeastern Greece had turned Socrates' questioning into a dogma. "Nothing," he declared, "can be known with certainty." Which view is right? How fallible are we? Can religion overcome human fallibility? These are some of the basic questions with which this book is concerned.

1

The Critical Way in Religion

There are two traditions in the religion of the West. On the one hand, there is a tradition with which we are all familiar, based upon the idea of truth given to humanity by divine revelation. This tradition is established, nurtured, and protected by the three great religions of the West: Judaism, Christianity, and Islam.

At the core of this tradition lies the concept of believing, of having faith in the truth of the revelation taught by one's religion. Notions of what these truths are often differ among the three great religions. Sharp differences often occur among various sects within the three great Western religions; but all alike are united in their approach to matters religious. That approach is confessional. It is based on believing. It is centered in faith, and is elaborated and defended by religious institutions—the churches and temples of the various religious groups.

There is, on the other hand, a second tradition in the West with which we are equally familiar, but which we have not been accustomed to associate with religion. It is a tradition of inquiry, of testing, of conjecturing, and of probing into the depths of all experience and all life. This second tradition is established, nurtured, and protected, not in our churches and temples, but in a newer institution in human society, the university. The university is the critical tradition institutionalized, as the church is the ecclesiastical tradition institutionalized.

These two traditions are basically antithetical, although they live together in apparent harmony. The confessional or ecclesiastical tradition holds that we already know final truth in certain fundamental areas of life. The critical or university tradition holds that we do not, that truth is something towards which we move in the future, not something given to us in the past. In the critical tradition every datum and every proposition of whatever kind, emanating from whatever source, and backed by whatever authority, is examined and tested in an attempt to determine its validity. There are no exceptions to this rule.

There is, of course, nothing novel in the careful examination and testing of religious teachings. The religions that are based on revelation follow this practice. How else are they to determine what is and what is not a true revelation? The critical tradition, however, carries the examining process one step further. It tests with equal severity the basic proposition upon which the several revelations of the several religions rest. The critical tradition examines with no less care the doctrine of revelation itself.

When such an examination is made and made rigorously, the doctrine of revelation does not come off very well. Subjected to the canons of judgment by which the university community is accustomed to accept or reject knowledge in all other areas of life, the doctrine of revelation disintegrates. And when that one single doctrine falls, all the revelations held by the various religions come tumbling down with it.

There is no more basic difference between the critical way in religion and the ecclesiastical way. Judaism, Islam, and Christianity (both Protestant and Catholic) rest upon this doctrine. Despite their many and often acrimonious differences, all three religions and the sects and divisions within each of them hold to this basic principle. All three depend, in the end, on the claim that God revealed to their founders his will and his truth.

Some Jewish and Muslim thinkers may object to being lumped together with the Christians as "confessional." In a technical sense the objection has merit. To "confess," meaning to declare one's faith, evolved in Christianity, and in the minds of many remains essentially a Christian idea.

In a more general sense, however, to "confess," meaning to declare one's faith, applies in Judaism and Islam no less than in Christianity. All three religions rest upon the single basic belief that God has revealed his will and truth to humanity. They differ as to where, when, how, and to whom these revelations have been made, and they differ as to what God is understood to have said on those occasions. But Christianity, Judaism, and Islam alike require their adherents to "confess" their belief in the truth of the revelations their particular religions hold.

The critical mind does not deny the possibility of revelation. It assumes neither that revelations have occurred nor that they have not, neither that God exists and breaks into human history nor that he does not. The critical mind asserts only that these matters should be looked into, and with far greater care than we have been accustomed to use in the past. The critical mind insists on examining every claim everybody makes in religion to see whether or not it is valid. This includes an examination of the doctrine of revelation itself.

As we shall see, many religious claims do not bear careful scrutiny. As we shall also see, the religions have not taken kindly to such scrutiny. They have not welcomed, they have resisted, the questionings of the critical mind. Often they have suppressed such probing with fire and sword, with torture and death. Almost always the ecclesiastical establishment has vilified and ostracized such questioners. Nevertheless, in the face of it all, the critical way in religion has continued to grow until, today, it is very widely followed even among the members of churches of the ecclesiastical way.

1. The Critical Way and the Ecclesiastical Way

We commonly speak of "traditions" in religion, but I shall also use the term "way." It is a metaphor, to be sure, but it is a vivid one. It is also very old and readily grasped, because it is universal in scope and is confined to no particular place or time, nation, or race. The Buddha spoke of the "eightfold *path.*" Hesiod, in his *Works and Days,* observed, "Before Virtue the immortal gods have put the sweat of man's brow; and long and steep is the *way* to it," and Parmenides divided his great poem on the trustworthiness of the senses into "The *Way* of Truth" and "The *Way* of Seeming."

From the earliest passages in the Old Testament through the latest in the New, "The Way of the Lord" is an ever-recurrent theme. The Dead Sea Scrolls reveal the fact that the Essenes called themselves "The People of the Way" or simply "The Way," and we learn from the Book of Acts that the first Christians also called themselves the people of "The Way."

What is the difference between the critical way in religion and the critical tradition in religion? The *tradition* is the thought and practice of those who, since ancient times, have approached religion in a critical manner. It consists in the persons, their writings, the ongoing stream of thought they represent, and the steadily accumulating body of teachings that has resulted from their work. The critical *way,* on the other hand, is conceptual—theological, if you will. People of the critical way approach religious questions in a critical manner. This in turn places them in the critical tradition, and the works they produce belong to and enlarge the critical tradition. In many cases the two words "way" and "tradition" can be used interchangeably. The difference is primarily one of emphasis. As an example, we could say that Socrates is one of the greatest figures in the critical tradition and that his thinking greatly advanced that tradition. We could also say that Socrates was of a critical turn of mind, that in religion, as in all things, he followed the critical way and that if we were to seek an exemplar of the critical way in religion, no figure would serve us better than he.

The idea of divine intervention in human affairs seems to have been a universal characteristic of primitive religion, a ready explanation for much that otherwise went unexplained. Primitive people believed in spirits, which were thought to play an active role in human affairs. If a tree fell on someone, it was looked upon as intentional, like the arrow from an enemy's bow. Traditions regarding spirits or divinities and how to bend their activities to human desire tended to acquire a sacrosanct status, nearly impervious to change. The divine was seldom, if ever, an area that invited experimentation. Once a point of view regarding such matters became established, it tended to remain unchanged.

But tribal lore, however complex, was never complete, never able to answer all the questions that might be asked. Always something went unexplained, or the explanations that were given did not hang together. In primitive times, as at present, no doubt a few thoughtful people were not satisfied with official explanations. As is true today, a certain restless, curious few were always poking into things, asking questions that lay beyond the answers they had been given; always trying to understand things in a broader and more comprehensive manner; always trying better to accomplish whatever task they might have in hand. Well back in prehistory, restless minds seem to have pondered the meaning of life and death, as they strove to fashion clothing, fishhooks, houses, and weapons.

Progress was no doubt more marked in the practical arts. A hook that would catch more fish than those currently in use did not have to be proven superior by argument. Nor would such an improved hook have appeared among tradition-bound people. The wheel was not invented by minds that believed all wisdom was derived from an earlier and more enlightened time. Surely the concept of a pole plunged through the center of two rotating discs emerged in the mind of some individual or group able and willing to think outside and beyond the tradition in which they were nurtured.

In the intellectual, moral, and spiritual realms, progress may have been slower, but the ability to see incongruity and sense injustice, the habit of testing human judgment by trial and error—these two were at work and played their part in bringing about change in supposedly unchangeable social, moral, and religious beliefs and practices. As an example, students of primitive religion agree that animal sacrifice, so common in ancient religion, in many instances represents the practice of human sacrifice, transformed by the moral enlightenment of people now lost to history.

"Would that I had known . . . sayings that are unfamiliar," wrote a priest of Heliopolis in Egypt as an introduction to some reflections on the state of society some four thousand years ago. Apparently conscious that he was thinking along new lines, he continued his prayer for "new speech that has not occurred before, free from repetitions, not the utterance of what has long passed which the ancestors spoke." After these introductory words he voiced what can be considered one of the earliest moral protests that has come down to us. "Righteousness is cast out; iniquity is in the midst of the council hall," he cried in cadences anticipating the Old Testament prophets who would appear fifteen hundred years later.

The difference in the attitude of the two traditions toward the Bible in Christianity will illustrate the basic difference between them. A mainline Protestant periodical, which lies squarely in the ecclesiastical tradition, recently asked in an editorial, "What do one's biblical commitments mean for the person who is politically aware?" Clearly the editor took it for granted that Protestant Christians have "biblical commitments" and that as Christians they must keep these commitments in mind when they enter the political realm. Those in the critical tradition have no such commitments. They are not committed to the Christian Bible, the Jewish Bible, the Bible of Islam, or to any other. In the critical tradition one's commitments are to a vision of truth and right, of human welfare, beauty, and goodness.

For those of the critical way, there is a bonus in such an approach. In the ecclesiastical tradition the arguments are endless and often acrimonious as to what one's "biblical commitments" are. The Bible is a rare and wonderful assembly of writings, seldom entirely clear in their meaning and far from consistent even where those meanings can be agreed upon. In the critical tradition questions about Bible meanings are surely to be pondered and debated, but the answer to such questions does not necessarily determine one's course of action. In the critical tradition one does not close off discussion by asking "What does the Bible say?" One asks instead, "What ought I to do?" quite apart from anything that is or is not in any Bible.

The difference between the ecclesiastical and the critical way in religion can also be seen in the reasons each gives for the beliefs it holds. In the ecclesiastical tradition you are asked to accept on faith the beliefs of a church or temple. In the critical tradition you are asked to accept beliefs, whether religious or any other kind, because of the evidence that supports them. In the ecclesiastical tradition you believe because you have faith. In the critical tradition you believe because you are persuaded; you cannot disbelieve even if you want to.

The contrast also appears in the attitude of the two traditions toward authority. In an address to the Roman Rota in 1971, Pope Paul discussed the source of the Catholic Church's authority and in particular the relationship between hierarchy and people in the exercise of that authority. The faithful "are the object, not the origin of the authority," the pope said. Authority "is established for their service and is not at their service." He went on to assert that some current thinking about authority might have dangerous consequences for the church—for example, the notion of giving the people powers that do not belong to them. The pope said that the church will never renounce its claim to make laws that are binding on the people, though there might well be a shift in style. The foregoing is an extreme instance of the role of authority in the ecclesiastical tradition; the role of authority in the critical tradition is the opposite. Any authority that is recognized there does not flow from a hierarchy. It flows from the views of the people who make up that tradition in concert with one another.

Another contrast has to do with what we call tolerance, with our attitude toward those whose religious beliefs differ from ours. Time was when the state involved itself in such matters, and tolerance consisted in the state's refusal to enter religious controversy. It meant that religious authorities could not enlist the power of the state in enforcing religious policies. In those days tolerance, when it occurred, meant that nation could not be pitted against nation in the name of religion, and it meant that religious differences within a nation could not be resolved by the use of governmental power. Happily, in the Western world today such tolerance is exercised almost everywhere.

The critical tradition has always stood in the forefront of the fight for tolerance of every kind. The fight to keep the power of the state out of religious controversy and to obstruct all ecclesiastical-power-seeking has been led by those of the critical way. The nearly universal adoption of this point of view in Western culture today is one of the most significant achievements of the critical approach to the question of ecclesiastical authority.

The old way, which we have inherited, was a clash of systems, of theologies, of religions, and of gods. The new way, the critical way, replaces the clash with interchange. Claims and counterclaims give way to comparison and contrast. Charge and countercharge are replaced by mutual inquiry and, above all, by mutual respect. The dissenter, the heretic, and the unbeliever become the critic from whom something may be learned, an ally in seeking the closest possible approach to truth. In the critical tradition we move far beyond the old concept of tolerance. We no longer persecute dissenters. We do not silence them, nor do we ignore them—a technique often more effective than direct censorship. In the critical tradition we listen to our critics in the hope of learning something from them.

John Milton once said, "God prefers the lush and many-tinted profusion of spring to the frozen conformity of winter." A. O. Lovejoy, in his *Great Chain of Being,* praised diversity as "the essence of excellence." Whitehead once remarked, "A clash of doctrines is not a disaster—it is an opportunity."

Still another contrast can be seen in the sources of religious knowledge to which the two traditions look. In the ecclesiastical tradition, the source of knowledge, in addition to direct inspiration, is the Bible or some other sacred, semi-sacred, ancient and hallowed writing, as well as ancient traditions not clearly recorded but recognized in practice. In the critical tradition, the source of religious knowledge is identical to the source of knowledge of every other kind. It includes direct inspiration as well as the hard data of experience. The difference is, in the critical tradition all supposed knowledge from every source and of every kind must be tested and verified. Such data as the Bible and other holy books contain are included, not excluded, but in the critical tradition, holy books are not given priority in veracity or authority. In the critical tradition there are no prior commitments.

One's commitment is to the inquiring process itself, whereby every principle and every assertion is subjected to the most searching examination possible.

The idea that there are special sources of knowledge when knowledge is "religious" results in an elitism, often found in the ecclesiastical tradition, that is foreign to the spirit of the critical tradition. An archbishop about to retire was asked about his private views on religion. Assured that he would remain anonymous, the churchman began speaking with great candor. Suddenly interrupting himself, he said, "I can't say things like these to the faithful people inside the church. It would offend them. They wouldn't be able to understand. It's a great pity. I have always told them what they were able to comprehend."

With a sigh he concluded, "Oh, if we could be open and completely honest with one another inside the church!"

The critical way in religion allows for no such judgment by a privileged few about what the many may and may not hear, and no decisions made for them about what they can understand and what might offend them. To the critical mind all such pre-empting of the decision-making process is abhorrent. The prayer of the archbishop, to be completely open and honest with one another *inside* the church, is the goal and commitment of the critical way in religion.

To those of the ecclesiastical way, the critical way often seems to be one of denial. To those of the critical way, it is a position of nonaffirmation only. This distinction is fundamental. The contrast is not between believers and deniers; it is between two sets of believers, those who are willing to believe the dogmas of established religion and those who think the case for such believing has not been made. The critical tradition does not reject Judeo-Christian, Islamic, Buddhist, or any other religious teaching. It rejects the Judeo-Christian-Islamic method of establishing the truth these teachings are said to contain. The critical way is neither one of dissent nor of heresy, neither of skepticism nor of scientism. It is a way of checking and testing, of exposing error, and of eliminating it wherever it is found.

The most fruitful aspect of the critical way is not the testing side, however. It is not the ferreting out of human deception, error, and inadequacy, important as this process is. The most fruitful side is the questing side and the new understanding of our world and of our human condition that results from it. This is the reason for inquiry in the first place. Its primary purpose is not the exposing of tears, patches, and threadbare spots in the tapestry of traditional religion. Its purpose is to fashion a new and better weaving to take the place of one that is worn, frayed, and not nearly large or complex enough to depict the scene it is designed to portray.

The critical mind not only checks every proposition in the most thoroughgoing manner, it also frames new propositions to replace those that are found to be false or inadequate. These in turn are also tested with the utmost severity in an attempt to determine how far they may be valid. Any new proposition, however inviting, that cannot meet such a test is either rejected outright or it is held tentatively until its validity can be more surely determined. A new proposition that tests out, however, is adopted tentatively at first but increasingly accepted as true, if it continues to test out over a period of time. This acceptance holds until a larger, clearer, more adequate, or more accurate proposition can be devised to take its place.

One of the most persuasive arguments put forward by the defenders of the ecclesiastical way is the sense of certainty it offers. Those who accept its teachings are said to *know,* whereas others have to face unanswered questions, uncertainty, even ignorance. Obviously, certitude in a world of doubt and change gives great comfort and support to the believer. But what of those who are not convinced that ecclesiastical leaders know what they think they know? Where is the certainty for those who find the religions less clear than natural science in the realm of knowledge and less valid than philosophy, psychology, and anthropology in the realm of value? For them the supposed certainties of religion are not merely uncertain; they are a delusion. They offer a false security because they claim to know what no one can know with the certainty they claim.

The critical way is the way of those who believe the certainty offered by the religions is unobtainable by anyone. They believe that ultimate questions must of necessity have open-ended answers. The experience of the race, at least down to the present time, has proved this to be true. As we shall see in Part II, experience has shown again and again that the supposed certainties of one generation of religious leaders are frequently modified and often abandoned outright by the leaders of the next. Much as we may yearn for certitude, continuous inquiry, not finality, seems to be our lot when it comes to ultimate questions.

While the critical way in religion has never really been identified, its presence has been sensed by many writers. Its essential character has sometimes been grasped, but for the most part it has been misunderstood and very often caricatured. Ideas associated with the critical way in religion include heresy, nonconformity, infidelity, dissent, protest, skepticism, liberalism, rationalism, agnosticism, atheism, humanism, secularism, positivism, scientism, empiricism, freethinking, The Enlightenment. Many of these terms originated as epithets. Many are epithets still. Consider, for example, the fact that "thinker" is an honored designation to apply to anyone. "Free" is one of the most precious words in the language. Yet "freethinker," a term often applied to those of an independent mind in religion, even today bears within it the sting of opprobrium and derision.

The critical way in religion is not encompassed by any of the foregoing terms. Each is too narrow, and most involve elements the critical tradition could not tolerate. How, then, is it to be described? It involves concepts like the following:

> Freedom, tolerance, and self-reliance;
> Inquiry, experimentation, and testing;
> Change, progress, growth, and evolution;
> Uncertainty and probability;
> Unity and universality;
> Consistency, integrity, and objectivity.

On the other hand, the way of questing and testing does not involve such concepts as:

> Total reliance on reason;
> Doubt that anything can ultimately be known;
> A declaration of the supremacy of man;
> Acceptance of the mechanistic hypothesis;
> A rejection of the idea of a religious or spiritual dimension in life;
> The view that science alone can bring us true knowledge;
> The view that whatever is known must be based solely on evidence.

Nor does the way of inquiry include many religious concepts long familiar in the West, such as God, Trinity, heaven, purgatory, hell, angels, devils, witches, miracles, redemption, salvation, immortality, resurrection, incarnation, transubstantiation, revelation, and petitionary prayer. The tradition of inquiry does not necessarily deny the validity of these concepts. Rather, it finds them of little help in understanding the nature of existence and human experience.

Perhaps the differences in our human temperament account for the differences between the critical way and the ecclesiastical way. Many people active in the traditional churches quite frankly say they do not believe the traditional dogmas of the church and derive little from its liturgy. Nevertheless, they continue on as members and are often very active. Why cannot all of us do this? We go to concerts we don't like, plays that offend us, lectures that bore us, and cinema that is revolting, and we watch television that is inane. Yet many of us will not go to church if we are either bored or repelled by it. Why?

The churches are constantly updating their doctrine and practice, although often at a seemingly glacial pace. Is that why we turn away? I do not think so. The reason is more basic. We can sit out an ill-performed concert or play if we must. But we *participate* in worship. In church what we hear, do, and say makes a difference. If we don't believe our own words as we say them or if we find the ceremonial in which we are involved empty, we have an uneasy sense of falsity, of posturing, and of pretending. While we concede that a certain amount of such conduct is necessary in polite social intercourse, with religion it is different. In the church or temple, at worship, it makes a difference whether what we hear and say is right or wrong, good or bad, valid or invalid. If a religious service lacks dignity, beauty, and integrity, we do not sit it out or sigh and turn away: we feel cheated. An empty or misleading religious exercise is not merely offensive; it is intolerable.

In the temple we must be wholly honest—with ourselves and with everyone else. There can be no dissimulation, no subterfuge, and no sham, even for a supposedly noble purpose. When we are truly at worship, we must be completely ourselves. We face up to our shortcomings—all of them—as best we can, as in traditional language we confess our sins. We measure what we are by what we would like to be, and what we have done by what we wish we had done. We seek strength to perform the tasks life lays upon us and we breathe our prayers of hope and aspiration for the days ahead. Both the critical and the ecclesiastical mind agree that there can be no pretense in the church. For the critical mind such pretense enters when the official beliefs of a church are not believed and when its ceremonial has become anachronistic.

2. Criticism in the Ecclesiastical Tradition

The distinction between the critical way and the ecclesiastical way is elusive and often escapes us because *both* are critical. All religious thought worthy of the name is critical. How else are religious thinkers to sift out what is valid in their tradition from what is not; what belongs, from what does not? Have they not examined every preachment and every premise a thousand times? Have they too not tested every argument to the point of exhaustion? Is it not the clergy, the churchmen firmly implanted in the ecclesiastical tradition, who have engaged in the critical study of the Bible? Are they not as critical as it is possible to be in examining the data bearing upon their faith? What is the distinction between criticism in the critical tradition and criticism in the ecclesiastical tradition?

In Christianity there is indeed a long and clear tradition of criticism, the roots of which are in the New Testament itself. Christianity arose as a separatist movement out of criticism of the forms of Judaism that prevailed in the first century A.D. Jesus' criticisms of the scribes and Pharisees, whether justified or not (many Jewish scholars claim they were not justified), dominate the Gospels. Paul did not hesitate to rebuke the new and struggling churches he founded. As an example, his first letter to the church at Corinth is both a plea and a remonstrance. "I appeal to you," he wrote, "that there be no dissension among you . . . for it has been reported to me . . . that there is quarreling among you." Paul's masterpiece, his hymn to love, is the climax of his denunciation of the divisions in the Corinthian church and his plea for mutual understanding and concern among the members.

Criticism like this continues to be the stock in trade of orthodox clergy and laity even today. The current phase of this mood among church people owes no small debt to Sören Kierkegaard, the nineteenth-century Danish theologian who has been high on the list of Protestant heroes ever since his rediscovery in the early twentieth century. A devout Christian himself, Kierkegaard condemned the church of his time for its "twaddle, twattle, patter, smallness, mediocrity, playing at Christianity, transforming everything into mere words."

Criticism of church practice has continued to be the fashion among religious writers ever since, particularly those in our theological schools. Uncounted books published during the last fifty years have in like manner roasted the church for its sloth, its folly, its softness, its caution, and its compromises. *The Comfortable Pew, The Noise of Solemn Assemblies,* and *The Suburban Captivity of the Churches* are typical recent titles. The burden of the entire genre is criticism—specifically, the failure of the Christian churches, in particular the Protestant churches, to live up to their own self-professed ideals. In the heyday of this sort of thing, a popular news magazine surveying the situation observed sardonically, "Such criticism has become a new kind of ritual within Protestantism, bringing the articulate critic instant headlines, crowded speaking schedules, and a rush of publishing offers."

Critical theological thinking has never been wholly absent from Christianity, Judaism, or Islam. The monumental struggles with doctrine that wracked the early Christian church were at least in part the result of thinking that was critical in character. The orthodoxies and heresies, the creeds and debates in council of that period resulted from attempts of the church fathers to make logical sense of the official teaching of their time.

In our own time, it has been the so-called liberals who have engaged in sustained criticism of traditional Christian doctrine. It was the liberals who brought biblical criticism out of the theological schools and into the churches. It was they who wrote the first "human" lives of Jesus, they who accelerated the modernizing of ancient dogma, they who led the effort, particularly in Protestant Christianity and in Judaism, to bring religious thought abreast of thought in other areas. It was the liberals who turned the attention of the faithful to the values to be found in other religions. It was they who led the fight for the acceptance of an evolutionary concept of the origins of the world and of man; they who conceded the presence of myths in the Bible; and they who insisted that a true Christianity demands social action.

Liberals of the ecclesiastical way, like their counterparts of the critical way, are critical of existing thought patterns and seek the freedom to change them. They want to loosen them, broaden them, "liberalize" them. In this they are one with those of the critical way. They are tolerant toward change and toward doctrines different from their own. They tend to be open-minded and open-hearted toward other religions, toward the various sects and divisions within their own churches, and even toward those with differing opinions within their own particular group.

As in the critical tradition, liberals in the ecclesiastical tradition tend to favor the participation of lay people as well as clergy in the decision-making process: they strongly favor the uses of freedom in the various aspects of religious endeavor. They oppose authoritarianism. They favor the questioning, testing approach to doctrine, dogma, and practice, and advocate changes that testing and questing suggest.

Liberals in the ecclesiastical tradition frequently advocated the same specific doctrines as those advocated in the critical tradition. As an example (in Christianity), those of the critical way and liberals of the ecclesiastical way might both reject the doctrine of the Incarnation or the idea that Jesus was the Son of God in a special sense. Both might agree that the Bible is an extraordinary religious document but not revealed from heaven in any direct way, not literally true, and not Final Truth. Both might reject such Christian doctrines as the Trinity, the Virgin Birth, and the Resurrection. As a result, liberals in Episcopal, Presbyterian, Methodist, Catholic, and other churches often assert that there is no significant difference between themselves and those who like to think of themselves as very, very liberal.

Nevertheless, beneath these elements that the critical way and liberals in the ecclesiastical way hold in common, there is a difference as basic as it is elusive. The confusion rises from the structure of Western thought itself. So deeply are Christian concepts woven into the culture of the West, that even those who might reject such concepts unconsciously make use of them. As an example, when we hear that a friend has joined a church with which we are unfamiliar, our response is apt to be: "Is that so? What do they believe?" On the surface the question seems natural enough, and lacking in any serious implications. On a little reflection, however, we can see that the question takes its rise from our belief in the importance of believing. Regarding a church with which we are unfamiliar, we ask what they believe as a means by which to place that church within the larger Judeo-Christian belief structure of Western thought.

Because Western religion, Christianity in particular, makes central the adherence of the individual to a set of beliefs, the Western mind thinks this way about religion almost instinctively. We tend to visualize religious belief as extending along a line beginning at one end with the strictest adherence to ancient teachings and extending on the other until it reaches a very broad, flexible, and nearly amorphous set of teachings. We think of this line as extending from the most conservative and orthodox beliefs on one end to the most liberal and radical on the other. In fact, one can say there is a kind of belief-chart imprinted on the Western mind, roughly resembling the one on the adjoining page.

Conservative-Liberal
Belief-Chart
of the American
Religious Community

- Jews: Orthodox especially
- Roman Catholics
- Eastern Orthodox
- Pentecostals
- Adventists
- Jehovah's Witnesses
- Lutherans: Missouri Synod especially
- Mennonites
- Baptists: Southern and Primitive especially
- Presbyterians
- Episcopalians
- United Church of Christ: member groups
- Methodists
- Friends
- Unitarian Universalists
- Ethical Culturalists
- Humanists
- Atheists

No two charts, of course, would be exactly alike, and none would be as exact or clearly drawn as the sample I have given. In fact, the complexity of the chart that any one of us carries in the mind could not be reduced to a printed page. To illustrate: my chart, even to approach adequacy, would extend Judaism alone from one end of the chart to the other. In terms of orthodoxy—namely, strict, inflexible, unchanging adherence to the articles of one's faith—vast numbers of fundamentalist Protestants would be regarded as more conservative than the majority of Roman Catholics or Jews. Members of Lutheran, Episcopal, Presbyterian, and Methodist churches, as well as of many other denominational groups, could quite properly be distributed across the entire chart.

Nevertheless, allowing for these exceptions, variations, and individual differences, the generalization still holds. Because of the emphasis in Western religion on principles of belief and belonging, the Western mind, as part of its thought structure, tends to arrange religious groups on a conservative-liberal scale. Usually vague, often inaccurate, but always present, that scale represents popular conceptions of the emphasis placed by particular religious groups on the acceptance of their particular teachings.

Many readers will want to quarrel with the accompanying diagram. They will want to rearrange the progression from conservatism and/or orthodoxy to liberalism and/or radicalism. I will gladly accept any such corrections, for the particular position of any church, sect, denomination, or philosophy on the chart is not the point. The point is that most members of Western culture think religiously more or less in accordance with such a chart.

Thus, when we say a church or a person is a liberal or conservative, it is to their place in the Judeo-Christian belief-structure that we are referring. A conservative, we think, holds to the familiar tenets at one end of our religious belief-system. A liberal, on the other hand, is one who belongs on the other end of the chart. He or she is one who is ready to adopt restatements, modifications, and even new formulations of it. Today, for example, the conservative Christians still maintain their belief in the Virgin Birth; liberals, on the other hand, tend to think of it mythically or poetically—in any case, not as literal truth. The very liberal or radical simply reject the idea outright.

The way this chart dominates our thinking is apparent in the writings of most "liberal" religionists. In 1974 a graduate student studying the Unitarian Univeralist denomination, usually regarded as one of the most "liberal" churches, sent a questionnaire to its ministers. As a final item on his inquiry he wrote:

> Please check the theological position with which you most closely identify yourself:
>
> Theist
> Religious Humanist

Liberal Protestant
Christian Theist
Christian Humanist

In his summary of the results, he dismisses with scorn "a few ministers who . . . objected to being categorized." He felt theirs was a quibble. The belief-chart of Western culture was so much a part of his thinking he was unable to take seriously those who rejected the structure itself and could not in conscience classify themselves according to the categories it set up.

A contemporary writer of orthodox persuasion falls into the same error. He says the underlying principles of liberalism are an emphasis (1) on continuity rather than *dis*continuity in the world; (2) on the autonomy of human reason and experience, rather than on authoritative divine revelation; and (3) on the dynamic rather than the static nature of life and the world. He quite fails to see that a true liberalism is not a set of doctrines, however broad. It is neither a theology, a metaphysics, nor an epistemology. It is a method by which we assess the validity of theological, metaphysical, and epistemological doctrines.

The critical way in religion is also not to be confused with "Radical Theology," which its advocates describe as a "theology of revolution." Radical theology tries to overthrow and replace the value system prevailing in the theology of its day and usually in society as well. Christian theologians love to use the word "radical" in this sense, applying it to the Bible and often to their own teachings as well.

Supposedly, a radical theology would be expected to fall at the far end of the belief-chart where the critical way is to be found. But it does not. "Radical Theology" is biblical and would fall closer to the other end of the belief chart. "Radical," these theologians point out, means "root." Hence, a theological position that goes back to the roots of its own tradition can legitimately claim to be "radical," even though it would be called conservative by any other standard. To the critical mind, such usage does not clarify but further confuses religious thinking.

3. The Critical Way and Liberalism

When we speak of liberals in religion, what do we mean? Who are we talking about? Ideas vary. A popular view holds that liberals have as their goal the adjustment of religion to secular thought and culture. An equally popular view holds that the central concept of liberalism in all its varieties is liberty, "an unshaken belief in the necessity of freedom to achieve every desirable aim. A deep concern for the freedom of the individual inspired (liberalism's) opposition to absolute certainty, be it that of the state, of the church, or of a political party. The fundamental postulate of liberalism has been the moral worth, the absolute value, and the essential dignity of the human personality."

Those who follow the critical way in religion usually think of themselves as liberals, and they are usually so regarded by those who follow the ecclesiastical way. But great numbers of people who clearly follow the ecclesiastical way also look upon themselves as liberals and are so regarded by others. What is the difference? Are both liberals?

The answer is yes, and this single fact, probably more than any other, explains the difficulty many people have in distinguishing the critical way from the ecclesiastical way in religion. Yet the difference is fundamental. Let us call liberals who belong in the ecclesiastical tradition modifying-liberals and those that belong in the critical tradition thoroughgoing-liberals. As the word "modifying" suggests, these liberals have as their goal the modification of the doctrines and practices of their churches in order to modernize and improve them. As the word "thoroughgoing" suggests, these liberals have as their goal the establishment of what they regard as the best possible doctrine and practice in the church. Superficially, the goal of both of these groups might seem to be the same. Nevertheless, the difference between them is fundamental. It concerns the question, How far is the modifying process to go? What, if any, limits are to be placed on it? The answer to that question divides the modifying- and thoroughgoing-liberals from each other.

To illustrate, let us return to the definition of religious liberals as those who attempt to "adjust theology to secular thought and culture." Many liberals, especially those who are commonly thought of as very liberal, have no such aim. Their purpose is not to adjust theology to secular culture or to anything else. That may be the result of what they do, but their purpose is to understand natural and human phenomena, whether secular or religious, and to state what they understand in the clearest language possible. They do not begin with an existing theology and try to adapt it to something else. They begin with the world and human experience and try to make of it what they can, quite apart from existing theological structures—Christian, Jewish, or Muslim, ancient or modern, theocentric or humanistic, sacred or secular.

For example, as far back as 1937 Sidney Hook of New York University, Senior Fellow of the Hoover Institution at Stanford, asserted that *the methods of critical inquiry* (italics mine) are essential to any sound social philosophy. Hook was writing as a Jew, but he was careful to point out that the methods of critical inquiry are valid in and of themselves. Liberal Jews support critical inquiry, he argued, not because the method favors the position in which Jews find themselves (as it does) but because the methods of critical inquiry are essential to the ideal human society. Such are the thorough-going liberals. Their goal is not to modify and improve a particular tradition but to seek truth and right beyond all cultural conditioning.

Modifying liberals, on the other hand, begin with a prior commitment to Christianity, Judaism, Islam—even Buddhism. They are liberal Protestants,

Catholics, or Jews—liberal Methodists, Episcopalians, or Presbyterians. They seek to adapt the thought and practice of their church, or of churches generally, to what they believe to be broader notions of truth, newer concepts of worship, and better standards of church government. But their basic loyalty is to the church and its teachings, and their basic purpose is the strengthening and improving of its doctrine and practice.

As a result, a curious reversal of roles comes about for modifying- and thoroughgoing-liberals. Modifying-liberals usually think of themselves as believers because they accept a large part of traditional doctrine and often stigmatize thoroughgoing-liberals as "unbelievers" because they reject so much of it. Yet the attitude of the modifying-liberal toward doctrine formulation is likely to be flexible, yielding, and broadly interpretative. The attitude of the thoroughgoing-liberal, on the other hand, is likely to be strict, unyielding, and far more literal. The modifying-liberal tends to leave the words of ancient credal formulations as they are and interpret them in order to update them and make their meaning more congenial. The thoroughgoing-liberal, eager that words should, as far as possible, be made to mean what they say rather than trying to retain and reinterpret ancient formulations, tries to put new creeds in their place or give up credal formulations entirely.

The modifying-liberal appears to have little anxiety lest religious words be misunderstood. For the thoroughgoing-liberal, however, the crux of the matter is the need to use words that are as clear as possible in their meaning, words that invite assent in and of themselves. For the thoroughgoing-liberal it is important to avoid words that turn people off because their obvious meaning is at best irrelevant and at worst abhorrent—words that have to be reinterpreted in order to become acceptable to the worshiper.

With the modifying-liberals, always there comes a point when they call for an end to modifying, an end to change, and a return to stability, pre-established order, and certainty. At that point they give up the development of new ideas and the rechecking of old ones. In the face of our human limitations, aware that we cannot know everything we should like to know, that the most profound questions will of necessity remain unanswered, they cease inquiry and step out on the venture of faith.

Thoroughgoing-liberals never reach such a point. No less aware of our human limitations, they nevertheless continue to test old concepts and search for new and better ones. They do not think that faith can answer questions inquiry cannot. Christians today who think themselves very liberal boldly declare that they no longer believe in the Trinity, the Virgin Birth, or the Resurrection, yet they hold to the central Christian dogma of the Christ who is known by faith. The thoroughgoing-liberal subjects even this basic doctrine to the same scrutiny to which liberals in the ecclesiastical tradition subject doctrines like the Trinity, the Virgin Birth, and the Resurrection.

For both, the goal is truth. The difference lies in the concept of truth each holds, and in the notions of each as to how truth of any kind is to be attained.

For the modifying-liberal truth is something religion holds and teaches; for the thoroughgoing-liberal, truth is a goal that forever recedes in religion as it does in every line of human endeavor.

Modifying and thoroughgoing-liberals have been difficult to distinguish from each other because the modifying-liberals themselves have often been unable to see that there was a point in the modifying process beyond which they would not go. In the peak period of the liberal movement, many of its leaders, with an exhilarating sense of freedom, proclaimed their faith as if it would, and indeed had, met and answered all questions.

Writings from the heyday of religious liberalism in the 1920s abound in examples of this principle. One minister wrote, "For several years the weekly calendar [of the church I serve as minister] has carried the following formulation of the ideals of the church: This church practices union; it has no creed; seeks to make religion as intelligent as science; as appealing as art; as vital as the day's work; as intimate as the home; as inspiring as love."

Who could ask for a more open approach to religion, with no previous commitments to any orthodoxy? But if we read the above statement a little further, we find that the writer doesn't quite mean what he seems to be saying. On the very next page following the above, with no consciousness of disparity, he writes: "The Church of the Disciples of Christ is 'based upon biblical authority or upon the authority of Jesus and His Apostles.'"

Harry Emerson Fosdick, one of the leaders of the Protestant "Modernist" movement in the 1920s, wrote in his autobiography: "What finally smashed the whole idea of biblical inerrancy for me was a book by Andrew D. White, president of Cornell University, entitled *History of the Warfare of Science with Theology in Christendom.* It was a ponderous two-volume work, but I devoured it. It seemed to me unanswerable. Here were the facts, shocking facts about the way the assumed infallibility of the Scriptures had impeded research, deepened and prolonged obscurantism, fed the mania of persecution, and held up the progress of mankind. I no longer believed the old stuff I had been taught. Moreover, I no longer merely doubted it. I rose in indignant revolt against it."

In his *Modern Use of the Bible,* however, published in his mature years, Fosdick insisted that the authority of the Bible must be acknowledged while its non-inerrancy was also recognized. As a means of doing both, he resorted to a device already well developed by others who had sought to achieve both ends at the same time: that of the transient and permanent in religion, a distinction between the things that pass and those that endure eternally. Theodore Parker, the Boston Unitarian antislavery preacher, had made use of it more than a century earlier in defense of a more liberal brand of Unitarianism he was then advocating. Shortly before that, David Friedrich Strauss in Germany had separated what he believed to be the transient from the permanent in defending his unorthodox views of Christianity.

Thoroughgoing-liberals would not deny that there are basic concepts we may accept as true. They part company with modifying-liberals, however, at the point where the latter stop asking questions and enter the realm of faith. With regard to the Bible, for example, they would feel compelled to ask what authority it may be said to possess and why. How do we know there is permanent truth in its pages, unless we test those truths to see how permanent they are? The distinction here is fundamental. Thoroughgoing-liberals do not question the reality of ultimate truth and right. They question the manner in which their ultimacy is established. Because we can so easily be mistaken, they want to examine with the utmost care the grounds upon which the permanency of any truth is said to rest.

Thoroughgoing-liberalism does not rest upon any external authority because it can find no foundation sufficiently solid to sustain so basic a claim. Thoroughgoing-liberalism derives its conclusions from those things an open mind can discover or a wide-ranging imagination conceive.

In the decades since Fosdick's time, the situation has not changed. *The Comfortable Pew* (1965), a volume highly critical of the churches, stated clearly that it was "not written for free thinkers." It was written for "those within the Church" who want to know why the Church has been losing ground. That is to say, it was written for believers—for people who regarded the teachings of the Church as authoritative. The validity of those teachings was never questioned; only the *manner* in which the Church and the churchmen conducted the affairs of organized religion came under criticism. Another highly critical volume, *The Suburban Captivity of the Churches* (1962), also stopped far short of questioning fundamental Christian doctrines and beliefs. Said the author: "The task of the Church is reconciliation of men with God and with one another in human society."

In the critical tradition, the second half of that sentence would be accepted because its meaning is relatively clear. But what does the first half mean? What are we saying when we say that men should be reconciled with God? In the critical tradition such a statement would not appear until as many questions had been asked about it as the author asks about reconciling people with one another in human society, particularly in the decaying central cities of America.

Unlike Kierkegaard and the host of loyal churchmen who have followed in his now well-worn pathway, those of the critical way are not primarily concerned with the failure of the churches to do all they might in city and suburb to provide for the material needs of people. These problems are not to be minimized. But churches and temples are human institutions, subject to the foibles of all human institutions, both religious and secular. Their shortcomings are not hard to find. Both modifying and thoroughgoing-liberals are eager to improve the churches and to make them more effective as instruments of social amelioration. But thoroughgoing-liberals would carry the improvement process further, beyond the institutional shortcomings and failures of the churches to the most fundamental of their teachings.

As an example, many modifying-liberals readily accept the doctrine of the Trinity and ably defend it. In this sense, the doctrine is believed. Thoroughgoing-liberals, on the other hand, reject the doctrine because to them it seems like a construct of the mind resulting from theological debate more than a statement about the nature of things. For this reason, thoroughgoing-liberals are very uncomfortable when asked to stand in a religious sanctuary and recite aloud with others the words "I believe . . .," followed by statements they quite literally do not believe. Modifying-liberals apparently have no such qualms. For them the official doctrines of their church are what they believe, and they are prone to dismiss as unbelievers any who say they do not believe. Thoroughgoing-liberals, on the other hand, take statements of belief far more seriously. They think creeds recited in public worship do not represent true belief but only assent to a form of worship. For the thoroughgoing-liberal, belief is what we feel to be true, deep in our hearts.

Modifying-liberalism has as its goal the liberalizing of the movements with which it is identified. In Christianity the result has been a more liberal Catholicism, Lutheranism, Presbyterianism, or Anglicanism—in short, a more liberal Christianity. The goal of thoroughgoing-liberalism, however, is not to liberalize any particular movement or all movements, although that is often the result of its activities. Its goal is the clarification of concepts quite apart from the particular tradition out of which they have come. Its goal is the adequacy of ideas, quite apart from their historic roots or any sacred origin that may be claimed for them. In the critical tradition the goal is clarity of thought, clarity of communication, sharpness of concept, and depth of understanding.

The thoroughgoing-liberal is one who follows the critical way in religion. The modifying-liberal ordinarily is a person of ecclesiastical temper, eager to modernize the church, but no less eager to preserve its essential teaching and practice. Accordingly, much as those of the critical way in religion might like to go on calling themselves liberals as they have in the past, it would seem that they cannot; at least they cannot if they wish to be known for what they really are. The critical mind is not necessarily liberal in the usual meaning of the term. Confronted by sloppy thinking, slippery concepts, or theological cant, the critical mind is anything but open-minded and tolerant. To be sure, the critical tradition has played a conspicuous role in the age-long fight for religious liberty. Complete freedom of thought and expression are central in the critical approach. In this sense, the critical tradition and liberalism are the same. Both would agree freedom is essential to critical thinking. But the critical tradition is more than the freedom to be critical. Freedom is a necessary precondition, the necessary means to the end the critical tradition pursues. But it is not the end itself. The end is truth, unlimited by any tradition and unclouded by any prior commitments.

2

Human Fallibility

The creature with whom we start, *homo religiosus,* the human animal, possesses a remarkable set of assets and liabilities. We begin with the liabilities. We begin with the fact that we can be wrong when we want desperately to be right. We can be in error even though forewarned, even though we have taken the most elaborate precautions to avoid it; and we can be dead wrong even when we believe with all that is in us that we are right. As one student of the problem asserted, "The story of man the thinker should not crowd out the yet more instructive career of man the blunderer. [We also need to] know something of the story of human error."

It is with this colossal, all-pervasive, ever-present fact that we start our attempt to identify, to understand, and to interpret the role of religion in human life. We begin here, above all, because the ecclesiastical way in religion, despite its emphasis upon the weakness and sinfulness of people, does not take human fallibility sufficiently into account.

Dogmas, authoritatively declared to be true; traditions, accepted because their ancient lineage is thought to endow them with a special sanctity; revelations, regarded as true because they are believed to have been delivered to men by God—none of these commends itself to critical minds. The critical way, on the basis of experience in every other field of human endeavor, feels the need to check and test to the uttermost every dogma, tradition, and revelation that any religion claims. For reasons we shall explore at length, organized religion talks and acts much of the time as if, in the area of revelation, the ordinary rules do not apply. Let us remind ourselves, then, of the ever-increasing mass of evidence of human fallibility with which any such view has now to contend.

1. The Problem of Error

As long ago as the fifth century B.C., the Greek thinker Parmenides apparently undertook to prove that the senses are not to be trusted. The record of his thought and its impact on his time is unfortunately hazy, but Parmenides' proof seems to have been a tremendous shock to his contemporaries, who were accustomed to rely on their seeing, hearing, smelling, and feeling, much as we do today, except when we remember that our sense impressions can be very unreliable indeed.

Consider, for example, the effect of hallucinatory drugs upon us. We know before we take them that under their influence we shall see things no one else can see, hear things no one else can hear, and sense things of which we alone are aware. We know, in short, that our experiences will be imaginary. No one else will share them with us. And yet, under the influence of the drugs, those experiences will be totally real to us, even though the sights we see and the sounds we hear do not exist in the real world. They are the result of psychological derangement due to the effect of the drugs on our nervous system.

As soon as our nervous system begins to function normally again, we know we shall readily accept the view the rest of the world held about us while we were drugged—that our experiences were imaginary, that in believing in their truth or reality we were mistaken. Alcohol will do the same thing to us in a milder way, as many more of us have learned from personal experience, some of it painful. This is particularly true for the young, whom experience has not yet taught how mistaken they can be in their perceptions and judgments when intoxicated, even though they are aware of the possibility and believe themselves to have guarded carefully against it. The tragic statistics on drunken driving show how error-prone any of us can be when intoxicated.

If all human error were traceable to artificial stimuli like liquor and drugs, our problems would not be so difficult. But the plain fact is we can be quite as mistaken about what is going on around us when we have imbibed nothing at all. Behavioral disorders known as delusions and hallucinations are a case in point. Among these, delusions of grandeur are familiar to most of us. Books on psychology are full of examples of people suffering from delusions of grandeur about themselves. Some think of themselves as saviors of the world. Some believe themselves to be religious, moral, political, or military leaders chosen to bring men into a new era. Some call themselves Lord Christ, the Virgin Mary, Joan of Arc, the Pope, Mahatma Gandhi, or some other sainted character.

The problem is complicated by humanity's frequent inability to distinguish its saviors from charlatans and would-be destroyers. Jesus of Nazareth was mockingly called "King of the Jews" and was executed. Socrates was accused of misleading the young and forced to drink the hemlock. Joan of Arc was burned to death as a witch. Did people like these suffer from delusions of grandeur? There is little evidence to support such a view. To be sure, many today question Jesus' view of himself as the promised Messiah, assuming that he believed this of himself—a point still under intensive debate. Many question the validity of the voices Joan of Arc heard in her garden, and they question the validity of the daemon Socrates heard speaking to him. There is a very fine line between a clearly identifiable delusion and the overpowering vision and sense of mission that characterizes great human leaders. One clear distinction, however, is that between self-identification with an historical figure—e.g., "I am Napoleon"—and a sense of mission and purpose on behalf of humankind. As in so many instances where human character is assessed, the presence of gray areas does not render invalid the distinct concepts the gray areas separate.

Again, the problem of human error would be greatly simplified if it were confined to those under the influence of drugs and those who are deranged. But we all know that delusions are only a matter of degree. To some extent we all have them. We need be neither neurotic nor psychotic to develop a messianic complex, see things that do not exist, hear sounds when all is silent, smell odors that are imaginary, or feel sensations of which we ourselves are the cause. Usually intense desire or deep anxiety is the real cause, but simple boredom is enough to cause us to fall into repeated errors, as a series of experiments undertaken during World War II demonstrated. Early in the war, the British became aware that their new secret weapon—radar—used for detecting submarines was not working reliably. Checking for mechanical failure, they found none. They then shifted their attention to the men who watched the radar screens on which the U-boats were detected. These men, they found, were highly trained and thoroughly dependable.

In the course of their studies however, the investigators made a revealing discovery. The radar-watchers usually worked alone and kept watch for several hours at a time. Uniformly, their best performance came at the beginning of their time on duty. After that their dependability fell off sharply. Through laboratory simulation of these circumstances using the same watchers as subjects, the investigators soon found that simple boredom, nothing else, was the cause of their failure to see submarines plainly visible on the screen before them. The dependability of the watchers declined sharply within half an hour.

Subsequent experiments have confirmed and greatly elaborated these findings. In a laboratory environment in which all outside stimuli—those of sight, sound, smell, and touch—were eliminated, it was found that prolonged exposure to a monotonous environment has very deleterious effects on our ability to report accurately what is going on around us. Normal functioning of the brain depends on constant sensory bombardment. Sensory stimuli have the general function of maintaining this arousal, but they rapidly lose their power to do so if they become monotonously repetitious.

Contemporary studies of participants in a movement known as transcendental meditation point in the same direction. Wrote one investigator:

"Oxygen consumption, heart rate, skin resistance and electro-encephalograph measurements were recorded before, during and after subjects practiced a technique called transcendental meditation. There were significant changes between the control period and the meditation period in all measurements. During meditation, oxygen consumption and heart rate decreased, skin resistance increased and the electro-encephalogram showed specific changes in certain frequencies. These results seem to distinguish the state produced by transcendental meditation from commonly encountered states of consciousness and suggest that it may have practical applications."

Investigators of transcendental meditation are no less clear that the results of the practice are measurably beneficial. The point with which we are concerned, however, is the fallibility of the human organism in judging what is going on in the surrounding environment. These experiments provide an explanation without entering the more treacherous waters of assessing the truth of the experiences that result from the bodily states they measure. Such changes in bodily state have long since been measured in the case of drug use. What is remarkable in transcendental meditation is that bodily changes no less striking can also be measured when the cause is not drugs but self-induced quiet. What is most arresting is the similarity between the conditions of mental and physical privation under which the mystics of old felt the presence of the divine, and the conditions under which visions, both religious and nonreligious, are being measured by modern psychology.

In addition to the vast area of error to which we are subject but within which we can apply corrective measures, there is another, far greater in extent, over which control is difficult, if not impossible, to maintain. Countless laboratory experiments have established the truth of this observation, none more valid and dramatic than those of Adelbert Ames, Jr., at Dartmouth College.

Ames suffered from faulty stereoscopic vision. The studies involved in designing proper corrective glasses led him into a series of experiments that made him a pioneer thinker in the area of sense perception analysis. Ames theorized that our knowledge of the external world is only in part what the individual learns about it through his senses. Another part, equally important, he contributes himself. Thus, what we see, feel, smell, and hear is not alone what is "out there." It is rather a construct of our sense-impressions interacting with the brain. Hence what we "know" is not alone what is "out there," but what we, interacting with it, are able to make out of it. In short,

Ames argued that human knowledge is a composite of stimuli from outside of us and whatever it is that we ourselves do with those stimuli in making them "known" to the self that we are.

To prove his point, Ames constructed his now-famous room. To a person entering it, the room appeared to be rectangular like any ordinary room. But the Ames room was, in fact, highly irregular in shape. One of the far corners was much farther away from the viewer than the other. Yet the room was constructed so that the two corners appeared to be equidistant from the viewer. Both floor and ceiling were tilted, yet, again, both were constructed to appear level. The illusion was created by designing the baseboards and window frames in such a manner as to provide the false perspective necessary to make it all look even and give the illusion of squareness and regularity he sought. All details by which the eye might overcome the illusion and correct its false impressions had been carefully eliminated.

From all of this an astonishing result followed, even for those who knew how oddly the room was shaped and that its purpose was to deceive the eye and the brain. Ames showed that, because of the false perspective the room gave, three people of the same height standing at the far end of the room looked radically different in height to the beholder and in photographs, even though the beholder knew he was being deceived. Experience, Ames showed, has so conditioned us to the rules of perspective that we cannot, without considerable effort and practice, overcome these habits of thought even when we know they lead to error.

The degree to which error is bound up with our own individual psychology has been shown in further experiments with the Ames room. Our emotions also play a part in our making mistakes and in our ability to overcome them. A set of experiments has shown, for example, that newlyweds with very strong emotional ties to each other are far superior to the rank and file of men and women in overcoming errors of judgment with regard to the size of a spouse seen in a distorted Ames room. The newlyweds, the experiments showed, were far better able to see each other in their true size than were strangers.

Another set of experiments has shown that the moral judgments we make tend to be more subjective than objective. Apparently, we always make such judgments in context. We severely condemn an evil act in the context of minor wrongs, but we rate the very same act less severely in the context of grave wrongs. If we were able to be as objective as we should like to think we are, we would expect to be able always to rate the same wrong as having the same degree of severity.

Research workers at the Massachusetts General Hospital have trained some patients to control attacks of a painful nature by employing the mind to raise their hand and skin temperatures. The technique is known as "biofeedback." By no means can every patient be so trained, but the fact that even a few can raises questions about our accuracy and dependability. If a patient can be trained to control one of his "involuntary" functions, in this case skin temperature on the hand, and so eliminate pain, has he or she eliminated the pain or merely the capacity to register it? Is there a difference?

The well-known fact that eyewitnesses are untrustworthy needs no restatement. Experiments in this field continually show how mistaken our firsthand observations can be. Yet our culture is built on the assumption that eyewitnesses can with certainty tell us what happened, who was there, and under what conditions an event occurred. Despite the ever-accumulating evidence to the contrary, our legal system rests upon this premise.

Another area where human error is common but seldom emphasized and often overlooked entirely is that of prediction. I am not referring to the fantasies or to the chicanery of fortunetellers, but to the inability of great minds to assess the potential in an existing situation. We need only recall two or three famous cases. For instance, Daniel Webster declared the acquisition of New Mexico and California by the United States an absurd idea: "I hold that they are not worth a dollar!" he said. Henry Ford in his autobiography wrote: "The Edison Company offered me the general superintendency of the company but only on condition that I would give up my gas engine and devote myself to something really useful." In 1936 Charles Lindbergh said, regarding Robert H. Goddard, pioneer in the development of rockets for space travel: "I would much prefer to have him interested in real scientific development than to have him primarily interested in more spectacular achievements which are of less real value."

A new field of study known as the "communications environment" tackles the problem of human error from the point of view of language. Writers in this field hold that the culture to which we belong determines our language and is in turn determined by it. Language largely determines thought, they say, and since language is filled with ambiguity, unexamined assumptions, and inaccuracies, so, willy-nilly, is our understanding. They back their conclusions with an impressive array of data and insist that accuracy and an understanding of the nature and extent of the errors by which we try to live and do our thinking must be our goal.

A standard text in the field argues that we are all wound up in verbal quandaries, that these quandaries are like verbal cocoons, and that the structure of these cocoons is determined in great measure by the structure of the society in which they are formed. The structure of societies, in turn, has been and continues to be determined significantly by the structure of language. Since we acquire all these patterns of thought unconsciously, we employ them unaware of the baggage of error and false implications they carry. The only cure for these ills is to strive for accuracy. We must learn to eliminate the complex of errors that language builds into our thought without our being aware of it.

Over and beyond the problem of error to which we are subject because of the hidden ambiguities of language is the problem of error in transmitting our thoughts to one another. The problem is a very old one. As we all know, it is easy to misunderstand what someone else is saying, in particular if we are in a noisy room. With the rapid expansion of mechanical means of communication—telephone, radio, and television—and with the development of computerized information processing, the problem of error in transmission and the need to correct it has become acute. To meet it, exceedingly complex systems of error correcting have been devised, some of them involving very sophisticated mathematical theory to understand and explain.

The key of all correction systems in communication, whether ancient or modern, appears to be redundancy. We disclose error by repeating the same message. We do it in ordinary conversation. If I don't understand what you say, you repeat or rephrase it until I do. We do the same thing with the common problem of balancing a checkbook. If you and the bank come out with the same balance, your repetition of their arithmetic assures you that both are error-free. It is the repetition of the process that is the error-detecting device. When your repetition of the bank's arithmetic results in a figure different from theirs, you know there is an error somewhere, either yours or theirs—usually yours. Again, it is the repetition of the process—the redundancy—that reveals the mistake.

As we might expect, the first error-correcting systems were devised to eliminate mistakes in the use of numbers.

Error is so pervasive an aspect of our existence that nature herself has been compelled to deal with it. For this reason, nucleic acids are used for the storing and transmitting of information in biological organisms. Nucleic acids are apparently among the most stable elements in the biological realm; hence, they are less apt to cause error as a result of changes in themselves.

Perhaps the most pervasive evidence of the problem of accuracy and error is to be found in science, the fundamental standard and goal of which is accuracy—freedom from error. That goal is now generally conceded to be visionary. Whether we peer down the most powerful microscope in search of the atom or lift our greatest telescopes to the stars, eventually we reach the point where things grow fuzzy and where accurate observation is no longer possible.

Dependable knowledge was the goal of science from the beginning, but by the early nineteenth century Karl Friedrich Gauss, a German mathematician and astronomer, had concluded that the goal was impossible to attain—that in the end we come up against limits of human observation beyond which we cannot, at a particular time, penetrate. We may continue to extend the frontiers of knowledge, as in fact we are constantly doing, but beyond these limits, wherever they are at any given moment, lies haziness, inaccuracy, and error.

Gauss noted this fact while reviewing the astronomical data already accumulated at that time. Because of the limitations of the instruments by which those data were gathered, the results varied. Gauss plotted these variations on a graph and came up with a bell-shaped curve. The most accurate observations, he concluded, were probably, but not necessarily, those that clustered in the center. In the end, he said, we remain uncertain.

Since his time our astronomical instruments have improved enormously. In many areas where Gauss was uncertain, we feel quite confident today. However, the problem he faced remains as acute for us as it was for him. We possess vastly more data about the heavens than he did, but at the outer reaches of our instruments lies the same scatter of errors that Gauss contended with, and beyond the frontiers of observation lies an area of uncertainty no less real for us than the area he faced was for him. Our knowledge may grow, but the fact of human error and the uncertainty that results from it remain.

We have before us, then, three fundamental conclusions:

1. We human beings make mistakes even though we are aware of the tendency in ourselves, and even though we strive to the uttermost to be accurate.

2. We can, however, eliminate a vast amount of error and greatly increase our accuracy by facing up to the pervasiveness of error and by taking every measure possible to avoid it, or to detect, correct, and eliminate it.

3. No area of life, including religion, is exempt from the operation of these principles.

2. Our Credulity

Human fallibility would not be such a problem but for the reinforcing factor of our credulity. We humanoids are perhaps the most gullible of all the creatures of the earth. I met this aspect of our nature quite forcefully and unexpectedly during the mid-1950s when the Dead Sea Scroll discoveries were first coming to the attention of the public. In the spring of that year, I did a series of lectures on the Scrolls in Boston. The attendance astonished me. More astonishing still was that a number of those present, perhaps 5 to 10 percent, had come with more or less well-developed theories of conspiracy, nondisclosure, forgery, and fraud with regard to the Scrolls. Details varied from individual to individual, but, in general, the theory seemed to be that the true story of Jesus was now revealed in the Scrolls; that it had long been known by the church, but had been concealed from the people. Here again the reasons varied, but there was unanimity on the supposed fact of suppression.

I was unprepared for the anger with which some of these people greeted my answers to their questions following the lectures. Confining myself carefully to the data the Scrolls contained and the deductions that could legitimately be drawn from them, I stated flatly that there was no evidence whatever of any secret story or any concealment of facts from the people. In the eyes of the questioners, that made me a part of the conspiracy. Obviously, in these questionings I was confronted not so much by the desire to learn as by paranoia, although of a mild sort. It was, however, a firsthand lesson in human credulity. In these amateur students of the Dead Sea Scrolls I found a readiness to believe, not what the data showed, but what, despite the data, they wanted very much to believe.

In order to see the problem of human credulity in perspective, let us look back in time to a belief we now know to have been false but which was once almost universally accepted as true, the legend of the unicorn. The origin of that mythical creature is unknown, but its beginnings can be traced as far back as the fourth century B.C. Quite obviously, the idea of the unicorn was derived from an imaginary combination of the rhinoceros, with a single horn protruding from his snout, and the horse, which the unicorn resembles in every other respect. The legend has no place in the classical history of Greece and Rome, but it continued to make progress after its first appearance, handed on from one writer to another with little notice or comment. Each writer seems to have accepted without question what he had found in an earlier source.

Those who are familiar with the King James Version of the Old Testament are aware of the many references to the unicorn to be found there. They appear in Numbers, Deuteronomy, Job, Psalms, and Isaiah. Modern scholars, however, think that "unicorn" is a mistranslation of the Hebrew *re'em,* which the Septuagint, a pre-Christian Greek version of the Old Testament, had rendered "monoceros," meaning "one horn." Contemporary opinion holds *re'em* should be translated "wild buffalo," and the Revised Standard Version does so. A reading of the passages in which references to the animal appear supports the surmise of the scholars. In each case the meaning of the passage is much more suited to the wild buffalo than to the gentle unicorn.

Widespread mention of and belief in the unicorn began with the publication of a volume in Alexandria in the third century A.D. entitled *Physiologus,* in which the author described many animals, including the unicorn, which he compared to Christ. Subsequently, the unicorn came to be associated with the Virgin, who was said to make the capture of the unicorn possible. This in turn explained why no one ever gained possession of the animal. Belief in the unicorn thus became a part of the living structure of the Christian faith for a time.

During these centuries men believed in the unicorn as they believed in the horse. Every day of their lives they came in contact with horses. They rode them, worked them, cared for them, bred them, and buried them when they died. In all that time they never saw a unicorn. Yet no one seems to have questioned the existence of the mythical creature with a slender horn growing out of his forehead. The educated and the ignorant, the wise and the simple, the noble and the peasant, all alike believed.

With the coming of modern science, the unicorn vanished into the limbo of myth and imagination whence he had come. When men ceased to rely on the writings of the ancients and turned their eyes to the world about them, they discovered that no such animal was to be found anywhere. They also began to see how unlikely was the presupposed biological structure of a horse with a horn on his forehead.

Not all the beliefs of antiquity are so easily given up, however, even when they lack any basis in fact. Astrology is a conspicuous example. Recognized as a pseudoscience even in ancient times, astrology today is enjoying an extraordinary revival. Part of the credence given to it derives from the fact that it is based on one of the oldest and most fundamental of all the sciences, astronomy. The study of the stars was a major human concern among men even before the dawn of history and in civilizations having little or no contact with one another. We are best acquainted with the work of the men of Babylon and Egypt in this area, but the succession of the seasons, the phases of the moon, the movements of the planets and the stars were subjects of intense thought and study among the Mayans of Yucatan, the Indians, and the Chinese. It has been determined that Stonehenge in England in Megalithic times was an astronomical observatory of surprisingly sophisticated character.

Astrology begins and astronomy ends when we attempt to relate the movement of the planets to events in their lives in the same direct manner in which the sun is known to influence the procession of the seasons and the moon, the rise and fall of the tides. This was the case in the ancient world when people believed the future could be foretold by those who knew the art of divination. Among the ancients astrology became the chief means of foretelling the future. The sophistication of Hellenistic civilization in the ancient world put no damper on the "science" of astrology. This pseudoscience "fell upon the Hellenistic mind as a new disease falls upon some remote island people," wrote Gilbert Murray, the classics scholar. "A great foreign religion came like water in the desert to minds reluctantly and superficially enlightened but secretly longing for the old terrors and raptures from which they had been set free."

The same thing happened in Renaissance Italy. There, once again, enlightened minds, accustomed to reason and, to some degree, to the testing of ideas in the real world, turned to astrology to answer questions about the future. A full-scale attack upon astrology by Pico della Mirandola has come down to us. Again, as in ancient times, astrology prospered in a period of upheaval and uncertainty. New and unsettling discoveries like those of Columbus and da Gama were being made. It was a time of war and social unrest, a time of changing mores and of new religious institutions challenging the old, familiar, and supposedly eternal ways of the Church. Said Gilbert Murray in an observation as applicable to Renaissance Italy as to the Greco-Roman world about which he was writing: "The best seed-ground for superstition is a society in which the fortunes of men seem to bear practically no relation to their merits." If he is right, perhaps the upheavals of our time—social, moral, and political—account for the resurgence of astrology among educated, intelligent people today.

A deep-seated need of which we are quite unaware often impels us toward beliefs we might otherwise reject outright. The *New Yorker* magazine for a time played upon our lingering, half-accepted, half-rejected belief in magic and myth. A favorite device in their cartoons, continuing through three decades, showed the well-known figures of ancient mythology in modern American settings. A typical cartoon pictured an outdoor symphony concert with the conductor warning the flutes to play the proper notes. In the shadows behind the stage we see the god Pan playing on his flute. A similar line of cartoon clichés included rainmaking, the magic carpet, and the genie who rises from a lamp. No one pretends to believe in these beings, yet some impulse deep within us responds when their existence is suggested. As we laugh at a sex joke because it plays upon our fears of inadequacy or upon our suppressed desires, so we laugh at a spook joke because it plays upon our fears or upon our primitive readiness to believe.

Even those who would haughtily reject any suggestion that they believe in magic or myth reveal the same tendency in subtle ways. Such an instance was reported during the development of the hydrogen bomb. Those with the scientific skill and insight to design and build such an instrument obviously were not men bound by the superstitions of an earlier day. They were, however, as the following story shows, subject, like all of us, to the tendency to toy with concepts formerly taken for granted but now no longer believed.

> One night, under considerable strain from waiting for news, Dr. Edward Teller, the director of the project, and his laboratory manager, Herb York, popped into Livermore's Golden Rule Creamery for dinner. On the counter Teller noticed an automatic fortune telling machine bearing a sign: "Swami. Ask me a question." Jokingly, he scribbled on a piece of paper: "Do we really understand what we are trying to do?" Back popped the answer: "There seems to be a trend of doubt." Teller tried again: "Will Ivy be a success?" The answer: "Why do you ask? Of course." Ivy was a success.

The preceding paragraph, quoted word for word from a widely read news magazine, makes it clear that the director of the H-bomb project had not the slightest belief in the ability of such a mechanism to predict the future. Left unexplained was the impulse that made him write questions of the most profound importance and feed them into the machine when he was extremely anxious and tired. More important, the account does not explain why he or his companion thought the result significant enough to tell anybody about it. More important still is the question why a national magazine, that thinks of itself as sophisticated and boasts of its educated readership, thought the story worth almost as much space as a picture of the exploding bomb itself. To what deep-seated human craving were the editors catering but the readiness to believe what we cannot prove, a readiness that lurks in us all?

A magician who spent forty years trying to track down the famous Indian rope trick found the explanation, not in the arts of the magician where he had been looking for it, but in the psychology of the human mind. The Indian rope trick is pure fiction, he declared, but mankind has always had an instinctive urge to manufacture the myth that it exists. It is rooted in the idea of a stairway to heaven and, he surmised, represents a universal dream. The Chinese have it in a folk tale called "The Theft of the Peach," and it appears in our story of "Jack and the Beanstalk."

Our readiness to believe in the face of countervailing evidence has been explained in many ways. Deep-seated emotional need is surely one reason. How easily we assume that we are loved, only to discover that we have been mistaken. The never-ending procession of popular songs on this theme testifies to the way our need to be loved outruns our judgment and our powers of observation as well.

The same need, projected on a cosmic scale, apparently explains a lot of theological believing. Sigmund Freud said that all religious doctrines, such as belief in a loving God, belief in future rewards and punishments, and belief in the forgiveness of sin, could be explained as illusions derived from human wishes. Our wishes need not be impossible to accomplish in order to fall into the category of illusion. Our experience, unrelated to reality, becomes an illusion when wish fulfillment is a prominent factor in its motivation. We can understand and accept this principle in ordinary matters, but not in religion. Our religion is too much a part of us. It is so precious to us that we are unable to see it objectively.

We are not usually so foolish, however, as to accept unsupported beliefs just because we need to believe them. In religion the cultural conditions that surround us often support our beliefs, and in that way our acceptance of them becomes easy and natural, in fact, almost inevitable. A belief that might otherwise seem outrageous can become quite plausible if everyone around us seems to hold it.

The "flying saucer" phenomenon, "unidentified flying objects" ("UFOs," as they are also known), provide a clear instance of the will to believe that can possess us in the face of very flimsy evidence. Some years ago Donald Menzel, at that time Director of the Harvard Observatory, undertook a number of public lectures to disprove and discredit the flying saucer idea. An irate believer wrote him as follows: "I wish that one of those space ships would land on top of Observatory Hill, and that a squad of the Little Men would seize you, put you in their ship and take you away to Venus. Then maybe you'd believe!"

Not all the flying saucer phenomena have as yet been disproved, but enough have to indicate that the burden of proof is still on the believers. As an example, supposed UFO sightings in Utah between 1965 and 1968 were probably spruce budworm moths migrating at night and set aglow by St. Elmo's fire, an atmospheric phenomenon that occurs when strong electrical fields are present. Such insect illuminations have been created in the laboratory. Two Department of Agriculture scientists noticed the high correlation between the UFO sightings and U.S. Forest Service records of severe budworm infestations. They surmised, apparently correctly, that the cause was massive night migrations of the budworm moths, occasionally seen glowing as they passed through St. Elmo's fire.

The flying saucer phenomenon illustrates the role played by cultural conditioning in our believing the otherwise unbelievable. For years science fiction in its various forms—on television and in the cinema, in books and comic strips—has been conditioning our minds to the acceptance of stories of spacemen coming to our planet. In 1938 Orson Welles produced a Halloween program in the form of a simulated news broadcast. The script, based on H. G. Wells's *The War of the Worlds,* called for the program to begin with an innocuous broadcast. Soon the announcer broke in with the "news" that spacemen had just landed in New Jersey. The program was exceedingly realistic and for this reason, it was punctuated from time to time with a reminder to the viewing audience that they were listening to a drama, not news. Nevertheless, millions of listeners across the country simply did not or would not hear the reminder and accepted the fiction as fact. Pandemonium reigned for hours until people finally could be persuaded that they had taken as reality what had been designed as entertainment.

The role of the climate of opinion in belief without evidence is nowhere seen more vividly and terribly than in the phenomenon of witchcraft, one of the darkest stains on the history of Western culture. Witchcraft is now usually dismissed as a collective fantasy. The conspiracy theory, however, supports it. The explanation now commonly given is psychological. A popular theory holds that the widespread persecution of witches can be explained away as Christian Europe's attempt to root out lingering pockets of secret paganism, but even this theory is being given up for lack of evidence to support it.

The witchcraft mania that swept the little New England town of Salem in the Province of Massachusetts at the end of the seventeenth century is as dramatic and thoroughly documented an example of cultural conditioning and believing without proof as one could hope to find. The story is very familiar, and to grasp its meaning in the context of human credulity, we need only recall a few details.

In 1689, when William and Mary became king and queen of England, they granted religious toleration never previously known to the British people. We might suppose that this would have been regarded by the colonists in New England as a very great boon, but the opposite was the case. The Puritans were not tolerant. They had come to America in order to worship God as they felt the Bible demanded. In order to achieve their goal, they left an intolerant Church of England and established a colony in the American wilderness. Once settled in North America, however, they established a holy commonwealth more intolerant than anything they had known under the English crown. William and Mary's edict, coming as it did more than fifty years after the Puritans had established their holy commonwealth, brought their particular type of church-state structure to an end, and with it, the dominance of the clergy in both religious and secular affairs.

If it was a blow to the Puritan hierarchy, the edict was welcomed by the people generally. A mood of religious tolerance had been quietly growing among the children and grandchildren of the first Puritan settlers. But those who hold power never seem to be willing to give it up, whether for good reason or bad. It was so with the Puritan divines of New England. To counteract the effect of the royal decree of tolerance, the ministers resorted to the jeremiad, the refuge of many a hard-pressed churchman both before and since that time. They began preaching vehemently about the dire results that would follow if the people should take advantage of the new tolerance accorded them and depart from the Puritan way.

Gradually, the clergy began predicting that a visitation of witchcraft would follow a relaxation in the stern Puritan standards. In an attempt to frighten the people into submission, the ministers, in effect, created an atmosphere in which witchcraft could appear, even though they did not intend such a result and had no idea it would follow. The sermons preached in the three years between 1689, when toleration was proclaimed in England, and 1692, when the Salem witch trials began, contained all the materials necessary to set the scene for the debacle. People began to look for witches. They began expecting to find them because they had been hearing so much about them. And what they looked for, they soon began to find.

Another factor in the situation was the acrimonious quarrels that characterized the oldest communities in New England at the time. In small, stable communities, quarrels are often accentuated into feuds and may be perpetuated for years. This seems to have been true to a remarkable degree among third-generation colonists in late seventeenth-century New England. The witch hysteria proved to be a sort of emotional release from this tension. The people of those days needed to believe in witches or some other external force in order to account for any ill will they felt toward one another, which as Christian people they deplored and which they were at a loss either to explain or control. Furthermore, there was nothing in seventeenth-century knowledge inconsistent with a belief in witches. There was no way to *dis*prove their existence. This made belief in them, backed by the fulminations of the clergy, both possible and respectable.

It seems to have been the simple honesty of a woman named Mary Easty that finally broke the hysteria in Salem. She was among those condemned to die as the witchcraft madness began to burn itself out. After her condemnation, she wrote to her judges from prison: "I petition Your Honors not for my own life, for I know I must die, and my appointed time is set; but if it be possible, let no more innocent blood be shed. . . . I question not but Your Honors do the utmost of your powers in the discovery and detecting of witchcraft and witches, and would not be guilty of innocent blood for the world. But by my own innocency, I know you are in the wrong way."

It does not take much imagination for us to see the effect of such a letter upon the judges, who by this time had begun asking questions of their own. Here was a woman respected by the entire community, with clemency to be expected by confessing implication in witchcraft, who nevertheless maintained a quiet but unshakeable claim to innocence. The judges had only the unsupported accusations of others as proof of her guilt. She made no protest against their right to condemn her. She knew them to be striving to do the best they knew how.

But Mary Easty had made an appalling discovery and she reported it to the judges, not for her own sake, but for the judges', and for the sake of those who might follow her to the gallows. Until her arrest and conviction, she, like most people, had doubtless believed that Salem had, in fact, been beset by an invasion of witchery. She believed it because so many people said they experienced the power of witchcraft upon themselves. In short, Mary Easty believed in witchcraft because everyone else believed in it. The ministers believed it on the same basis and because of what they had read in writings of medieval divines who were acknowledged authorities in such matters. All alike agreed that witchcraft was a devious ill, centered in deceit that had to be met and rooted out with ruthless force.

Mary Easty, however, knew that she was not a witch. She knew that she had made no compact with the devil. She knew herself to be quite as normal and sane and honorable as the next person. Because of this, she made her appalling discovery: the notion that Salem had suffered from an invasion by the Devil was false. It was her letter, and the assertions of others like her, that brought that dread phase of American history to a close.

Mary Easty was among the last of those condemned to death as witches, but her words lived on to condemn those who condemned her. She had not asked to be acquitted on the ground that she was innocent. She had not begged for mercy on the ground that death by hanging was cruel, as well as disgraceful to her family and her own good name. Instead, she had written a letter, hoping to persuade the magistrates that they were in error and so to put a stop to the whole mad business. "By my own innocency," she had written, "I know you are in the wrong way." In the face of such clear-headed, forthright courage, the will to believe in witches could not stand.

An arresting and very persuasive new explanation for the sudden appearance and the equally sudden disappearance of witchcraft in Salem has recently been put forward by a young student of psychology. Apparently a fungus that grows on rye produces LSD. Conditions appear to have been right for a flowering of the fungus at the time of the Salem outbreak. The records of the town, which are abundant, support the surmise that the rye fungus, called ergot, could have been the true cause of the witchcraft phenomenon. Cultural conditions found in witchcraft provide a ready explanation of the delusions caused by the LSD fungus. Hysteria and human gullibility did the rest.

Is this student of psychology right? Very possibly. Should her explanation turn out to be the correct one, and should it turn out that the madness that possessed a small New England town in the late seventeenth century was due to the then-unknown drug LSD, how fragile a thing our human belief-structure becomes. In the light of that story, and such a possible explanation of it, anyone who advocates believing without also advocating the most scrupulous checking and testing will find himself or herself on very insecure ground. In no small part it is in protest against such believing that the critical way in religion became a living tradition in the West.

3. The Will to Deceive

Our fallibility, extended by our gullibility, would not be half such a problem for us, were not both reinforced by the will to deceive. There seem to be but few of us who will not at some time and in some way deceive others to their hurt and to our own gain. This tendency seems to have been with us for a very long time. For this reason, treachery, guile, and double-dealing have long been the concern of religion East and West. Judaism and Christianity are both clear in their demand for honesty and in their denunciation of deceit. In the Psalms we read:

> Why do you boast, O mighty man,
>   of mischief done against the godly?
> You worker of treachery,
>   you love evil more than good,
>   and lying more than speaking the truth.

In the Psalms God is invited to vent his wrath upon all liars and deceivers. He is implored to save the Psalmist from the deceiving ways of other men. "A righteous man hates falsehood," we read in the Book of Proverbs, and, "Bread gained by deceit is sweet to a man, but afterward his mouth will be full of gravel." The denunciations of the prophets against all deceivers are equally vehement.

The New Testament is even clearer on the matter; the Gospels and the Epistles condemn deceit of any kind and for any purpose. Falsehood is nowhere condoned, no matter how great the object toward which it is directed. Paul wound up his great letter to the church at Rome with a denunciation of those who try to deceive the hearts of the simple-minded;

he condemned the deceiver again in his second letter to the church in Thessaly, and to the church at Ephesus he wrote: "Therefore, putting away falsehood, let everyone speak the truth to his neighbor." To the church at Colossea he wrote, "Do not lie to one another, seeing that you have put off the old nature with its practices." The revelation to John on the island of Patmos consigns all liars to eternal hellfire.

The idea that deceit is a grave moral wrong is apparently relatively new, however. Evidence for quite a different attitude is to be found in the older strata of the Old Testament, notably in the Jacob stories. Although most of us were introduced to these tales in our church schools, few of us discovered that they relate a series of deceptions which follow one upon another in rapid succession, and include the most infamous ruse of all by which Jacob deceived both his father and his elder brother Esau, to secure for himself the birthright that belonged to his brother.

It is interesting to see how contemporary Christianity deals with the problem of deceit on the part of a Bible hero. *The Interpreter's Bible,* a huge compendium of textual analysis and interpretation, does not hesitate to condemn the deceptions of Jacob, but it struggles to justify them or explain them away. One of the contributors to the work tries to absolve Jacob by pointing out that it was his mother Rebekah who conceived and executed the plan. Jacob was only a reluctant accomplice. "Upon me be your curse," Rebekah said to Jacob as she spurred him on to the deception.

It is folly to judge the stories in Genesis by the moral standards of today, although it must be done if ancient Bible tales are to be used for the moral instruction of the young. The reason for dealing with this material here is not to pass judgment on the morals of an earlier time but to show how relatively recent present-day standards of deceit are, and to remind ourselves that the Bible we call "Holy" contains such tales. Cunning and guile were honored not only in Israel but almost universally in ancient times. We remember the wily Odysseus in Homer. Diogenes, we recall, was famous because he went about, lantern in hand, searching by night and by day for an honest man.

Deception by the priesthood marked the religions of the ancients. A striking instance was turned up some years ago during archeological excavations in ancient Corinth. The diggers first made their way down to the pavement of the Agora, the marketplace in the center of the city. Having noted and recorded every detail, the excavators then took up the paving stones and discovered that originally there had been a spring or fountain in the center of the marketplace, probably the reason the town had been located at that particular spot in the first place. In those long-forgotten days, the overflow from the fountain had been carried in an open duct into a small temple built at the side of the marketplace. There the water poured over a stone altar and disappeared under the temple floor. From that point it flowed in an underground conduit some thirty feet long to a terrace wall, where it emptied into a large stone jar on the outside.

As civilization spread through Greece, the ancient spring had dried up. The fountain and the temple also had been abandoned some four centuries before the time of the Christian era and the whole marketplace paved with stone. All this was more than clear to the archeologists, but being puzzled about the little temple and the water conduits in and out of it, they carefully removed the paving stones of the temple floor also. As they expected, this revealed the channel through which the water had been carried from the altar to the terrace wall outside. The channel had been carefully plastered in order that no water might be wasted. But they also found something that they did not expect at all. A small tunnel had been cut under the temple floor, just large enough for a man to crawl through on his hands and knees. It reached a point under the altar where it stopped dead. There was a double door at the other end through which the tunnel was entered. An inscription notified any possible intruder that he would be liable to a substantial fine if he were to venture inside.

And so the picture was complete. Ancient records tell us that in the worship of Dionysus, the god of wine, the miracle of turning water into wine was quite common. Here before the eyes of men living more than two thousand years later, the means by which the "miracle" was performed lay exposed. When the temple ceremonies called for turning water into wine, one of the priests crawled through the little tunnel under the floor, stopped the flow of water temporarily, and poured wine into the channel, which then flowed out of the temple wall and into the stone jar on the terrace, to the delight and astonishment of the common people.

This story from ancient Corinth is by no means a solitary instance of the pious frauds of the religious men in ancient times; unhappily, it is typical. In Egypt and Greece, Palestine and Mesopotamia, countless examples of the deception of the faithful have come to light. The Egyptians were particularly adept at contriving magical events having to do with worship. They made temple doors to swing open mysteriously, fires to start up apparently spontaneously, water to flow and stop, thus demonstrating to the unsuspecting worshiper beyond any possibility of doubt that the god of the temple was present and willing, on special occasions, to show his power.

We could perhaps set our minds at rest on this matter on the ground that these were all ancient and all pagan priests who stooped to such devices. It seems to be a human characteristic rather than merely an ancient or pagan one to deceive the pious in furthering their piety. Christianity was by no means exempt from this practice, as we can see from the "Donation of Constantine" and the "Decretals of Mercator." The Donation of Constantine was a document purporting to have been issued by Constantine in gratitude for his being healed of leprosy by Pope Sylvester I. By it he forever granted to Pope Sylvester and his successors spiritual supremacy over all other patriarchates and over all matters of faith and morals. The decree also granted to the pope temporal power over Rome, Italy, and the "provinces, places and civitates of the western regions." It is now universally agreed that this document was a forgery, drawn up in the papal chancellery probably during the third quarter of the eighth century.

How such a fabrication came about makes a fascinating story. It begins in the year 756 when Pepin, king of the Franks, deeded to the pope certain lands he had conquered in Italy. In the complexities of medieval politics, this had the effect of completing the separation of the eastern and western branches of the Church. In effect, then, Pepin's gift of land to the pope established, finally, Rome's independence of Byzantium.

As the pope began to exercise the authority of a secular prince over his newly acquired lands, and as the validity of Pepin's "donation" enjoyed increasing recognition, apparently the idea of a contrived "Donation of Constantine" suggested itself by analogy. The original intent was not to provide documentary evidence for the supremacy of the church over the state, but to support by an instrument even more impressive than the Donation of Pepin the claims of the Roman Church against those of Byzantium. If Constantine himself had granted the western lands to the Bishop of Rome, what standing could Byzantium's claim have? It was only later, when the medieval popes found themselves in a struggle for power with the rising monarchies of the West, that the Donation of Constantine came more and more into use. Gregory VII, Innocent III, Boniface VIII, all used it with telling effect. For seven hundred years it was one of the chief weapons employed by the Church in its pursuit of political power. In the fifteenth century, however, as the Renaissance produced new patterns of thought, Lorenzo Valla, an astute and resourceful scholar, began a critical study of the Scriptures. He examined many another basic document with the same critical eye and concluded, among other things, that the Apostles' Creed could not have been written by the Apostles and that the writings attributed to Dionysus the Areopagite could not possibly have been written by him. Valla then published a study showing that the Donation of Constantine was a forgery. No scholar has since challenged his conclusions. "It is not my aim to inveigh against anyone," he once wrote, "but to root out error from men's minds." And he added, "To give one's life in defense of truth and justice is the path of highest virtue."

Apparently the success of the Donation of Constantine tempted the papacy to strengthen its claim to supremacy with further documentation. In the middle of the ninth century a series of decretals was published in the neighborhood of Tours. They purported to be documents issued by popes who had reigned before Constantine and by church councils of the same period. They were attributed to one Isidore Mercator, a specialist in canon law who was supposed to have compiled them. As a result, the "Isidorian

Decretals" became a part of the canon law of the Church and remained so until they too were shown to have been a forgery.

Unfortunately the deceptions and trickery of the churchmen were not always so highly motivated. Nor were they confined to the high-ranking officials of the Church. The practices of many of the pre-Reformation clergy are too well known to require review here. The lesson to be learned from it all is that even religion is not exempt from fraud, and that fraud is a problem with which theologians and churchmen must deal. Religion lends itself to deception as do most aspects of the human enterprise. Despite the high purposes to which it is dedicated, religion does not lack for devotees who will bend its offices to their own low ends, or who will, in furthering its influence, resort to deception and prevarication.

What then of our own time? As I write, reports are appearing in the press about a boy evangelist who enjoyed and still enjoys fabulous success. Having grown to manhood, he now says it is all a fraud designed to take money from the gullible. He estimates his childhood "take" as having been in excess of three million dollars. What he has been doing is bad, he admits, but defends it on the ground that others do things that are wrong, too. Now he yearns to turn his talents as an audience spellbinder to straight entertainment.

Contemporary instances of deception in religion are not always as clear-cut as were those of an earlier day and are therefore much more difficult to assess. An example is the problem of alleged miraculous cures. On the outskirts of Mexico City stands a great cathedral at the shrine of Guadalupe. Since the time when a simple Indian, Juan Diego, had a vision of the Virgin there, Guadalupe has been a mecca for pilgrims from all over Mexico. In front of the great church is a broad plaza paved with stone. Somehow the belief has grown up over the years that an ailing penitent who crosses the plaza on his or her knees will be miraculously healed. A visitor to the shrine on almost any day can see the procession of supplicants slowly making their way across the plaza with the aid of their loved ones. It is a pitiful sight. By the time the supplicant reaches the church door his knees are often bloody. Some say they have been miraculously cured; more say they have not. The Church frowns on the practice but still it goes on, and the cathedral coffers are filled with the gifts of believing pilgrims.

Are they deceived? In this case, who is deceiving whom? The clergy, the church that keeps its doors open and its coffers ready at hand? Or are the ignorant poor deceiving themselves? Do the lame, the halt, and the blind come to Guadalupe eager to believe that adequate penance will confer on them the miracle of healing?

Without trying to pass judgment on any particular instance, we can say without qualification that man's will to deceive his fellow man is a problem from which religion has never been free and is not free today. Deception has always pervaded all of life. There is no need to cite here the instances of deceit and misrepresentation of which there is so much evidence today. We are deceived and manipulated by government, industry, entertainment, and the news media, and who knows how much else. The contemporary literature in this field is enormous. Apparently art forgery goes back thousands of years. Even science, which prides itself on its integrity and, in fact, depends upon it, is not free from those who try to achieve by dissimulation what they cannot achieve by merit, the Piltdown Man hoax being perhaps the most famous instance. This does not mean that all religion is a sham, but it does suggest that in assessing the claims of religion we need to take the will to deceive into account. Religion, despite its high purposes and noble ideals, is not exempt from human frailty.

One of the most encouraging aspects of contemporary culture is the accelerating frequency with which a famous line from Oliver Cromwell is quoted: "My brethren, by the bowels of Christ I beseech you, bethink you that you may be mistaken." The earliest modern reference I have come across is to be found in Alfred North Whitehead's *Science and the Modern World,* published in 1925. Perhaps it was he who first dug the quotation out and started it on its way. In any case, we can be grateful for the frequency with which it is repeated today, for the problem of human error is fundamental, and we ought never to permit ourselves to forget it.

The critical tradition in religion is a reflection of this fundamental aspect of human nature, an aspect that may be fundamental to the universe itself. We are fallible and there are no exceptions to this rule. Accordingly, in religion, as in all things, we are required to test, retest, and test yet again every alleged "fact" that is laid before us and every principle anyone proposes, no matter who does it or how high the authority on which it is said to rest. Our fallibility also requires us to test and retest, often to reformulate or to conceive anew, the concepts by which we seek to understand and interpret experience. In the graceful words of the English philosopher and critic, Leslie Stephen, our task is to "strengthen the fitful and uncertain influence of a sound intellect upon the vast and intricate jumble of conflicting opinions in the world at large."

PART II

The Critical Tradition in the Religion of the West

To attempt to outline the story of the emergence of the critical way in religion is a formidable undertaking. The sheer bulk of the available material is staggering. Primary documentary sources exist in abundance, and these in turn have been subjected to uncounted interpretative studies, the more recent of which are based upon a first-hand review of all the extant records relevant to a carefully delineated area of investigation. Beyond these are studies of the various periods into which the history of the West conveniently falls—the Renaissance and Enlightenment, for example. The attempts of still other scholars to distill and to relate to one another what they discern as the most basic elements in Western culture add further to our understanding of the whole.

But, though formidable, the task is not impossible. The exceedingly high standards of accuracy that prevail in contemporary scholarship make for a high degree of reliability in the historical writing being done in our time. Nowhere is the competition for accuracy and adequacy more fierce. No group diligently searches the work of fellow members for errors of omission and commission, judgments based on surmise rather than data, misunderstandings, misinterpretations, and so on. No group more quickly exposes such errors to common view.

As a result, scholars today can and do rely upon the work of one another, as I have done in the pages that follow. Since no one could ever read all the original documents relevant to the critical tradition in the religion of the West, I have relied, in no small part, upon the writings of scholars who have devoted their lives to a study of the sources in special fields. These students are the first to admit that the best of them will have his or her analysis colored by the views current in his or her own time and that they will inevitably be colored to some degree by the particular tastes, often by the prejudices, of the author as well. The relative accuracy of such writing is, however, protected by the varying points of view to be found in all the rest and by the readiness of each writer to point out errors, omissions, and personal opinions in the writings of others—and often, but not always, even in their own. The goal in historiography is not so much perfection—unattainable in any human enterprise—as it is an adequate telling of the story within the limits of human fallibility and the bounds of one's own cultural conditioning.

A second difficulty in recounting the emergence of the critical way in religion as a living tradition in Western culture is the problem of selection. In such a welter of material, who should be chosen for special mention? What periods, what trends should have extended consideration? My guiding principle has been the evidence of independent creative and critical minds and spirits. I have chosen for special treatment thinkers, periods, trends bearing this mark.

The story of Western culture in its religious aspects shows that the rebels, the nonconformists, the prophets, the critics, and the protesters had much in common with one another. The discernible thread of continuity between them, the movement in thought from one to another, as when the Enlightenment went back to Pyrrho of Elis, or when Galileo, less consciously but more directly, built his thought on the work of Copernicus—all these connections and relationships, taken together, make up the critical tradition in the religion of the West.

The story that follows is, of course, not complete, nor can it be expected to be wholly error-free. New data are constantly being discovered and greater understanding of the meaning of the vast complex of data we already possess is constantly being achieved. The best possible account pieced together in our time will inevitably yield to a better, soon to follow.

My story will have served its purpose if, to some degree, it can show how a tradition in religion, which I have called critical, has been growing in the West for some twenty-five centuries. It will be enough if those who react to this story, whether in a positive or negative way, discern more clearly that there has long been, and that there continues today, to be a critical tradition as well as an ecclesiastical tradition in the religion of the West. It will be enough if the story told here can give religious seekers in our time the realization that they are not alone; that they stand in a long and honorable line of men and women, who, down through the ages, have sought a better religion than the churches and temples of their time were able to provide.

John Henry Newman, Oxford don, Cardinal, and redoubtable defender of the traditional approach to religion, once wrote: "The medieval schools were the arena of as critical a struggle between truth and error as Christianity has ever endured. . . . Scarcely had the humanities risen into popularity when they were found to be infected with the most subtle and fatal form of unbelief; and the heresies of the East germinated in the West of Europe and in Catholic lecture rooms with a mysterious vigor upon which history throws little light."

The point of view of the critical way in religion is exactly opposite to that of Newman. The critical mind rejects outright the idea that the beginnings of questioning in medieval universities can be compared with infection and disease. It would shift the metaphor to that of a landscape slowly disclosed to the eye as a new day dawns, slowly suffusing everything with light and making ever more distinct the details of the scene.

As to history, the critical mind would sharply dissent from Newman's view that history "throws little light" upon the vigor of the questioning that arose in the high Middle Ages. In history the critical mind finds the answer to many of its questions. With regard to the vigor of the questioning process, the critical mind would argue that there is nothing mysterious about it, as the following pages will show. Indeed, that is the purpose of Part II, to outline the origin and the development of the critical way in religion as it became pervasive, first in Western thought and more recently in human thought worldwide.

3

The Critical Tradition Is Born

Many thinkers have commented on the sudden burst of bold, original thinking that took place in the world in the middle of the first millennium B.C. It was as if our humankind, slowly making its way out of the jungle into civilization, suddenly reached a new level of understanding. In that period various cultures, widely separated from one another, broke through age-old ways of thought and practice and, apparently independently of one another, established basic new patterns of thought and practice. For this reason it has been called the "axial" period. Among the figures whose work contributed to this sudden surge in human thought and understanding, the following are often named: Confucius, Lao-Tzu, the authors of the Upanishads, Gautama the Buddha, Zoroaster, Elijah, Isaiah, Jeremiah, Deutero-Isaiah, Homer, Thales, Xenophanes, Parmenides, Heraclitus, Plato, Thucydides, and Archimedes.

One of those most often cited as making a sudden departure in the thought of the West is Thales, a figure of the sixth century B.C. He remains somewhat hazy owing to the paucity of our records. If what we know is at all reliable, however, we could hardly choose a better person with whom to begin an account of the growth and development of the critical tradition in the religion of the West.

1. Insight in Ionia

In the seventh and sixth centuries B.C. there was a thriving civilization at the eastern end of the Mediterranean Sea. Not the least of the cultures flourishing there at the time was that of the Greeks. It centered around the shores of the Aegean Sea from the Peloponnesus to the west coast of Asia Minor, known as Ionia. One of the greatest of the Ionian cities was Miletus where, as far as we know, Thales lived his entire life. It was a leading commercial center and was evidently a leading cultural center as well. There at the hands of Thales came one of the most basic shifts in human thinking of which we are aware.

We have no reason to think he alone brought about such a shift. Perhaps he was the most articulate member of a group of thinkers who had begun to speculate on basic questions of origin and causality. As far as we can now see, he was not a reformer. He was not trying to liberate the mind from old fears and superstitions, he was trying to work out new explanations of the nature of things. Apparently those that were offered by the authorities to whom people in his time were accustomed to turn, namely, Homer and Hesiod, did not satisfy him. In their writings natural phenomena and human events were either taken for granted or looked upon as resulting from the activities of the gods. If a man drowned in a river, it was because the river god was angry with him. If he was victorious in battle, it was because Ares intervened to help him. If a thunderstorm occurred, it was because Zeus was angry.

This manner of explaining things was not questioned by anyone in Hellenic culture until Thales' time, at least as far as we know today. Seen now in the perspective of time, Thales seems to have made a nearly incredible leap of the imagination when he attempted a natural explanation of his world. The particular formula he hit on—that water is the basic substance from which all things are derived—is not what is important about him, although our present-day knowledge of the role of water in the physical structure of the world shows something of his genius. It was the fact that this suggestion constituted a wholly new approach to an old and accepted set of ideas that makes Thales stand out as one of the giant intellects of all time, if indeed we are justified in attributing such a basic insight to a single individual. Few at the time or since have agreed with him that water is the basic substance in nature, but that is of no consequence. Virtually all of the thinkers who came after him agreed with his major premise that speculation and analysis will give you better answers to fundamental questions than stories about the activities of the gods. Thales replaced narrative with philosophy.

Another citizen of Miletus, a near-contemporary of Thales, a pupil, in fact, stands next in line among the great Greek natural philosophers. His name was Anaximander. The basic substance of which all things are made is not water, he asserted; it is "The Boundless," or the infinite. As with Thales, what is important about him is not his particular solution to the problem with which these thinkers were wrestling. Anaximander's greatness lies in the fact that he, the pupil, like his master, abandoned the practice of citing ancient authorities and struck out on his own. This included his rejecting Thales' formulation.

Anaximenes, also a citizen of that remarkable city, Miletus, and a younger contemporary of Anaximander, continued the new speculative tradition. He suggested that the basic substance is air. But he, like his two predecessors, is not important because of his particular theory; it was soon replaced by yet another. Like Thales and Anaximander, Anaximenes was important because he developed further the speculative approach to cosmological questions.

What sort of men were these pioneers in the realm of thought? How do we explain their apparently sudden appearance in Ionia? We know that their ancestors were Hellenes. We know that the Hellenes had been driven from their homes on the mainland of Greece by the invading Dorians. We know, too, that when settled on the shores of Ionia, across the Aegean Sea, they slew the men then living there, took the women and children captive, and settled down with them.

We know the invaders of Hellas were Indo-Europeans. They worshiped sky gods, symbolizing vitality, rather than the earth gods, symbolizing fertility, to whom most of the peoples of that time gave their allegiance. Perhaps this is part of the explanation of their superiority. The gods the Hellenes worshiped, unlike most of the deities of the ancient world, called upon people not to humble themselves, but to display their virtue and power as persons.

These ideals are central in Homer, and it may be that their predominance in his writings explains, at least in part, the emergence of the critical way in religion in ancient Greece. We know the fundamental role that Homer played in the formation of Greek character. Perhaps—in his continual holding before the Greek mind the virtues of self-reliance, of individual prowess and achievement in his positive approach to life—we have a key to the boldness and originality of the Greek mind in this period.

The contrast with ideals being instilled into other peoples in the same general area at the same time is very great. Elsewhere the virtues of humility, subservience, and submission to authority prevailed. Compare, for example, the basic attitude of the *Iliad* and *Odyssey* with that of the older passages in Genesis. Obedience and submission to divine commands, not self-reliance and daring, are the dominant themes in the stories of Adam and Eve, driven from Eden because they disobeyed God in seeking knowledge; of the builders of the Tower of Babel, who also sought knowledge and were also punished for doing so. The story of Noah makes the same point, as do uncounted subsequent tales, by showing how well the Lord God rewarded those who obeyed his commands, and how severely he punished those who did not.

Another factor contributing to Ionian superiority was the wide-ranging trade developed by the Greeks of this period. Their cities flourished, Miletus being foremost among them. As has so often happened in human history, material prosperity produced leisure; leisure resulted in the development of learning and in the practice of speculation, contemplation, and reflection. Again, as has so often happened in the past, commercial prosperity brought with it a change in the class structure. This in turn resulted in the breaking of old social customs and taboos. The result was an atmosphere of freedom in which fresh thinking was possible and new ideas could be expressed without danger of political reprisal or social ostracism.

All of these factors need to be seen in the wider context of Near Eastern life and culture if they are to be fully understood. Behind the burgeoning Greek civilization of that period lay at least two millennia of Mesopotamian and Egyptian culture, perhaps much more. Before the Greek period, Sumer and Akkad had risen and fallen; so had Ur, Babylon, Hurria, Mitanni, and Assyria. The Egyptian Empire was twenty-five centuries old at that time. The culture and learning of all of these nations was the heritage of the Greeks. Beyond these lay the empires and cultures of India and China.

True, the invading Hellenes were barbarians, but the wives they took in the new land they occupied, who became the mothers of their children, had grown up in a culture already ancient at the time. All of this was the heritage of the children's children of the invading barbarian Hellenes, of whom we learn in the Homeric epics. Perhaps the vitality and self-confidence of the barbarian invaders combined with the learning of the ancient Near East to produce the unique cultural tradition that developed first in Ionia and later on the mainland of Greece.

At about this time the alphabet, one of the most basic inventions of the human mind, was worked out. Scholars have now traced the development of the alphabet from Minoan Linear A, which appeared in the second millennium, through Minoan Linear B, which appeared around the fourteenth century B.C., to the alphabet which the Greeks adapted from that of the Phoenicians in the eighth or ninth century B.C.

The oral narratives of Homer and Hesiod were reduced to writing soon afterward. We can easily imagine the impact of that extraordinary event on the Greek mind. When at last those great and beloved works could be read at leisure and their meaning pondered line by line, then, for the first time, a thoughtful mind could set in juxtaposition the details of a complex tradition. Before that, the Homeric epics swept past the listener in a single afternoon or evening or perhaps a series of them. Homer, pondered in the cold light of day, must have seemed quite different from Homer heard in a great gathering through the highly skilled and dramatic voice of a minstrel.

It is a legitimate surmise that alert minds, reading Homer and Hesiod for the first time and having the opportunity to reread what they had read, might have found these accounts of the causes of things inadequate. Newer and better ideas might well have come into their minds as they read, and the kind of speculation we see for the first time in Thales may well have been the result. From such records as have come down to us, it now appears that following Hesiod's attempt to find a unifying principle for the gods, Thales found a single unifying principle for the world of nature, a principle having nothing to do with the gods.

The result was the emergence of a new type of figure—the man the Greeks later named the philosopher—the thinker, the man who was supposedly inept at practical affairs, who seemed not to care for riches, family, fame, or even bodily comfort, but who, lost in thought, formulated ideas of which no one had dreamed heretofore. These were the forerunners of the critical way in religion. With them the formulation of the critical way in the religion of the West can be said to have begun. Few of these thinkers directly attacked the established religious beliefs and practices of their time, but their speculations on the physical nature of things and on the manner in which the natural world operates marked a basic departure from the older religio-mythical approach. The difference was fundamental. Heretofore, thinking had been based upon the premise that events happen as a result of the intervention of the gods. Such an assumption is wholly absent from thinking in the critical way in religion.

2. The New Philosophy and the Old Religion

Xenophanes of Colophon, a city on the western edge of what is now Turkey, first drew out the implications of Ionian thought for the cosmology of Homer and Hesiod. More than all the rest taken together, Xenophanes set the new philosophy in juxtaposition to the old mythology. He apparently was the first to grasp the fundamental inconsistency between the two points of view. At least among those of whom we have any record, he was the first to state it. Xenophanes had the insight and the courage to attack the theology of Homer and Hesiod with the philosophy of Thales and Anaximander. As far as our records show, he was the first to point out how far from the god-ideal were the dwellers on Olympus, whose antics Homer describes in such glowing detail.

Hear now Xenophanes himself, as his words have come down to us in fragmentary form.

> 1. God is one, supreme among gods and men and not like mortals in body or in mind.
>
> 2. The whole of God sees, the whole perceives, the whole hears.
>
> 3. Without effort he sets in motion all things by mind and thought.
>
> 4. Mortals suppose that the gods are born (as they themselves are) and that they wear man's clothing and have human voice and body.
>
> 5. But if cattle or lions had hands, so as to paint with their hands and produce works of art as men do, they would paint their gods and

> give them bodies in form like their own—horses like horses and cattle like cattle.
>
> 6. Homer and Hesiod attribute to the gods all things which are disreputable and worthy of blame when done by men; and they told of them many lawless deeds, stealing, adultery and deception of each other.

There is no evidence that the Greeks were alarmed by the writings of Xenophanes any more than they had been by the speculations of the other Ionian philosophers. Perhaps a basic tolerance prevailed in Ionia in the sixth century B.C. It is also likely that the implications of what Xenophanes was saying had not yet been fully understood as an implicit denial of the existence of the gods of Homer.

In Pericles' time, however, there emerged an overt conflict between free speculation and established religion. It came through the person of Anaxagoras, a brilliant thinker, a teacher and friend of Pericles, of Euripides, and probably of Socrates as well. Not surprisingly, Anaxagoras, too, grew up in Ionia, where he doubtless was steeped in the tradition of independent speculation that still prevailed there. While still a young man he went to Athens, where he remained for the major part of his life. Anaxagoras' teachings seem extraordinary to us even now. He sought to reconcile Ionian natural philosophy with Homeric religion by asserting that the gods were abstractions. He also said that the sun, to which all Athenians were accustomed to address prayers every morning and evening, was not a deity but a mass of flaming matter of enormous size. He suggested that both animals and man originally sprang from warm, moist clay. The moon shines not by its own light, he said, but by the reflected light of the sun. He taught the atomic theory of matter, and was among the first to insist that change is real. Like Thales, he successfully predicted an eclipse of the sun, and to his wide-eyed observers, demonstrated that air is not mere empty space but a compressible reality.

All this gave Pericles' enemies the opportunity for which they had been waiting. They first secured the passage of an anti-blasphemy law, then, as an oblique attack on Pericles, brought his tutor and friend to trial for attacking the gods of the state. Anaxagoras was convicted, fined, and banished. He was saved from execution only by the intervention of Pericles himself.

Protagoras, a contemporary and fellow Athenian, was also exiled for blasphemy. Nothing of his work remains today except a single sentence from his essay entitled "On the Gods." Nevertheless, those few words undoubtedly summarize his basic viewpoint. He wrote, "Concerning the gods, I am unable to say whether they exist or not, nor, if they do, what they are like; there are many things which hinder us from knowledge; there is the obscurity of the subject and the shortness of human life."

Today we have little trouble agreeing with Protagoras' doubts about the deities in the Greek pantheon. Like him we can find no reason for believing they ever existed, and like him, we have no basis upon which to attempt any kind of description of them. We would also readily agree with him that many things hinder us from acquiring such knowledge, among them the obscurity of the subject matter and the fact that none of us has sufficient time to investigate it, owing to the shortness of our lifespan.

If, however, we are to grasp the startlingly contemporary character of Protagoras' thought, we have only to apply to the divinities of our own time what he said about the divinities of ancient Greece. Recasting his words to apply to ideas that prevail today, we might find Protagoras saying, "Concerning God, I am unable to say whether he exists or not, nor, if he does, what he is like. Many things hinder us from knowing all that we might like to know about God, among them the fact that his nature is obscure and that a single lifetime is not enough to enable us to penetrate such a mystery."

Protagoras was not an atheist; he was an agnostic. He did not deny the existence of the divine. He said only that he had no firsthand knowledge to rely on because the subject matter was too obscure to permit any clear and positive statements about it. Even in our own post-Death-of-God days, such a statement would sound extreme.

Euripides dealt with the problem of belief in the Homeric gods from the moral point of view. In his *Heracles,* the hero cries: "I do not believe the gods commit adultery, or bind each other in chains. I never did believe it; I never shall; nor that one god is tyrant of the rest. If god is truly god, he is perfect, lacking nothing. These are the poets' wretched lies."

Plato, in *The Republic,* expresses the same idea. In teaching young boys, he says, the tales of Homer and Hesiod should be censored. Like Euripides, he insisted that stories about the wrongdoing of the gods are lies. He writes, "The doings of Cronus and the sufferings which his son in turn inflicted on him, even if they were not true, ought certainly not to be lightly told to young and thoughtless persons." After detailing at length the pictures of the gods that must be rejected, Plato declares, "God is perfectly simple and true both in word and deed; he changes not; he deceives not either by sign or word, by dream or waking vision." And he concludes, "Although we are admirers of Homer, we do not admire the lying dream which Zeus sends to Agamemnon."

The speculations of the Ionians on the nature of the physical world seem childish to us now, but such an observation misses the point. What is important about them for us is not their answers but their questions. The Ionians were questioning the old explanation of things and putting forward new answers of their own. Pythagoras is one of the more famous of the Greek thinkers who grew out of this tradition. Socrates, to whom we shall presently turn, was the most famous of them all. We can go on adding to the list: Solon, who introduced the concept of the rule of law; Heraclitus, who grasped the fundamental character of the fact of change; Democritus, who developed a cosmology that bears remarkable resemblance to modern concepts of the atom; Pericles, who did not feel himself to be tradition-bound in government; Phidias and Praxiteles in their natural yet ideal representations in art—and so on and on.

The art of the Greeks expressed this spirit in a truly remarkable way. One scholar, describing Greek statuary, writes: "The Olympic Hermes is a perfect human being, no more, no less. Every detail of his body was shaped from a consummate knowledge of actual bodies. Nothing is added to mark his deity, no aureole around his head, no mystic staff, no hint that here is he who guides the soul to death. The significance of the statue to the Greek artist, the mark of the divinity, was its beauty, only that. [For the artist] the Word had become flesh. . . . He never had an impulse to fashion something different, something truer than this truth of nature." The artist's notion of the eternal was what real men and women actually were or might become.

By the time of the classical period, the educated Greek mind had ceased to believe in the gods. The gods were not thought of as abstractions or myths or symbols or representations. They were regarded as the constructs of the mind of an earlier time. Belief in their reality was not sustained by trying to humanize them or to demythologize them. And unlike our own time, which is so similar in so many ways, no one undertook to declare that they had died.

One final example must serve to round out the implications of the new departure in human thought initiated by the Ionian philosophers. It is taken from the field of medicine and is from Hippocrates' tract, *On the Sacred Diseases.* Writing on epilepsy, which the Greeks before him had considered divine, Hippocrates said:

> The Sacred Disease appears to me to be not a bit more divine than other diseases, nor more sacred; it has a nature and a cause. Men believe it something divine through ignorance and their sense of the marvelous. Yet while its divinity is sustained because of an inability to comprehend it, this is really disproved by the simplicity of the manner in which the disease is cured, to wit, by purifications and incantations. But if it is to be held divine because marvelous, many will be the sacred diseases and not one, for I will demonstrate the existence of other diseases no less marvelous and portentous which no one considers sacred. . . . And they who first ascribed this disorder to the gods must have been like magicians and purifiers, charlatans and quacks of our own day who claim excessive piety and more than average knowledge, while they use divinity as a pretext and a shield for their own inability to produce a cure.

Where shall we find in any literature or any language a clearer sense of the worth of observation and the need to divest ourselves of ancient erroneous ideas that persist because they became associated with man's belief in the divine? Such is the critical tradition, and such are its origins in ancient Greece. In this tradition, all principles, all experience, the whole fabric of life are to be examined to see what there may be of wisdom in it all, and what there may be of folly.

3. Socrates

Occasionally there appears a mind so great that, in retrospect, it can be seen as a watershed in human history. Such was Socrates, universally recognized as among the greatest persons of genius the world has produced.

Students of Greek culture generally agree that fifth century Greek thought, character, and institutions represent an extraordinary level of human achievement. They agree, too, that Socrates, standing at the apex of this development, is nevertheless a pivotal character in his own right. One scholar says he belongs to "that small number of adventurers who from time to time have enlarged the horizon of the human spirit." Another has called him "the dividing point." Before him everything was looked on as impersonal, ruled by fate. After Socrates, responsibility centers in the individual: *he* makes the judgments. Still another, after delineating the "electric atmosphere" of Athens at that time and the atmosphere of freedom that prevailed there, went on to say that Socrates "was a unique event in the history of the Greek spirit." He found in him "the first appearance in the west of the problem . . . of state and church . . . a problem not peculiar to Christianity. . . . It is the tension between citizenship in an earthly community and one's spiritual subjection to God."

No iconoclast, but one who held the traditions of his people in great reverence, Socrates was above all else a seeker of the truth. Keenly aware of human limitations and frailty, with the fact of human fallibility and venality ever before him, he sought knowledge that was sure and formulations of truth that could stand the test of criticism. Thus, although he never wrote a word of his own as far as we know, his words, recorded by Plato, Xenophon, and others, became part of the basic structure of Western thought. "Know thyself," he used to say; "Virtue is knowledge." The key to his life and thought is found in an admonition quoted by Plato in the *Apology*: "The unexamined life is not worth living."

Students of Socrates often say that he turned philosophy from the study of nature to the study of human life. The remark is accurate concerning the emphasis of his thought, but it misses the most fundamental contribution he made: his introduction of the Socratic method. Socrates was above all the critic. He tested the validity of Greek naturalistic philosophy of his time, but he tested with equal severity human thought about the human creature. He spent little time examining naturalistic philosophy because he did not think the exercise profitable. In Socrates' time the naturalistic philosophers had sufficiently exposed the weaknesses of one another to spare anyone else the need to do so. It is another way of saying that by the fifth century B.C., the first great adventure in speculating on cosmological questions had spent itself and had become a cacophony of conflicting theories. In many instances speculation had given way to dogma. Still virtually untouched by speculation and criticism, however, lay the whole world of human ideals and human motivation. It was to this that Socrates turned his attention. His greatness was that he seems to have been the first to apply a thoroughgoing method of examination and criticism to human thought and ideals.

To understand him we have always to keep in mind the purpose to which his method was devoted. The "Socratic method" was a means to an end. The end was truth and right, knowledge and understanding. The means was the closest possible examination of any assertion in order to discover whether or not it was true. In the popular mind Socrates is often confused with the Sophists. He was similarly confused with them in ancient Greece. There is indeed a superficial similarity. Both sought to make their points in oral debate. But there the similarity ends: the goals of the two were exactly opposite. The Sophists engaged in argument in order to best an opponent—in order to win in a forensic encounter. Socrates engaged in argument in order to expose error and inconsistency in the pursuit of truth and understanding.

At his trial Socrates was condemned for (1) "not worshipping the gods whom the State worships, but introducing new and unfamiliar religious practices," and (2) "of corrupting the young." He denounced both accusations as false, but they made sense to most Athenians. As the people saw it, the corruption of the youth followed directly from his use of the critical method, and it was a simple matter of fact that Socrates did not follow the cult practices observed in Athens in his day.

Socrates is a nearly perfect exemplar of the critical way in religion. Deeply religious in his devotion to the values men and women seek in their lives, he was nevertheless unwilling to accept any value until he had first tested it in every way possible. Plato, Socrates' perhaps even more brilliant pupil, purported to reproduce in dialogue form the debates of the master with the citizens of Athens. In the early dialogues in particular, Plato followed virtually the same format in each. A proposition was set up; then step by step it was examined in every conceivable way, and its ambiguities, shortcomings, and errors brought to light. Implicit if not explicit in the Platonic dialogues was the conviction that critical thought is fundamental in the truth-seeking process. This is the first principle of the critical way in religion.

The law of criticism has no exceptions. If we are to move toward truth we must examine our own thought with the same care we bestow upon the thought of others, and we must encourage them to be no less scrupulous in their examination of ours. Anyone who would seek the truth by means of the critical method must see that the method itself is subject to criticism. So too is the principle by which it is justified. Socrates saw this also.

Accordingly, he stood for the open and public discussion of all matters. It was, he insisted, the best guarantee that truth in any area may be attained. At his trial he said, "In me you have a stimulating critic, persistently urging you with persuasion and reproaches, persistently testing your opinions and trying to show you that you are really ignorant of what you suppose you know. Daily discussion of the matters about which you hear me conversing is the highest good for man. Life that is not tested by such discussion is not worth living." This is the second of the principles articulated in Socrates that is fundamental in the critical way in religion.

But there was a deeper dimension to Socrates' belief in the value of open discussion. He believed in the full right of freedom of speech, to put the concept in our language, quite apart from its truth-yielding aspect. Socrates' emphasis here was bound up with his doctrine of the soul, and this aspect of his thought is better described by our phrase "freedom of conscience." Again to quote his words (as reported by Plato) when he was on trial for his life: "If you acquit me . . . upon condition that I may not inquire and speculate any more . . . I shall reply: Men of Athens, I honor and love you, but I shall obey God rather than you, and while I have life and strength, I shall never cease from the practice and teaching of philosophy. . . . I do nothing but go about, persuading you all, old and young alike, not to take thought for your persons or your properties, but first and chiefly to care about the greatest improvement of the soul." In this declaration we have a third principle that is basic in the critical way in religion made articulate by Socrates. In contemporary language we would speak of the right of self-expression, of self-fulfillment focused in one of the most precious of all freedoms, the freedom of conscience.

Socrates cast into clear, bold, unmistakable language a fourth tenet of the critical tradition: you cannot delegate to someone else the decision as to what is true and right. You can, of course, in the technical sense. You can let the state or the church make these decisions for you, but you still have not escaped the requirement life lays upon you to decide for yourself. You have only pushed it one step further back. The initial decision, that church or state shall decide these questions on your behalf, is still yours. You and you alone can declare yourself incompetent to decide and give over to church or state the privilege of resolving these questions. You and you alone make *that* decision. There is no way you can delegate it.

Truth, wisdom, virtue, the good of one's own soul, the welfare of the state—all these principles animated Socrates' thought. In his eyes they laid upon him, and by implication upon all men, the duty to speak, the duty to make such wisdom as had been given to him available to all men. Athens at that time was far from granting to all the right of freedom of speech. And yet the principle was practiced to a remarkable degree, as we can see from the fact that Socrates was unmolested up to the age of seventy even though his teachings and his public disputations rankled many a public dignitary. His description of himself as a gadfly was probably quite accurate.

Such was Socrates. In speaking of him as a watershed figure in human thought, I do not suggest that he stands alone. Great men are like great mountain peaks. Everest, the tallest of them all, rises from the Himalayas, the greatest of all the mountain ranges of the earth. So with Socrates: the largest part of his significance is derived from Greek culture taken as a whole in the fifth century B.C. He is the epitome of the thought of his contemporaries and immediate predecessors. He is a watershed because he was clearer, more forthright, and more explicit than anyone else. After Socrates, the critical method was a part of the apparatus of human thought. After his time people were clearer as to the method of testing and criticism, and they were clearer as to the ultimate authority of the individual. He established the principle that truth is best attained through public discussion, and that we cannot delegate the power to decide what is and what is not the truth.

Why, then, did Athens, the greatest democracy the world produced until modern times, condemn and execute such a man at a time when democracy in Athens can be said to have been at or near flood tide? In the eyes of the citizens, Socrates was a threat to the social structure under which they lived and which they believed to be the guarantor of the way of life they cherished. His searching, questioning approach to everything, including belief in the gods of Homer, would, they feared, result in open disbelief in the gods, and that, in turn, would undermine the state. As we shall see, the ancient Athenians were not the only people to hold that formal adherence to the official gods of their time, quite apart from one's inner conviction, is a necessary ingredient of social stability.

It is another way of saying that the Athenians did not believe in the power of truth to the degree that Socrates did. Nor did they believe in the critical method to the degree that he did. Like so many supposed devotees of the critical tradition who have followed them, the Athenian citizens believed that criticism must not be carried "too far." They insisted that it stop short of questioning the concepts implicit in Homer. That Athens permitted Socrates openly to pursue the critical method until he was seventy years of age is the measure of her clarity of mind and tolerance of spirit. That in the end she felt compelled to silence him shows how novel and how narrowly supported were the concepts he had invited the Athenians to embrace.

4

"Right" Belief

While the critical tradition was becoming articulate and gaining prominence in ancient Greece, the beginning of the ecclesiastical tradition, as we know it in the West, was taking place in ancient Israel. Where the critical tradition centered in testing, questing, and speculating, the ecclesiastical tradition centered in structures, practices, beliefs, and laws derived from sources, both oral and written, assumed to be authoritative.

The contrast between the Greek attitude toward Homer and the Israelitic attitude toward the Bible provides us with a striking instance of this difference. The Greeks held the *Iliad* and *Odyssey* in the highest esteem. In the classical period many looked upon Homer as the educator of all Greece. They saw him not merely as a poet of supreme quality, but as a guide for living as well. Yet the Greeks did not sanctify Homer in the way that Israel sanctified the Bible. Although the *Iliad* and *Odyssey* are replete with stories of the gods and of their interference in the affairs of men, the Greeks did not believe that Zeus or any of the other members of the Olympic pantheon had revealed to Homer the words that he spoke. And Homer made no such claim for himself.

With the Israelites and their sacred writings it was quite another matter. There, the idea that the deity spoke directly to men seems to have appeared very early, and with it the claim that those to whom he had spoken were his chosen emissaries. When their words were committed to writing, the writings became sacred in the eyes of the Israelites, and the directives they contained came to be regarded as authoritative, divine law. This in turn led to a doctrine still current and troublesome in our time: the doctrine that there are, in religion, beliefs that are to be accepted, followed, and never questioned because they are divine in origin, having been revealed to men by no less an entity than the Lord God himself.

1. True and False Prophets in Israel

In Israel the belief that God speaks directly to men can be traced at least as far back as the prophet Amos, and there is ample evidence that the tradition goes back much further. Amos is the first prophet of whom we have a sufficiently complete and accurate record to be able to speak with confidence. Presumably, in our Bible, we have Amos's own words. Preaching, he declared that his words were not his own, but those of Yahweh, God of Israel. That is why his words, nearly three thousand years old, have been preserved to the present day. Men believed them to be God's own. Many still do.

"The Lord roars from Zion," Amos declared boldly. "He utters his voice from Jerusalem." With this startling introduction he then went on to tell the people of Israel what God was saying. Apparently the people believed that Amos knew, for they listened. When he told them that he, Amos, had heard the words he uttered on God's behalf from the very lips of the Almighty, apparently they believed that, too. All the great prophets, each in turn, offered himself to Israel as a kind of conduit for God's will.

"Hear O heavens and give ear O earth," Isaiah cried, "for the Lord has spoken." Isaiah then went on to tell the people what the Lord had said to him and, again, the people believed. Jeremiah did the same and was even more explicit in assuring the people that his words were God's own. "Behold, I have put words in your mouth," he declared, uttering the words he believed God had spoken to him.

Lest there be any doubt on the matter, we read later on in Jeremiah's writings: "In the fourth year of Jehoiakim, King of Judah, this word came to Jeremiah from the Lord: 'Take a scroll and write on it all the words that I have spoken to you against Israel and Judah and all the nations . . .' Then Jeremiah called Baruch [who] wrote upon a scroll at the dictation of Jeremiah all the words of the Lord which he had spoken to him." We could hardly ask for a more explicit statement of the doctrine that the very words of Scripture come to men directly from God himself.

This belief was by no means confined to Israel. In ancient times generally, people seem to have had little trouble believing that God or the gods spoke to mortals through specially appointed emissaries, and the further back we go in human history, the more general this view becomes. As a natural extension of the nearly universal belief in spirits, gods, demons, and supernatural forces, it was to be expected.

A problem lay at the heart of the concept of prophecy, however, and it showed itself very early. In ancient times there seems to have been no lack of candidates for the role of prophet or spokesman for the divine. Many people seem to have offered themselves as vehicles by which the will of various supernatural agencies could be transmitted to creatures of earth. But was every claimant to such a crown to be accepted on his or her own say-so? How was one to tell? On what ground might a purported prophet be rejected as a dissembler, a mere crank, or a lunatic?

The question is raised by implication in the Book of Amos. It is explicit in Jeremiah. In an obvious attempt to discredit competing prophets, Jeremiah repeatedly warned his hearers against false prophets: "The Lord said to me 'the prophets are prophesying lies in my name; I did not send them nor did I command them or speak to them. They are prophesying to you a lying vision, worthless divination and the deceit of their own minds.'" Jeremiah reiterates the point many times. Like all prophets, he faced the problem of credibility. In order to get his message across, he had to establish himself as an authentic prophet in the minds of the people. To brand all competitors as false prophets seems to have been the standard procedure.

In the seventh century B.C., the period of the Deuteronomists, Israel sought to resolve the problem of who was and who was not a false prophet by laying the severest penalty upon all impostors. The Deuteronomists wrote: "If a prophet arises among you, or a dreamer of dreams and gives you a sign or a wonder and the sign or wonder . . . comes to pass . . . you shall not listen to him . . . for the Lord your God is testing you."

But how were the people to tell who was and who was not false? On this point the Deuteronomists are perfectly clear. They were at that time busily codifying the traditional teachings and practices in Israel and they made use of the doctrine of the false prophet as a device by which to reinforce conformity to the self-consistent system they sought to devise. Whoever rose up with teachings contrary to their system they branded as a "false prophet" and a "dreamer of dreams." He was not to be listened to, they declared, even though he was able accurately to foretell the future and to perform signs and wonders as well.

A careful reading of the Book of Deuteronomy shows that the false teachings the authors had in mind relate to the worship of gods other than Yahweh, God of Israel. "You shall walk after the Lord your God," the Deuteronomists commanded. "Fear him, keep his commandments and obey his voice. . . . The penalty for being a false prophet is death. . . . If your brother . . . or your son or your daughter or the wife of your bosom or your friend who is as your own soul entices you secretly, saying let us go and serve other gods . . . you shall not listen to him . . . but you shall kill him . . . you shall stone him to death with stones."

The children of Israel are to remain loyal to the religious tradition then prevailing and being codified by the Deuteronomists. Belief in Yahweh, Israel's god, was central. Belief in the existence of all other gods and in their power, as well as worship of them in any form, was to be rejected on pain of death.

The principle of prophecy, however, by its own nature, is not subject to systematization and codification. Once we admit the principle that God speaks directly to men, who can say with assurance when or whether such a transaction has taken place? Israel never resolved the question of how you tell a false prophet from a true one. Neither did Christianity. It plagued the first Christians, as the New Testament clearly shows. Matthew's Gospel is replete with dire warnings against being led astray by false prophets. "Many will come in my name," Jesus warns his disciples on the Mount of Olives. "If anyone says to you, 'Lo, here is the Christ!' or 'There he is!' do not believe it. For false Christs and false prophets will arise and show great signs and wonders, so as to lead astray, if possible, even the elect."

The Book of Acts relates an incident in which Paul came across a prophet named Bar-Jesus who purported to speak on God's behalf. Paul's denunciation of him matches in vehemence anything to be found in the Bible. "You son of the devil," he cries, "you enemy of all righteousness, full of all deceit and villainy, will you not stop making crooked the straight paths of the Lord?" Then, to confirm his curse, he strikes the man blind.

The fury of the early church toward false prophets—that is, toward those who claimed messiahship for someone other than Jesus—is evident throughout the Book of Revelation. In one passage, three foul spirits like frogs are said to issue from the mouth of the false prophet. In another, the false prophet was thrown alive into a lake of fire that burns with brimstone. Finally, the devil himself was thrown into the lake, where both were to be tormented day and night forever. These judgments on the false prophet show how greatly the early church believed itself to be threatened by those outside its structure who also claimed to be authentic spokesmen for God.

Thus Christianity was born as a believing religion. Descending as it did directly from Judaism, which had at its heart the problem of right and wrong belief, Christianity from the start found itself in the same situation. In Judaism and later in Christianity the problem of "right belief" extended from the prophets, apostles, and other visionaries to their writings. An authentic prophet might have writings attributed to him that were false. They might have been erroneously transcribed. Since the words of a prophet were thought to be the very words of God, it was important to know. There could be no mistake on such a matter. Moreover, once the validity of a prophetic writing was established, it was of crucial importance that its precepts be followed to the letter. That in turn meant that these writings must be understood clearly and that any ambiguities in them must be resolved accurately.

It was in this manner that the religion of Israel, and later Christianity and Islam as well, became "religions of the book." The writings in which God's words spoken to the prophets had been set down became sacred. So too did the books in which the acts of the people were recorded, and God's acts in conjunction with them, also become sacred. Such was the origin of the Old and New Testaments. They are writings that originated in a wide variety of places and times, and for a wide variety of reasons, but which for other and often quite different reasons came to be looked upon as sacred in character. Gathered together as a unity and authoritatively declared to be sacred, with other candidate manuscripts authoritatively excluded, these writings became the sacred books of these religions.

2. The Essenes and the New Covenant

We can see the role of "right belief" sharpening in the religion of Israel if we turn to the Dead Sea Scrolls. These manuscripts, dating to the first and second centuries B.C., were almost miraculously preserved for more than two thousand years in caves above the Dead Sea and discovered in the 1940s and 1950s. The Scrolls were compiled by a sect known as the Essenes, a Jewish heretical group that developed in the brief period of Jewish independence immediately preceding the beginning of the Christian era.

It was a time of high expectancy among the Jews, a time when apocalyptic ideas enjoyed wide currency and the coming of God's kingdom on earth was thought to be at hand. As any reader can easily see by consulting the Bible, expectations of this sort had been the daily fare of devout Jews at least since the time of "Second Isaiah," the unknown prophet or prophets whose words are found in Isaiah chapters 40–66. They are words of hope, spoken to Israel when her people were in exile in Babylon. The great prophet Isaiah, like Jeremiah and Ezekiel, had pictured in lurid detail the punishment God would visit upon Israel and all the nations for failing to follow his law. "Second Isaiah" told the exiles in Babylon that Israel had been punished enough. He was not a prophet of doom like the first Isaiah, but a prophet of hope. His message begins with the familiar words:

> Comfort ye, comfort ye my people, says
> your God
> Speak tenderly to Jerusalem, and
> cry to her
> That her warfare is ended, that her
> iniquity is pardoned

The unknown prophet then goes on to tell the Children of Israel that a great new day now awaits them. He continues:

> A voice cries
> In the Wilderness prepare the
> way of the Lord
> Make straight in the desert a
> highway for our God.

Then, as if to assure the people of the reward that would be theirs when they had prepared "the way of the Lord," Second Isaiah proclaimed in words that are very familiar to us:

Every valley shall be lifted up
and every mountain and hill be
made low
And the glory of the Lord shall be
revealed.

The ecstatic promises of glorious things to come continue to mount as we read on through to the end of the Book of Isaiah. Here is Second Isaiah's description of the new Jerusalem that is to come:

O afflicted one, storm tossed and
not comforted,
Behold I will set your stones in antimony
And lay your foundations with
sapphires.
I will make your pinnacles of agate,
your gates of carbuncles
And your wall of precious stones.

In that great day, nations and kings shall bow before Israel, the unknown seer continues, and he cries:

Arise, shine for your light has come
And the glory of the Lord has
risen upon you
And nations shall come to your light
And kings to the brightness
of your rising.
Foreigners shall build up your
walls
And their kings shall minister to you.

He concludes:

For behold I create new heavens and
a new earth
And the former things shall not
be remembered
or come to mind.

By the second and first centuries B.C., these prophecies and others even more concrete in character had crystallized into the expectation that the God of Israel was soon to intervene in human affairs on Israel's behalf. All that was necessary to bring it about was for Israel to live up to her half of the covenant she had made with God long before. By that covenant God had agreed that he would be Israel's God and that they should be his people.

Israel on her part had only to obey God's law to bring God into history and usher in the great new day.

As a result, the second and first centuries marked a period of great religious fervor in Israel. The attempt to follow God's law as recorded in Israel's ancient holy books became almost an obsession. Accordingly, a great amount of effort went into determining what that law was and how it was to be interpreted. In an attempt to determine exactly what God expected of them, the religious leaders of Israel searched out and examined with the greatest care every nuance of meaning that could be derived from their ancient holy books.

In such movements there are always those who think that even the most rigorous and devout are still not rigorous and devout enough—that yet more is required. The Essenes appear to have originated in this manner. As far as we can now determine, they were a group of fanatically devout Jews in Jerusalem who, in the early second century B.C., gave up on the less devout members of their group and went out into the desert down by the Dead Sea, there in seclusion to do what they believed God required of them. They took literally Second Isaiah's words: "In the Wilderness prepare the way of the Lord." Wilderness, in that passage, means what we call desert. At a site we know today as Qumran, above the cliffs at the north end of the Dead Sea, they established a colony and built a house, where through the sheer force of their own piety they expected to become the agents by which the kingdom of God on earth could be brought in.

In their thought about Israel and about themselves, the Essenes evolved the idea of a New Covenant to be contrasted with the Old. Long ago, in Noah's time, according to Jewish teaching, God had made a covenant with Israel, which he later renewed with Abraham. By it he was to be their God and they were to be his people. That covenant, the Essenes asserted, had been broken because of Israel's misbehavior, and a new covenant had taken its place.

They found the concept in Jeremiah where the prophet said: "Behold the days are coming says the Lord when I will make a new covenant with the house of Israel and the house of Judah." Jeremiah's idea was inward and spiritual. "I will put my law within them," he quotes the Lord as promising, "and I will write it upon their hearts." The Essene view was much more legalistic. Apparently unaware of this basic difference, however, the Essenes saw themselves as the people of the New Covenant and they believed devoutly that through the keeping of this Covenant God would intervene and bring the new day to pass.

In short, the Essenes were a company of believers, and at the heart of their thought lay the concept of right belief. Clear as to what they believed, they were no less clear as to the importance of their believing it and of their not believing something contrary to it. Their very identity was derived from their beliefs about themselves, about their role in human history, the role they were to play in its ending, and the reward that would be theirs when these apocalyptic events came to pass. Although not stated that way, with the Essenes, right belief had become the basis of admission into the group. A rejection of these beliefs meant rejection by the group as well.

3. Christianity: "Unless ye believe . . ."

With the emergence of Christianity the role of belief becomes explicit. Where Israel spoke of false prophets, the worship of false gods, apostasy; where the Essenes built their movement on the acceptance of their New Covenant status, the Christians took the position that one must believe in order to be a Christian and they began very early to spell out what those beliefs should be.

The Christian attitude toward belief, as well as the movement itself, seems to have had Essene origins of a more or less clearly defined sort. Not all authorities agree, of course, that there was such a connection, but many have been led by the evidence to the conclusion that the connection was very close, if indeed the Essene community at Qumran and the beginnings of Christianity in Jerusalem were not two successive phases of the same movement. If this should eventually prove to be the case; if it could be shown that Christian origins do in fact lie in Essene thought, practice, and community organization, then the emphasis on right believing in the early Christian church could more readily be understood. It would mean that the concept—and its application—was not fashioned by the Apostles, but that it evolved in the Essene community out of earlier Judaic origins and was bequeathed to the early Christian Church in the well-developed form in which we find it there. The fact of such a connection would provide us with a much more plausible explanation of the thought-pattern evident among the first Christians in the Book of Acts.

It is fashionable today to think of Christians as followers of Jesus' way, but it was not so in the first century A.D. The Gospels give little attention to followers versus nonfollowers of his moral teachings. Discipleship was not measured by loyalty to his ethical ideals. The Gospels center on belief and nonbelief in his Messiahship. They stress the role of the man Jesus as the Lord's anointed, come at last to bring in the Kingdom of Righteousness. They concern belief in Jesus as the Christ.

The early Christians held other beliefs closely associated with their basic concept of the person of the Nazarene, but they had nothing to do with his ethical message. For example, Jesus had foretold the early coming of the Judgment Day. He had promised that when it came he would return on the clouds of Heaven to judge between those who were to be saved and those who were to be damned. These, too, were among the beliefs of the early Christians. But far more significantly, they believed in the importance of these beliefs. They held that whoever believed these things would be among the saved when the Judgment Day came, and whoever did not would be damned.

In short, Jesus himself, or at least the Gospel writers, looked on right believing as absolutely necessary. Mark, the oldest of the Gospel accounts and our earliest written source, records Jesus' first words as he begins his ministry as follows: "Now after John was arrested Jesus came into Galilee preaching the Gospel of God and saying, 'The time is fulfilled and the kingdom of God is at hand; repent and believe in the gospel.'"

Paraphrasing these words in contemporary concepts, we might read: After John the Baptist had been arrested for teachings that were contrary to the accepted theology of the time and for preaching insurrection, Jesus came into Galilee as an itinerant preacher. His message was similar to that of the Baptist. "The long-promised Day of the Lord is soon to come," he said. "On that day the world as we know it will end and the Kingdom of God will take its place. Therefore repent of your evil ways while there is still time. This is God's good news for all people."

Throughout his story Mark exhibits such an emphasis on belief. When a ruler of the synagogue asks that his sick daughter be healed, and it is reported that the girl has died, Jesus says to the man, "Fear not, only believe."

When a woman with an issue of blood touched Jesus' garment, according to Mark's story, she was immediately healed. Jesus' explanation was very simple: "Your faith has made you well"; that is to say, your belief. "It is because you believed I had the power to cure you that I was able to do it."

"All things are possible to him who believes," Jesus said on another occasion when asked to cure a child possessed by a dumb spirit. The father's honest response was, "Lord, I believe. Help thou mine unbelief." In the same vein Jesus is reported to have said to Peter, "Have faith in God. Truly I say to you, whoever says to this mountain, 'Be taken up and cast into the sea' and does not doubt in his heart but believes that what he says will come to pass, it will be done for him. . . . Whatever you ask in prayer, believe that you will receive it and you will."

The point comes through most clearly in John's account, the latest of the Bible biographies. There, belief is pivotal. John's entire Gospel can be seen as a tract on right belief. Its whole purpose is to persuade the reader to believe that the events recorded there actually happened and that they derive their meaning from the fact that Jesus was the Messiah, the Christ, the Son of God, the Word of God.

The second paragraph of John's Gospel, which reads like the opening paragraph of an earlier edition, begins: "There was a man sent from God whose name was John. He came for testimony to bear witness to the light that all might believe through him." As John sees the Gospel story, that is its purpose—to persuade men that Jesus was the Christ and to persuade them of the importance of believing what he, John, says.

It is in John's Gospel that we find the story of "Doubting Thomas," a man who has become a symbol for skepticism in Western literature. According to The Fourth Gospel, Thomas was not with the disciples when they first saw Jesus after he rose from the dead. When they told Thomas about it, he said, "Unless I see his hands, the print of the nails, and place my finger in the mark of the nails and place my hand in his side, I will not believe."

Later, according to John's account, Jesus confronted Thomas and said to him: "Put your finger here and see my hands; and put out your hand and place it in my side; do not be faithless, but believing." Thomas could only say, "My Lord and my God!" But Jesus pressed him further: "Have you believed because you have seen me?" he asked. "Blessed are those who have not seen and yet believe."

The point of the story is plain: It is of the utmost importance that Christians *believe* that Jesus rose from the dead. Even Thomas, who doubted his Lord, came to believe when he was presented with physical proof. More faithful still are those who can believe in the resurrection without physical proof, which is now no longer possible. Such is the obvious import of the story. But lest the reader miss the point, John, who seems to be writing more of a polemic than a biography, continues: "Now Jesus did many other signs in the presence of the disciples which are not written in this book; but these are written that you may believe that Jesus is the Christ [i.e., the Messiah expected by the Jews], the Son of God, and that believing you may have life in his name."

It was a lot to believe about a man who was executed for blasphemy and inciting rebellion. Gradually, however, others joined the little band of believers. Soon the beliefs they held began to grow both in number and extent. Public acceptance of these beliefs—"confession," as it was called—was the basis for admission to the group. Only believers could be baptized into the faith. Only believers could become "Christians."

If we turn to the Book of Revelation we find there an expression of the most intensely partisan view of the importance of believing official Christian teachings. Toward the end of the book we are told that the "faithless," that is to say the *un*believers, are to be cast with the false prophets into "the lake that burns with fire and brimstone, which is the second death." Accompanying them also are to be "the cowardly, the polluted, murderers, fornicators, sorcerers, idolaters and liars."

As the early church grew, as it spread through the Roman world, as its teachers grew in numbers, so did its teachings. Soon it became clear that, while the primitive church in its doctrine of right belief had a highly effective organizing principle, it also had a lion by the tail. Questions of interpretation arose. Definitions and delineations became necessary. Arguments developed because those with the authority to interpret could not agree.

Who was right? When two men of equal authority disagreed, how should the issue be resolved?

In an attempt to deal with this problem, the church early developed the use of creeds or statements of faith. They originated as baptismal confessions made by the convert as part of his initiation into the fellowship of Christians or as a redeclaration of faith on the part of those who already were members. In fact, the practice of unison redeclaration of faith became widespread just because of the problem of "falling away." This had earlier become standard practice in the Essene community at Qumran and for the same reason.

The first major compilation and condensation of the confession of the early church is still widely used today—the so-called Apostles' Creed, which dates to the third century A.D. A leading authority and a devout churchman speaks of "the extreme unlikelihood of the Apostles having drafted an official summary" of the faith. It is clear, he says, that the Apostolic church did not "possess an official, textually determined confession of faith." But creeds of a lesser sort appeared very early in widely scattered areas. As time went on, they tended to increase in similarity and to become more stereotyped. For example, most of the later confessions contained assertions of belief in the virgin birth, in Jesus' suffering and death under Pilate, in his resurrection on the third day, in the fact that he sits on the right hand of the Father, and that he is soon to return to judge the living and the dead, although such material is usually lacking in the early baptismal confessions. Gradually, too, the creeds became part of the liturgy of worship.

It was out of the conflicts that produced the creeds that the idea of orthodoxy or right belief, and that of heresy or wrong belief, arose. The struggle for supremacy among the prophets was repeated among the interpreters of Scripture. To be sure, the prophets were looked upon as God's emissaries, while the interpreters of Scripture were not. But there the difference ended. In both cases the spokesman was held to be either totally right or totally wrong. There was no middle ground. In neither case was it thought possible to be partially right and partially wrong. The doctrine of revelation and that of divine inspiration permitted no gradations, no exceptions, no probabilities, and no approximations. Either God did or he did not reveal his truth to prophet A or apostle B. The interpretation of Scripture offered by thinker C was totally right or it was totally wrong, not partially right and partially wrong, among other reasons because thinker C was looked upon as a personage with authority, or without it, as the case might be.

In any doctrine of revelation or inspiration, authority makes itself felt very early. Otherwise there is no way to tell the true spokesmen for God from their imitators. This was one of the principal factors in the development of institutionalism in Christianity. Only a priesthood possessing acknowledged authority in religious matters could resolve the disputes that arose as to which prophet was truly God's spokesman, and which thinker truly understood the meaning of Holy Writ. Some were recognized as God's chosen. The rest were rejected and were labeled outcasts, blasphemers, and heretics.

Theological controversy among the early Christians was quite as much political and social as religious. Their zeal for their cause was derived from the conviction that they were doing God's will, but it could not have been hampered by their knowledge of the rewards of victory. Thus, groups of believers tended to gather around a particular thinker, and often they came to constitute what was in effect a political party. Devoutly believing in the validity of their views, they contended fiercely with one another in an attempt to gain supremacy for their views. The first three centuries of Christianity produced, among other theological groups, the Gnostics, the Docetists, the Eutychians, the Marcionites, the Montanists, the Monarchians, the Novatians, the Donatists, and the Arians. Each of them at first vied for supremacy, but in the end each was adjudged heretical, having failed to persuade sufficient numbers of the faithful that theirs was the true and right opinion.

By the fourth century A.D. the problem of right belief had become a critical one in the Christian churches. Charges of heresy flew back and forth and controversy between leading theologians and their supporters became intense. W. E. H. Lecky, in his *History of European Morals*—although inaccurate in minor detail, perhaps—nevertheless conveys an acceptable impression of the situation in the church during the first three centuries of the Christian era. He writes:

> The eighty or ninety sects into which Christianity speedily divided, hated one another with an intensity that extorted the wonder of Julian and the ridicule of the Pagans of Alexandria, and the fierce riots and persecutions that hatred produced appear in every page of ecclesiastical history. There is, indeed, something at once grotesque and ghastly in the spectacle. The Donatists, having separated from the orthodox . . . refused to perform their rites in the orthodox churches which they had seized til they had burnt the altar and scraped the wood, beat multitudes to death with clubs, blinded others by anointing their eyes with lime, filled Africa, during nearly two centuries, with war and desolation, and contributed largely to its final ruin.
>
> The Catholics tell how an Arian emperor caused eighty orthodox priests to be drowned on a single occasion; how three thousand persons perished in the riots that convulsed Constantinople when the Arian bishop Macedonius superseded the Athanasian Paul; how George of Cappadocia, the Arian bishop of Alexandria, caused the widows of the Athanasian party to be scourged on the soles of their feet, the holy virgins to be stripped naked, to be flogged with the prickly branches of palm trees, or to be slowly scorched over fires til they abjured their creed. The triumph of the Catholics in Egypt was

> accompanied (if we may believe the solemn assertions of eighty Arian bishops) by every variety of plunder, murder, sacrilege, and outrage . . .
>
> In Ephesus, during the contest between St. Cyril and the Nestorians, the cathedral itself was the theatre of a fierce and bloody conflict. Constantinople, on the occasion of the deposition of St. Chrysostom, was for several days, in a condition of absolute anarchy. After the Council of Chalcedon, Jerusalem and Alexandria were again convulsed, and the bishop of the latter city was murdered in his baptistry. About fifty years later, when the Monophysite controversy was at its height, the palace of the emperor at Constantinople was blockaded, the churches were beseiged, and the streets commanded by furious bands of contending monks. Repressed for a time, the riots broke out two years after with an increased ferocity, and almost every leading city of the East was filled by the monks with bloodshed and with riots.
>
> Together with these legislative and ecclesiastical measures, a literature arose surpassing in its mendacious ferocity any other the world had known. The polemical writers habitually painted as daemons those who diverged from the orthodox belief, gloated with a vindictive piety over the sufferings of the heretic upon earth, as upon a Divine punishment, and sometimes, with an almost superhuman malice, passing in imagination beyond the threshold of the grave, exulted in no ambiguous terms on the tortures which they believed to be reserved for him for ever.

Lecky is often criticized for having been too extreme in his account, but a very recent biography of Saint Jerome, translator of the Vulgate, the standard Latin text of the Bible in the Catholic Church for fifteen hundred years, amply corroborates his words. Jerome, it seems, took after his theological opponents with venomous fury. "Grunting pig" was his favorite epithet for a lifelong friend with whom he had a falling out. Legends more and more adorned Jerome's name after his death, as the immense value to the Church of his translations of, and commentary on, the Bible became known. But in his lifetime, the revered saint battled with vituperation and calumny, and with scant attention to the veracity of his language.

When the Emperor Constantine was converted to Christianity early in the fourth century A.D., he determined to put a stop to religious controversy in the realm. Among his motives in adopting Christianity had been his desire to bring unity and strength to his empire. Accordingly, in the year 324 A.D., having reunited with the Roman Empire politically, he summoned the first Ecumenical Council of the Church. It met at Nicaea in Asia Minor the next year, 325 A.D., with the purpose of establishing a single formula of belief for all Christians.

The immediate purpose of the Council was to settle a dispute then raging in Alexandria between a priest named Arius and his bishop, Athanasius. Arius held that Christ was of a different substance (in the Aristotelian sense) than God; the bishop held that Christ and God were of the same substance. To us it seems an empty metaphysical distinction, but to the contestants the question was basic. The Athanasians demanded to know: if Christ was of a different substance than God, then he was not really divine, and if he was not divine, how could man be saved? As they saw it, only the sacrifice of God himself, in the person of Christ, made man's salvation possible. The Arians, on the other hand, were trying to devise a doctrine that was self-consistent. To them the Athanasian position, that Christ had been wholly God and wholly man both at the same time, was absurd.

Abstruse as all this seems to us now, it was of fundamental importance at the time and to some degree remains so today, for the divines at Nicaea were debating what turned out to be one of the most fundamental teachings of the Christian Church: the doctrine of the Trinity. We find it hard to believe now that so crucial a matter was resolved by a mere majority vote, but that was the case. By vote of the Ecumenical Council at Nicaea in 325 A.D., the doctrine of the "consubstantiality" of the Father and the Son became the true and authoritative belief for Christians. In many Christian circles today that doctrine is still officially held to be the correct view.

Constantine apparently was naive in attempting to end theological turmoil with a great Church Council. After Nicaea the churchmen went right on arguing, as many a scholar attests, if anything more fiercely than ever. Nevertheless, the result of the Council, the so-called Nicene Creed, not only canonized the Trinitarian Creed; it also, and far more importantly, canonized the idea of a creed as the way to resolve theological disputes.

Thenceforth, in the eyes of the Church, the Nicene Creed was the right way to state certain theological principles, and all others were wrong. Such is the role of authority in the institutions of religion where problems of revelation and inspiration are concerned. The power to choose among the contenders is given to the Church. Whom the Church chooses is thereby declared to be right, while those who remain unpersuaded are declared to be in error, no matter how convinced of the truth of their position they may be.

While the Council of Nicaea settled some of the problems having to do with the nature of God, it left untouched many having to do with the nature of Christ. One of the most hotly debated concerned the relationship between his divine and human natures. This was settled by the Council of Chalcedon in 451 A.D., where it became clear past all doubting that in Christianity what is true and what is false is not necessarily that which men are persuaded of. It is that which the Church declares to be true officially, despite what the members may privately think. Thus, after Chalcedon the position of the Church was greatly strengthened. Whereas Nicaea reached its conclusions only after extensive debate and by a vote of the clergy in attendance, the conclusions of Chalcedon were dictated by the Bishop of Rome, who by that time had acquired the title of Pope. It was adopted without debate because the Bishop of Rome, as Pope, now enjoyed the full support of the emperor. The interlocking of church and state, so characteristic of Christianity for so long, may well be said to have begun at Chalcedon in 451 A.D.

In this way, the idea of right belief (orthodoxy) and wrong belief (heresy) became part of the living fibre of Christianity. Thereafter all the resources of the Church, usually aided by the secular rulers, the kings and emperors of the nations, were bent to enforcing acceptance of official doctrine. So deeply ingrained did the importance of right belief become, the Protestant Reformation more than a thousand years later did not depart from it. To be sure, the great reformers, Luther and Calvin, developed certain doctrines that differed from Roman Catholic teaching, notably that regarding the supremacy of the pope, but they never departed from the more basic conviction that right belief is the heart of Christianity.

5

Defenders of the Faith

The Sacred Scriptures of Judaism and Christianity were the prime source by which "right belief" was determined. By the first or second century A.D. both had established which of the writings in their particular traditions were to be included and which were to be left out of the Bible. While these decisions ended one set of controversies, others raged on. Writings deemed to be sacred are no less obscure in their meaning, and no more self-consistent than other writings. They are equally subject to different interpretations, each seemingly legitimate. Which is the right one? How are we to tell? Who is to say?

The problem is further complicated by the tendency of groups to form in support of various particular interpretations. Such groups, marked at the outset by genuine differences of theological opinion, often coalesce into political parties. Their purpose then shifts from accurate interpretation to the achievement of power and authority.

In Judaism, Christianity, and Islam the niceties of theological debate have often become bludgeons in a power-play. The question then shifts from What is right? to Who is right? Those who win determine what the "true" interpretation is to be. "Might makes right" can apply as well in theology as in politics. The Council of Nicaea, where the Athanasians defeated the Arians, is the best known Christian example of a theological conflict become political. There are innumerable others less well known.

But even after a great council has fought theological questions through to a resolution, controversy is seldom stilled. The victory of one political party over another merely moves the battle one step further along. The resolution of one problem seldom accomplishes more than to reveal yet other ambiguities, inconsistencies, or unbelievable doctrines that must then be dealt with.

Where beliefs rest on revelations, and the revelations are recorded in a Holy Book, the debate as to what these revelations really meant simply goes on and on, generation after generation and century after century.

A further complication results from the mere passage of time. The words and thoughts of one generation often become archaic to the next. Any formulation, whether the report of a revelation or an interpretation of it, inevitably involves the thought-pattern of the time out of which it comes. As conditions change, so do the thought-patterns of the people. As a result, both the written records of any period and later interpretation of their meaning grow obscure, irrelevant, or both. Their implications are ill-understood. They may be altogether unknown by a later age. Yet the sacred words must be kept. They must be believed and they must be used as a guide for conduct.

The problem is nearly as severe in the absence of a theory of divine revelation as we can see in the struggle of the Greeks of the classical period with the writings of Homer. As we have noted, in Periclean Athens the *Iliad* and *Odyssey* were looked upon as very nearly sacred. But the wisdom and moral principles the Greeks found in Homer could not be detached from his words, and, as we have seen, this created a problem for those who were attracted to Ionian naturalism and Socratic inquiry. Classical Greece was too clear-headed to give up the way of questing and testing: it made too much sense. But Homer, the molder of the ideals of Greek culture, could not be given up either.

1. Interpretation and Allegory

In an attempt to keep their Homer intact, and at the same time to offer the people a religion that made sense, the Greeks resorted to one of the most ancient forms of thought and speech, that of allegory. It was an easy and natural thing for them to do. Poetry, which is the stuff of allegory, symbol, metaphor, and imagery, was one of the supreme accomplishments of the Greek spirit. Allegory is but the formalization of the images of the poets, their metaphors, their symbols, and their similes. All language, in fact, is but a set of symbols. Of this the Greek mind was well aware, and the conclusion that Homer could better be understood if he were "interpreted" was almost inevitable. The process was given further impetus by the practice that prevailed throughout ancient Greece of using Homer as a textbook for the educating of the young. Out of this method of teaching, incessant discussions of Homer's true meaning arose.

But what of his bloodletting stories? What of his bizarre cosmology? What of the patent immorality of his deities? The process of correcting Homer and adapting his thought to the tastes of a later day began as early as Hesiod, a near contemporary. The end result was the formalization of the allegorical method of interpretation of the *Iliad* and *Odyssey*. This stage seems to have been reached with Anaxagoras. He argued that the Homeric gods were not real and were not intended to be so understood. They were, rather, intended as symbols of the mental powers and moral virtues of men. Zeus, he said, was mind and Athene, art.

With that the floodgates opened. Now that a method had been devised by which Homer could be made fully acceptable to minds familiar with Greek philosophy and science, there was no limit to the meanings Homer could be made to yield. Metrodorus, a pupil of Anaxagoras, in the fifth century advanced the allegorizing process to a clear naturalism. He interpreted the Homeric stories as symbolic representations of physical phenomena. The gods were really not deities, he said; they were the powers of nature. For Metrodorus the gods and all their doings represented the interplay of natural forces. Homer should be read at two levels, he would have argued in today's language: on the surface as beautiful myths and stories, but at a deeper level as a presentation of the clash of the forces of the natural world. Heraclides declared that "Homer would be impious if he were not allegorical"; that is to say, Homer could only be accepted as the educator of Greece if his obvious meanings were first explained away. The purpose of much theological allegorizing has never been more clearly stated.

The method of allegory was in turn adopted by Judaism. Hellenized Jews of the Diaspora in classical times were having the same difficulty with the Old Testament that the Greeks had been having with Homer. The Old Testament did not belong to the world of thought that Greek philosophy had created, any more than did the *Iliad* and the *Odyssey*. The later Israelites found the mores of the early Old Testament no more to their liking than was much of Homer to the Romans and Greeks. Accordingly, Jewish thinkers, like their Greek counterparts, also turned to the allegorical method as a means of keeping the Old Testament intact while holding to their sharpened moral standards and the picture of the natural world that classical science and philosophy had worked out.

Philo (first century B.C.–first century A.D.), was the great allegorizer for Judaism. In order to keep intact the ancient thought and language of the Bible (for him, the Old Testament) he made the assumption, then very common, that Scriptural texts have a twofold meaning: the literal and obvious, and the underlying, or allegorical. The latter, he argued, is obscure to the many, but clear to the few. Philo makes use of the allegorical method without reservation in order that Bible meanings might become clear to all. He regarded virtually everything in the Bible as allegorical—names, dates, numbers, stories of historical events, even rules of conduct. Thus Hellenistic Jews, steeped in Greek critical philosophy, were enabled to reconcile the questions their philosophical minds were asking with the demand that their Sacred Scriptures, believed to have been revealed by God, be kept literally intact, their divine origin and character unquestioned.

In Christian theology this kind of reasoning is known as apologetics, the art of defending, by whatever means can be found, a theological doctrine, the truth of which is taken for granted at the outset. It begins with Paul. Although theological schools do not usually stress the fact, Paul was a persistent but not very skilled allegorist. Even Martin Luther once took him to task for an allegory he developed in his letter to the Galatians. Attempting to deal with the problem of the Law for gentile converts to Christianity, Paul wrote, "You who desire to be under law, do you not hear the law? For it is written that Abraham had two sons, one by a slave and one by a free woman. But the son of the slave was born according to the flesh, the son of the free woman through promise. Now this is an allegory: these women are two covenants. One is from Mount Sinai, bearing children for slavery; she is Hagar. Now Hagar is Mount Sinai in Arabia; she corresponds to the present Jerusalem, for she is in slavery with her children. But the Jerusalem above is free, and she is our mother."

Paul, in another allegory fundamental to his theology, taught that in one man (Adam) all men sinned and through one man (Christ) all men are saved. Christian theologians following him found that through the allegorical method they could solve almost any exegetical problem. Here, for example, is a typical passage from the Song of Songs in the Old Testament, attributed to Solomon:

> O that you would kiss me with the
> kisses of your mouth
> For your love is better than wine.

No ordinary person has any difficulty understanding what that passage means. It describes an exceedingly intense and well-nigh universal experience. The remainder of the Song of Songs, some of which seems startingly modern, is equally unmistakable in its meaning and equally descriptive of feelings and experiences that come to all of us.

Oh, but you are mistaken, says the allegorist. Yours is but a shallow understanding of a richly symbolic passage of Scripture. This is not the love poem that you think it is. You are deceived by its surface imagery. To understand and appreciate its true meaning you must see that it is really an allegory. Its true meaning, say the Jews, is God's love for his people, Israel, while the Christians say its true meaning is Christ's love for his church. And, say both religious groups, these concepts are so mystical in quality that we could never grasp them unaided. This explains why such lofty thoughts were cast in such very human terms.

Christian allegorizing began in earnest with Clement of Alexandria, A.D. 150–220. Origen, his pupil, carried the practice further. It reached its fullest development under these two men. Saint Augustine made extensive use of the allegorical method and it continued on long after his time.

A parallel development took place among non-Christians. The Emperor Julian (A.D. 361–363) provides us with a striking instance. Confronted by increasing turmoil in the empire, he sought to reassert the old Roman virtues and bring about stability by restoring the former state religion. To make the Graeco-Roman myths palatable to his sophisticated subjects he turned to one Sallustius who produced a treatise entitled *Concerning the Gods and the Universe.* It was a masterpiece of allegory. The gods, Sallustius asserted, never lived. They are abstractions only; but they symbolize deeper truths. The stories told about them never happened, he concludes, "but these things always are."

Despite the elaborate allegories developed by Sallustius, Julian's attempt to restore the old Roman religion failed utterly. As far as we can now learn, *Concerning the Gods and the Universe* was never published. At the conclusion of Julian's brief reign, Christianity was restored and the emperor, at the hands of Christian writers, has become known to history as "Julian the Apostate."

Reading the bizarre reconstructions of the allegorists we wonder that any one took them seriously, but their work is the more instructive to us just for this reason. It enables us to understand the distortion of Bible meanings that are given serious consideration in our own time. Strict allegorizing has long since been given up in Christianity, but the substitutes we use are little different in character from those employed by the ancients. Today, for example, we search out "levels of meaning" in Scripture; we seek the "core of truth" that Bible myths are said to contain; we speak of the "biblical message" that is to be found in miracle and other stories and we say that a Bible story or myth contains, in addition to its obvious factual details, elements that are transcendent and universal. Such stories "refer at one and the same time both to matters of fact, and to what transcends matters of fact." As with the Greeks and Homer, with Philo and the Old Testament, the Romans and the Graeco-Roman pantheon, the purpose is to keep the ancient words intact, to use the stories for the instruction of young and old alike and so to permit change while nothing changes at all.

Many ancient writers saw how highly arbitrary the allegorizing process can be. The problem made itself felt in Christianity very early among the Gnostics, a heretical sect that appeared in the first century A.D. and gained great strength. As with so many of the allegorizers, they sought to reconcile religious teachings and philosophy. In their case they stressed knowledge rather than faith and tried to reconcile the Old Testament with the teachings of the Greek philosophers. In an attempt to demolish their heresies logically, Irenaeus, one of the great churchmen of the second century, turned the full power of his intellect against them. In his book *Adversus Haereses* he wrote: "They gather their views from other sources than the Scriptures and then they endeavor to adapt with an air of probability to their own peculiar assertions the parables of the Lord, the sayings of the prophets, and the words of the Apostles, with the result that by transferring passages, and dressing them up anew, and making one thing out of another, they succeed in deluding many through their wicked art in adapting the words of the Lord to their opinions." Such Christian railing against allegories of which they did not approve accomplished little, however. It was easy to separate out heresiarchs like the Gnostics, but there was no good way to control the allegorizing of the faithful.

Non-Christian Romans were as aware as the Christians that the allegorizing method can represent the thinking of the allegorizer far better than that of the author he allegorizes. A neo-Platonist of the fourth century A.D., Maximus of Tyre, observed that God, being greater than time and eternity, is in fact unnameable. To get around this problem, said Maximus, we employ various helpful names, concepts, pictures, and stories by which to describe him and we name all that is beautiful after him.

Maximus noticed that the allegorizing or abstracting process is carried on in all religions and moves toward the same ultimate concepts in each. He realized that the allegorizers in the several religions were moving out of the particularities of their own faith to universal principles common to all religions. Maximus heartily approved of this tendency.

If allegorizing always led to the universals Maximus of Tyre perceived, we should have here a clear instance of the critical way in religion making itself felt in the Graeco-Roman world. Unfortunately the opposite was the case. In the ancient world the allegorical method was not used as a method of inquiry or for the discovery of new ideas. It was used to reconcile religion and philosophy, to stifle inquiry, and to win acceptance by critical minds of outmoded teachings and practices.

A very important distinction should be made at this point. Reading congenial contemporary meanings out of archaic writing is one thing. Recognizing the profound and moving symbolism present in such writing, because it was present in the mind of the writer, is quite another. With the goddess Athene, for example, no allegorizing process was necessary for Greeks in the classical period. They may have doubted her literal existence, but they lived by all that she symbolized for them.

As Gilbert Murray reminds us, Athene is at once an ideal and a mystery, the ideal of wisdom, of incessant labor, of almost terrifying purity, seen through the light of some mystic and spiritual devotion similar to, but transcending, the love of man for woman. But is she really the goddess of the *Iliad* and of Sophocles? he asks in all candor. "The truth is," he answers, "she is neither one nor the other . . . the goddess, that is, of the best and most characteristic worship that these idealized creations awakened."

Few, if any, would quarrel with the need for poetic imagery or the uses of levels of meaning in writing, whether or not the writer is aware of them. Often a writer, whether poet or prophet, scientist or theologian, is reaching for ideas that, at the moment, can only be dimly perceived. The critical mind in no way questions the practice of trying to probe such insights to their uttermost depths. Questions about the legitimacy of the allegorizing process arise only when an attempt is made to read back into extant writings meanings that could hardly have been in the author's mind at the time of composition. To be sure, there is a fine line between the legitimate and illegitimate use of allegory. But the presence of a gray area in no way affects the validity of the distinction. The critical mind holds it to be fundamental that we sharply distinguish between (1) the allegorizing of Homer, the Bible, or any other writing in order to make them acceptable, and (2) the use of poetic imagery or the reaching for new concepts through analogies to things we already understand.

The critical way in religion lost out in the Graeco-Roman world because, among other reasons, of the allegorizing method. The allegorists provided a palliative, not a solution. It was a detour around, not a confrontation of, the problem. They avoided the hard issues before them by giving old words and concepts new and often quite different meanings. For devout Christians and Jews, steeped in Hellenistic culture, allegorizing was an enormously effective instrument by which to move easily into an otherwise puzzling and intellectually difficult religious faith.

2. Saint Augustine

The allegorical method played an important part in the life and thought of the greatest intellect of the ancient Church, Saint Augustine. The scope of his thought, however, went far beyond the narrow aspect of apologetics. Augustine has been called the architect of Western thought for a thousand years after his time. Certainly his influence is felt even today. He has also been denounced as the thinker who provided the Church with the thought-structure by which it suppressed independent thinking and enforced doctrinal conformity down to the Reformation period and beyond. In the few paragraphs that follow, no over-view of Augustine's thought will be attempted. Many studies have failed in such an attempt. The scope and complexity of his thought is not the only problem. He also had a way of changing his mind on basic issues. However, no understanding of the collapse of critical thought in the West is possible without some knowledge of the role he played in it.

Saint Augustine was born in Africa in A.D. 354, but forty years after Constantine had made Christianity the official religion of the Roman Empire. While still a young man, a Roman citizen and not a Christian, he became a convert to the Christian heresy known as Manichaeism. The Manichaeist allegories appealed to him as a valid means of reconciling

Christian teachings and classical philosophy. From age twenty to twenty-nine, Augustine was a passionate member of the Manichaean sect. Then he went to Rome. Not much attracted to the Manichaeans there, he broke with the sect and began to study neo-Platonism. From that he turned to a study of the Christian scriptures under the inspiration of Bishop Ambrose of Milan.

Ambrose, first a churchman and only secondarily a theologian, had adopted the method of allegory in order to interpret difficult passages in the Bible, notably in the early Old Testament. The young Augustine found this much to his liking. For a former Manichaean the method was wholly familiar. Like Augustine and Ambrose, the Manichaeans had been puzzled as to how early Old Testament stories could be accepted as the word of God. Understood as allegories of noble and profound truth, however, these tales, often bloodthirsty and immoral as well, could be accepted. Ambrose found full justification for the allegorical method in the words of Paul. "The letter killeth but the spirit giveth life," the Apostle had written, meaning that Bible passages are not to be read literally but figuratively. As we have seen, it was Paul himself who set the pattern of allegorizing in Christianity.

Until this time Augustine had been far from ascetic in his habits. Now, however, began an internal struggle with the flesh, as he later described it in his *Confessions*. His conversion to Christianity followed when he was thirty-two years of age. From then on, he was a devout and unquestioning believer in the Christian revelation, and he became its most redoubtable defender.

Augustine first took on his old friends the Manichaeans. Returning to North Africa, he settled at Hippo, where he eventually became bishop. After the Manichaeans, he directed his fire at a schismatic movement, the Donatists, and from them turned to still another, the Pelagians. When he died he was by far the most influential thinker in the Church, and he remains today among the very greatest of its leaders. By sheer force of intellect Augustine fashioned the Christian Church as an institution in accordance with its stated ideals and purposes as he understood them, and also in accordance with the needs of the Church to survive and prosper.

In Augustine's time the Christian Church was vigorous and fluid. Neither its institutional form nor its doctrinal position was yet so fixed that anyone could be certain in which direction either might grow. It can be said with accuracy that in the fourth century A.D. the structure and doctrine of the Church had been largely determined and that both only awaited the mind of an Augustine to establish them more or less permanently. In any event, this is the role Augustine played and it is why he is so important in any attempt to understand the virtual disappearance of the critical tradition in the religion of the West.

We take nothing from the greatness of Augustine as a churchman and as a thinker when we point out that his thinking was the antithesis of the critical way in religion. He is authoritarian where the critical tradition is free. He holds to the doctrine of revealed truth where the critical tradition asserts that truth is discovered. Augustine looks to the wisdom and authority of the ancients where the critical tradition looks to the authority of the self. One looks to revelation, the other to reason; one looks to God's free grace, the other to personal responsibility; one looks to the strength of an institution he regards as holy, the other looks to the untrammeled human mind and spirit. Like many a great theologian since his time, Augustine used his enormous reasoning powers to persuade the faithful that they were not to rely upon reason except as it supported their faith.

At each point Augustine moved the Church in the direction of institutional strength. That meant institutional authority. While the effect of his work was the establishment of a relatively immobile orthodoxy, at the same time he created a social organism that was able to endure through the chaos of the disintegrating Roman Empire and so to bring some measure of stability into the lives of people who had very little else to count on.

Augustine's starting point was complete and unquestioning acceptance of the idea that God reveals his will and truth to men, and an equally unquestioning acceptance of the content of those revelations. On that premise he built a doctrine of sin in which the living God was involved with men. He combined the category of God with the sacraments of the Church. Thus personal piety was institutionalized. He taught complete surrender to divine grace but he also insisted that grace comes to us through the offices of the Church, since sin is the natural manner of life for all of us. God has redeemed us in Jesus Christ. All that is required is contrition based on complete faith and trust. That means belief in the Christian revelation, belief in Christ's redemption, belief that our sins will be forgiven on confession and contrition, and belief that the Church is the earthly agency through which all this is made possible.

In the controversy with the Manichaeans, Augustine used reason to show that reason was not to be trusted. Reason was highly trusted in the ancient world, and the Manichaeans, as a part of that world, had taken the position that truth comes to man through reason. No, said Augustine. The Roman Church has the truth. God gave that truth to the founders of the Church and the Church holds it in its keeping. Men come to know the truth only by following rigorously the discipline of the Church. Only the pure in heart can expect to know what that truth is.

The Church teaches morality, Augustine said, so that a man's knowledge of the truth will not be obscured by sin. Faith is the next step, but it comes in the name of authority, not of reason. Since authority is fundamental in the world, we should expect to find it in the Church as much as anywhere else. But how, Augustine asked, do we know that authority in the Church is divine in origin? Because, he answers, it comes direct from Christ, is attested to by converts to the Church and by the happiness they find in their conversion. The authority of the Church is further attested by the continuity of its tradition descending from Christ himself.

The way in which Augustine made the place of the Church central for Christians and its authority unquestioned among them appears again in his controversy with the Donatists. Where the issue with the Manichaeans was the right of the individual to seek the truth for himself, in the Donatist controversy the right of the civil arm to enforce religious conformity was at issue. Augustine had at first opposed civil interference in religious affairs. Gradually, however, he moved to the opposite position. In the year 391 he was still arguing for freedom from coercion. In 400 he merely called for tolerance for dissenters. By 405 he was saying that heresy is a crime, equal to murder and rape, but he still opposed using violence against heretics. By the year 420 however, he had reached a position of complete intolerance. The only thing he refused to concede was the death penalty. That, he said, should never be used against heretics. "Compel them to come in," Augustine urged, citing as his authority Jesus' parable of the man who compelled people to attend his feast. It was the doctrine on which the Inquisition was built and the doctrine by which all its horrors were justified. Technically the death penalty was administered by the state, after the Church had condemned the alleged heretic and had asked for mercy that was not expected to be given.

In the third of the great controversies in which he became involved, that with Pelagius, Augustine, as before, championed the Church against the individual. Although we know little about Pelagius, he appears to have been a true exponent of the rights and needs of the individual, of the critical way in religion. Apparently he held singularly modern theological opinions. The views of this redoubtable fourth-century British monk, when expressed by twentieth-century clergymen, win both notice and approval, as if to assert such views requires clear and bold thinking even today. Here are some of them:

1. *Adam was an ordinary man. He would have died an ordinary death whether or not he had eaten of the forbidden fruit in Eden.*
   Official Catholic doctrine then as now held that Adam, by his disobedience, brought sin and death into the world and that had he not disobeyed God's command, he would have been immortal.
2. *The sin of Adam did harm to no one but himself.*
   Official Catholic doctrine held that owing to Adam's disobedience all men have since borne the stain of Adam's sin.
3. *Children are born sinless.*
   Official doctrine held that they are born guilty of Adam's sin.

4. *Even before the coming of Christ there were men who had been entirely without sin.*
   The official view has always been that none save Christ is sinless.

Here again the basic issue was the authority of the Church against the freedom of the individual. Pelagius held that man has within himself the capacity to become righteous. No, said Augustine, that makes God superfluous, a redeemer superfluous, and the Church superfluous as well. Man, Augustine insisted, is helpless; grace is God's free gift; man cannot earn it; if he can help himself, then Christ died in vain; these benefits are available to man only through the Church. To Augustine, above all others, we owe the doctrine: "No salvation outside the Church," even though Cyprian, not Augustine, first expressed the formula.

Perhaps the most interesting aspect of the controversy between Augustine and Pelagius, fought out as it was in theological terms, is the contrast between the personalities of the two men. Augustine—emotional, self-indulgent, unable, by his own confession, to resist the lusts of the flesh; Pelagius—a stern, self-disciplined Celt from the monasteries of Scotland and Ireland. Augustine, in vain seeking asceticism in the midst of the moral lassitude of the later Roman Empire, until through a conversion experience, God's grace came upon him; Pelagius, visiting Rome as a young man, shocked by the moral conditions he found there among professed Christians, including the clergy. For Augustine the disciplines exacted by the Church came hard. Pelagius took them in stride as the obligations one accepted if one chose to become a son of the Church.

Pelagius found, to his amazement, that Roman Christians justified their moral laxity on the ground that God asks more of us than we on our own can accomplish. This, in fact, had been Augustine's own personal experience. Yearning for the ascetic life and unable to achieve it, he begged God in prayer for the strength to do his will and then invited God to demand of man as much as he cared to. "Give what thou commandest; and command what thou wilt" was his prayer.

Pelagius took the opposite position. He wanted to place moral responsibility on man and to hold him to account for his actions. "Everything good and everything evil, in respect of which we are either worthy of praise or of blame, is done by us, not born with us," he argued. "We are not born in our full development, but with a capacity for good and evil; we are begotten as well without virtue as without vice, and before the activity of our own personal will there is nothing in man but what God has stored in him." His meaning, if not its exposition, has a contemporary ring.

Augustine was a church-builder, an institutionalist; Pelagius was a man-builder. He centered his thought in what man can do and in the obligations that fall upon him because of that fact. Against his will he was drawn into the discussion of a variety of theological questions. He had no heart for it because he felt, as do those who belong in the critical tradition, that the conceptual scheme a man develops by which to resolve metaphysical questions is far less important than the life he lives. It is in this sense that Pelagius belongs in the critical tradition and he is among the last of its exponents in the ancient world of whom we have much knowledge.

The result of Augustine's work was the virtually complete suppression of freedom of thought and expression on doctrinal matters. There were, of course, other contributing factors, notably the barbarian invasions and the slow disintegration of the Roman Empire. As the Church grew increasingly powerful, as its structure more and more became intertwined with the state, its general philosophy came to be enforced by the state, and freedom of expression died out altogether. We tend to forget that thought and expression had been remarkably free in ancient Rome. As in Greece, the leaders of the people, including the emperors, were unbelievers. They supported and indeed often enforced formal obeisance to the ancient gods of their culture, but they did so not out of belief but because they thought such worship was important in maintaining the fabric of society.

The same point of view has often been expressed in Judaism and Christianity. We often hear even today that religion is useful in maintaining good behavior. But such a view is the mark not of belief but of unbelief. For this reason it is often accompanied by a very wide tolerance of diversity in religion. After all, if the purpose of worship is to maintain civil order, what does the particular character of the worship matter? In such a view the worth of a religion is not determined by the validity of its theology but by the degree to which it controls conduct.

In Rome there was little suppression of independent thinking unless it was thought to be politically seditious. Lucretius' attack on religion in *On the Nature of Things* created no stir, nor did Lucian's satire, *Zeus in a Tragedy Part.* The Emperor Tiberius, questioned about these matters, remarked, "If the gods are insulted, let them see to it themselves." Rome was even tolerant toward exclusionist sects like Judaism. Its quarrel with Christianity stemmed from the unwillingness of the Christians to offer incense to the Emperor as a god. The grounds for this were political, not religious. The Christians were persecuted for their political obstinacy, not their theological doctrines.

Rome ended its persecution of the Christians in A.D. 311 with the First Edict of Toleration. It was followed by a second, two years later, the Edict of Milan. By it, the Emperor Constantine decreed that all who professed Christianity were to be permitted to continue, and that at the same time all others were to be allowed the free and unrestricted practice of their religion.

This was the high-water mark of religious tolerance in the ancient world. Once Constantine had made Christianity the official religion of the Roman Empire, he was immediately subjected to pressure to outlaw all other faiths. This the tolerant old Roman steadfastly refused to do. In the end, however, the Christians became sufficiently powerful to force their views on everyone. The mind of Augustine the thinker fashioned the formula by which this philosophy was justified. The will of Augustine the churchman made it an accomplished fact.

The number of scholars who have detailed the disappearance of liberty, independent thought, and criticism in the Christian Church after it gained the support of the Roman Emperors is legion. None is more eloquent and none more indignant than Francesco Ruffini, an Italian Catholic of the "Modernist" movement at the beginning of the twentieth century. He wrote:

> The deplorable revolution in the traditions of the primitive church was carried out at the time of Augustine, and it constitutes one of the strangest and most decisive points, not only in Augustine's individual psychology, as well as in the general doctrine of the psychological motives for religious intolerance, but also in the history of the Church itself, indeed of humanity as a whole.
>
> So long as the heretics had a preponderant position in Africa, Augustine was the most fervent supporter of the orthodox liberal tendencies; but afterwards he did not scruple to invoke the aid of the civil power against the Donatists, and decidedly and explicitly to repudiate the principle of liberty of conscience. "When man prevails," said Augustine, in justification of his position, "it is right to invoke liberty of conscience. But when, on the contrary, the truth predominates, it is just to use coercion." Under the Emperors Gratian and Theodosius, inspired by St. Ambrose, official status was taken from the pagan religions of Rome. Successive restrictions were imposed until, under Theodosius II and Valentinian III, all liberty was taken away from them. Under the code of Justinian, the denial of the Trinity and the repetition of baptism was made punishable by death.

Why did Augustine, whose mind was so clear and competent, choose the ecclesiastical way in religion rather than the critical way in which he had been reared? No doubt the clue lies in the social and political turmoil of the period in which he lived. It was a time of great political and social upheaval, a time of conquest and civil war within the empire over the right of succession to the throne, and a time of barbarian invasions as well. First came the Visigoths in southeastern Europe. When Augustine was fifty years old, the Vandals overran Gaul and the Romans abandoned Britain. The Huns under Attila began to ravage the empire. In the year 410 Alaric sacked Rome. Augustine died in 430 while the Vandals stood at the gates of his home city of Hippo in North Africa.

Augustine was seeking stability in a world of chaos. He was fashioning a structure with the capacity to deal with internally divisive elements. He was seeking a unity that could overcome splintering diversity, a means by which to control the centrifugal forces that threatened to tear the church of his time apart.

This raises the interesting question whether those who advocate the critical way in religion would do so in a less stable place and time than our own. My own answer is that the critical way in religion, if it is valid anywhere at any time, is valid everywhere and always. There certainly are ages in which the need is more for unity than diversity. But there can never be a time when the critical mind should be silenced because of other supposedly more important considerations. If we humans are truly to communicate with one another; if we are to root out error and falsehood, injustice, oppression, and fear; if we are to increase our understanding of ourselves and our world; if we are to live life to the full, then the critical mind must be free to probe where it will. To prove its case the critical mind need only point to the Christian Church and to Western culture in the centuries during which the Church followed the path of repression in the interest of unity. It was not until the chains were broken that the mind really began again to grow. The beginnings of that movement came in the Middle Ages and reached a climax, first in relatively narrow circles in the Renaissance, and subsequently much more broadly and powerfully in the period of the Enlightenment.

The human spirit will not be downed. Neither torture, imprisonment, nor threats of death will prevent us indefinitely from thinking for ourselves and giving voice to our thoughts. However severe the measures of suppression may be, and they were severe indeed in the ancient and medieval Church, eventually, it seems, someone, somewhere, will begin again to ask questions, begin again to think for himself, begin again to test the supposedly sure and certain tenets of his religion and culture. When he does so; when he finds them wanting; when the old ideas in which he was nurtured cannot stand the test; when the questioner conceives of broader, better, more accurate ideas, he will speak.

If the time be right he will be heard and a new era will dawn because of his vision and courage and because there were others of vision and courage who saw the truth in what he said. This happened in western Europe many centuries after Augustine's time, and yet more centuries after the allegorizing process had run its course. Not surprisingly perhaps, the spokesman of the new movement was another Celt, another product of the stern, disciplined monasteries of Scotland and Ireland.

6

The Rebirth of the Critical Tradition in Europe

Historians know that the periods into which they divide human history are inevitably arbitrary. At best, they designate times of more rapid transition or more complete stagnation than usual. The so-called "Dark Ages" are a case in point. From the disintegration of the Roman Empire—say the fifth or sixth century A.D. to the time we know as the Carolingian Renaissance in the ninth century—the light of learning and of critical, independent thinking burned very low in the West. Political, social, and economic chaos was the order of the day. Because of this turmoil people were concerned with the effort of just staying alive more than with anything else, and as a result very little was accomplished in any field. In his *History of the Franks,* Gregory of Tours (538–593) gives a picture of the barbarization of the Church itself in a world of barbarism and violence: "The towns have let culture perish; learned men are not to be found. Woe to our times."

1. The Slender Thread

There is some risk in singling out for special attention the Roman nobleman of the fifth century, Boethius, and the Celtic Christian ascetic of the ninth century, Erigena. And yet, in the light of our present knowledge of those remote and turbulent times, who can better stand as symbols of the slender thread that connects the critical tradition of the ancient world with that of medieval and modern times?

Quite apart from his role in the critical way in religion, Anicius Manlius Severincis Boethius (480?–524?) stands out as a figure of great significance. For a millennium he exercised a profound influence on the thought of western

Europe. Down to the Renaissance his works were known and read by all educated men. A scion of one of the leading families of the Roman Empire, Boethius was steeped in ancient Hellenistic culture. He was educated both in Rome and in Athens, and as a result, in a time when knowledge of Greek was rapidly fading in the West, he was as much at home in the one as in the other. A thorough student of both Plato and Aristotle, he proposed the translation into Latin of all the works of both men, together with commentaries in which he hoped to reconcile the differences between the two Greek intellectual giants.

Boethius was the last of a vanishing class. He lived during the very period many historians today, in the light of fifteen hundred years of hindsight, identify as the time when the ancient Roman Empire at last ceased to exist. Half a century before his birth, Alaric the Visigoth had taken and sacked Rome, an unthinkable event for the "Eternal City." He was still a lad when the Ostrogothic leader Theodoric invaded Italy at the invitation of the Emperor. In the year 510 Theodoric appointed Boethius consul and their relationship appears to have been close. Less than fifteen years later, however, he was executed without trial at Theodoric's command. The charge was treason.

Because of his involvement in affairs of state and his death at a little more than forty years of age, Boethius accomplished little of his grandiose plan of translation and commentary on Plato and Aristotle. He carried his project far enough, however, so that the works he did translate formed the basis of western Europe's knowledge of Greek thought for almost a millennium. His *Consolation of Philosophy,* written in prison with the sentence of death hanging over his head, proved to be no less important, and, for the critical way in religion, crucial. He composed it as a dialogue after the manner of Plato, using but two characters, himself and a figure he called "My Lady Philosophy." The issue they debate is the one uppermost in Boethius's mind as he asked such questions as: Why do the innocent suffer? How is a good man, ruled by tyrants, to think of life? It was Job's old question: why does a good God, all-powerful and all-wise, ever reward the evil and torment the good?

Boethius' answer to these questions is hardly that of the critical mind. He is far too rationalistic for that, far too Aristotelian in his reliance upon logic as a means of reaching the truth. Boethius is important for the critical tradition in religion, nevertheless, because he forms a link of great consequence between critical thought in ancient times and its reemergence in western Europe in the high Middle Ages.

Boethius was a thinker in a time when people seem virtually to have stopped thinking. He had an inquisitive mind. Not content with the answers the Church Fathers had given to profound questions, he sought answers in the clarity of his own mind and in the depths of his own soul. His answers are not distilled from the writings of the Fathers, of which an abundance had been accumulated in his time, including those of the great Saint Augustine. In fact, Boethius writes as if that great body of sacred literature, the Bible included, did not exist. Boethius' God is not Christian but Platonic. Boethius' answers to his own questions are not biblical but philosophical. He asks Job's question but does not give Job's answer or even mention his name. It was Lady Philosophy, not the Lord Christ, who brought him consolation as he approached the day of his execution.

Boethius had implicit if not explicit faith in the ultimate rationality of the world. The moral principles that can be perceived operating in the world were for him completely rational and were a part of the whole. For him it was all a unity, a unity that could be perceived by thinking through the elements in the structure.

Today the critical mind would insist on weighing the wide variety of data that life lays before us, an idea that never crossed the neo-Platonic mind of Boethius. As the transition figure between the ancient and the medieval critical mind, he could not be expected to be a full-blown exemplar of the critical way in religion. Living as he did in a time when allegiance to ecclesiastical authority was the order of the day, it is enough that for twenty years of his adult life he thought and wrote as a free spirit, as one who found his inspiration, not in Christian ecclesiastical dogma, but like the ancient Greeks he so much admired, in rigorous thought and in philosophical speculations.

"I want to educate present society in the spirit of Greek philosophy," Boethius said. That he did not succeed is beside the point. As learning began to revive again in the tenth century after the chaos of the Dark Ages, it was to Boethius that men first turned. The first to take full advantage of his translations was Gerbert of Aurillac, who later became Pope Sylvester II (972–982) half a millennium after *The Consolation of Philosophy* had given what hope and support it could to its author as he went to his execution.

How far the Church attempted to carry its control of men's thinking and actions can be seen in the following (taken from a Decree of the Council of Nicaea in 787 A.D. with regard to painting). "It is not the invention of the painter which creates a picture," said the Council solemnly, "but the inviolable law and tradition of the Church. It is not the painter but the Holy Fathers who have to invent and dictate. To them manifestly belongs the composition, to the painter only the execution."

2. The Universities Emerge

Meanwhile, profound changes had taken place in the economics, politics, and social structures of western Europe. It was in early medieval times that a new institution in human society first began to take form—the university. It is surprising how many of the structural elements that evolved as the new universities came into being in the early Middle Ages remain with us today. Even the vocabulary is the same in many instances. *Universitas,* from which our word university is derived, originally meant all the teachers and students taken together as a unit. They were headed by a *chancellarius*; our word is chancellor. The areas of study and students in those areas were divided into colleges (Latin *collegia*). These were in turn administered by deans (Latin *decani*), also called rectors, since they were always churchmen. In each college the faculty offered a prescribed curriculum on a prescribed schedule, as is the case today. And again, as with us, academic degrees were awarded to students who, upon examination, were able to show that they had successfully completed the prescribed set of courses.

Since it was out of the universities that the critical tradition came, we shall not be surprised to learn that the universities, like the critical way in religion, find their roots in ancient Greece. We can follow this development at least as far back as Plato, under whose aegis formalized education seems to have had its beginnings. Our word "academy" is derived from Academia, the name of an area northwest of Athens where Plato, about 387 B.C., began lecturing in his own house and garden to a circle of advisers and friends. Like Socrates, his teacher, Plato charged no fees, but he gave courses of lectures and conducted disputations extending over a three- or four-year period.

The step taken by Plato that distinguished him from Socrates and the other thinkers of the time was simple, but it was fundamental in two respects. First, he settled down and did his lecturing and disputing in one place, a place he himself provided. Secondly, he pursued his topics through a series of lectures or disputations over an extended period of time, as a result of which his hearers got some grasp of the broad range of material he was dealing with. Heretofore Socrates and the other great minds of Greece had lectured and debated wherever it pleased them, usually but not always in public places, on whatever subject came to mind at the moment, and only as long as circumstances might determine.

Through the Socratic Dialogues as set down by Plato we gain a clear picture of the practice as it prevailed before the establishment of the Academy. Each dialogue had a setting of its own. These included various public porches, the homes of private citizens, and the prison of Socrates. Plato's institution of the Academy marks the beginning of higher education on a formal basis in Hellas. Before his time, instruction of the young had been individual and personal. After his time, education at the upper level gradually became organized and institutionalized on a group basis.

His Academy continued on for several centuries after his time until the year A.D. 529, when the Roman Emperor Justinian closed it as a part of his program of suppressing all heresy and all vestiges of paganism. As we move into the Middle Ages, nothing like the educational system that prevailed in the ancient world is to be found in western Europe. The continuing effort, like that of Justinian, to reduce all independent thought to silence, coupled with the social turmoil resulting from the barbarian invasions and civil wars, brought discussion, experimentation, and progress in learning to a standstill. Only the monasteries, scattered like small islands in a turbulent sea, kept the vision of knowledge and education alive.

The story of the rebirth of learning in western Europe begins with a man we ordinarily associate with war, conquest, and romantic poetry: Charles the Great, king of the Franks, known to history as Charlemagne. He brought about no such educational revolution by himself. The makings of it were already at hand and so were the men who could assist him. Among these was a monk named Alcuin (735–804), a product, like Pelagius, of the stern but learned Christianity of Britain. In one of his letters to Charlemagne at the time the educational revival was being planned, Alcuin wrote: "If your intentions are carried out it may be that a new Athens will arise in France and an Athens fairer than of old, for our Athens, ennobled by the teachings of Christ will surpass the wisdom of the Academy." Obviously, the new learning sponsored by Charlemagne did not rise directly out of the old learning of Greece, yet the presence of the Athenian ideal and its impact on their planning is clear.

Under the leadership of Charlemagne there occurred in western Europe, beginning in the ninth century, a movement scholars know today as the Carolingian Renaissance. It was an intellectual awakening that drew scholars from all over Europe. The center of the revival was the Palace School that Charlemagne set up and which he himself attended. Those who gathered there were true scholars. They sought books wherever they could be found, laboriously making copies for themselves and others. They created original works of their own. They undertook to replace the often corrupt texts then in circulation with more accurate ones. The influence of the Palace School spread widely. As a result of it, libraries were established in monasteries where before there had been but few books. Those libraries became centers for the production of yet more manuscripts, which in turn spread learning yet more widely through Europe.

It was out of the milieu established by the Palace School that the first clear reaffirmation of the critical tradition came, formulated by John Scotus Erigena (815?–877?) also called John the Scot. Born and reared in Ireland, Erigena, like Pelagius and Alcuin, was a product of the Celtic church. We know very little about that church, but from Erigena's writings we can assume that in his time it was a thriving institution which encouraged independent thought and discussion. He was among the earliest of the medieval scholars to know Greek. Erigena is best known among historians for his translation of *Pseudo Dionysius,* a fifth-century neo-Platonist work, and for his *De Divisione Nature,* a speculative system in which he develops his own theological views. On the basis of the latter he has been called "the first eminent philosopher of the Middle Ages" and "the first great thinker since Augustine." Over a five-hundred-year period apparently only he attempted a theological system of his own.

For the critical tradition, Erigena's importance does not lie in the particular philosophico-theological system he worked out, but in his attitude toward the process by which systems are constructed. "Authority is the source of knowledge," he wrote, as any loyal churchman would. What he meant was this: those things we can be said really to know depend upon the authority of the Church. The Church has the authority to declare them to be true, and so we believe them. "But," he continues, "our own reason remains the norm by which all authority must be judged."

This is the critical tradition in essence. Whoever would claim authority in any realm must persuade reasonable people that he has the authority he claims. While Erigena did not say it in so many words, he seems clearly to have placed what we know through experience above what we suppose ourselves to know through revelation, the source of knowledge upheld by the authority of the church. "Authority sometimes proceeds from reason," he wrote, "but reason never from authority . . . true reason . . . is established in its own strength." Elsewhere he acknowledged the authority of Scripture, also a thoroughly orthodox view, but he went on to observe that since everyone acknowledges the authority of Scripture, no further emphasis upon it is needed. Consequently he would emphasize reason. And he did.

His critical approach appears almost incidentally when he attempts to reconcile the inconsistencies in the writings of the Church Fathers. He first professes reverence for them, then he shows the inconsistencies in them; but he then goes on to blunt any application of the critical principle by attempting to show that the seeming inconsistencies do not really exist after all. Perhaps this is what he believed. It is also possible that in daring to expose inconsistencies in the writings of the Church Fathers he felt he had gone as far as a man could. In any event, he was so far ahead of his time and so clear in stating the problem that the Church officially condemned his chief work, *De Devisione Natura,* at the Council of Sens in 1225, nearly four hundred years after he wrote it.

Berengar of Tours, an eleventh-century French ecclesiastic, went so far as to argue that no true miracle took place when the bread and wine were blessed during the eucharist; in short, he held that the eucharist was only symbolic. Such a view would not necessarily place him in the critical tradition, but his reasons for holding that view would. Berengar insisted that since nothing could be seen to change during the eucharist, nothing did.

"It is a part of courage to have recourse to dialectic in all things," wrote Berengar, "for recourse to dialectic is recourse to reason, and he who does not avail himself of reason abandons his chief honor, since by virtue of reason he was made in the image of God." He clearly put reason above authority. "When authority and reason conflict," he continued, "one must follow reason, inasmuch as no authority can supersede reason in a mind capable of discovering truth." This was too much for the medieval Church, deeply entrenched as it was in its own doctrine of authority. Berengar of Tours was declared a heretic and forced to recant. He spent the remainder of his life as a recluse.

When we read about such forced recantations, we find ourselves wondering who was fooling whom. This pattern prevailed throughout the Middle Ages and even into Reformation times. Did anyone suppose that such retractions meant an inward change in belief? To ask such a question is to misunderstand the medieval Church's conception of itself and what it sought in enforcing such conformity. The purpose was the purpose Augustine had sought to achieve: unity, conformity, institutional strength, the prevention of schism and of acrimonious, divisive debate. The coercive measures taken by the medieval church were severe, thoroughgoing, and effective. That is why men like Berengar and Erigena stand out. More than nine hundred years ago Berengar of Tours, with clarity of mind and with the courage of his convictions, took an honored place among those who revived the critical way in the religion of the West.

3. The Critical Tradition in the Middle Ages

Medieval universities arose in response to a felt need. By the twelfth and thirteenth centuries a considerable body of learning had been accumulated, of which most people were only dimly aware, but about which there began to be a rising curiosity. As the news began to get around that a vast literature created by the Greeks and Romans, known only to a few scholars, lay hidden in Europe's libraries, the desire to get at it was kindled. The desire to read it, to acquire the knowledge the ancients had, mounted. In addition, by the time of the high Middle Ages, medieval "science" had developed a lore all its own. An expanding body of law was developing in both ecclesiastical and civil courts. Beyond these areas of learning there were the fields of medicine and mathematics, engineering, astronomy, and, of course, astrology—all of which required special training to enter.

The universities were both the cause and the result of the reawakening of the mood of inquiry. They prospered because of the thirst for learning that was felt throughout Europe at this time, stimulated by the knowledge that there was much learning to be acquired. There, men with knowledge taught those who lacked but wanted to acquire it. From this an unexpected result followed. Inquiring minds, gathered in one place, generated questions. The students not only stimulated one another, and their teachers as well; they also gained support from one another in their questioning and in the development of answers that were new and different from those they had heard before. These answers in turn generated yet more questions from which still more answers came, and so on.

The corruption and lassitude that had eaten its way into the medieval Church also contributed to independent thought. The wealth, the high living, the immorality that characterized the Church generally in this period produced a mounting succession of protests, all from within the Church itself. In the Middle Ages the common people and most clerics had little understanding of the arguments by which Augustine had established the authority of the Church, but they had no difficulty whatever understanding the immorality and self-indulgence of the clergy. These practices were denounced, not only in terms of Catholic doctrine and Scripture but also in terms of common decency.

When men began to challenge the Church and the churchmen on the basis of Scripture and by their own sense of what is fitting and proper, it was but a short step to the raising of doctrinal questions as well. When the moral questions came and the questions themselves were not denounced, the intellectual questions followed soon after. Questions beget questions, no matter what they are about. It is a habit of mind: a kind of mental set. If answers of any sort follow, then there are still more questions, and so on.

At the time when the great ferment we know as the Medieval Renaissance and Reformation was in full flower, Christian Europe made contact with Islam. In many aspects of knowledge and culture, Islam in the eleventh century was much further advanced than western Europe. Two hundred years earlier Abd ar-Rahman III had pacified the turbulent Iberian peninsula. Marked commercial and industrial progress followed. Conspicuous among these enterprises was the manufacture of paper, for which there was now a great demand, both in Islam and western Europe, owing to the revival of learning in both areas. The Arabs were skilled in metal work. The cloth they wove is still known to us by Arabic names: muslin, damask, gauze, cotton, and satin. They led in the science of agriculture.

Most important for Western culture, the Arabs possessed the treasures of Greek literature and thought that had come into their hands by means of two Christian heretical groups living within the confines of Islamic culture, the Monophysites and the Nestorians. With their access to Greek manuscripts through Byzantium, these heretical sects had translated many Greek works, particularly Aristotle, into Arabic. As a result, the Muslims knew and perfected the Greek astrolabe, the predecessor of the sextant, for observing the position of heavenly bodies. They knew the Greeks had concluded that the earth is round, not flat as the Christian West believed at that time. Geometry, logic, astronomy, medicine—all these they learned from the Greeks. By the ninth century, when the influence of Charlemagne's Palace School first was felt, the whole corpus of Greek scientific and philosophical writing had been translated into Arabic.

Because of the fanaticism that has characterized many Islamic military campaigns we tend to think of Muslim religion as intolerant. It was so only in part. The period following the great expansion of Islam, around the eastern and southern shores of the Mediterranean and into Spain on the west, was marked by an unusually tolerant spirit for those times. Beginning in the eleventh century the trade barriers between the Christian and the Islamic world went down and a remarkable interchange between the two cultures took place. In this exchange the West gained access to the vast storehouse of Greek learning and culture, and it came fortunately, at a time when a newly awakened desire for learning suffused the West. Here again, effect was cause and cause was effect. New discoveries in learning in turn stimulated the desire for yet more learning.

As has happened often in human history, when the political barriers at last had been broken down, the first to take advantage of the new freedom and opportunity were the traders. In the wake of the traders came the scholars. One of the earliest of these and one of the greatest was an Englishman, Adelard of Bath (not to be confused with his better-known near contemporary, the Frenchman Abelard). Adelard was a product of twelfth-century English university life then centered at Oxford. The movement boasted such men as Robert Grosseteste, Roger Bacon, Duns Scotus, and William of Ockham. Its strength lay in mathematics and science more than in theology.

The earliest of the thinkers of the English school, and the most original as well, appears to have been Adelard. He also seems to have been at least as energetic as any in the pursuit of knowledge. On hearing of the achievements of the Arabs in science and mathematics, he went to Sicily, where Christian and Muslim cultures mingled. Thence he traveled to North Africa, to western Asia, then to Greece, and finally to Spain. What he sought and what he discovered through his travels was the learning of ancient Greece. To avail himself of it he mastered Arabic and soon began the translation of these sources into Latin. Among them was Euclid's *Elements of Geometry.*

As with so many of the most alert minds of this period, their increasing knowledge put an increasing strain on the faith and trust demanded of them by the Church. It was the old question with which the ancient world had struggled and which the Church had solved by giving up the ancient learning of Greece and Rome and confining its teachings to the Bible and the writings of Christian scholars. Adelard's solution to the problem is contained in a letter, happily preserved for us, to his nephew. He advised the young man to accept the teachings of Christianity on faith. You can't accept them on the basis of reason, he wrote. Too many of them are irrational. Study the natural world, he advised, and use reason rather than authority as you do it. Seek natural causes for events, not supernatural ones.

Adelard told his nephew that he had learned this distinction from the Arabs. It was a formula that became standard in the Middle Ages and was invoked for hundreds of years afterward. Whoever wished to pursue the path of inquiry and yet be able to assure the authorities of his loyalty to orthodox Church teaching took this position. The truth gained from reason and from observation of the natural world was only rational truth, they said. Revealed truth is of another sort, attained neither by observation and experiment nor by the use of reason, but accepted on faith. Whether justifiably or not, Europe dubbed this teaching the doctrine of "double truth."

4. Ibn-Rushd (Averroës)

Adelard was accurate when he said he had learned from the Arabs the distinction between truth arrived at by reason and observation and truth attained by faith. There was one Muslim thinker in particular from whom this idea came, a man known to the Christian West as Averroës (the Arabic form of his name is Ibn-Rushd). He is in all probability the key figure in the establishment of the critical tradition in western Europe. Ibn-Rushd was born in Cordoba, Spain in 1126. He died in the same city in 1198. At that time Cordoba was a leading intellectual center. Great libraries had been gathered there; schools of philosophy, poetry, music, mathematics, and medicine flourished. Much if not most of the impetus for this sudden burst of learning came through the discovery of the rich intellectual resources of ancient Greece and Rome. Great numbers of these works were searched out, translated into Arabic, widely discussed, taught, and used.

Ibn-Rushd was very much a part of the surging life that existed at Cordoba. He became a great legal scholar, as his grandfather before him had been. Through most of his life he enjoyed great favor at court. However, when he was sixty-nine years of age he was banished because of his heretical views, even though he always professed complete loyalty to Islam. He was allowed to return shortly before his death.

In Ibn-Rushd, we have a direct connection between classical Greek thought of a critical character and the reappearance of that kind of thinking in western Europe in the Middle Ages. In his youth he read in translation all of Aristotle's writings he could obtain, and that meant most of those now known to us. In the true sense of the word, he became a disciple of the ancient Greek philosopher. *The* Philosopher, he called him. He concluded that all wisdom and truth lay with Aristotle, and wrote an extensive commentary on his works.

However, Ibn-Rushd's study of Aristotle created a great problem for him. As a loyal Muslim, fully accepting the Islamic faith, how was he to square the supernatural elements of his religion with the natural philosophy of Aristotle? It is not surprising that Ibn-Rushd, struggling with this problem, reached the same conclusion to which his Christian contemporaries were being driven: that since truth is one and comes through revelation, knowledge acquired through the study of nature and philosophy is of a lesser sort. It was assumed that if we knew enough, we could see that the inconsistencies were more apparent than real. Ibn-Rushd carried on a stout defense of Aristotle without ever questioning the validity of the Islamic faith. When al-Ghazzali, the great Muslim leader, suspecting that heresy was in the air, wrote a book in defense of Islamic faith entitled *Incoherence of the Philosophers,* Ibn-Rushd responded with a tract entitled *Incoherence of Incoherence,* in which he took the Aristotelian approach.

Al-Ghazzali had seen correctly, however, that no matter how Ibn-Rushd might protest his loyalty to the orthodox Muslim faith, his devotion to Aristotle made him suspect. How could he call Aristotle "The Philosopher" and not see that his philosophy was in conflict with the revealed religion of Islam? Perhaps in his heart Ibn-Rushd could not. The record does not show. But it does show that that was what Adelard of Bath got out of studying and translating his work. In any event, whether rightly or wrongly, Ibn-Rushd, under the name Averroës, came to be regarded in the West as the source of the doctrine of "double truth." The Averroists, as his Christian followers were called, began teaching that there are two roads to truth: the one through revelation (in this instance Christian, not Muslim), the other through reason and observation.

As one of the earliest exponents of the critical way in religion in medieval Europe, Averroës is a figure of sharply contrasting principles. An exemplar of the critical way in his adoption of the natural philosophy of Aristotle, he is at the same time an exemplar of the ecclesiastical way in much of the rest of his thought. For example, in defending the role of the Qur'an as the source of revelation for Islam, he used an argument widely employed by Jews and Christians even today. Sacred Scripture (the Bible or the Qur'an) is not to be taken as a book of natural history, he said, but as a revelation of the moral principles by which we are to live. These principles are not to be examined intellectually; they are to be taken on faith. The Qur'an is a book of truth, and we must believe. Philosophy, on the other hand (i.e., the science of Aristotle), does not deal with moral precepts; it deals with the natural world and with modes of thought. In this limited sense philosophy may be regarded as the highest form of truth, but it is a body of truth different from that of moral precept. Such was his teaching.

At the same time, Ibn-Rushd's capacity for original and independent thought showed itself in areas outside theology and philosophy. As an example, he noted and protested against the lowly role assigned to women in Islam. "Women are kept like domestic animals or house plants for the purpose of gratification," he wrote. "They should be allowed to take part in the production of material and intellectual wealth."

In his attitude toward the common people, however, Ibn-Rushd was reactionary and patrician. Like the Christians Duns Scotus and Erasmus, he was deeply concerned lest the speculations of the philosophers upset the faith of the uneducated masses. He seems to have been alarmed at the possible impact of the thinking of Aristotle on minds less well endowed than his own. He insisted that heretical ideas, even though they can be refuted, should be kept from the multitude. We dare not present such views as alternatives and trust ordinary people to choose wisely among them; better not to let them hear such upsetting views at all.

This idea is one of very ancient lineage, as we saw in connection with the religions of Greece and Rome. Plato felt that only the philosopher-king was sufficiently endowed with wisdom to be able to govern properly. Since the most ancient times it has been held that religion, even when laden with superstition and error, must be maintained as a means by which to keep the masses in order. It was a common opinion among the Roman Stoics. Cicero voices it clearly. Machiavelli is perhaps the best known exponent of the idea. Ibn-Rushd, in his patrician view of life, is neither the first nor is he likely to be the last of the great exemplars of the critical way in religion to fail to apply exacting standards to every aspect of his own thinking.

There was a parallel development of the critical way in Judaism, contemporaneous with that of Averroism. Devout Jews faced the same problem as did Christians and Muslims: how to reconcile ancient religious teaching with contemporary thinking derived from Aristotle and dictated by reason and observation. Moses ben Maimon, a Hebrew physician known to the West as Maimonides, a contemporary of Ibn-Rushd, and like him a citizen of Cordoba, undertook the task of reconciling reason and faith for Judaism. Like Ibn-Rushd and the Averroists at the University of Paris, he argued that Aristotelian philosophy should be restricted to the things of earth. The things of heaven could be known only through revelation, he asserted, and were available to men only through the Word of God. Moses ben Maimon published a *Guide to the Perplexed* in which he attempted to spell all this out. The result was, of course, that he, like Ibn-Rushd, became identified with the doctrine of double truth. The idea that there are two sources of truth available to us was a compromise. It was one of the many attempts we find in the history of religion to reconcile reason and faith. Loyal Muslims, Christians, and Jews accepted the precepts of their several faiths as truth that was not to be questioned since God was its source. But they were at the same time unwilling to give up the conclusions toward which both reason and observation impelled them. The doctrine of double truth solved the problem for them to this degree: it enabled them to pursue the critical method freely while professing complete loyalty to their particular religious traditions. This loyalty, they maintained, had been established in advance and was not to be questioned.

But the compromise did not work. However well the idea of double truth may have served to meet the needs of medieval rationalists, it satisfied official Christianity, Judaism, and Islam not at all. Each stoutly maintained that truth was one, and that any supposed truth discovered through the use of reason or observation must be wholly consistent with the truth that religion already held through God's previous revelation.

The reaction of the Christian Church to the idea of double truth eventually went beyond argument. One of the so-called Averroists, David of Dinant, was burnt at the stake; another, Amalric of Bena, was forced to recant. Others were pursued in various ways as the Church tried, unsuccessfully, to prevent the reading of Averroës and all of Aristotle as well, excepting only his *Logic*. The Averroist movement ultimately was crushed and the principle of double truth condemned in A.D. 1277.

It was Thomas Aquinas who resolved the problem for Christianity. In his massive *Summa Theologiae* he undertook to reconcile faith and reason in all their many related aspects. He did so to his own satisfaction and that of the medieval Church and he did it by means of Aristotelian logic. But the history of the Church in the West makes it clear that Aquinas succeeded only for a time. The Protestant Reformation did not solve the problem either. The authority of revelation remained unquestioned in the two major divisions of the Christian Church, and in Judaism and Islam as well. At the same time the challenge of reason continued to grow more insistent. Observation and experiment, the testing and checking of everything against the evidence, against inconsistencies, against error, and against the possibility of deception, slowly increased. No one ever found an answer to the contradictions between the two.

Ibn-Rushd and his problems with Islam, Moses ben Maimon and his problems with Judaism, matched those that plagued Christianity. In all three religions we see the same conflict with traditional theological views. In the reaction in all three to the new approach we can see what the critical way is and what it is not. It is not anti-Christian, anti-Muslim, or anti-Jewish. It is anti-authority. It is anti- any teaching that is to be accepted, like the revelations of Judaism, Christianity, and Islam, on the authority of an institution that declares them to be true. The critical tradition does not declare dogmatically that no revelation is possible, nor does it declare dogmatically that any or all revelations are false. It holds only that any such claim must meet the same standards for acceptance as those by which we judge every other claim. Adelard of Bath and Ibn-Rushd did not go so far, but they paved the way for those who did.

7

The Renaissance

Over a century ago the Swiss scholar Jacob Burckhardt published *The Civilization of the Renaissance in Italy.* In it he developed the thesis, widely accepted today but novel in 1860, that "a new and unique civilization called 'the Renaissance' existed in Italy in the fourteenth, fifteenth and sixteenth centuries." Seen in the light of the critical tradition in the religion of the West, Burckhardt's concept takes on added validity and significance. He argued that the development of individualism was the primary distinguishing characteristic of the Italian Renaissance. In the Middle Ages, he said, "Man was conscious of himself only as a member of a race, people, party, family or corporation—only through some general category." In Renaissance Italy, however, "Man became a spiritual *individual* and recognized himself as such." As Burckhardt saw it, the sense of one's individuality resulted in the capacity to view the world objectively. No such conscious division of experience between the subjective and the objective had existed in the Middle Ages.

The special character of the Italian Renaissance disclosed by Burckhardt's genius can also be seen as a sharp advance in the critical way in religion and in life taken as a whole. The two go hand in hand. To be conscious of the self as an individual is to wish to express one's thoughts openly, even when they differ sharply from ideas that prevail in one's own time. Only someone aware of his own selfhood, his own individuality, would think to challenge a commonly accepted idea.

1. Medieval Pioneers

It was during the Renaissance that many of the principles of the critical way in religion attained full formulation. Among the most basic of these is the practice of independent thinking coupled with the opportunity to express such thoughts openly. Today, we call this freedom of speech. No such concept existed in the medieval mind, but the elements in the conflict out of which the principle at last emerged were gestating at that time. They had been, since the time of Socrates in Athens and the Edict of Toleration in ancient Rome. In medieval times the conflict is most vividly seen in the church's struggle with heresy.

The idea of heresy can be traced far back in human history. Some writers begin an account of the subject with Amenhotep IV, King of Egypt, who reigned from 1372 to 1354 B.C. There is ample evidence to support the surmise that this remarkable ruler who took the name Akhenaten or Ikhnaton was among the earliest of the dissenters from the established orthodoxy of his time, and one of the earliest to set up a new religious movement in competition with the old. Recent speculation centers on his queen Nefertiti (again with variant spellings), who was as beautiful as Akhenaten was ugly.There seems to be good reason to believe that the Queen and not the King was the the moving force in the reform they attempted to bring about in the ancient and well-established religion of Egypt. Nothing came of the movement, however. Accordingly, those interested in the origins of heresy shift their attention to Greece, where Anaxagoras was exiled and Socrates paid for his dissenting views with his life.

Heresy, more strictly construed, begins with Christianity. It begins with an organization with the power to establish officially accepted views and to suppress dissenting movements by force. As the Church slowly became centralized, as the Bishop of Rome slowly became the most powerful figure in the Church, dissenting groups were systematically brought into line or eliminated. The process was quite as much political as doctrinal.

From the beginning heretics were hunted out and dealt with, often with great severity. In 1233 Pope Gregory IX formalized the procedure by creating within the Church a new institution, called The Holy Office or Inquisition. We need not pause to review its horrors. Torture, imprisonment under appalling conditions, death at the stake—all these are well enough known to spare us another review of them here. They are a part of our story only in the negative sense that they were the dread means by which medieval society, Church and state alike, sought to suppress the emerging independence of thought. Such suppression was looked upon as a means of stabilizing social order.

The Church was not loath to use argument in its defense, either, and in the area of disputation it never lacked champions of the greatest skill. They were needed, for those who were asking questions were men of great talent also. Abelard (1079–1142), for example, known to most of us through his tragic romance with Heloise, was a skilled dialectician and a very popular teacher as well. Crowds of students flocked to him wherever he went. "The first key to wisdom," he wrote, "is called interrogation, diligent and unceasing. By doubting we are led to inquiry and from inquiry we perceive truth." Abelard took his own advice. In his *Sic et Non* he collected the writings of the Church authorities on many topics and set them in opposition to one another. His aim was to show that there was disagreement among them on almost every basic issue. He then tried to resolve these conflicting views. Nevertheless, he let the contradictions stand against each other and invited his students to attempt such answers as they could. The emphasis he thereby placed on the contradictions among the Church fathers could have no result other than to undermine ecclesiastical authority. Most scholars feel, however, that his purpose was not to discredit the Church but to find an explanation for the discrepancies.

Thomas Aquinas resolved to the satisfaction of the Church the questions raised by Abelard, the Averroists, and all the other questioners, experimenters, and thinkers of the high Middle Ages. In his *Summa Theologiae,* as we have seen, he sought to reconcile the demands of faith and reason. He did not agree with the anti-Averroists who said that Islamic writings should not be read by devout Christians. In an attempt to reconcile the demands of faith and reason, he made a distinction which had been implicit if not explicit in many of the thinkers who preceded him—a distinction between revealed and natural theology. His was not the distinction of the Averroists between two kinds of truth which could not be reconciled. For Aquinas truth was one, but had two sources—one natural and the other revealed. Both, he held, yield the same truth in the end. Aquinas brought the natural philosophy of Aristotle into the Christian orbit and welded the two into a Christian orthodoxy. It was a singular and monumental achievement of the mind.

What Aquinas did, however, was far from introducing the critical way into Christian philosophy. It was the opposite. The basic metaphysical concept by which Aquinas achieved a unity of outlook was the controlling presence and will of God. For Aquinas, God was both the source of revelation and the source of all that occurs in the natural world as well. In Aristotelian language, of which Aquinas made great use, God was both the first and final cause of everything that happened. His knowledge and will directed all events and, as needed, he would disrupt natural processes for his own purpose.

When Abelard began pointing out the inconsistencies that lay in the sacrosanct writings of the Church Fathers, by no means everyone saw the danger to the thought-structure of the Church latent in his method. He was careful always to resolve such apparent inconsistencies in favor of the established faith. But when his pupil Arnold of Brescia declared boldly that all Christian dogma must be grounded in Scripture, not in the writings of the Fathers, when Arnold openly condemned the luxurious lives of priests and prelates and engaged in political activity directed against the power of the papacy as well, the Church had little trouble deciding what to do with him. Arnold was hanged, his body burned, and his ashes thrown into the Tiber in 1155.

Despite the extensive control exercised by the Church, there was during the medieval period freedom of thought and expression to a surprising degree. Certainly the body of writing that has come down to us in particular from Italy during the fourteenth, fifteenth, and sixteenth centuries—the Renaissance period—shows remarkable lack of restraint by medieval standards. It was the Counter-Reformation in the mid-sixteenth century that re-established and enforced the earlier standards of uniformity, the hunting out and persecution of all who deviated from the norm.

Explanations for this attitude on the part of an extraordinarily powerful church vary. Some ascribe it to the moral laxity that characterized many medieval churchmen, and from time to time, ecclesiastical institutions as well. Others see it as part of the general laxity that often accompanies great power. Church authorities in the later Middle Ages did not feel the need to be as severe in dealing with new ideas as their predecessors had.

Still others have a subtler explanation. They argue that it was easy for the Church to identify and deal with heretics like Pierre de Bruys (executed in 1126) who asserted the primacy of Scripture above the authority of the Church, and with Arnold of Brescia for the same reason. The heresy of both was an ancient one, easily recognized by the dullest cleric. Essentially it was an assertion of the right of the individual's direct access to God, and of his right to independent private judgment.

It was quite another matter, however, when men raised questions that had not heretofore been formulated. And such questions were continually being raised at that time by churchmen, apparently loyal to the organization and to the intellectual traditions of the Church as well. For a very few independent thinkers it was a time of great creativity, a time when a handful of bold and gifted minds sought to come to terms with reality, to understand it, to interpret it in a manner that took into account such data as those minds were then able to distinguish, and to answer such questions as those minds were then able to formulate.

From the ninth to the seventeenth centuries, while the thought of the Church Fathers, in particular, that of Augustine and, later on, with a good admixture of Aristotle, gave form to the medieval mind, the ever-endemic critical way in religion made itself felt. We can see it clearly in the life and work of an Englishman whose original turn of mind and whose influence on those who came after him undermined the very foundations of medieval thought. But because the men of his time could not foresee the long-range impact of his teachings on Catholic theology, he attained great prestige among his contemporaries and was never threatened or harmed by the Church. His name was Robert Grosseteste (d. 1253). His approach to both ecclesiastical and secular matters was that of the critical mind: a hard-nosed examination of the data upon which people relied in defense of the things they said and the things they did.

In Grosseteste's time, churchmen were accustomed to rely upon the documents they happened to have in hand, never thinking to question their validity. Grosseteste wanted to know what authority those manuscripts possessed. He wanted to know where those manuscripts came from. Obviously they were not the originals. Did the copyists who prepared the manuscripts circulating in the Middle Ages have the originals before them? he asked. Obviously not. Then what copies did they have? Where had those copies come from? Above all, how reliable were they?

When Robert Grosseteste asked questions, people paid attention. He was a person of consequence: Chancellor at Oxford and a man who seems to have exerted profound influence on the then very young university. From the meager records that have come down to us he emerges as a very great and original mind. A student of Aristotle, he was nevertheless brought to essentially Platonic views through his studies of Saint Augustine and Pseudo-Dionysius. He was a voracious reader of the writings then making their way into Europe from the Arab world. Out of this complex of influences and his own interests he bent Oxford toward a somewhat modern and scientific approach to knowledge. He was a student of astronomy, meteorology, optics, physics, and linguistics. Anticipating modern standards of scholarship, he continually stressed the importance of reading authors in the original tongues.

Roger Bacon (1214–1294), Robert Grossteste's famous pupil, acclaimed the older man as "the great master, the most learned man of his day." Whether Bacon was the precursor of modern science, as some have asserted, there is no doubt that he was a man of erratic and irascible genius. He was outspoken in his criticisms of scholasticism, and became the most insistent medieval advocate of the role of experiment in acquiring knowledge. Some notion of the scope of his imaginative work can be gathered from a passage from his writings in which he mentions "machines for navigating . . . without rowers, so that great ships suited to river or ocean guided by one man may be borne with greater speed than if they were full of men. Likewise cars may be made so that without a draught animal they may be moved with unthinkable speed. . . . And flying machines are possible so that a man may sit in the middle turning some device by which artificial wings may beat in the air in the manner of a flying bird."

Such thinking is remarkable by any standard, given the mentality of the Middle Ages. Some students, in criticism of Bacon, have stressed the bitterness of his attacks upon contemporary theologians. Others say he was erratic; others point to the fact that he appears to have been a loner. They fault him for his failure to see the nonscientific basis of astrology and alchemy, to which he devoted much time and attention.

But how much are we to expect of a man who, in the closed cultural world of medieval times, could insist on the importance of observation, experiment, and testing, the standards by which our civilization functions today?

Who in the thirteenth century would have been the likely confidant and friend of a man who envisioned, however vaguely, steamships, automobiles, and airplanes? Roger Bacon, with all his shortcomings, epitomizes the critical way. Seven hundred years ago he saw the limitations of theology, denounced them, advocated and practiced observation, experiment, and testing as the means of gaining knowledge that was exact and dependable. He was the explorer and the critic, the destroyer of the false and inadequate, the builder of a better way as best he could see it.

On the one hand, Roger Bacon, throughout his life, loyally accepted the standard medieval view that reason and knowledge must be subordinate to faith. On the other, his views were so radical in so many ways, they were looked on with suspicion and they did not gain wide acceptance. Some fourteen years before he died Bacon was imprisoned because of the heretical views implied in his teachings. He is but one of the many bold spirits out of whose clear mind and personal courage the university tradition grew to the place of power and prestige it now enjoys in the Western world.

Despite his professed orthodoxy, which may well have been completely sincere, Roger Bacon is of importance to us because his emphasis on the empirical was out of all proportion to the mood and practice of his time. In harmony with academic standards that prevail today, he insisted that scholars should go to the sources. They should cease to rely on what some earlier authority had said, and find out what they could for themselves. If they were to rely on earlier authorities, he said, again in a thoroughly modern vein, they should go to the authorities themselves, read them and quote from the original, never from a secondary source. In that way, Bacon argued, they could avoid misquotations and quotations out of context.

In accordance with this point of view, he was highly critical of the scholars he had heard lecturing at the University of Paris, and denounced them for using Peter Lombard's *Sentences,* a book about the Bible, rather than the Bible itself. He criticized the Vulgate, the Latin text declared by the papacy to be official, then in use at Paris. It is, said Bacon, demonstrably faulty at various points. His conclusions, like those of Bible scholars today, were derived from his knowledge of ancient languages, which enabled him to compare the Latin Vulgate with the original Hebrew and Greek.

Roger Bacon's insistence on the importance of observation and experiment is his most significant contribution. Argument, he held, does not lead to conclusions that are certain and can be relied upon, but observation and experiment do. For this reason we should test by observation and by experiment whatever conclusions we reach by argument.

It may seem surprising to find this aspect of the critical way articulated so early. Yet here it is—a very large part of it, at any rate—written out and supported by reasoned argument in the middle of the thirteenth century. At Oxford, in Roger Bacon, we see the critical way being institutionalized in the university. Bacon wanted the standards of the critical way to prevail in university teaching. They prevailed at Oxford, he felt, at least to some degree, but not at Paris and at other universities where scholasticism held sway. As it is with most pioneers, his contemporaries were slow to understand what he was saying, and slower still to adopt and make use of his point of view. But eventually the world of scholarship did so, and eventually too the university and the Western world in which it evolved, learned to go to the sources, to test all supposed knowledge, to devise experiments by which to do so, and to frame new concepts by which these observations could be understood.

2. Freedom of Speech

As the writings of ancient non-Christian authors, Plato, Aristotle, Lucretius, Cicero, Seneca, began to circulate in Medieval Europe, the medieval mind was stirred to new activity. To grasp the reason for the force of this impact we today need to remember how closed in and stultifying (by our standards) scholasticism was. What the medievalists caught from the ancients was an exhilarating sense of freedom and thought. More than any particular fresh idea, they sensed the basic concept of questioning and testing all ideas, the practice of reaching out for new ideas through which to conceptualize their thought and experience.

Petrarch, the Italian poet of the fourteenth century who is often described as the father of Renaissance humanism, exhibits this sense of release, of excitement, and discovery. In his "Ascent of Mount Ventoux" he writes, speaking to himself as he reflects on his climb: "What you have so often experienced today while climbing this mountain happens to you, you must know, and to many others who are making their way toward the blessed life. This is not easily understood by us men, because the motions of the body lie open, while those of the mind are invisible and hidden. The life we call blessed is located on a high peak."

We today can readily identify the new sense of freedom of expression in the Renaissance. But we need to remember that it is far clearer to us than it was then. The men of the Renaissance did not talk in terms of freedom of thought and expression. That came later. Yet it was the fact of the new freedom to read, think, write, and speak that gave late medieval and Renaissance thinkers their sense of purpose and achievement. Even though it was during this period that the Inquisition was instituted, remarkable freedom prevailed in Renaissance Italy until after the Protestant Reformation. The writings of the independent minds of the time were not, for the most part, anti-Christian. The pioneers of the time were usually loyal churchmen. Some actively sought to reconcile the ideas of the ancients with Christian teachings.

Robert Grosseteste and Roger Bacon were among those who, within medieval society, found themselves able to think independently. Grosseteste was able to do so without arousing the ire of the Church; Bacon was not. Nevertheless, as a result of the work of both, that of Grosseteste more than Bacon, their successors were able to see avenues of inquiry of a very novel character opening up to them.

William of Ockham (1300–1349), another Englishman, was among those who discerned the way the work of his fellow countrymen had pointed. Marsiglio of Padua (1290?–1343), an Italian, was another. Both were products of medieval university life. William of Ockham was a product of the remarkable tradition that prevailed at Oxford. Marsiglio of Padua represents the high level of learning and independent thinking achieved in Italy at the time. Both men believed in the capacity of the human mind for valid and fruitful independent thought, and both reached the conclusion that the Church should not be permitted to suppress such thinking. Cutting through questions about the orthodoxy or heresy of specific doctrines, both men concluded that limitations could and should be placed on the temporal power of the Church. Marsiglio said the Church should be confined to a religious role and that the state should be left free to govern the affairs of men as it thought best. He went so far as to insist that the Church should not be governed by the pope, but by councils summoned by the secular ruler. In his *Defender of the Peace* we have one of the earliest clear statements of the principle of the separation of church and state. Because of his heretical teaching, Marsiglio was forced to flee from the University of Paris where he had been teaching and of which he had been made Rector. The next year he was condemned and excommunicated by Pope John XXII.

Marsiglio was no democrat, however. When he said the people were to determine the laws, he meant the aristocracy whom he thought were alone competent. As the king must rule under law established by the nobles, so, he argued, the pope and clergy should govern the Church under rules established by a general assembly of the Church. He advocated a council of the aristocracy in which both laity and clergy would participate. The Bible, not the pope and not the clergy, said Marsiglio, is the source of authority in the Church. Since interpretation of Scripture is necessary, however, he would assign this task to reasonable and learned men, as not everyone would be equal to so exalted a task.

William of Ockham held much the same view of church, state, and the role of secular power. He was, said one student of the period, "the great iconoclast clearing the encumbered ground of the Middle Ages and preparing a beachhead for the philosophers of the Renaissance." Like Marsiglio he accepted without question the prevailing view that Scripture was the highest authority. Therefore, said he, even the pope and the higher clergy were subject to it. He was, another scholar asserted, "a daring thinker . . .

one of the half dozen British philosophers who have profoundly influenced the thought of Western Europe." Still another declared in connection with his work that the period which he did so much to shape "was the most extreme and unorthodox in the history of medieval thought."

Familiarity with the problems of post-exilic Judaism would have enabled Marsiglio and William to understand the difficulties involved if Scripture were in fact to be made the final authority. So would a knowledge of the theological turmoil in the early Church. Both Judaism and early Christianity solved the problem of how the Bible was to be interpreted by giving it into the hands of the professional priesthood. The medieval clergy had no intention of giving it back to the people and they dealt summarily with anyone who advocated such an idea.

Among the men who grasped the fundamental character of the issue was a younger contemporary and fellow countryman of Ockham, John Wyclif (1320?–1384), yet another product of Oxford, where he was famous for his skill in theological disputation. He contended that if the Bible and not the Church was the authority in Christianity, then all men should be able to read it for themselves. Accordingly, he sponsored the first translation of the Bible into English. Like Ockham, he denied, on the basis of Scripture, all the claims of the papacy to temporal power, and was sustained in his position by the schism in the papacy that occurred at this time.

Happily, Wyclif, like Ockham, was not made to suffer death for his views. Although accused of heresy by the pope and summoned before the bishop in London to clear himself of the charge, Wyclif was never sentenced. He was, however, seriously curtailed in his activities during the latter part of his life. The Council of Constance, in 1415, a generation after his death, condemned him. His body was dug up, burned, and the remains were thrown into the River Swift.

Wyclif's younger contemporary and disciple, the Bohemian John Hus (1369?–1415), was not as fortunate. He paid with his life for advocating similar views. Like almost all the other leaders with whom we have been dealing, Hus was a product of and a participant in university life. Educated at the University of Prague, he began lecturing there before he was thirty. While still in his thirties he became successively Dean of the Philosophical Faculty and Rector of the entire University. Because his preaching was thought to undermine the authority of the Church, Hus was forbidden to preach at the great church erected by the citizens for him in their capital city, Prague. He refused to obey the command and demanded to know, "Where is there authority in Holy Writ for forbidding preaching in so public a place? I avow it to be my purpose to defend the truth which God has enabled me to know." In Hus we find a clear assertion of the principle of independent judgment and the right to give it voice.

In another instance when a papal legate demanded his cooperation in the sale of indulgences, a favorite method of raising funds for the papal treasury at that time, Hus refused:

"Will you not obey the apostolical mandates?" asked the legate.

"My Lord," Hus replied, "I am ready with all my heart to obey the apostolical mandates. But I call apostolical mandates the doctrines of the apostles of Christ; and so far as the papal mandates agree with these, so far will I obey them most willingly. But if I see anything in them at variance with these, I shall not obey, even though the stake were staring me in the face."

Eager to vindicate himself and the Bohemian reform movement, Hus went to the Council of Constance, armed with a safe-conduct granted by the Emperor. At the Council, however, he was summoned to a hearing before the cardinals, placed under arrest, was condemned for refusing to recant his "errors," and finally was burned at the stake. It was the same Council of Constance that condemned Wyclif posthumously. The Church is not required to keep faith with heretics, the churchmen explained. Who can now say how much of the impetus for the Reformation came from that single dramatic breach of faith on the part of a church calling itself the instrument of Christ on earth?

3. The Critical Way in the Renaissance

With John Hus we are fully in the period of the Renaissance. One of the areas in which the Renaissance mind sought hard, verifiable knowledge, in place of the rationalistic structures of medieval scholasticism, was that of documentation. It began with the Bible because of the place the Bible had in medieval thought. Not always consulted, its contents not always known, the Bible was nevertheless regarded as divine revelation—if not the source of the authority of the Church, certainly the sacred record of how that authority had been established. During the later Middle Ages and the early Renaissance, more and more attention was given to this remarkable document.

In Robert Grosseteste at Oxford in the thirteenth century we saw the beginnings of this development. It was with Lorenzo Valla, however, whose work we noted in connection with the forged "Donation of Constantine," that serious philology and literary criticism really begins. He even dared to question the authenticity of certain passages in the Vulgate. It was faulty, he asserted, in the light of the older Greek texts from which it had been translated.

Like the other leaders in the movement that became the critical way in religion, he too was a product of medieval university life. Educated for the priesthood at Rome, he early showed a clear, bold, and original turn of mind. As a young man he was a very popular lecturer and moved from university to university according to his mood, as was the custom at the time. He was a little past thirty when he published his shattering treatise demolishing one of the fundamental bases of papal claims to temporal authority, the "Donation of Constantine." Considering the impact of this revelation on the Church, one would expect Lorenzo to have been condemned and executed as a dangerous heretic and a threat to the very foundations of society. But not in Italy in the fifteenth century. Apparently the Church, its officials being themselves imbued with the mood of the times, either could not or did not care to bestir themselves to silence him. Perhaps most important of all, he did not use his discoveries to develop a political movement aimed at displacing those in authority.

In addition to discrediting the document on which the papacy rested its claim to temporal authority, Valla impugned the divine character of the Scriptures themselves. Where Marsiglio, Ockham, Wyclif, and Hus accepted the Bible as God's word, Valla asserted that the writings contained in it could not have been divinely inspired in any literal sense. They were, he said, too filled with inconsistencies and absurdities. Valla was the first to apply the method of literary criticism to the Bible rigorously. Today many orthodox scholars support his conclusions but they were startling indeed in the fifteenth century. Through a similar line of reasoning, Valla showed that the Apostles' Creed could not have been written by the Apostles, again as modern scholarship has conceded. Valla even went so far as to accuse the great Saint Augustine of heresy. Nevertheless, quite unbelievably, he was later appointed apostolic secretary to Pope Nicholas V, which would seem proof enough of the urbanity of the Church in his time. Apparently the Renaissance Church felt itself strong enough to accept the criticism of some of its most basic teachings and at the same time to make use of the most brilliant minds it could find.

Typical of Valla's writing is the following passage in which he tells of an encounter with an Inquisitor one day in Rome. Valla challenged some of the things the Inquisitor was saying, whereupon he demanded that Valla recant. Valla refused. "Revoke," shouted the Inquisitor. "Show me why," Valla replied. Then he asked, "Are you trying to change my mouth or my mind? What good will it be if I confess with my mouth what I do not believe with my mind?" Here we see the critical mind at work. Interested neither in power, except as it corrupts, nor in conformity, except as it does the same, Valla was concerned about the truth. He felt strongly that forcing a man to say what you want him to neither makes a believer of him nor moves anyone toward the truth. But the idea was new and little understood by his hearers, who thought of truth in religion not as something you discover but something you already have, and that need not, must not, and in fact cannot be questioned.

While Valla greatly advanced the understanding of the Bible and of certain basic doctrines of the Church, he never once challenged its authority. He tried to set right what he found to be wrong, without impugning the institution—the Church—which not only had made the mistakes and deceptions but also had greatly profited by them. Accordingly, because of the mood of confidence and tolerance in the Church in Italy in the fifteenth century and because of the manner in which Valla wrote and conducted himself, he died peacefully in his bed, even though his work was ultimately far more damaging to the authority of the Church than that of many a heretic who was committed to the flames.

The search for hard knowledge based on observation expressed itself not only in the study of manuscripts and their origins but in other areas as well. Students of Renaissance art report the same developments as do the students of intellectual history. It was in this period that artists began taking a closer look at the world around them in an attempt to see more clearly and to depict more accurately what they saw. It was the artists who discovered perspective, not the scientists, and they did so as a direct result of their effort to paint the world as they saw it. They carried on extensive anatomical studies of the human form for the same reason—in order to be able to paint lifelike human beings inside the clothing draped around them.

Another concept implicit in the critical tradition in religion appeared among the Renaissance humanists: that of the "perennial philosophy," as they called it. In the middle of the sixteenth century Augustino Steuco developed the idea of a deeper wisdom and unity that pervades all separate ideas as they come and go. For him, the perennial philosophy happened to be Platonism, but the basic concept that there is such a fundamental philosophy, an ultimate self-consistent truth behind all particular truths, lay at the heart of his thinking. Pico della Mirandola, to whom we shall come in a moment, gave the idea its fullest expression.

Humanist thinkers developed another concept that is only just now gaining currency and is central in the critical way: that of the universality of all religions. Again, Pico is the leading spokesman of the idea. He held that all religious and philosophical traditions share in a common universal truth. Nicholas of Cusa, half a century before, was among those who helped to give that idea currency. "The King of Kings decreed," he wrote, "that under the names to which they were accustomed, all people [Jews, Arabs, Mohammedans, Turks, Persians, Tartars, and Christians] should hold one faith in perpetual peace."

Another concept that is central in the critical tradition in religion appeared in the Italian Renaissance: that of the interrelatedness and interdependence of all people. It emerged in the thought of Marsilio Ficino, a Platonist of the mid-fifteenth century. He was a loyal Christian, yet he came close to developing a theory of natural religion. He thought it possible to reconcile the demands of reason and the articles of the Christian faith. Out of his Platonic concept of love came a belief in what he called the "solidarity of mankind." He used the Latin word *humanitas,* a term the ancient Roman Stoics employed to express their ideal of cultural refinement and respect for other people. But to Ficino the term meant our mutual obligation to one another as members of the human race. Ficino said we need to love one another because we are human and, conversely, that one who is inhuman and cruel removes himself from the community of mankind.

A final instance of a critical principle first stated in the Renaissance is found in the writings of Pietro Pomponazzi, a younger contemporary of Ficino. An Aristotelian rather than a Platonist, he developed the belief that one should be concerned with *this* world rather than the next—a novel, indeed a radical, idea in the celestially oriented Middle Ages. In a treatise on Immortality, Pomponazzi said he could find no evidence for the idea of a future life, but added piously that we must believe it as an article of faith. We are therefore left, he concluded, with the ideal of moral virtue not as a means of gaining the joys of heaven or of avoiding the pains of hell, but of moral virtue pursued for its own sake. Therefore, he argued, we should center our interest on the present life lived on earth here and now.

"The essential reward of virtue is virtue itself," Pomponazzi wrote in peculiarly modern fashion. "It makes men happy. Human nature cannot attain anything higher than virtue. . . . The opposite applies to vice. The punishment of the vicious person is vice itself which is more miserable and unhappy than anything else. Punishment inflicted by the state is less heavy than a sense of guilt," he wrote. "By the same token, when we are rewarded for virtue, the virtuous act seems less perfect than when it stands alone on its own merits." A good deed done without hope of reward is better than a similar deed for which a reward is expected. In the same way, a wicked act which is punished seems less wicked than one that goes unpunished. When a penalty is added to guilt, our sense of guilt decreases.

How like one of our contemporary "new" theologians he sounds. How many people, clergy and laity alike, are heard to voice these sentiments today in the belief that they are saying something quite radical and new?

4. The Dignity of Man

Consciousness of the self as an individual, rather than the submergence of the self as a servant of the community—as Jacob Burckhardt saw, a shift in the psychology of the West—was central in the period we now know as the Renaissance. Coupled with it was a consciousness of freedom: the opportunity to express one's innermost thoughts openly, to go about more or less as one chooses, to be the kind of person one aspires to be and do the kind of things one would like to do. These concepts, too, belong to Renaissance psychology.

Because we in the West take this so much for granted today, it is difficult for us to understand the sense of exhilaration the change brought about in western Europe in the thirteenth, fourteenth, and fifteenth centuries. The courage to criticize what had been taken for granted (even dogmas and documents regarded as holy in some sense); attention to the stubborn facts of daily life; the use of mathematics to establish similarities and differences among the data of experience; notions of a single eternal truth underlying all particulars; the notion of a corresponding human interrelatedness, whereby every individual is required to be deeply concerned with the welfare of every other individual; the concept of a kind of universal religion underlying all the particular religions; and finally the conviction that since we know nothing beyond the life given to us to live here on earth, we had best live it to the full and find our rewards and punishments here and now: all these concepts, ideas, and attitudes are closely interrelated and can be gathered under a single head. This the men of the Renaissance did. It is the doctrine of the dignity of man.

Like every other supposedly "new" idea, the idea of human dignity was an outgrowth of an earlier pattern of thought. This particular concept, to no small degree, emerged not as a development from, but as a reaction against an older concept. A concrete example will make the point clear.

The most powerful prelate the Roman Church has ever known was Innocent III, who reigned from 1198–1216. During the more leisurely years before his elevation to the papacy, he wrote a book entitled *On the Contempt of this World.* It epitomized the official attitude of the Church and of ecclesiastical thinking in medieval times. In Book I he describes "The Miserable Beginnings of Human Existence." Job's lamentations that he had ever been born provided appropriate scriptural quotations for the theme. With these anguished cries spelled out for the reader, Innocent says he will "consider in tears" certain questions. He then continues: "Verily, man has been formed of dust, has been conceived in sin, was born to punishment. In his actions he is evil, disgraceful and deceitful. He does what he ought not do, whatever is shameful and not profitable to do. Man will become fuel for fire, the food of worms, a mass of putridity."

After this warm-up he continues: "Let me elaborate on this point. Man has been formed of dust, clay, ashes and, a thing far more vile, of the filthy sperm. Man has been conceived in the desire of the flesh, in the heat of sensual lust, in the foul stench of wantonness. He was born to labor, to fear, to suffering and, most miserable of all, to death. His evil doings offend God, offend his neighbor, offend himself. He defiles his good name, contaminates his person, violates his conscience through his shameful acts. His vanity prompts him to neglect what is most important, most necessary and most useful. Accordingly, he is destined to become the fuel of the everlasting, eternally painful hellfire; the food of voracious, consuming worms. His destiny is to be a putrid mass that eternally emits a most horrible stench." The remainder is in similar vein.

It was four hundred years before anyone attempted a refutation of the great pope's thesis. About 1452 Giannozzo Manetti, an Italian humanist, published *On the Dignity of Man.* In it he does not hesitate to name his adversary Innocent III and other illustrious writers whom he also undertakes to refute. Manetti is perfectly clear as to his purpose. "I thought it important," he says, "to refute what has been written by many ancient and modern writers on the goodness of death and the misery of human life." He finds these authors "repugnant," "frivolous," and "fake."

Was Manetti's a stroke of bold and original genius? Did he, even in medieval times, out of the blue as it were, perceive that man, for all his misery, has another side to his nature? By no means. Again our indebtedness is to the ancient Greeks, whose works Manetti had read with care. A millennium and a half earlier they had worked this doctrine out in some detail. Perhaps no one either before or since ever stated the idea more eloquently than Sophocles had in his Ode to Man in *Antigone.* What was new in the Renaissance was Manetti's restatement of it over against the prevailing medieval Christian doctrine. In fact, Manetti relied principally on Cicero and Lactantius, who were inheritors and re-interpreters of Greek thought.

Manetti's work was part of the growing articulation of the classical doctrine of man at the hands of the Italian humanists of the Renaissance. It was an attempt to understand and interpret what was happening among the Italian humanists to human thought about the human condition, but it was also an attempt to gain acceptance for a concept of humanity that was tantamount to a denial of the then-prevailing traditional Christian view.

We have an outstanding statement of the Renaissance doctrine of the dignity, as against the depravity, of man in a tract by a Florentine thinker of the fifteenth century named Giovanni Pico della Mirandola. A loyal churchman, he was, nevertheless, cited for heresy but cleared of the charge during his own lifetime. After the manner of medieval times, Pico posted nine hundred theses dealing with theology and related topics which he intended to defend publicly in debate against anyone who chose to question him. As a sort of introductory statement for his theses, he prepared a document which he entitled "Notes and Documents of the Dignity of Man: Oration of Pico, etc." Some of the theses he proposed to defend were declared heretical and the public disputation was never held. The *Oration* was not published until after his death. It had enormous influence, however, and stands today as the high-water mark of Italian humanist thought regarding man's abilities and the opportunities that lie before him.

Pico's own words are so strong and vivid they are worth our recalling even today. As we might expect, he begins biblically, outlining the creation process as it is set down in Genesis. Then, boldly placing himself in the mind of God, he retells in Renaissance rather than biblical language what God was thinking about after he had finished creating the world. "God was not tired when he had finished," Pico asserts. "When it came to creating man as the crown of creation, God placed man in the middle of the world. He gave Man the function of a form not set apart [i.e., he was truly a part of creation, both earthly and celestial]. Then, says Pico, not fearing to put words into God's mouth:

"I have given thee neither a fixed abode nor a form that is thine alone, nor any function that is peculiar to thyself. According to thy longing and according to thy judgment, Adam, thou mayest have and possess that abode, that form, and those functions which thou thyself shalt desire. The nature of all other things is limited and constrained within the bounds of laws prescribed by me; thou, coerced by no necessity, shalt ordain for thyself the limits of thy nature in accordance with thine own free will, in whose hand I have placed thee. I have set thee at the world's center, that thou mayest from thence more easily observe whatever is in the world. I have made thee neither of heaven nor of earth, neither mortal nor immortal, so that thou mayest with greater freedom of choice and with more honor, as though the maker and moulder of thyself, fashion thyself in whatever shape thou shalt prefer. Thou shalt have the power to degenerate into the lower forms of life, which are animal; thou shalt have the power, out of thy soul's judgment, to be reborn into the higher forms of life, which are divine."

At this point the effort to understand what was really going on in the Renaissance mind often vanishes in current arguments about its optimism or pessimism. So to be led aside would be to misconceive the situation as it was at that time. In their own minds the humanists were neither optimists nor pessimists. As they saw themselves they were realists, and the judgment seems to have been accurate. They asserted the dignity of man as against an older view typified by Innocent III, not because they lived by the dogma of eternal progress but because they considered the doctrine of man's dignity a more accurate appraisal of what they found men saying and thinking and doing. They found man far less miserable, far less helpless, and far less forlorn than Innocent had depicted him. The humanists did not ignore the misery and pain that is often man's lot on earth. Their position was: it is not the whole story.

Those who today espouse the critical way in religion are seldom heard to pay tribute to their Renaissance forebears. They are apt to cite nineteenth and twentieth-century thinkers in support of the views they hold. It is time the critical way in religion acknowledged its debt to men like Robert Grosseteste and Roger Bacon, Giannozzo Manetti and Pico della Mirandola. The humanists, drawing their inspiration from Greece and Rome, were able to break through the closed system of medieval Christian dogma and to set Western thought free again. They were neither pagan nor anti-Christian. They were humanists. Their interest centered in man's life on earth. Loyal churchmen, at least in the formal sense, none seems to have had a desire to damage or destroy the Christian Church, neither its ecclesiastical structure, its intellectual accomplishments, its social role, nor its economic foundation. What they intended and what they accomplished was to advance human thought and aspiration beyond the confines within which it had become bound by the scholastic philosophy and theology of the Middle Ages.

8

Erasmus and Castellio

With the coming of the Protestant Reformation in the midst of the mounting Renaissance in Western Europe, there are so many exemplars of the critical tradition that further choice among typical individuals becomes almost impossible. To conclude this overview, then, we shall consider but two more thinkers. Both stand in the front rank of those who formulated and gave impetus to the critical way in the religion of the West. The one, Desiderius Erasmus, a Dutchman, is world famous. The other, Sebastian Castellio, a Frenchman, was scarcely known to the world of scholarship until very recently.

1. Desiderius Erasmus

We turn first to Erasmus, a man who resembles Lorenzo Valla in many ways. Erasmus admired Valla and republished his *Annotations on the New Testament.* Like Valla, he was no fighter and has often been criticized for not leaving the Catholic Church and joining the Reformation. He had no taste for martyrdom, he said, being content to leave that honor to stouter souls. "I do not think myself worthy of that dignity," he once remarked, and added that he hoped he would be willing to die for Christ but not for the paradoxes of Luther.

On the other hand, Erasmus, like his Italian predecessor, was a man of exceedingly independent mind. Basically a reformer, eager to ferret out errors in human thought, whether clerical or lay, he was yet unwilling either to repudiate the Church or to weaken its authority. Rather than make a frontal attack on the desultory ways of the clergy in his time, Erasmus chose the way of satire. With consummate skill he ridiculed the morals, the self-indulgence, and the pretensions of the clergy. His book, *In Praise of Folly,* published in 1519, makes stimulating reading even today and of all the writings of that time is among the few that still enjoy a general readership.

More than that of any figure discussed so far, the life of Erasmus is centered in the growing universities of the West. His interests, his standards, and his achievements exemplify the critical tradition as it was steadily evolving in the centers of learning of the late Middle Ages. His passion for learning, his love of independence, and his scrupulous standards of scholarship were acquired in the course of his education in his native Netherlands. Later he attended the University of Paris and went from there to England, where he was associated with Oxford University, whose role in the development of the critical tradition we have already noted.

By this time Erasmus was devoting all his energies to his studies, occasionally taking pupils to expand his meager income. But in England, as elsewhere, he declined to teach publicly. From Oxford he turned back to the life of an itinerant student, moving from place to place as the occasion suggested, accepting sustenance from anyone who would provide it, yet unwilling to be beholden to anyone as to where he should live, what he should do, or to what matters he was to turn his attention.

In middle life Erasmus went again to England, this time not to Oxford but to the younger, smaller university at Cambridge. His gentle, tolerant, inquisitive, scientific spirit may well have had a profound effect on the rapidly changing academic community there. Insignificant compared with Oxford down to the sixteenth century, Cambridge had begun to grow rapidly in prestige and size beginning with the Reformation, with which it was closely associated. To aid in its development, Erasmus, the universal scholar, had been deliberately sought out. There is a tradition, now seriously questioned, that he became Lady Margaret Professor of Divinity in 1511. Although direct evidence is lacking, it seems obvious he played an important if not a definitive role in establishing the traditions of scholarship, scientific objectivity, philosophical inquiry, and speculation that have characterized Cambridge ever since.

Typical of his endeavors during this period was the publication, in 1505, before he went to England, of a new edition of Lorenzo Valla's *Annotations on the New Testament.* A year later he brought out his own *Enchiridion Militis Christiani,* a plea to return to Christian sources. In it he also advocated a return to Christian practice as it is seen in the New Testament. Erasmus, the Christian mystic, was pleading for a high level of moral conduct. *The Enchiridion* embodies much of the piety, anti-intellectualism, and mysticism current in the Renaissance period, and in particular voices the outlook of the Brothers of the Common Life, a mystical group by whom he had been educated. Erasmus the scholar was pleading for an equally high commitment to an accurate reading of the sources on which our understanding of the New Testament Christian Church is based.

While at Cambridge, Erasmus worked on a fresh translation of his Greek New Testament into Latin. In the perspective of history the New Testament in Greek has proved to be his most important scholarly work. Originally published in 1516, the work sought to establish a correct Greek text from which translations into Latin (or into the vernacular) could then be made. The problem to which Erasmus addressed himself was a particularly vexing one in his time and to some extent remains so today. None of the original documents of the New Testament—or of the Old Testament, for that matter—are any longer in existence. All that remains is a wide variety of copies, some early, some late, some seemingly accurate, others obviously careless copies of copies of copies. All of these early manuscripts are in Greek or they appear to be translations from Greek originals. How to choose among them? Which were the earliest, which the latest, which the closest to the original, which sloppy, error-filled copies?

In his travels about Europe, Erasmus had diligently sought out every New Testament manuscript in Greek he could find. He knew that our oldest manuscripts for the most part go back only to the fourth century. Unfortunately for him he did not have access to one of the most basic biblical documents, Codex Vaticanus at Rome. Nevertheless, from such sources as he had, he assembled a text that was remarkably accurate for his time and the standards he set, by which the worth of ancient manuscripts is to be assessed and a composite basic text established, remain today.

Really to understand the man Erasmus, we should give some attention to his motives in producing his Greek New Testament. Sound scholarship was surely one of them. But just as surely, piety was another. Jesus' life and teaching, the thought and practice of the early church fathers, held a commanding place in his personal philosophy. He took the New Testament at face value. For him it was the Christian way, the path of moral duty and a guide to personal salvation as well. This conviction was the moving force behind his concern with an accurate Bible text. What did Jesus do? What had he really said? What was the true Gospel record?

Erasmus had no interest in theological debate. He was not concerned to choose among the many interpretations of Jesus' life and teaching that had proliferated by his time. He wanted to make the Bible useful as the source book of Christianity that he believed it to be. To this end he wrote paraphrases of the New Testament which were really homiletical commentaries. He published one for every New Testament book except Revelation. It is interesting to notice that he omitted so fanciful a writing from his collection, but not difficult to see why. No doubt he wondered whether it really belonged in the canon of the New Testament at all. The external evidence was against it, yet he included it in his Greek New Testament, which makes his omission of it from the Commentary the more eloquent.

In pursuit of the truth there was no compromise in Erasmus. He omitted from his Greek New Testament I John 5:7 which is the basis of the doctrine of the Trinity, as central a concept as Christianity espouses. It was a bold and brave thing to do, and it created a furor. But Erasmus did it, not in a spirit of contentiousness or as a means of attacking the Church he loved and sought to serve, despite the morals of its clergy which he deplored. Erasmus omitted that crucial passage from his Greek New Testament as he omitted many others, simply because it did not appear in the earliest manuscripts. Obviously, he concluded, it had been inserted later, by a pious scribe who felt that such an emendation of the text was both necessary and proper.

His tolerant spirit appears in a letter he wrote to a friend a decade before the Protestant Reformation set all Europe ablaze. Following a visit to Rome he wrote: "Had I not torn myself from the city of Rome, I could never have resolved to leave. There one enjoys sweet liberty, rich libraries, the charming friendship of writers and scholars, and the sight of antique monuments. I was honored by the society of eminent prelates, so that I cannot conceive of a greater pleasure than to return to the city."

It was the city, the Church, and the climate of opinion of the Italian Renaissance of which Erasmus spoke: tolerant, urbane, and free, in the sense that a man who spoke critically but not caustically was heard and the validity of his thought was weighed and considered. With the polarization brought on later by the Reformation, the Inquisition in Spain forbade the reading of several of Erasmus's books. The Council of Trent condemned some of his work. In 1559 Pope Paul IV put Erasmus in the first class of forbidden authors, which meant that all his works were condemned. In 1584 an expurgatorial index of passages to be deleted from his works was issued. It was fifty-five quarto pages long. A new list was issued in 1640 that had fifty-nine folio pages, each with double columns of entries.

Happily, when this torrent of condemnation fell upon him the gentle, peace-loving Erasmus was safely in his grave, beyond the power of human vituperation and ecclesiastical vengeance. During his lifetime, however, he was called upon continually to defend his right to criticize the Church and to try to determine the authenticity of its sacred writings. But he was never summoned before an official tribunal. Without trying to guess what Erasmus might have done had he been brought to trial for his heresies, we can say that his arguments were forceful weapons in the struggle that went on in the Reformation period to permit men to state publicly their honest beliefs about religious questions. Erasmus took the principle enunciated by Socrates when he was on trial for his life and applied it to the savage practices of the Reformation period. "By terrorization," he observed, "we drive men to believe what they do not know. That which is forced is not sincere."

On another occasion, speaking of the practice of burning heretics at the stake, he remarked, echoing Valla, "It is no feat to burn a little man. It is a great achievement to persuade him." And again in his *In Praise of Folly,* he asked, "What authority in Holy Writ commands that heretics be consumed by fire rather than reclaimed by argument?" Abelard had said it long before: "Heretics should be compelled by reason rather than by force." Lorenzo Valla had said the same thing. But the Church seems not to have heard. At any rate it chose not to act.

2. Sebastian Castellio

It was Sebastian Castellio, a Frenchman, who pinned this principle down in a single historic instance that shook all of Europe. When John Calvin, the Protestant Reformer, reverted to the ways of the Inquisition and sent Michael Servetus to the stake for heresy, the principle at last became established and thereafter was questioned less and less: the principle that you cannot win an argument by force. All that you can do is to silence or make hypocrites of the opposition. When you resort to force, you really display your own weakness. You confess publicly that you have run out of arguments and that, since you cannot persuade your adversary by threats, torture, or even death by fire, you will wring from him, if you can, words he would not otherwise utter, words that he himself does not believe.

Did Castellio win such a concession from the mind of Europe, long steeped in the belief that with heretics the Church should "compel them to come in"? Was he alone responsible? Surely not. But he seems to have been a pivotal figure in bringing about the change that took place during the Reformation period in the thinking of the West on this question. Not everyone is persuaded even today that this is how one goes about learning the truth. But it is the mood of our time as it was not in Castellio's.

It is legitimate to ask whether a thinker who even today is so little known could have had any influence at all. Until very recently you would have found few and but very brief references to him in the history books. The 1958 edition of the *Encyclopedia Britannica* merely notes that he was one of three opponents of Calvin. The reason is that those in authority in his time took the most extreme measures to suppress his writings. So successful were they, few contemporary copies of any of his books are to be found in the world's libraries today, although originally many copies seem to have been in circulation. His final work, *The Art of Doubt and Belief, of Knowledge and Ignorance,* was not published until our own time. It is plain from his writing, however, that among those who made articulate the critical way in religion none ranks higher than Castellio.

Sebastian Castellio was born just before the Reformation broke, in 1515 in Dauphine, a country bordering on Switzerland, France, and Savoy. When he was twenty-four years old he witnessed the burning of a group of heretics at Lyons under the aegis of the Inquisition. The experience marked him for life. Appalled at what he had seen, he left for Strasbourg, where he joined John Calvin and the Reformation, although he had been a devout Catholic. Twenty-five years later, another burning, that of Michael Servetus, wrung from him a clear and unequivocal assertion of the idea of tolerance in religion, of freedom of speech, of the capacity of truth to sustain itself in open debate; of the arrogance and error of any who think themselves infallible; and of the evil and folly of using force to settle a theological argument.

Castellio, attracted by the then young Calvin's belief in tolerance, as set forth in an early edition of the *Institutes of the Christian Religion,* agreed to go with him to Geneva. There he became first a teacher in and then Rector of the Municipal Reformed College. Because of his outspoken manner he soon found himself in conflict with his mentor, now theocratic dictator of Protestant Geneva. When Calvin prevented his ordination, Castellio left for Basel, where he was living when Calvin committed Servetus to the flames. There Castellio engaged in an arduous program of writing and in the translating of ancient books, most importantly the Bible. As a result he was appointed to the Greek chair at the University of Basel. It was while he held this post that he published his attack on John Calvin for the role he played in sending Michael Servetus to the stake.

Calvin had been summoned by the Protestants at Geneva to bring civil and religious turmoil to an end. At the outbreak of the Reformation the city of Geneva had experienced social upheaval which no one seemed able to quell. John Calvin succeeded in calming down the populace, but he accomplished the feat, not by following early Reformation doctrines of individual freedom, but by enforcing conformity in doctrine and practice in the Genevan Church and state. In doing so, Calvin believed he was implementing God's plan for human society. Castellio was a threat to the civil and religious order that Calvin had established as a means of implementing God's will, something he had accomplished through the exercise of political power and theological skill.

The reaction to the burning of Servetus, which spread throughout Protestant Europe, was so severe that Calvin felt called upon to issue a defense of what he had done. In the same year, 1554, Castellio anonymously published an attack on Calvin entitled: *Concerning Heretics: Whether They Should Be Persecuted and What Should Be Done About Them.* Castellio's argument was basically that of Valla and Erasmus. "When Servetus fought with reasons and writings," Castellio wrote, "he should have been repulsed by reasons and writings. To kill a man is not to protect a doctrine but only to kill a man. Those who are armed with wisdom, desire no other weapons. They fear not to fight openly, and to withstand all comers, provided there be a just and legitimate discussion. They know that truth is an invincible weapon. The others employ the sword, after the manner of the world, and conclude with iron the discussion they began with words, for they well know that without the sword they would be defenseless."

Castellio demanded to know further how Calvin could be so sure that he was right in his interpretation of Scripture—sure enough to send to the stake a man whose interpretation was different. Doctrines that have been in dispute over a long period of time, he asserted, obviously are not clear enough to justify so drastic an action. Then, in a final burst of outrage against all churches in their barbarous efforts to control heresy, he cried to the Lord Christ: "O Creator and King of the world, dost thou see these things? Art thou so changed? When thou wast on earth, none was more mild, more forgiving, more patient in injury. . . . Can it be that those who do not understand thy precepts as the mighty demand, shall be drowned, cut with lashes, . . . dismembered, roasted at a slow fire, tortured to death as slowly as possible? Art thou an-hungered for human flesh? If thou Christ, do really command these things, what is left for Satan to do?"

Castellio was not seeking martyrdom. He wanted, rather, to undermine by argument the tyranny at Geneva that made Servetus' death possible. He was back to the fundamental question Socrates had asked when on trial for his life: where does the state get the authority to dictate what a man should say and what he should think? As if to prove that Castellio was right, that he could not be defeated in an open exchange of ideas, Calvin took steps to suppress Castellio's *Concerning Heretics.* He gave wide circulation, however, to a savage polemic of his own in which he compared Castellio to the Devil. "May God destroy you, Satan," was Calvin's concluding line.

Calvin's position was clear. Officially he held that the state had no right to dictate what a man's religion should be. On the other hand he deeply believed that there was one true faith, namely the Christian religion. He believed that his interpretation of it was the correct one. Finally, he believed that the Christian religion was the will of God as contained in the Scriptures. To Calvin that meant church and state alike should seek to implement God's will as the Scriptures revealed it. That, however, meant in fact the Scriptures as John Calvin interpreted them—a claim the validity of which no one outside his own household of faith was willing to acknowledge.

Why did John Calvin, the great Protestant reformer, ranking with Martin Luther in power and effectiveness, revert to the ways of the Inquisition when confronted by heresy? His own answer made at the time was that he did it to maintain order and harmony in Church and state and for the advancement of the Kingdom of God. Calvin had seen at first hand the disruption that theological controversy can cause. He was determined not to let this happen in Protestant Geneva. As soon as the authority of Rome was displaced by the authority of the Bible, sharp and furious debate broke out as to the meaning of various passages and the manner in which the doctrines and creeds of the Church were to be understood. In fact, Calvin had written his great *Institutes* for this very purpose: to allay further controversy among Protestants as to how the Bible was to be understood.

As an example, in the early days of the Reformation both Luther and Calvin had objected to the word "homousious" (meaning "sharing one being with the Father") in the Nicene Creed because it is not to be found in the Bible. But, like the Church fathers at Nicaea who introduced it, they too soon found themselves forced to revert to it. "Homousious" was exact and excluded argument where the Bible was vague and invited it. To bring to an end the controversies that swirled about them as to how "God's Word" was to be understood, the Protestants were driven to do as the ancient church had done. They too began drawing up official creeds, although they did not always label them so. The Lutherans, in solemn council, agreed upon the Augsburg Confession. The Calvinists, on the basis of the *Institutes of the Christian Religion,* drew up one confession after another, of which the Westminster Confession is perhaps best known to us, in the various countries into which they spread. The Church of England adopted the Thirty-nine Articles. Almost all Protestant churches avowed the Apostles' Creed. Even the very liberal Minor Church in Poland at this time found it necessary to formulate its views in what came to be known as the Racovian Catechism.

The problem, as in ancient times, was that theological controversy is seldom merely theological. Whatever their origins, theological differences soon become rallying points for those seeking political power in the church and often in the state as well. In the Reformation period as in ancient times, many of the contenders passionately believed in the doctrines they espoused. More often, perhaps, whatever their true beliefs, they were concerned with power and authority in the Church as well. In any case, the result was turmoil and the victor, however he achieved his victory, was able not merely to force his views on the vanquished, but was able to control the ecclesiastical organization also.

The outcry that arose following Castellio's attack on Calvin far surpassed in fury the somewhat restrained criticism of Calvin for being party to the execution of Servetus. Castellio had made three points: (1) We do not know enough to be entitled to execute one another because of theological differences. (2) We ourselves are not good enough to be entitled to take such drastic measures. (3) In any event, force does not persuade; all it does is make one lie. These three points amounted to a doctrine of tolerance which undercut the fundamental Christian notion of "right belief." As we noted in Chapter 4, the doctrine of "right belief" is as old as Christianity itself. The very structure of the Church rested upon it. Catholics and Protestants alike took Castellio to task for undercutting it.

A second aspect of his thought reinforced the fierce reaction against his doctrine of tolerance. Clearly apparent from his earliest writings was the fact that he held heretical views on many doctrines. For example, like most scholars today, Castellio regarded the Song of Songs as a secular love poem which might or might not be thought an allegory of Christ and the Church. Like Pelagius of old, he did not think Adam's sin in the Garden of Eden forever stained the human race. This meant a rejection of the doctrine of original sin, on which the Church had rested since the time of Saint Augustine. Everyone should read the Scriptures for himself, he urged, harking back to the Italian humanist view. Let each reader see for himself what the Bible actually says. Whoever does so will discover how complex, how obscure, how inconsistent, and how much in need of interpretation it is. This in turn should caution anyone against thinking that his own interpretation of Scripture is necessarily the only one possible.

It is clear from the literature of the Italian Renaissance that Castellio's heresies were mild compared with many that had enjoyed open expression in the fifteenth and early sixteenth centuries. Overt expressions of independent thought in Protestantism soon faded out, however, after the Reformation had become established. The same thing happened in Catholicism following the Counter-Reformation. By the time Castellio died at age forty-eight he was under indictment for heresy. Whether he too would have been sent to the stake none can now say. Many quietly defended him, and the university where he taught gave him an honorable burial.

It is difficult to assess the role that Castellio played in the growth of the critical tradition in religion in the West because heretofore there has been so little evidence on which to base a judgment. We have always known that his works circulated clandestinely. Through the new interest in him among Reformation scholars, increasing evidence of his influence is accumulating. It is now known, for example, that in the seventeenth century, the influential English philosopher John Locke planned to publish Castellio's works in translation.

The impact of Castellio's thought was chiefly felt among the Arminians in the Netherlands, where in the latter part of the sixteenth century there was an increasing protest against strict Calvinism and an effort to replace the Calvinistic theocracy with a consistory government. In 1578 the control of the Catholics had been thrown off. The strict Calvinism that replaced it seemed little better to the self-reliant Dutch. As they moved toward religious tolerance and the ideal of self-government, they found in Castellio's writings a clear articulation of their mood. Dirck Coornhert, then Secretary of State, translated Castellio's writings into Dutch and so made them available to the common people.

In Castellio, even more than in Erasmus, we find the critical way grown articulate. His roots, like those of Erasmus, are in Italian humanism and German mysticism. No doubt he imbibed much of this philosophy at Lyons, but he also may have been well grounded in it in his home as a youth. Among his other works is a translation of the widely popular *Theologia Germani.*

Like the work of so many of the leaders of the critical way in religion, Castellio's thought was forged in the heat of controversy. As a result, he grasped basic issues and stated them clearly. His *Concerning Heretics,* for example, caps five hundred years of struggle on the part of those who exemplified the critical tradition in western Europe. In it he laid down two of the fundamental principles on which the critical tradition stands: first, that no man and no church or any other institution has the capacity to state with finality what the truth is; second, that you cannot persuade a man's mind by force. All that you can do is maim him, kill him, reduce him to silence, or make him lie. Castellio, out of his own personal experience, restated the principle asserted by Socrates so long before, that truth is never achieved by force. For an articulation of the second half of this Socratic principle—that truth can be achieved only through the open and free encounter of mind with mind—Europe had to wait for the coming of the Enlightenment.

9

The Enlightenment

Most of the principles of the critical way had become articulate by the middle of the sixteenth century. Both the Renaissance and Reformation were, in part, expressions of it. That these principles achieved statement at all is remarkable when we consider the fierce opposition they evoked. Yet the practice of independent thinking, once begun, could not be stopped. Neither the terrors of the Inquisition in Catholic countries nor the repressions among the Protestants were sufficient to deter men from asking questions, seeking knowledge, and reading forbidden writings.

The result was a development known to students of Western culture as the Enlightenment. A many-faceted movement, it was, above all, intellectual in emphasis, attempting to understand, in the broadest sense, the nature of man and his world. The definition of philosophy given by the Enlightenment was "the organized habit of criticism." Thus, in the Enlightenment, the critical way can be said to have reached maturity.

1. Excitement and Change

We cannot now know how much reading matter circulated clandestinely in the Renaissance-Reformation period, but it was evidently considerable. The Bible, for example, at first kept from the hands of the common people, was much sought after as soon as translations in the vernacular became available. Despite the banning and burning of unauthorized translations and the punishment visited upon those caught with them, copies of the Bible continued to circulate ever more widely until official translations at last were made and permitted to circulate freely. Luther translated the Bible into

German in the early sixteenth century. The first official Bible in English, the King James Version, appeared in 1611.

What happened with regard to the Bible typifies what was happening in the church as a whole during those centuries. A basic change in attitude toward religious thought and expression was taking place. Rigid control was slowly giving way to freedom of expression. The churches were becoming tolerant of inquiry. Slowly, grudgingly it seemed, they permitted factual data, objectively established, to modify ancient teachings. By the eighteenth century, independent thinking in religion might produce social ostracism and economic privation, but it rarely brought on the physical barbarities that marked the Middle Ages and the early Renaissance.

Why? Had the Church become powerless to assert its authority? Had the monarchies of Europe ceased to support the demands of the clergy that the civil arm support them? The answer to both questions is: yes, to some degree, because of a fundamental change that was taking place which neither state nor church could control. As in the Middle Ages, the steadily accumulating body of knowledge and the steadily increasing ability of people to distinguish truth from error had its effect. Both together were responsible for the new shift in policy. Now that people had begun to see how much there was to know; now that they began to see how much yet remained to be discovered; now that they were learning the techniques by which truth could be distinguished from error, and fact could be separated from fancy, they were impatient with any attempt to suppress thought and expression. They wanted to *know*—even if knowing meant a loss of faith, or meant a rejection of traditional religion.

There was great excitement in the process, both for the onlookers who got the benefit of it and the participants who made the discoveries. Even today we can sense the fervor that possessed Copernicus when it dawned upon him that the sun, not the earth, was the center of the universe. We need only read the writings of Galileo to see it. In 1610 Galileo published his first work, setting forth the observations he had made through a telescope he himself had designed and built. The opening paragraphs read:

> Great indeed are the things which in this brief treatise I propose for observation and consideration by all students of nature. I say great, because of the excellence of the subject itself, the entirely unexpected and novel character of these things, and finally because of the instrument by means of which they have been revealed to our senses. Surely it is a great thing to increase the numerous host of fixed stars previously visible to the unaided vision, adding countless more which have never before been seen, exposing these plainly to the eye in numbers ten times exceeding the old and familiar stars.
>
> It is a very beautiful thing, and most gratifying to the sight, to behold the body of the moon, distant from us almost sixty earthly radii, as if it were no farther away than two such measures—so that

> its diameter appears almost thirty times larger, its surface nearly nine hundred times, and its volume twenty-seven thousand times as large as when viewed with the naked eye. In this way one may learn with all the certainty of sense evidence that the moon is not robed in a smooth and polished surface but is in fact rough and uneven, covered everywhere, just like the earth's surface, with huge prominences, deep valleys, and chasms.

In Galileo we have a late example of the battle which was by that time some five centuries old—the battle between men who sought a new understanding of familiar things, and the Church, which felt threatened by the expression of such views. Although Galileo became famous throughout Europe because of his discoveries, he was dragged before the Holy Office and forced to make a humiliating recantation of his discoveries when he was seventy years of age and blind. He spent the few remaining years of his life as a prisoner.

Those who have found lack of character and courage in Galileo's recantation and in the whispered addendum "but it is true," that he is supposed to have spoken at his trial, might better save their criticisms for the small-minded men who condemned him. Neither the truth nor the falsity of Galileo's discoveries was established by threatening an old man with torture to force him publicly to deny what he knew to be true. All that was accomplished was the humiliation of a great man because he dared to express ideas that conflicted with the established religion of his day.

The increasing thirst for hard, dependable knowledge that possessed western Europe in the sixteenth, seventeenth, and eighteenth centuries can be accounted for by a number of factors. Scholars have listed a great many of them. They include the increase in trade taking place at that time, the growth of towns, the shifting of economic power to the north and west where the Enlightenment centered, the Protestant Reformation, the end of Roman Catholic dominance, the cultural revolution brought about by the printing press, and the widespread increase in education that resulted from it. All these and other factors taken together constitute the mood of the times which both produced the full expression of the critical way and were at the same time the result of it.

As the Church discovered that it could no longer maintain uniformity of thought through suppression, it gradually increased its dependence on argument—in particular in England, France, and Germany, where by the eighteenth century the advance of knowledge had become the most rapid. Few seem to have been aware at the time that so basic a change was taking place. Such things are most often seen only in the perspective of history and the evidence for it is now abundant. In the sixteenth century the battle had raged over the right of men to say what they believed in religion even though it might differ from ecclesiastical pronouncements. Castellio and Erasmus had said that men ought to be persuaded by argument rather than by imprisonment, torture, and the threat of death. Two hundred years later, independent thought had won by argument this fundamental battle. In the eighteenth century, expression was relatively free. The center of the battle had shifted from prison, gallows, and pyre to books, pamphlets, and the public platform.

2. Great Enlightenment Thinkers

While the Enlightenment is primarily an eighteenth-century movement, its beginnings are clearly discernible in the seventeenth century and even earlier. If we were to pick a single individual with whom to begin, for most students of the period it would be that delightfully urbane Frenchman, Michel de Montaigne. A sixteenth-century Renaissance Reformation thinker, he nevertheless best typifies the mood and character of the Enlightenment. Why? Because he got into language the single most basic question the Enlightenment wrestled with.

"What do I know?" Montaigne asked. It is the central question of the critical way in religion, formulated at a later stage as *How do I know?* How does anyone know? It is the problem of certainty, the problem we all face by virtue of the fact of our human fallibility. Montaigne faced up to it squarely.

The question was an old one. The ancient skeptics had formulated it and traced its origins to a shadowy figure, Pyrrho of Elis, who lived 360–275 B.C. None of Pyrrho's writing has survived, but fortunately we have a full account of his teachings in a work of one of his disciples, Sextus Empiricus. Pyrrhonism, as this philosophy is known, rested upon the single principle that nothing can be surely known. The Pyrrhonists worked out a method of doubting, a step-by-step procedure for ridding the mind of beliefs heretofore accepted as true but seen to be doubtful after careful examination. The method, when systematically and scrupulously followed, leads to an ultimate and total skepticism: the view that nothing can be known to be true for certain. Everything, if examined carefully enough, can be legitimately called into question.

The influence of the legendary Pyrrho on Montaigne, arching over a period of some eighteen hundred years, provides us with a vivid illustration of the fact that the critical way in religion is a tradition. It lives and grows from person to person and from land to land. Suppressed, ignored, forgotten, the critical way, given the opportunity for expression, makes an immediate and powerful appeal to the seekers of knowledge. Montaigne came upon a copy of Sextus' work on Pyrrho, at a time when he, Montaigne, was trying to defend a writer on natural theology. The uncompromising form of Sextus' argument and the clarity of his mind plunged Montaigne into a period of profound soul-searching. In his "Apology for Raymond Sebond," Montaigne worked through his own problem, and resolved to his own satisfaction the relationship between reason and faith. He did so in quite as uncompromising a manner as had Sextus and, no doubt, Pyrrho himself nearly two millennia before.

In the end Montaigne concluded that Sextus had been right: that no certain knowledge is possible. But he did not stop there. As so many thinkers had done before him, Montaigne turned to the Christian faith as a sure source of knowledge in religious matters. He did not, however, come out with the medieval doctrine of two truths or of two ways to truth. Montaigne insists that there is but one road to final truth—the Christian way, through the faith given to us by revelation, and held for us by the Church. All else must remain in doubt because of the weakness and unreliability of our human faculties.

What did Montaigne really think about the issue of faith as against reason and experience? The argument on this point still goes on and it concerns many medieval, Renaissance, and Enlightenment figures in addition to Montaigne. How many of them sought to hide secular skepticism behind a mask of Christian piety? Probably we shall never know. What is clear with Montaigne, however, is the power of his argument for skepticism, despite his declaration of loyalty to the Christian faith. His thought became the basis of a sharp and sudden advance in the critical way in the religion of the West. After Montaigne, there was no escaping the question *How do you know?* After Montaigne, those who wanted to rest human knowledge on a firmer basis than the doctrine of revelation had first to explain how our human fallibility was to be overcome.

While Montaigne was a "philosophe," he was not a philosopher in the sense that Descartes, his compatriot, was. And yet, with an assist from Pyrrho via Sextus Empiricus, he forced the mind of western Europe to face up to a question no one has since been able to answer with finality: how can we be sure that we know what we think we know? It has since become one of the most basic problems of philosophy. Called "epistemology," a word derived from the Greek, coined a little over a century ago, it is the study of how we know and of the limits of our knowing.

René Descartes lived some two generations later than Montaigne, but he is usually given the credit for first formulating the epistemological problem and for systematically seeking an answer to it, although it was recently learned that an earlier thinker, Pierre Charron, a disciple of Montaigne, may actually deserve the credit for it. In any event, true to the format set by Sextus long before, Descartes began by establishing a method by which to check every assertion anyone might make. The result was his monumental *Discourse on Method,* published in 1637. Even today it is a refreshing experience to read him. After noting at some length the evidence of our human fallibility, Descartes says: I resolved "to accept nothing as true which I did not clearly recognize to be so . . . to accept nothing more than what was presented to my mind so clearly and distinctly that I could have no occasion to doubt it." According to his own lights he stuck by that resolve. Determined to find a way out, he found it in himself. The one thing he could be sure of, he asserted, was that he himself existed. He concluded that this was so on noting the fact that it was he himself who was asking the doubting questions, whereupon he reached his classical statement *cogito ergo sum,* "I think, therefore I am."

Today the answers Descartes gave to his questions are not nearly as important as the questions themselves, and the clarity and determination with which he addressed himself to the fact of human fallibility. His obvious piety and the centrality of God in his philosophical system kept him out of trouble with the Church despite the fact that his method of doubt was threatening to faith. The Church soon came to agree with his critics. Only thirteen years after his death, Descartes's writings were placed on the Index. It was clear to the Church, even if not to Descartes, that for most people his work led to skepticism, not to faith. His proof of the existence of God was deemed not nearly as persuasive as his insistence that one must ask for verification of whatever is said until further checking becomes impossible. It did not take the Church long to see that despite Descartes's protestations of faith his method led to its dissolution instead.

Although René Descartes is seldom quoted in books on religion, he holds a central place in the critical tradition. He asks the question that is crucial for the critical mind and he puts it in the most uncompromising manner possible. Why then did not the critical way in religion gain wide acceptance as a result of the writings of Descartes? Probably, more than anything else, because Descartes himself did not grasp, or at least did not spell out, the full import of his own questionings for organized religion in his time. He found certainty in the fact of his thinking, and through that, certainty in the fact of his own existence. Like Montaigne he found ultimate certainty in God, whose existence he thought he could prove. But it remained for David Hume, the Scotsman, a century later, both to ask the ancient question of Pyrrho and also to see that, pressed far enough, the question: What can I know with absolute certainty? has no answer.

In 1684, before the Enlightenment can really be said to have got under way, Pierre Bayle, the French encyclopedist, published a *Philosophical Commentary on the Text, 'Compel Them to Come In'.* Bayle, who grew up as a Huguenot, was directing his fire at Louis XIV for revoking the Edict of Nantes, which had guaranteed equal political rights to Protestants even though curtailing their religious liberties. Bayle's publication was designed for use as a weapon in the struggle of the French Protestants to retain the religious liberty they had held so long and at such great sacrifice. It was only secondarily a theological tract, but was more effective in that role than in supporting the civil liberties of the Huguenots. Bayle attacked the doctrine "Compel Them to Come In," which had been developed by Augustine a thousand years before to justify the persecution of the Donatists. Augustine's argument was the main justification offered by the French Catholic clergy for the revocation of the Edict of Nantes, suppression of the Huguenots, and the appalling Massacre of Saint Bartholomew's Day.

In his tract in defense of the Huguenot position, Pierre Bayle put into clear, unmistakable language one of the basic principles of the Enlightenment and of the critical tradition as well: that the greatest obstacle to truth is not ignorance but partial truth or untruth which is held to be the truth. "Dogma, not error, is the foe of truth," he said. "Error can be corrected. Dogma cannot because it is declared to be true on the basis of authority. The mind is full of prejudice. Superstition is the common enemy of both knowledge and faith."

Bayle solved the problem of what to do with religious faith in a manner that harked back to Montaigne and even to Averroës. Take it on authority, he said, but do not try to persuade me to believe by the use of reason. And do not try to persuade me by force. Reason teaches that to force a man to believe what seems to him to be false is irrational, as well as immoral. No truth is certain enough to justify forcing anyone to accept it, he said, restating, whether he knew it or not, Castellio's argument, "there is no truth sure enough to justify persecution." No one can judge the reason of another; each must do this for himself—another principle of the critical way. We must not dogmatically reject even those beliefs we judge to be in error, because they might in the end turn out to be right. Force can only make a man a hypocrite, he declared with Erasmus and Castellio; it cannot change his mind. We may suppress only those doctrines which threaten public safety. The state must tolerate everything but intolerance.

Bayle's argument rested squarely on the Pyrrhonist position that we cannot be as certain about ultimate things as we might like. In his view the state must not, indeed cannot, even with all the authority in the world, force people to believe what they do not believe. In his famous *Dictionary,* published in 1697, he juxtaposed authoritative but inconsistent assertions. The device by which he accomplished this was that of the cross reference. By inviting the reader to compare one passage with another, he demonstrated to the alert mind without any comment that the two could not stand together: that if the one was true, the other must be false and vice versa. He used the same method with regard to Bible passages on which he commented freely, always inviting the reader to ask questions of his own.

A single example will suffice to show Bayle's method, his entry on Pyrrhonism. In it he was careful to point out the limits of the method of doubt. Pyrrhonism does *not* mean incomprehensibility, he insisted. The Pyrrhonists were examiners. They were inquirers. They suspended judgment until they could be certain. This, said Bayle, shows that they thought it possible to find out truth. Pyrrho, Bayle continued, found reasons to affirm, but he also found reasons to deny almost everything. He therefore suspended his assent to any proposition, if after examining the arguments pro and con he could reach no certain conclusion about it. "Let the matter be further inquired into," Bayle advised.

Bayle's method of subtly ridiculing ecclesiastical pretentions is also evident in his entry on Pyrrho. Pyrrhonism would seem to be dangerous to religion, he observes, because religion is founded on certainty. But it is really no threat at all, he continues, because of the grace that God has given the faithful to go on believing despite all the questions the inquiring mind may ask. Then, lest anyone miss his point, he adds, "but Pyrrhonism is not very dangerous to natural philosophy, since man can never find certainty there anyway." Our human faculties are too limited. Here he has abandoned the formula worked out by Montaigne and has gone back to the medieval doctrine of the Averroists: that there are two roads to truth, reason and revelation. But Bayle, without stating it in so many words, makes it clear that he thinks we have only one choice to make. Those who wish to submit their minds to authority may attain a sense of certainty, he is saying, but it will be a false certainty. As for himself, Bayle says he proposes to go on inquiring since the certainty the churchmen promise can never be achieved.

In 1689, five years after Bayle published his attack on the doctrine "Compel Them to Come In," John Locke in England published his *Letters Concerning Toleration.* His position and his argument were essentially the same as Bayle's. Locke's tract also had a political context to the then-new English Revolution, which he attempted to justify. For him the church was to be looked on as a free and voluntary society, and, for all the reasons stated by Bayle, could not be controlled by the state. Locke powerfully restated them. The government is purely secular, he declared; it has nothing to do with saving souls and must therefore follow a hands-off policy as far as religious doctrine and belief are concerned.

François Marie Arouet de Voltaire (1694–1778) is the next great name in the slowly widening and deepening critical tradition in religion. Like his fellow countryman Montaigne, he was not a professional philosopher but an essayist, an urbane writer on a wide variety of subjects, including religion. His writings are probably the best known of all Enlightenment thinkers. He was not a creative thinker: his great contribution was to expose the errors and follies of people, churchmen not excepted, and he did so by the use of every literary device known to the forensic art. Satire, ridicule, sarcasm, straight clear reasoning—he was master of them all and used them with telling effect.

A modern writer says of Voltaire: "He wanted to show: (a) that it is absurd to suppose that an omnipotent God, creator of Heaven and Earth, had chosen the Jews, a small tribe of Bedouin nomads, as His chosen people; (b) that the chronicle of that race (the Bible) was packed with incredible facts, obscenities, and contradictions (he took the trouble to publish, under the title of *La Bible Expliquée,* a survey of the biblical text with countless notes); (c) that the Gospels, although more moral than the

Old Testament, were nevertheless full of the gossipings of illiterate nobodies; and finally (d) that the disputes which set the sects at each other's throats throughout eighteen centuries were foolish and unavailing."

Voltaire was a deist but he was also an agnostic. He spoke often of belief in God, but it is clear from his writings that his theism was formal only. On the other hand we cannot say: therefore, he believed in man. We must guard against falling into the popular cliché that since Voltaire did not believe in God (in the traditional sense) he believed in man. He did not, in the doctrinaire meaning of that formula.

Voltaire constantly pointed out the very limited powers we humans possess and it is this that makes him so outstanding an exemplar of the critical way in religion. He insisted no less emphatically that we face the fact of human suffering, the degree to which we ourselves cause these sufferings and the degree to which we could, if we would, eliminate them. He was never more fierce in his satire than when he attacked the churchmen for the persecution of those who differed with official church dogma. "History is little else than a picture of human crimes and misfortunes," he once wrote. Those who continue to dismiss the Enlightenment as a movement of rosy unrealistic optimism need to reread their Voltaire.

The long struggle of the Western mind with the patent fact of human fallibility reaches its final point of development in the philosophy of the Scottish thinker David Hume. As Descartes had cast into philosophical form the piercing insights of Montaigne on this question, so Hume cast into philosophical form the yet more direct thought of Voltaire. Addressing himself to the question *How do you know?* Hume asked it continually until he found himself forced to answer "I don't know." We have no infallible grounds for believing what we do, he concluded. We have no way of knowing for sure whether or not the things we believe are really true. In his *Treatise of Human Nature* Hume declared with seeming finality that there is nothing of which we can really be sure, not even Descartes' famous "I think, therefore I am." The conclusions he reached have never been definitively refuted, though many have tried. Nevertheless, the great Scottish philosopher had common sense enough to admit that his was a philosophy for the closet and that on emerging from it we become believers again, if for no other reason than that we have to in order to live.

What was the Enlightenment? How shall we sum up this remarkable period which was not religious in any technical sense, yet profoundly influenced religion in the West and the world around? There have been many attempts to delineate it. Perhaps the best of them summarizes the Enlightenment as a loose, informal, wholly unorganized coalition of cultural critics, religious skeptics, and political reformers, who were widely scattered geographically and among whom, despite minor differences, a harmony of viewpoint prevailed. They were united on a program favoring secularism, humanity, cosmopolitanism and, above all, freedom in all its forms.

Enlightenment thinkers wanted freedom from arbitrary power, freedom of speech, freedom to trade, freedom for each person to realize his own talents, freedom of artistic response—in short, the freedom of a moral man to make his way in the world. Immanuel Kant (1724–1804) seems to have compressed the essence of it into a sentence when he wrote, "Dare to know: take the risk of discovery, exercise the right of unfettered criticism and accept the loneliness of autonomy."

10

The Legacy of the Enlightenment

For the critical way in religion an understanding of the influence of Enlightenment thinking in contemporary culture is crucial. We will now consider how Enlightenment ideas slowly entered Western religious thought. They entered silently for the most part, their origin unacknowledged by those who took them up. We shall note the degree to which these ideas have become a part of our thought today. In Christian circles in the eighteenth century there was a great hullabaloo over the threat to religion posed by Enlightenment thinkers. To some extent, as we shall see in the next chapter, that supposed threat is still being countered today. The battles of today are well publicized, as were those of the eighteenth and nineteenth centuries. What passed unnoticed then, and still draws little attention, is the matter to which we now turn: the silent acceptance by organized religion of Enlightenment ideas.

1. The Power of the Christian Church

The emergence of the Enlightenment is often seen as evidence of the weakness of an aging Christian Church, but it was nothing of the sort. The writings of the philosophes, the deists, and the rationalists of the seventeenth and eighteenth centuries left the structure of the Church unimpaired, its theology intact, and its power little diminished. When their work was done, people thought a little more freely about the problems implicit in Scripture and dogma, but their faith in traditional dogmas was scarcely lessened. They were made more familiar with the arguments pro and con, but they did not desert the Church. They did not turn away from its sacraments or cease to provide for its support. There was no dramatic drop-off in Christian institutional vitality as a result of the Enlightenment. It merely carried further and very slowly the ongoing process of erosion of the Church's power and prestige that had begun in the high Middle Ages.

One of the reasons for this was the intellectual and social status of many Enlightenment thinkers, the Deists in particular. Sir Leslie Stephen, in his *English Thought in the Eighteenth Century,* describes in a striking paragraph the contrast between the English deists and their orthodox opponents: "The names of the despised deists make but a poor show when compared with the imposing list [of the defenders of the faith]. They are but a ragged regiment, whose whole ammunition of learning was a trifle when compared with the abundant stores of a single light of orthodoxy. In speculative ability most of them were children by the side of their ablest antagonists. Swift's sneering assertion, that their literary power would hardly have attracted attention if employed upon any other topic, seems to be generally justified. But few of the deists, indeed, claimed respect as men of rank and of pretensions to taste."

A more basic reason why Enlightenment thinking made so little impact on the ecclesiastical way in religion was the role that traditional religion plays in human life. It concerns so much that is precious to us, and purports to answer so many fundamental questions, that only the most powerful motives will persuade us to question it. For most people in the eighteenth century who were touched at all by Enlightenment thinking, the reassurances of the local parish priest no doubt were sufficient. The faithful were told to ignore the blasphemous writings of the philosophers, which they did, and the Church, its doctrine intact, continued on its way.

Yet another reason was that education in the Enlightenment period, particularly at the university level, was still narrowly confined. It was a privilege that few enjoyed. Thus, while it is true that to a marked degree the critical tradition had by this time become the tradition in the universities of western Europe, the mood and temper of the universities had little effect upon religion because so few people were exposed to the critical tradition directly by attendance at universities. Another reason, even more important, was that so few university men, whatever their private views, ever set Christian dogma in juxtaposition to scientific findings that seemed to contradict it.

The great Sir Isaac Newton, for example, is now known to have held views that were quite heretical for his day, though not for ours. He read and studied the Bible, in particular the New Testament, and according to the standards of the critical way based the conclusions he drew from his reading on the evidence the Scriptures contained. On the basis of his studies he wrote an essay showing that the famous verse in I John 5:7, spelling out the doctrine of the Trinity, was spurious. The tract was entitled "An Historical Account of Two Notable Corruptions of the Scriptures, In a Letter to a Friend," but he never published it. Newton also spotted the two types of writing present in Daniel, and concluded the book had been written by two different people. This he discussed in his *Observations on the Book of Daniel.*

The debate still goes on as to whether Newton was an Arian, a Socinian, or a Unitarian; it is beside the point. What is important for our purposes is that during his lifetime he suppressed his religious views and became very angry when others sought to reveal them. More important, still, perhaps is the fact that his heresy (by seventeenth-century standards) is largely unknown even today.

The same thing is true of John Milton. Known by virtually everyone as a front-rank poet, he is less well known as a powerful pamphleteer who fought for various human rights; recall, for example, his ringing defense of freedom of speech and the press in the *Areopagitica.* But John Milton is scarcely known at all for his heterodox religious views, the chief reason being that he voluntarily suppressed those views during his lifetime and avoided religious controversy.

Late in life Milton wrote a *Treatise on Christian Doctrine* in Latin but did not publish it. When the manuscript was discovered among his papers in 1823 and was published two years later, it created a sensation. By our standards today the *Treatise* contained nothing startling but, because it was strictly biblical rather than doctrinal, it differed at many points from the orthodox theology of the time. These differences aroused a storm of criticism, a storm that would have been even more severe had the work appeared a century and a half earlier, during Milton's lifetime.

Evidence that heterodox views were voluntarily suppressed by men like Newton and Milton is supported by the very recent discovery of the writings of an Elizabethan scientist, heretofore virtually unknown, named Thomas Hariot. He seems to have been a scientific genius. But he was also quite unorthodox in his religious opinions, and he too was very careful to keep his views from all but a few intimates.

In their own eyes and those of their contemporaries, neither Newton nor Milton nor any of those who avoided religious controversy lacked courage. Rather, they chose what seemed to them to be the path of prudence and charity. Although they adopted the critical way in religion, for themselves they chose to maintain an outward mien of orthodox adherence and piety. Benjamin Franklin once expressed this point of view with characteristic grace. Asked by the President of Yale University about his religious views, Franklin, in a brief note, stated his position quite candidly. Then he added this postscript: "I confide that you will not expose me to criticism and censure by publishing any part of this communication to you. I have ever let others enjoy their religious sentiments, without reflecting on them for those that appeared to me unsupportable and even absurd. All sects here, and we have a great variety, have experienced my good will in assisting them with subscriptions for building their new places of worship; and, as I have never opposed any of their doctrines, I hope to go out of the world in peace with them all."

In the Enlightenment period and on into the nineteenth century, this point of view prevailed among thinkers great and small, known and forgotten. As a final example, Hermann Samuel Reimarus (1694–1768), a highly respected teacher in Hamburg, Germany, during his lifetime gave minute attention to a study of the Scriptures. As a result, he was led to some quite radical conclusions. Having written them out, like Newton, he circulated them among his friends but never published them. Reimarus died an honored and respected man. Soon after his death, however, Lessing, the great German dramatist and critic, came upon the manuscript, and finding Reimarus' views similar to his own, published fragments of the manuscript under a pseudonym.

The following excerpt gives something of the flavor of Reimarus' style. In this passage he undertakes with facts and figures to show that the most famous miracle in the Old Testament could not have occurred. He writes,

> If we look at . . . the miracle of the passage through the Red Sea, its inner contradiction, its impossibility is quite palpable. Six hundred thousand Israelites of military age leave Egypt, armed, and in battle order. They have with them their wives and their children and a good deal of rabble that had joined them. Now, we must count for each man of military age, four others at least; partly women, partly children, partly the aged, partly servants. The number of the emigrants, therefore, in proportion to those of military age, must be at least 3,000,000 souls. They take with them all their sheep and oxen, that is to say a large number of cattle. If we count only 300,000 heads of households, and give each of them one cow or ox and two sheep, that would add up to 300,000 oxen and cows, and 600,000 sheep and goats. In addition, we must count on at least 1,000 wagon loads of hay or fodder; to say nothing of the many other wagons containing the golden and silver vessels which they had purloined, and piles of baggage and tents needed for such an enormous army—even if we count only 5,000 wagons, which is one wagon to sixty persons.

Reimarus continues in similar vein at some length and the irony mounts as he goes along. Putting all the details together, in particular the time span within which the events are supposed to have taken place, the story as it is recounted in Exodus becomes ridiculous. Reimarus does not need to point out the moral. It is all too evident. He is saying the central miracle of the Old Testament simply could not have happened.

2. The Churchmen Counterattack

When Lessing published these fragments from Reimarus, he enjoyed a position of the highest eminence in German and in European letters and culture. But it was not enough to save either his or Reimarus' reputation from the wrath of the church or the censure of the state. Heretofore not troubled by the censorship that prevailed at the time, Lessing now found himself subject to it. Accordingly, he discontinued the publication of Reimarus' work. Except in France, nearly all of those who expressed such views during the seventeenth and eighteenth centuries, and even into the nineteenth, suffered from the same censure.

While certain Enlightenment thinkers, Voltaire for example, seem to have been motivated by the desire to destroy religion in all its forms, most of them criticized religion in order to save it. In fact, most of them hoped to strengthen it. They believed that if the various errors, foibles, and downright evils of religion could be eliminated, its usefulness and credibility would be greatly increased. Enlightenment thinkers attacked mythical ways of thinking, not because they were religious myths but because myths cannot be verified. There is no harm in a myth, they said, unless it is taken literally, which it was never intended to be.

The defenders of the faith could not believe this. They easily fell into the ancient canard, fostered by the Church down the ages, that whoever questions what the Church says or does is moved by hatred and that his purpose is not to improve religion but to destroy the Church. Any observer of the history of the West can only be dismayed by the persistence of this idea.

An eighteenth-century book defending the orthodox faith against deism breathes "an uncompromising spirit of hostility," according to a leading authority on the English Enlightenment. The author "treats his opponent as a fool and a knave . . . and obviously believes him to be both. 'Contempt' and 'hatred' are blended in every paragraph of this churchman's work."

We should suppose that today we could consign such theological utterances to the oblivion they deserve, but the mood of vituperation and scorn for the "skeptic" continues, not only in the writings of the churchmen but, more surprisingly, in those of supposedly dispassionate scholars. For example, among the writers on the development of the idea of tolerance in the West, none is more competent, none is more scholarly, and on the whole, none is more dispassionate and fair than Wilbur K. Jordan in his monumental *Development of Religious Toleration in England.* Yet Jordan, characterizing Herbert of Cherbury (1583–1648), uses such phrases as "contempt for institutional religion," "cold materialism which pervaded all his thought," "coldly analytical spirit," "absence of genteel piety and mystical devotion," "hostile criticism," "a complete and almost naive confidence in the efficacy of reason," "a darkly hostile detestation of clericalism," "far nobler men had long since broken the way," and so on.

In the light of so severe a judgment one would wonder why a respected scholar would pay any attention to Lord Herbert. In the same passage from which I have drawn the above phrases, Jordan tells us why he does. He says of Herbert (the italics are mine): "He laid a *firm philosophical basis* for

English rationalism. He approached the manifold problems of religion in a thoroughly secular and *critical spirit*. . . . He was the first thinker *in England* to undertake a *thoroughly comparative study* of religion and in this effort he *maintained a remarkable objectivity*. . . . In his *vigorous denunciation of all forms of ecclesiastical tyranny* he was to cut away the reasonable basis for the theory of persecution."

Jordan has yet higher praise for the man he says is animated by materialism and hostility toward religion. "Herbert," he continues (italics mine), *"proposed to examine religion with a strictly objective method designed to reveal the nature of truth."* He speaks of "Herbert's *devotion to the sanctity of the right of private judgment*," and adds that he *"surveyed the nature of truth and reason with a critical and dispassionate examination."* He quotes Herbert as saying, "It is the task of the critic to examine religious systems dispassionately and comparatively in order to detect which elements are true and which false."

Another competent and respected contemporary scholar falls into the same pattern of contempt for those who question traditional doctrine. In a paragraph summarizing the character of skeptics, he refers to them over and over again as a "tribe" and concludes by referring to "the whole horde of free thinkers, agnostics, materialists, rationalists and secularists of more recent vintage." The derogatory tone is evident. One can hardly imagine a respected scholar speaking of the Lutherans, say, as a *tribe*, or of the Catholics as a *horde*.

Because most of the issues argued by the Enlightenment are still being argued today, and because people still feel as deeply about them as ever, it is difficult to find an objective account of the movement in the history books. Those who seek to tell its story seem hardly able to avoid taking sides, and expressing their views with quite unscholarly fervor. As one scholar reminds us, "for the last half century or more, intellectual historians, students of literature and political theorists have worked to restore the Enlightenment to its true stature, to rescue it from its admirers nearly as much as from its detractors. . . . The Enlightenment has been held responsible for the evils of the modern age and much scorn has been directed at its supposed superficial rationalism, foolish optimism and irresponsible Utopianism. Compared to these distortions . . . the amiable caricature drawn by liberal and radical admirers of the Enlightenment has been innocuous: the naivete of the left has been far outweighed by the malice of the right." What I am attempting here is neither an encomium nor a demolition. The aim is rather to see as objectively as possible what the Enlightenment was and how it advanced the critical tradition

3. The Ecclesiastical Retreat

A study of the Enlightenment shows that the fury of the defenders of Christianity was among the strongest factors leading in the end to the acceptance of Enlightenment ideas. The doctrine of the Trinity was jeopardized by divisions among its defenders more than by the relatively few attacks of Enlightenment thinkers upon it. One scholar speaks of the "foot soldiers of the Enlightenment": thinkers of modest endowment possessed of "a stubborn integrity that made them continue to ask questions." Many of these, in fact, thought of themselves as defending the old way, but their arguments had the form and flavor of Enlightenment views. Hence they were impressed into the army of the Enlightenment in spite of themselves.

Accordingly, the tide of ecclesiastical dogma slowly receded. Beginning in the Middle Ages, gaining momentum through the Renaissance and Reformation, traditional, supposedly indubitable and unchangeable dogmas were modified, and some fell into disuse. Whether Enlightenment thinkers took the way of caution, like Milton, Newton, Reimarus, and Hume, or whether they took the way of boldness and plain speaking, like Voltaire, and later on Thomas Paine, the process of attrition set in. Yesterday's heresy became today's theological commonplace. This aspect of the conflict was silent as far as the Church was concerned. Churchmen seldom acknowledged and perhaps did not notice that a battlefield once hotly contested had been relinquished to the foe. Yet throughout this period they steadily narrowed the province they claimed as their own, while the area of life they acknowledged to be subject to the investigative process steadily widened. To be sure, when the Enlightenment period closed, religion had much ground still to relinquish, as we shall see in the following chapter. But it was during the Enlightenment period that the pattern was established. It was then that the claims of faith began steadily to yield to the results of observation, speculation, and testing.

Half a century ago Alfred North Whitehead described this process in a passage now classic as well as prophetic: "The religious controversies of the sixteenth and seventeenth centuries put theologians into a most unfortunate state of mind. They pictured themselves as the garrison of a fort, surrounded by hostile forces." As Whitehead saw it, the process has been continuous since that time. He wrote,

> A series of novel situations caught religious thinkers unprepared. In each case, after struggle, distress, and anathema the old doctrines were modified and reinterpreted. The next generation of religious apologists then congratulated the religious world on the deeper insight which has been gained. The result of the continued repetition of this undignified retreat, during many generations, has at last almost entirely destroyed the intellectual authority of religious

> thinkers. Consider this contrast: when Darwin or Einstein proclaim theories which modify our ideas, it is a triumph for science. We do not go about saying that there is another defeat for science, because its old ideas have been abandoned. We know that another step of scientific insight has been gained. Religion will not regain its old power until it can face change in the same spirit as does science. Its principles may be eternal, but the expression of those principles requires continual development.

The retreat actually began in the later Middle Ages, when the Church was forced to deal with the changing economic, social, and political conditions in Europe as the Renaissance came on. Finding it could no longer exert the control it had enjoyed under Popes Gregory VII, Innocent III, and Boniface VIII, the Church slowly withdrew many of the claims to power it had formerly made and increasingly confined its role to matters that were more spiritual. The erosion continued after the Reformation and again accelerated in pace in the nineteenth century, the period Whitehead describes so incisively.

The process is well illustrated by the controversies that took place in western Europe over the Bible, in particular in Protestant countries where the Bible was looked upon as the central authority for the Christian faith. As we have seen, the practice of examining the Bible closely but objectively goes back at least as far as Adelard of Bath and Arnold of Brescia. With Lorenzo Valla and Erasmus the study of the manuscripts from which our Bible text is derived took a central place. Nevertheless, biblical criticism, as we know it, did not attain full development or full acceptance until the late nineteenth century. Work in the field is still going on, although today the results are no longer as startling or significant.

The full story of how the Bible, once looked upon as God's literal revelation to men, became the human document most churchmen believe it to be today, is long and detailed. A brief outline will sufficiently serve our purposes. The story really begins in the Enlightenment period when a congeries of new information relating to the Bible forced thoughtful men to reconsider the traditional view of the holy books of Christianity and Judaism. Not only were they confronted by the literary critics and the textual critics; they had also to contend with the findings of astronomy, anthropology (primitive as the science was at that time), geology, and biology.

The critical study of the content of the Bible contrasted with the question of the text, which goes back to Erasmus, can be said to have begun with Reimarus, as we have seen. It was another German, however, David Friedrich Strauss, who today is credited with establishing the modern critical study of the Bible. His *Life of Jesus,* published in 1835, aroused a storm of protest and vilification. Only today, nearly a century and a half later, is his greatness at last being recognized in the ecclesiastical tradition. A review of one of the current books about him speaks of "his exclusion from a university professorship by a combination of dogmatic woodenness and petty politics" and credits him with changing "the direction of New Testament exegesis by exhaustingly demonstrating that the mystical nature of the sources prohibits a biography of Jesus."

Even a generation ago such an appraisal of Strauss by a mainline churchman would have been surprising. For a century his work was either ignored as incompetent or denounced as destructive. Today, when Rudolf Bultmann has made the presence of myth in the New Testament a respectable point of view, Strauss at last is no longer seen as a destroyer of Christianity but as a pioneer in developing new insights into New Testament studies. The story of this development provides yet another example of retreating theologians viewing their most recent concession to the critical tradition as a victory for religion and a new insight into its meaning.

A German philosopher, Ludwig Feuerbach, took up where Strauss left off. Strauss had made the radical assumption that the events in Jesus' life were to be understood naturally, not supernaturally. Feuerbach, in his *Essence of Christianity,* published six years later, made the same assumption with regard to all religious phenomena. He asserted that myths, legends, miracles, and dogma tell us more about the men who produced them than they do about the events they supposedly record. This distinction became fundamental in the critical tradition. Hume had stated the principle with simple clarity. "A miracle is a violation of the laws of nature," he wrote. "It is something we know cannot happen because it is contrary to all human experience." Voltaire had said the same, calling a miracle "a contradiction to the eternal laws of nature."

It was one thing for Hume to state the principle. It was quite another when Strauss showed what happens when you apply it to religious doctrines held sacred by the church. The life story of Jesus as recorded in the Gospels changes dramatically when it is interpreted naturalistically. Nevertheless, what Strauss said made sense to a widening circle of thoughtful people. While loudly denounced at the time and while Strauss himself was personally vilified, the views he presented slowly gained acceptance and eventually were proclaimed as having brought new light and understanding to the person of Jesus and the times in which he lived.

Karl Marx, better known for his social and political philosophy than for his religious views, drew from Feuerbach his famous line, "Religion is the opium of the people." Traditional religion, he said, by promising justice, mercy, and all good things in heaven, helps to make people content to endure injustice, cruelty, and want here on earth. Recent scholars, examining Marx's writings apart from the dogmas of political communism, have stressed the basically religious character of his thought and the fact that Feuerbach was the chief source of his inspiration.

Discoveries of archeologists in the latter part of the nineteenth century and particularly in the twentieth only aggravated the problems that resulted from the new critical studies of the Bible. To the delight of the churchmen, many excavations corroborated the historicity of the Bible. They revealed that many of the forgotten cities referred to in the Bible had once existed, and that conquests described there had in fact taken place. But the excavations also showed that much of the Bible, once thought to have been original and unique, was secondary and derivative. A reconstruction of the history and literature of the ancient Near East showed what an objective historian with no Christian commitments might expect: that Israel had not been unique. It was but one of many small nations in the Near East that had risen to prominence and gained a sense of identity in the first millennium B.C. and that had been very much a part of and reflected the general development of civilization in that region at that time.

Conjoined with the results of the other disciplines, biblical criticism further undermined the concept of the Bible as God's literal revelation to men. The first five books—the Pentateuch—proved a particularly fruitful field for the literary critics. They showed quite conclusively that these books were composed of at least four separate documents, written under different circumstances, by unknown authors often separated from one another by several centuries. Out of these studies, backed by references to history, archeology, and other sciences, came a vast amount of information about the sources of the material in the Bible. Beyond the demonstrable conclusions lay a far broader area of hypothesis and ultimately guesswork. Nevertheless, what did become clear to all but the most determined believers was that the Bible is a very human document; that it is made up of writings set down in a wide variety of places and times by a wide variety of men and for a wide variety of purposes.

The discoveries of the astronomers only added to the problems of the strict biblicists. They moved the Earth and the solar system established by Copernicus and Galileo, first to a universe of galaxies, and then to an expanding universe, the entire structure being incredibly large and incredibly old. In it our little planet with its precious life-sustaining character, and even humanity itself, seemed infinitesimal—a speck of matter in a speck of space for only a moment of time. None of these conclusions did very much to sustain the biblical view of man and his earth as the center and focus of all creation. Nor did it give much support to Christianity's doctrine of a personal God dwelling in heaven, loving and caring for each of us, and ready to receive us into his heaven at death, provided we had believed as we should and had lived a virtuous life as well. The studies of the biologists fully supported the astronomers with regard to man's place in nature. They soon found him to be a mammal, and the mammals to be one with the entire animal kingdom, the animal kingdom to be one with all life, and life itself to be an integral part of the physical universe. As a result, the view that man is the darling of God, his special creation and his special care, became less and less tenable.

A new discipline known as comparative religion, with its roots in the Enlightenment, developed in the nineteenth and early twentieth centuries, and further undermined the biblical view of man as holding a unique place in the natural order. The study of other religions, especially those of the ancient world, showed Christianity to be but one among many religions, each of which, like Christianity, claimed uniqueness for itself. Often the similarities among the religions, both ancient and modern, were striking.

Then too, the blemishes in Christianity were all too clear to scholars. They were familiar with the bloody and often shameful history of the Christian Church in its struggle for supremacy, a struggle that was often more political than spiritual. When the idealism of other religions was added to the list of comparisons, Christian claims to superiority and uniqueness no longer seemed so persuasive. It was hard to see, for example, in what sense the Sermon on the Mount was divine while the eightfold path of the Buddha was merely human. When James Frazer showed how much of Christianity could be traced directly back to pagan origins, many believers in the Christian revelation and Christian uniqueness had a most difficult time of it.

Standard histories of Christian thought, in particular Protestant thought, where the issues were most sharply drawn, tell the tale of the retreat of the churchmen in the face of the onward march of science. The persuasive power of the scientific method proved irresistible. The steadily accumulating data from geology and biology, archeology, paleography, and literary criticism brought about, one by one, the modification or abandonment of once sacrosanct and supposedly eternally true Christian doctrines. And as each was abandoned, each in turn was declared by the churchmen not to have been essential, but a misunderstanding of the deeper religious truths with which the discoveries of science were really in no conflict at all.

4. The Critical Way Enters Organized Religion

The retreat of the churchmen before the objective, speculative, and experimental methods of science was accompanied by the slow acceptance of Enlightenment ideas. They were but two aspects of a single development in the religion and culture of the West. We cannot point to a particular time when the critical way in religion began to gain acceptance. Since it is indigenous to our patterns of thought, in a very real sense the critical way has always been present within as well as outside organized religion. Nevertheless, it is clear that beginning in the Enlightenment, and slowly gaining momentum since that time, principles of the critical way in religion have steadily gained acceptance in both Judaism and Christianity. The process is still going on today very much as Whitehead described it: first, anathemas by the churchmen; then slow, often grudging but increasingly articulate acceptance; and finally the proclamation that the acceptance of the new principle is a great gain for religion because of the new understanding of old problems that such acceptance makes possible.

To illustrate, again we turn to the Bible and the problems attendant upon understanding it as God's word. From Arnold of Brescia (who went behind the writings of the Church Fathers to the Bible itself) through Erasmus (who went behind the text of the Bible to the manuscripts from which it was derived) on through Lorenzo Valla (who went behind every text to test its intrinsic validity as a piece of writing) on to Reimarus (who tested the validity of the text by naturalistic standards), we move to the severely critical position held by all scholars of good repute today: that Bible history, Bible manuscripts, Bible data, Bible content, and Bible interpretations are all to be approached with total scientific objectivity.

A contemporary author writes: "When the new sciences showed that Biblical *history* was in error . . . the understanding of what Biblical truth was had perforce to change." Continuing in the Whiteheadian vein, he declares, "We need to recognize the immense impact developments in science made on [Biblical theology's] self understanding." Another writer speaks of "the new insight gained from secularism." A third adds: "The struggle over evolution initiated a process of secularization of the Bible. This made possible a recovery of the Bible in its authentic historical categories." Still another, after reviewing the transformation of theology that took place as a result of Enlightenment thinking, concluded, "This movement enriched theology."

The years since the Enlightenment have seen the very widespread acceptance of another of its doctrines: the application of Judeo-Christian moral teaching to life as we live it. From the beginning, both Judaism and Christianity have had an inescapable moral dimension. Certain lines from the prophets and from the Gospels readily come to mind: "Let justice roll down as the waters." "Sell all thou hast and give to the poor." "Blessed are the merciful." "Love your enemies and pray for those who persecute you." "Whatever you wish that men would do to you, do so to them." And, of course, the parable of the Good Samaritan.

Ernst Troeltsch in his *Social Teachings of the Christian Churches* speaks of 'the concentration of [medieval] Christianity, specifically Thomism, upon the inward, personal and religious aspects of life." But, he adds, "There was still no idea of the need for a systematic transformation of the social order. . . . The Christian social doctrine of the Middle Ages was as far removed from being a program of social reform as was the social teaching of the Early Church, although for different reasons." Troeltsch argues that the concepts of brotherly love, of personal assistance to those in need—far beyond mere almsgiving—and, finally, of the reordering of society, appeared among the sects of the medieval and Reformation period, not in the Roman Catholic or in the larger Protestant churches. By the word "sect" Troeltsch meant small, self-organized religious groups marked by piety and fellowship and indifferent or hostile to the state.

In any event, Enlightenment thinkers were quite clear in their views of the matter. Many of them argued that the then-existing social order was unjust-and ought to be changed. They were equally clear that their views contrasted sharply with those of the Church. The misery, in the midst of which so many people live, is not due to original sin, they insisted. It is a result of the evils of society. As a remedy, Enlightenment thinkers introduced the concept "benevolence" to replace the older Christian concept "charity." In place of almsgiving they advocated social change. To bring their demand into focus, they introduced another new concept, "humanity". As a substitute for traditional Christian piety, centered in the self and the salvation of one's own soul, they advocated unselfish labor dedicated to the welfare of others and the transformation of the social structures that both caused and sanctioned the widespread sufferings of the time.

During the nineteenth century, as the Enlightenment concepts of benevolence and humanity began to make their way into the minds of thinking people, the more liberal churchmen began preaching these doctrines and demanding that they be carried out in practice. This was particularly true among urban ministers facing urban problems. It was a movement in which Unitarian ministers in northeastern United States took the lead. Many now outdated and outmoded social service organizations were founded in these cities at that time by wealthy parishioners. Ironically, they seem to have been quite unaware that the state of ease and plenty that made their benevolences possible was derived in part from the very conditions they denounced and sought to alleviate.

One of the earliest clerical voices in the awakening of the social conscience o America was that of Francis Greenwood Peabody. A Boston Unitarian clergyman, Peabody in the latter part of his life became professor of Christian Morals at the Harvard Divinity School. There, during the last quarter of the nineteenth century, he introduced a course entitled "Studies of Practical Problems: Temperance, Charity, Labor, Prison Discipline, Divorce, etc." It was a pioneering effort and established a policy which is now almost universally followed in the theological schools of the land. Out of the course came Peabody's most influential book, *Jesus Christ and the Social Question* (1900). It was straight, clear Enlightenment thinking.

Beginning in the twentieth century, a great change came over most of the American churches with regard to the relationship between theology and social questions. The movement became fully articulate with the publication in 1907 of Walter Rauschenbusch's *Christianity and the Social Crisis,* which established the idea of the "social gospel" in Protestant churches generally. Since that time the demand for Christian social action has increased steadily in the United States, rising to a clamor in the 1960s. It was a clear adoption within the ecclesiastical tradition of one of the basic tenets of the critical way in religion.

In the United States in the post–World War II period another of the Enlightenment teachings, pluralism, achieved acceptance among most of the churchmen. During that period Protestants, Catholics, and Jews, with increasing cordiality, began publicly to accept one another and to make common cause against such common enemies as "materialism," "secularism," and so on. Pluralism meant that there was to be more than one religious way in the United States, recognized by the churches themselves. It meant a mutual agreement on the part of the three established "faiths," Protestantism, Catholicism, and Judaism, to live and let live, and increasingly to cooperate with one another in areas of common concern.

That the principle had been written into the Constitution of the United States was no accident. The American Constitution was drawn up during the Enlightenment period by Enlightenment thinkers. Nevertheless, it was not until the 1950s, nearly two centuries later, that organized religion generally began openly to advocate pluralist principles.

Such pluralism had been achieved as early as the sixteenth century in both Romania and Poland by governmental decree. In Romania the Diet of Torda passed a decree in 1557, renewed it in 1563 and again in 1568, which provided that, "in every place the preachers shall preach and explain the gospel each according to his understanding of it, and if the congregation like it, well; if not, no one shall compel them, but they shall keep the preachers whose doctrines they approve."

In Poland, Unitarians, Calvinist Protestants, and Roman Catholics maintained a precarious coexistence under a series of enlightened rulers until the Counter Reformation swept through the country in the mid-seventeenth century and restored the former hegemony of the Roman Catholic Church. In 1573 the Polish diet passed an edict which read in part: "We senators of the . . . united republic of Poland . . . shall make oath to preserve and defend universal peace among dissidents in religion. . . . We who differ in religion will maintain peace among ourselves, and on account of difference in faith and rules of worship, will shed no blood, inflict no penalties. . . . If anyone shall oppose this contract and disturb the peace . . . we will rise up and destroy him."

Unfortunately these enlightened decrees did not represent permanent gains in the re-establishment of tolerance in Christianity. They were soon repealed or nullified, in the rising Counter Reformation that swept through Europe in the sixteenth and seventeenth centuries. Yet they were harbingers of things to come, as the doctrine of tolerance slowly gained acceptance within the ecclesiastical tradition.

Today many Roman Catholic as well as Protestant churchmen worldwide openly advocate a philosophy of tolerance that contrasts sharply with traditional views. Jewish writers, as members of a minority group, have always advocated tolerance. In fact, the principle of pluralism—tolerance, to use the older and more familiar term—has now been pushed to the point where it involves the advocacy of yet another Enlightenment principle. At the present time many Christian clergymen are openly proposing that mutual understanding, respect, and cooperation be extended to non-Christian religions, as well as to the various sects and divisions within Christianity.

Tolerance toward religions other than one's own is hardly a new idea. As we have already noted, it was the theory and practice of the Roman Empire. Stoics, Epicureans, and neo-Platonists all advocated and practiced mutual respect. The desirability of a generous attitude toward religions other than our own was never stated better than by the neo-Platonist of the fourth century A.D., Maximus of Tyre. Seeking to explain the difficulty of comprehending the nature of the deity, he wrote: "God, himself, the father and fashioner of all that is older than the Sun or the Sky, greater than time or eternity and all the flow of being, is unnameable . . . [and so we] use the help of sounds and names and pictures . . . naming all that is beautiful in this world after his nature. . . . If a Greek is stirred to remembrance of God by the art of Phidias, an Egyptian by paying worship to animals, another man by a river, another by fire . . . I have no anger for their divergences; only let them know, let them love, let them remember."

Intolerance was a Christian concept, fiercely pursued and enforced for a millennium. Nevertheless, the tolerance-idea again gained currency in Renaissance Italy. In the fifteenth century Nicholas of Cusa, whose independent and critical turn of mind we have already noted, made an eloquent plea for tolerance in his *De Pace Fidei.* There is but one religion, he argued. The deity is called by different names, and the rites by which the deity is worshipped differ from one another, but God is One and there should be no conflict between the several faiths. Herbert of Cherbury, more than a century later, was explicit on the point.

Today many churchmen openly advocate a philosophy of tolerance that contrasts sharply with traditional views. A Roman Catholic writer has suggested, for example, that "Christ is already manifesting himself [in non-Christian] religions. It is entirely possible that with the help of [Christ's] revelation elsewhere [i.e., in non-Christian religions] we shall discover new depths of meaning [again Whitehead's formula] in our own deposit of faith. Such a Catholicism would be one that had integrated all the true insights of the other religions into a comprehensive vision of the total Christ. . . . It will be the work of the Holy Spirit to help Christians understand the evidences of Christ's working beyond Christianity and at the same time to help non-Christians realize that he whom they call the Beloved [or the Supreme Reality] under different names is none other than the timeless Christ."

In 1973 a prominent Protestant clergyman and scholar declared, "I will not write off Zen or the Taj Mahal or druidic worship or the Koran as 'theirs.' They are mine too. . . . I will not let the Catholics keep St. Theresa, or the Unitarians have Michael Servetus or the Jews have Martin Buber or the Hindus have Lord Krishna all for themselves. . . . Within a span of weeks I have sensed the presence of the holy at an Apollo Temple in Delphi, a Toltec pyramid in Xochicalco and a Moslem mosque on the isle of Rhodes."

In 1974 Harvard University appointed a special committee to review the work of its Memorial Church. Agreement was not total, but a majority recommended expanding the ministry of the Church "to include a Jewish rabbi and a Catholic priest, and that other religions represented at Harvard ought to have a larger role at the Church." Many a college and university across the United States has long since taken a similar position, often much broader than that of Harvard's divided committee. So slowly does the university community attain its own objective standards when it deals with organized religion.

As a final example, the Enlightenment doctrine that heaven and hell are not real places is now enjoying open and widespread acceptance among mainline churchmen. But the idea was given clear expression at least as far back as our old friend Nicholas of Cusa in the fifteenth century. We do not go to either place when we die, according to this doctrine; if heaven and hell exist at all it is in our minds here and now. A popular news magazine ran a story on this development less than a decade ago and printed as news such Enlightenment views as the following:

> The traditional views of heaven and hell are about ninety-five percent mythology . . .
>
> —a Jesuit

> You make it or break it right here . . .
>
> —a rabbi

> Hell: not some external or arbitrary punishment that gets assigned for sin, but simply the working out of sin itself, as it destroys the distinctively personal being of the sinner . . .
>
> —a Protestant theologian

To see churchmen in various traditions openly advocating Enlightenment doctrines is to see the deep inroads critical thinking has made in ecclesiastical thinking in the West. Only a short time ago their predecessors in office roundly condemned such teachings. Even now persecution for holding such views is not far behind us. But it is astonishing almost never to see a reference to the brave and bold thinkers who first gave open expression to these ideas, except in scholarly works where the rootage of ideas is being traced.

The contrast is most vividly seen when we note how the theologians in various households of faith search out the writings of the ancients in their own traditions that support their views. Augustine and Aquinas, Luther and Calvin, Francis of Assisi and John Wesley, and a host of others are constantly appealed to for support and cited with gratitude. On the other hand, indebtedness to those who were once called "heretics," "infidels," "unbelievers," "skeptics," "agnostics," and "atheists" is seldom if ever acknowledged. When or where do you ever see a statement by an ecclesiastical leader to this effect: "The doctrine I am now advocating was first put forward by Renaissance or Enlightenment thinkers some two, three, or even four hundred years ago," naming the thinkers? Every scientist gives due credit to his intellectual forebears. Every competent scholar does the same. The critical mind would require that in religion a standard no less exacting be maintained.

11

Modern Times

Words have a way of changing their meaning despite the efforts of dictionary-makers to fix them more permanently. An example is the word "modern." For many years it has meant "contemporary." But we are now beginning to find that movements we have been calling "modern" flourished and died out so many years back they cannot be considered contemporary in any realistic sense. The "Modernist" movement in Roman Catholicism, which appeared just after 1900, has long since disappeared. "Modernism" among Protestants emerged in the United States in the early 1920s and died out soon after. Accordingly, being quite arbitrary about it, for convenience and for clarity of concept, I shall use "modern" for twentieth-century movements through the 1960s and "contemporary" for the present.

1. Liberalism and Modernism

The fundamental conflict between the critical way in religion and the ecclesiastical way entered a new phase in the movements in the twentieth century known as "Modernism." In Roman Catholicism the movement was suppressed by a papal decree in which Pius X branded the modernist movement as the "sewer of all heresies." In the Church of England and in the United States the contest was less dramatic and less abruptly ended, but the issue was the same: holding more strictly to traditional language, forms and practices, as against modification, in an attempt to square religious and secular thought with each other.

Although the name "Modernism" is no longer used, the same contest continues today. The Roman Church in the late twentieth century is experiencing a far more disruptive reform movement than that with its "Modernists" a hundred years ago. Notices of such changes appear regularly in the press. The following is a fair sample:

> "Priests Urge Probes of Mistreatment of Priests by Archbishops."
> "Pope Says Church Dissent Is 'Practically Schismatic.'"
> "Bishops Rebuffed: Pope, in Rejecting Synod's Advice, Reasserts his Supreme Authority."
> "Mass Absolution Is Granted to Catholics in Tennessee Rite."
> "Catholic Bishops in U.S. No Longer Speaking in a Single Voice"
> "Former Maryknoll Priests, Many Married, Joining in New Ministry"
> "A Broader Role for [Roman Catholic] Laity Is Stressed at Parley on Coast"
> "American Catholics Beginning to Find Their Bearings After Years of Upheaval"

Numerous books on the subject also appeared during the 1970s.

In the United States, Roman Catholic Modernism amounted to little, but in Protestantism a movement by that name created quite a stir. It emerged as a result of the impact on traditional theology of rapidly accumulating new knowledge in virtually every field of human endeavor. The situation is vividly portrayed in a set of autobiographical studies published in the early 1930s. In these retrospective writings we observe the unquestioning faith of devout young theological students dissolving under the impact of biblical criticism and the more liberal outlook of their teachers.

A typical passage by a leading theologian of the 1930s, Walter Marshall Horton, reads: "What impressed me most about Professor Lyman [of Union Theological Seminary] was his absolute intellectual integrity: his willingness to follow 'withersoever the argument leadeth' and his eagerness to apprehend new truth even if it required the revision of all his former theories. . . . One day in one of his classes it suddenly came over me that it was possible to be a Christian and remain intellectually honest at the same time. Subconsciously I had been half doubting it for years."

Horton's tribute to a beloved teacher shows the inroads the critical way was then making into the doctrinal structure of Protestant orthodoxy, and the conflict that resulted in the religious outlook of pious, believing young men. The passage shows, with equal clarity, how profound a problem critical standards posed for traditional faith and how inadequate the solutions were. What Horton failed to see was that the solution he found was not available to everyone. He was able to reconcile the unlimited pursuit of truth with his own Christian faith because he, personally, felt no need to pursue the questioning process very far. The basic tenets of his faith were never in jeopardy because he never felt the need to question them.

This became clear when, soon afterward, he repudiated his youthful liberalism and reverted to the evangelical faith in which he had been reared. "Liberalism as a system of theology has collapsed," he wrote, apparently more in relief than in sorrow. "It rationalized away the deepest Christian truths. It was only a romantic illusion." We could hardly ask for a better example of the problems liberals face when they apply the critical method in theology, stop part way along in the questioning process, yet lack a principle on the basis of which to justify their stopping.

The same flaw mars the writings of the two leading spokesmen of Protestant Modernism, Harry Emerson Fosdick, the nationally known New York preacher, and Shailer Matthews, Dean of the Chicago Divinity School. Both attempted to set apart what were considered to be the basic doctrines of the Christian revelation that should remain inviolate, while modifying in accordance with modern knowledge teachings that were not. Neither, however, dealt with the basic question, one that Christianity had been struggling with for nearly a thousand years: by what standard do you decide that certain doctrines can be modified or discarded while certain others cannot? By what standard do you determine how far the modifying process can go? The Modernists were never able to say.

Meanwhile, another religious phenomenon, also as old as the questions Modernism sought to answer, made its appearance in Protestant Europe: the "Crisis Theology" of Karl Barth. His was a clear call to the faithful to return from the vagaries of Modernism to the truths and certainties of traditional Christianity. Within a decade Reinhold Niebuhr in the United States, while he never accepted Barthianism uncritically, sounded what was essentially the same call. Others joined him; liberalism melted like summer snow and neo-orthodoxy became the order of the day. So successful were the neo-orthodox, and so completely did they dominate the religious scene for the next generation, for many years there was little attempt to deal with the problem of the conflict between the teachings of religion and the ever-widening circle of knowledge in other fields. The problem was not met; it was avoided. The arguments of the liberals were not countered; they were ignored.

A trivial incident will illustrate the situation. At a ministers' meeting in Boston in the early fifties, one of those monthly meetings that are held in cities and towns all over the country, where the clergy of various denominations meet to discuss their mutual problems and concerns, a minister introduced a paper he was to read with these words: "Now I don't want anybody to ask me whether or not these passages in the Bible with which I shall deal are true. I am not interested at the moment in whether the Bible is true; I am interested in what it *does.*" And that was the gist of his paper—the sense of well-being, of purpose and meaning that comes into your life when you believe, in this case, what Paul had written to one of the churches he founded.

In this instance, the critical mind would want to know whether that minister would advocate the same standards when dealing with his church budget. If he was running a deficit, would he demand an optimistic report in order to encourage the members and keep up their confidence? Or would he ask that the true facts be laid before them so that the problem could be dealt with realistically? In the critical tradition the standards that apply to talk about God also apply to paying the minister's salary and fixing the furnace.

2. The Dead Sea Scrolls

Writers on theology seldom stress the impact of the discovery of the Dead Sea Scrolls on Christian and Jewish thought in the twentieth century, but it was of profound importance to vast numbers of people. When the ancient Essene writings were discovered in the early 1950s, Bible scholars and theologians alike seemed to have matters pretty much back in hand. The slow process of adapting traditional faith to the findings of modern science and to those of biblical criticism had largely been worked through and resolved. To be sure, the Zadokite Fragments (also called the Damascus Document), discovered in 1895, had anticipated the Scroll discovery. But scholars had almost uniformly dismissed the Fragments as having no bearing on basic matters of faith.

Then in 1950 came the announcement by the American Schools of Oriental Research of the remarkable discovery in the caves at Qumran. Jewish and Christian scholars alike were quick to proclaim the importance of these discoveries for Old Testament studies and for a better understanding of Jewish sectarian life in the early Roman period. However, very little attention was given to the evidence in the Scrolls of similarities between the Essene Community at Qumran and the young Christian community in nearby Jerusalem. At first, questions about a possible relationship to John the Baptist, to Jesus, to the Gospel writers—Matthew, Mark, Luke, and John—were ignored by nearly all except A. Dupont-Sommer, the French scholar.

In 1955, however, Edmund Wilson, the critic and literary journalist, after prodigious study on his own, set the probability of such a connection before the reading public in a series of magazine articles. The response was like an explosion. Any Bible scholar might have done what Wilson did, and with greater authority than he could command in the highly specialized field of Old Testament and intertestamental studies. None but Dupont-Sommer had done so.

The popular clamor following the publication of Wilson's work brought some of the experts, Jewish and Christian alike, before the reading public. They, however, devoted most of their energies to the differences, not to the similarities, between the Scroll writings and the New Testament. As loyal adherents to their several religious communities, both Jews and Christians, with few exceptions, sought to open as deep a gulf as possible between Judaism, the Essene Community at Qumran, and the early Christian Church at Jerusalem. In public addresses, interviews, magazine articles, and books of many kinds, the scholars assured the people that nothing had changed and that Protestant, Catholic, and Jewish belief remained intact despite these discoveries. Preempting the field for themselves on the ground that they alone knew the languages prerequisite to Scroll study, they held to their religious faith while examining, in the most thoroughgoing critical manner, the data revealed by the Scrolls.

Summing up the accepted point of view, one scholar wrote: "The man of faith believes that God reveals himself and fulfills his purposes precisely in history. Faith is trusting this kind of God." For such a person, he concluded, the disclosure of errors in the Bible by archeologists or anyone else affects his faith in no way. The true believer will go on believing in the God who reveals himself in the Bible, whether or not the record proves faulty and whether or not other discoveries prove the Bible to be demonstrably in error.

Another scholar, engaged in a study of Christian and Jewish religious writings of the first and second centuries B.C. and the first and second centuries A.D., put the point in a broader context. Pressed by a reporter as to the possible impact of his studies on religion he said flatly: "The Pseudepigrapha [the scholarly name for these non-biblical writings] do not challenge any religious beliefs." He might have added, "provided, of course, you are among those who today increasingly accept the close interrelatedness of sectarian Judaism and primitive Christianity," a view by no means agreed upon either in Judaism or Christianity.

A generation later the formula was complete. The close relationship between the Essenes and the early Christian Church was acknowledged, but a basic distinction between the two was found in the "resurrection experience" of the first Christians and in the "scandalous" claim that flowed from it—that Jesus Christ was the promised Messiah of Israel. Declared one scholar, "There is nothing in the Scrolls even remotely like such an outrageous claim."

The widespread public interest that followed upon the revelation of the Essene Community at Qumran and their library of scrolls reminded the churchmen and the general public once more that theology, like all branches of human endeavor, must always come to terms with demonstrable facts. The Scrolls discoveries reminded everyone that such facts have a way of rising unexpectedly when everything seems to be settled.

What happened when theological debate turned from doctrines of sin and grace to the meaning of the similarities between Jesus' teaching and that of the Essenes? What happened to the uniqueness of Christ and his Church when the Dead Sea Scrolls revealed the existence of a community similar in many respects to the first Christian Church, a community close to Jerusalem and nearly contemporaneous with the earliest Christian community? What happened when orthodox scholars found passages from the New Testament reproduced in an earlier manuscript emanating from sectarian Judaism?

The answer is: far more than met the eye. In the United States civil rights activism soon caught the attention of theologians and the public alike and the Scrolls were forgotten. Yet the impact of the discovery remained. Those of critical temper had been alerted to the fact that yet more data now called into question the dogmas of uniqueness and special status with which both Judaism and Christianity are interlaced, dogmas that, since the Middle Ages, had been questioned by those of critical temper.

3. Dietrich Bonhoeffer

Among twentieth-century men of faith who sought fully and completely to address themselves to the problem set for religion by the critical tradition, none is more important than a young German theologian named Dietrich Bonhoeffer, a pivotal figure in twentieth-century Christian theology and a powerful force in the German resistance movement. Bonhoeffer was eventually taken prisoner by the Nazis. His courage, his sweetness of temper, and his ministry to his fellow prisoners won the respect of his jailers, and as a result many letters written to his parents and to certain friends were smuggled out of the prison and have been preserved. They are a remarkable set of writings.

Throughout his prison stay Bonhoeffer spent his time under the shadow of the gallows, and it is this that gives his writings special power and special meaning. There had been some review of his earlier letters by prison authorities, but there was none of his later letters. Those written to his friend Eberhard Bethge, who later edited and published them, are of particular interest for it was to Bethge that he expressed his deepest thoughts and anxieties. Bonhoeffer, like many of his contemporaries, had long been struggling with his true thoughts about God. Now, in a long letter dated July 16, 1944, realizing that the gallows stood just beyond, he wrote to Bethge what he *really* thought: "There is no longer any need for God as a working hypothesis, whether in morals, politics or science. Nor is there any need for such a God in religion or philosophy. In the name of intellectual honesty these working hypotheses should be dropped or dispensed with as far as possible."

"At this point," Bonhoeffer continues, "nervous souls start asking what room there is left for God now?" He answers his own question by detailing the various escape routes the theologians have devised in order to keep plausible the role Christianity had always assigned to God in the affairs of men. But, Bonhoeffer concludes, it can't be done. There is no way back to the old thought-structure except "at the cost of deliberately abandoning our intellectual sincerity. The only way is that of Matthew 18:3 i.e., through repentance, through *ultimate* honesty." (The italics are his.) Then follows the classic passage, quoted ten thousand times since, in which Bonhoeffer gives his view of the role of the God-hypothesis in today's world: "The only way to be honest is to recognize that we have to live in the world *etsi deus non daretur* [as if God did not exist; literally, is not given]. And this is just what we do see—before God! So our coming of age forces us to a true recognition of our situation *vis à vis* God. God is teaching us that we must live as men who can get along very well without him. The God who is with us is the God who foresakes us (Mark 15:34). The God who makes us live in this world without using him as a working hypothesis is the God before whom we are ever standing. Before God and with him we live without God."

Bonhoeffer was very much a product of the critical tradition. His father, a noted physician and psychiatrist, taught at the University of Berlin. His mother was the granddaughter of a professor of church history at Jena. As a child Bonhoeffer played with the children of the "universal theologian," Adolf von Harnack. Bonhoeffer grew up to study under Harnack and other great teachers at the University of Berlin. After a year of study at Union Theological Seminary in New York he began teaching at Berlin and continued on at that post until silenced by the Nazis.

In his letters from prison we see Bonhoeffer, steeped in the critical tradition, which in Germany in the 1930s had been absorbed totally into the university tradition. In his letters he is not saying that he had given up belief in God. His belief in God's love, care, protection, and purpose in all things was profound. What Bonhoeffer is trying to deal with is the conclusion that the role assigned to God traditionally can no longer be sustained; that there is no place for such a deity in our present thought-structure, and we simply have to face the fact.

Bonhoeffer is honest enough and scholar enough, to see that he has reached the conclusion the men of the Enlightenment reached. He is among the very few theologians to have done so and said so. Bonhoeffer is also aware of the antecedents of the Enlightenment in the Renaissance and Reformation period and he speaks of that as well. In short, while not using the words "critical tradition," he, as a product of German university life, seems to have attained a clear understanding of the movement with which we are dealing and of its inconsistency with traditional theology.

Bonhoeffer writes,

> On the historical side I should say there is *one* great development which leads to the idea of the autonomy of the world [i.e., a world explained without a belief in God]. In theology it is first discernible in Lord Herbert of Cherbury, with his assertion that reason is the sufficient instrument of religious knowledge. In ethics it first appears in Montaigne and Bodin with their substitution of moral principles

> for the ten commandments. In politics, Machiavelli, who emancipates politics from the tutelage of morality, and founds the doctrine of "reasons of state." Later, and very differently, though like Machiavelli tending toward the autonomy of human society, comes Grotius, with his international law as the law of nature, a law which would still be valid, *etsi deus non daretur.* The process is completed in philosophy. On the one hand we have the deism of Descartes, who holds that the world is a mechanism which runs on its own without any intervention of God. On the other hand there is the pantheism of Spinoza, with its identification of God with nature. In the last resort Kant is a deist, Fichte and Hegel pantheists. All along the line there is a growing tendency to assert the autonomy of man and the world.
>
> In natural science the process seems to start with Nicolas of Cusa and Giordano Bruno with their "heretical" doctrine of the infinity of space. The classical cosmos was finite, like the created world of the Middle Ages. An infinite universe, however it be conceived, is self-subsisting *etsi deus non daretur.* It is true that modern physics is not so sure as it was about the infinity of the universe, but it has not returned to the earlier conceptions of its finitude.

Bonhoeffer was hanged by the Nazis in April 1945, only a few days before the Allies reached Flossenburg, the little town to which he had been removed from Berlin. After the war the letters were published in Germany but created little stir in the English-speaking world until January 1952 when a few excerpts, including the lines quoted above, appeared in translation in *The Ecumenical Review.* In theological academic circles they created a sensation. A young professor of systematic theology, recalling years later the effect of those excerpts upon him, wrote: "I read them just before attending a meeting in New York City, where I ran into a couple of other people who had also read them. I remember that we agreed, as though we shared some guilty secret, that these pages held a sort of desperate importance for us. But just what it was we did not then understand." He found their meaning later in what he realized was the slow deterioration within himself "of that good old world of middle-of-the-road, ecumenical neo-orthodoxy." Bonhoeffer had put into words a question that an untold number of the clergy had quietly been asking themselves: where was the place for the God of traditional theology in the structure of modern thought?

Roughly three answers were given to this question. All of them attained prominence in the 1960s and they were very nearly contemporaneous. Two came from the academic community and one from the church. They were the "Death of God" movement, the "Honest to God" movement, and "Christian Secularity." No one would claim that Bonhoeffer alone was the cause of these movements. The cumulative effect of a thousand years of thought and scholarship is the explanation. Bonhoeffer's part lay in the fact that he, a devout Christian clergyman and a scholar of impeccable reputation, put into clear, unmistakable language the dilemma to which a millennium of independent thinking had at last brought the religion of the West. His words were the more shattering because he had written them from the valley of the shadow of death. When Dietrich Bonhoeffer asked what role the traditional God plays in modern life, the question could not be ignored. It hit with all the more force if the reader had secretly been asking such questions himself.

4. The Death of God and Christian Secularism

The "Death of God" was the earliest of the movements within the mainline churches to attempt an answer to Bonhoeffer's question. Starting from the metaphor of Nietzsche, a small group of Christian scholars declared that the traditional God of the West had died and that some new vital and equally comprehensive concept was now needed as a substitute. The movement went up like a skyrocket, for a brief period lit up the night sky of theology, and, like a skyrocket, soon vanished from everyone's sight, including apparently that of its own advocates.

The idea of the "Death of God" was still echoing around theological circles in 1967 when William Hamilton, a leading exponent, openly admitted his disappointment and frustration at trying to use the news media to communicate theology to the masses. Another leader of the movement, Thomas J. J. Altizer, nearly a decade later no longer spoke of the death of God. Instead, he summoned Christians back to the fullness of the biblical faith. Paul Van Buren, another of the leaders, openly repudiated the movement in an Easter sermon preached in New York City. With wide notice in the press, he declared that the Death of God movement had really been an admission of defeat. "It left out of account the fundamental thing the Gospel is about. It is about God. If we can't understand 'God', that is our problem. We have to be willing to talk about God as something we don't understand."

The Death-of-God people were reaching toward a fundamental truth, but they chose an unfortunate metaphor through which to express it. The God whose death they announced was by definition eternal and could not die. They were really saying not that God had died but that the concept of God long held by Christianity and Judaism is now obsolete for great numbers of people. In this they were right, but they would have conveyed their meaning more clearly had they said it that way: that our *concept* of God had undergone a drastic change. They might better have said: "Beginning as a kind of superman who walked in Eden in the cool of the day, God in the mind of the West grew from multiple tribal dieties into the one God of all. Thence he grew into the God of the planets, the moon, and the spheres of classical Christian times. Meanwhile, his miracles became remote, his heaven grew more distant and at last he himself became so vague that the God-concept lost all meaning. With that, the traditional God vanished except as an ultimate principle in a philosophico-theological system, the Unmoved Mover of Aristotle, the Principle of Concretion of Whitehead, or the God beyond God of Tillich."

Superficially the Death-of-God movement might seem to be an aspect of the critical tradition, since the proponents of the idea were asking searching questions about the God-idea and were giving remarkably critical answers to their own questions. But the movement had at its center the same flaw so many other liberal movements have had: an unwillingness to pursue the questioning process all the way to the end. The Death-of-God writers, in various ways and in varying degrees, kept what seemed to them to be the major Christian commitments. The movement had a second major flaw, the metaphor—the death of God—through which they sought to express themselves. It was dramatic, attention-getting, but essentially misleading, for none of the group believed that God had once lived and now was dead. All they meant was that certain older ideas of God were no longer held by themselves or by large numbers of other people. It was scarcely a new idea. All that was new was their flamboyant use of Nietzsche's startling announcement made back in the 1880s that God is dead and that it is we who have killed him.

The greatest surge of Bonhoeffer-type thinking resulted from a thin, easy-to-read paperback written by a bishop of the Church of England, John A. T. Robinson. Having pondered Bonhoeffer's words he published his reactions in 1962 under the title *Honest to God.* He, too, was a scholar; former Dean of Clare College, Cambridge, and Chaplain of Wells Theological College. His book became a runaway bestseller for both clergy and laity. In it vast numbers of people found release for their religious anxieties and also, a method of dealing with their unspoken doubts about the traditional deity. Robinson made two points that were very welcome to his readers: (1) None of us any longer believes in the God of tradition. (2) Not merely church people, but the church itself must become active in the world for the improvement of human society. Both of these should be recognized as Enlightenment principles.

Like the Death-of-God movement, the Honest-to-God movement also faded out before the end of the decade. It ended according to Whitehead's formula, with a less restricted view of ancient dogma than had prevailed heretofore, but with the assertion by the churchmen that nothing basic had changed and that new light had now been shed on the old problem of God's relation to the world. And like so many contemporary religious thinkers, Robinson also embraced Enlightenment principles once bitterly denounced by orthodox clergymen, but without acknowledging that he was doing so. Speaking of Christ as the revelation of God above all others, Robinson wrote: "Yet there are other faces of God, other aspects of reality reflected in other great religions and in various facets of humanism." In this he harked back more than three hundred years to Herbert of Cherbury.

The third movement that grew out of the writings of Dietrich Bonhoeffer and the accelerating disbelief of the post-war period was called Christian secularism or "secularity." Gabriel Vahanian, whose book *The Death of God* set going the movement of that name, had spoken of the secularization of Christianity. By it he meant the entry of the Church into the world; in short, the social gospel. This was in 1961. The idea, not new with Vahanian, culminated in Harvey Cox's *The Secular City* (1965), another theological bestseller that came out of the academic community. Cox, too, advocated the entrance of the Church into the world, and like the other Christian secularists, made no acknowledgment of his Enlightenment roots or even of Walter Rauschenbusch, the first great advocate of the Church's participation in the secular world. Like its predecessors, Christian secularity also soon faded from sight. Harvey Cox, for example, turned his attention to more aesthetic and liturgical matters. The torrent of books on Christian secularism had virtually dried up by 1968.

One final aspect of the upheaval of the 1960s was *aggiornamento* in the Roman Catholic Church, the sweeping movement of reform instituted by Pope John XXIII. Out of his spirit came Vatican II and the many changes resulting from it. One of the most noteworthy was the new mood of amity and cooperation with other churches that now characterizes the relationship of the Roman Church and its clergy with other churches and clergy. Heretofore exclusionist, the Roman attitude is now one of mutual tolerance, respect, and cooperation. Nevertheless, as in Protestantism, a recession has set in with a new attempt to reassert the old doctrines and practices and to bring the reform movement to a halt.

Judaism appears to have been little affected by current theological upheavals. Jews speak of attrition, the loss of active adherents, particularly among the young, but the strength of the movement as a religion appears to continue. Today only a very small organized movement consonant with the critical tradition exists in Judaism. Its leader is Rabbi Sherman T. Wine of Birmingham, Michigan, who calls himself a humanist. The movement publishes a small quarterly but appears to have limited influence as yet.

The chief problem "Humanistic Judaism" faces is the same as the one liberal movements in Christianity have faced: that the critical principle once taken up cannot be set down again. In Christianity the unwillingness to give up belief in certain doctrines considered to be basic marks the point at which the critical approach is abandoned. The point varies from group to group, but in each case the critical way stops at the point where a prior commitment to certain articles of faith begins. In Humanistic Judaism it is the same except that there the prior commitment is not theological but parochial. As one contributor to the humanistic quarterly wrote, rejecting membership, "I personally hope that some day everybody will abandon the parochialism of his religion and his nationality."

None of these controversies can be said to have been resolved. Instead in the United States they sank from sight in the more vivid concerns of the civil rights movement. This can be said really to have begun in the 1950s with the bus boycott organized in Montgomery, Alabama by a young black minister named Martin Luther King, Jr. While the Christian clergy were debating the Death-of-God movement, the Honest-to-God movement, and Christian secularism, the blacks, at first joined by a few committed whites, and subsequently by large numbers of clergy, were out in the streets, marching, picketing, protesting, conducting sit-ins, kneel-ins, and pray-ins. Out of the bruises and bloodshed, out of the speeches and pamphlets of that movement, arose a clamor for legislation to improve the lot of the black people in the United States. This social upheaval and the writings in theology that were contemporaneous all go together. The one is not understandable without the other. The two taken together mean the translation of moral principles into action, the translation of religion into life.

Conclusion

In an attempt to identify the critical way in religion, to delineate its character, and to assess its importance, we have now completed an overview of its history. The account, necessarily, has been rapid. Inevitably, it is also cursory. Nevertheless, we may now ask: what does the story tell us? Seen in the perspective of twenty-five centuries, what principles emerge? What characteristics of the critical way in religion does the story enable us to identify?

Above all else, perhaps, in the critical tradition in the religion of the West, we see the demand for freedom of thought and expression, the right to be critical, to point out errors, mistakes, and moral wrongs even when committed by those of high rank in church and state; the right to dissent from the claims of civil and ecclesiastical authority and the right to introduce new ideas even when they threaten to disrupt the existing order.

We see the demand for freedom coming as a direct result of the stubborn opposition of the Church to criticism and innovation. The story of the development of the critical tradition in the West presents a picture familiar to all students of culture: that of a human institution, in this case the Church, striving to maintain order, continuity, regularity, stability, and authority, but tending to congeal in the process, as human institutions seem always to do. The hardening process in turn aggravated the conflict with the critical tradition in which new ideas were generated and criticism of the old gained expression. The more rigid and repressive the Church became, the more urgent became the protest of imaginative and critical minds.

The continuing attempt to suppress innovation and criticism, both without and within the Church, resulted in the continued re-fighting of old battles, in apparent ignorance of earlier, nearly identical conflicts. History never repeats itself exactly, but in the long struggle between the ecclesiastical and the critical tradition in the West, it has often done so in a general sense, and still does with impressive regularity. The same issues appear again and again in different places and at different times, and the same arguments in slightly different guise are used over and over.

The story of the struggle between the critical and the ecclesiastical tradition shows yet another tendency in religious institutions. Movements that begin in criticism, reform, and innovation, protesting against the intransigence of established religious thought and practice, either disappear or, when they become stabilized, they too grow resistant to change. Until the Protestant Reformation all such movements were either crushed by the Church, as with the Albigensians, or they were enveloped by the Church, as were the monastic movements like the Franciscan Order. With the coming of the Reformation a dramatic break occurred, but the change it brought about was short-lived. Churches with their origins in protest and rebellion, once they had established their independence began to regularize their own thought and practice, while protest, innovation, and change were lost sight of or suppressed altogether.

The resulting growth pattern of organized religion in the West resembles that of the hemlock tree, a pattern that is nearly unique among the evergreens. Pines, spruces, and firs grow by sending skyward a single central vertical shoot. Hemlocks, on the other hand, grow by sending skyward a small delicately curving branch. The growth patterns of the two types of tree may be diagrammed as follows:

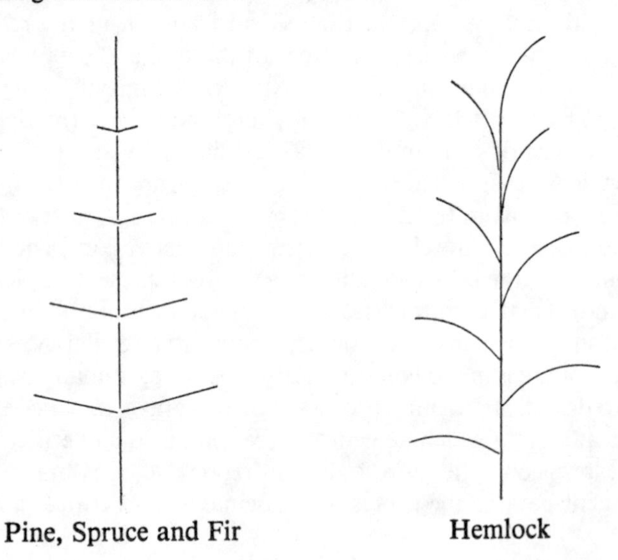

Unlike the pines, spruces, and firs the topmost tassle ("leader" in forestry language) on a hemlock does not eventually become a section of the main trunk of the tree, with side branches growing out of it. With the hemlock, the topmost tassle or leader eventually becomes a side branch. Thereafter, that branch remains permanently where it is, never moving up or down the main trunk, no matter how large or how old either grows to be. Meanwhile, the tree itself grows upward by sending out a single new shoot from the base of its topmost branch. The base section, in turn, eventually straightens up and becomes a part of the main tree trunk. On the analogy of the hemlock, the story of the growth and development of religious institutions in the West can be diagrammed as follows:

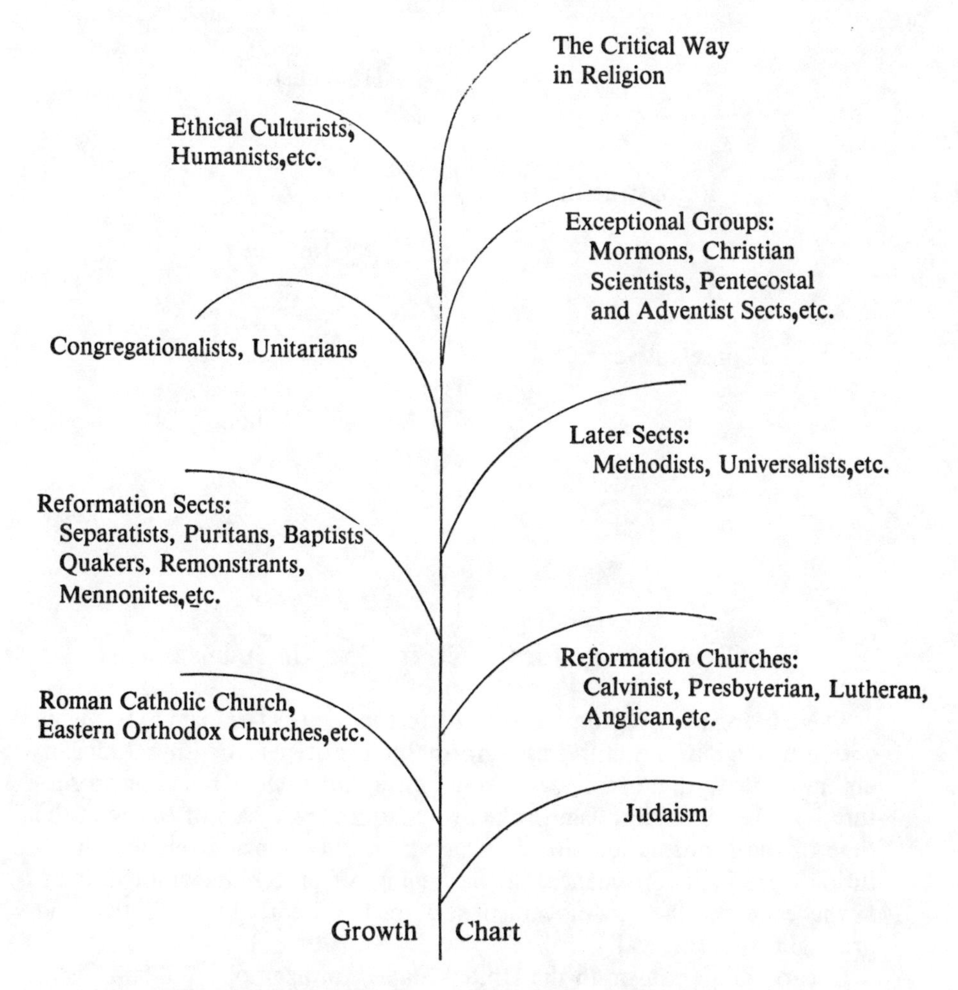

The Critical Way in the Religion of the West

Some may find this diagram pejorative. They may ask why their particular religious affiliation is regarded as a side branch on the tree of religious institutions, while other churches and temples that seem to them to be inferior are placed at the growing point at the top. There is a sense in which almost any ecclesiastical organization may be likened to the growth pattern of the hemlock tree. Let us take Judaism as an example: In the accompanying diagram, for historical reasons only, Judaism is the lowest branch on the religious institutional tree since, chronologically, Judaism came first. Like most organized religions, however, Judaism is far from being the stable, uniform, thoroughly established institution such a diagram implies. Instead, Judaism, like most organized religious movements, can be said to duplicate the pattern of the hemlock tree in its own pattern of growth.

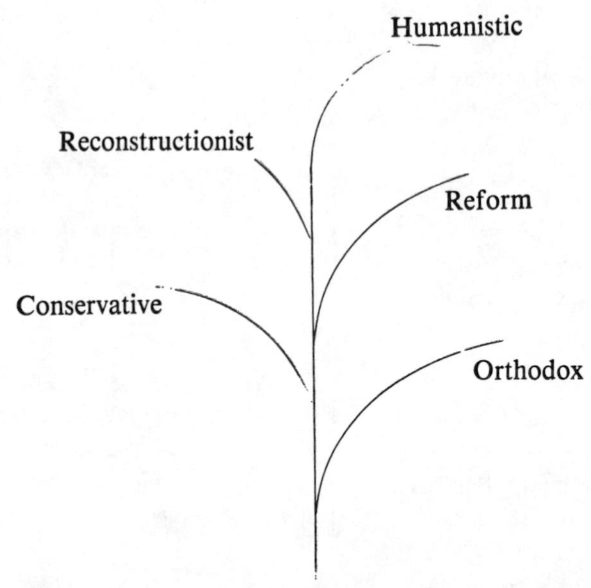

Growth Chart for the Critical Way in Judaism

There is apparently a fundamental difference between reform movements within a religious structure, as Reform Judaism remains within Judaism, and movements that break away from or are thrust out of the parent structure, as when Protestantism broke away from the Church of Rome at the time of the Reformation. But it is apparent only. Once a religious institution gains its independence, the hardening-off process inevitably sets in, as the leaders of the new movement seek to stabilize it, give it identity, and provide for its survival.

In early Unitarianism in the United States, for example, William Ellery Channing, its founder, was dismayed by an attempt to peg the thought and practice of the movement at its point of origin. "Old Unitarianism must undergo important modification or developments," he insisted. "This I have felt for years. . . . It began as a protest against the rejection of reason—against mental slavery. It pledged itself to progress as its life and end; but it had gradually grown stationary, and now we have a *Unitarian orthodoxy.*" On the other hand, the Roman Catholic Church, now some nineteen centuries old, found it necessary in 1976 and 1977 to discipline a cardinal who objected to the attempts of the Second Vatican Council to modernize the practice of the Church.

Like the hemlock, the critical way in religion produces one new branch after another, each growing out of the main stem of organized religion in the West. Like the hemlock, each new movement of protest and creativity is for a brief time the growing point of institutionalized religion. Then, like the hemlock, the growth pattern of the new movement shifts from the vertical to the horizontal. It becomes a branch rather than the growing point on the main stem of organized religion. Its form becomes fixed, and while as a branch it may become very large, its growth afterward is lateral rather than vertical.

No analogy is ever complete or wholly adequate, and I do not pretend that this one is. But the point it is designed to convey is not thereby invalidated. It is not my purpose to attempt a diagram of ecclesiastical history in the West, but rather to stress a single aspect of that history of fundamental importance to the critical tradition; namely, the tendency of reform movements, especially in Christianity, to harden off. The hemlock analogy is designed to show how reform movements in religion in the West, after initially embracing at least in part the liberating, reforming principle central in the critical tradition, tend to abandon it, once the new movement becomes established. Meanwhile, new developments come out of the main stem of Western religion under the continuing impact of critical thought.

PART III

The Ecclesiastical Way and Human Fallibility

12

Belief and Faith

In Part II we saw how the critical tradition in religion arose in reaction to the uncritical standards of the ecclesiastical tradition. We saw the clash between the two approaches to religion, once fierce and bloody, slowly grow quiescent as critical standards gained ever wider acceptance among the organized churches. Today critical standards are acclaimed in large areas of the ecclesiastical tradition. Nevertheless, the clash with the critical tradition continues at the point where its application threatens basic articles of religious faith.

From one point of view, no conflict whatever should be expected. Both the critical and the ecclesiastical mind take our human limitations as their point of departure. The critical mind thinks of the human creature as error-prone and easily deceived and therefore badly in need of some corrective device. The ecclesiastical mind thinks of the human creature as finite, mortal, limited, unable to know the truth, do the right, or act wisely without divine help, usually delivered through ecclesiastical channels.

At this point, however, agreement ends and the clash between the two begins. The critical mind thinks that our limitations belong to us as organisms inadequately equipped to do all we might like to do and know all we might like to know. It holds that we can best overcome these limitations by the constant unrelenting process of checking, testing, and reconceptualizing what we suppose ourselves to know.

The ecclesiastical mind, on the other hand, thinks of the human creature as finite, mortal, weak, and helpless, in contrast to God who is thought to be infinite, omniscient, immortal, and omnipotent. Christianity in particular has centered its teaching on what it thinks of as our "fallen" state, our consequent sinfulness and our inability to help ourselves unless we are aided in all these things by God's grace.

Organized religion in the West resorted to the concept of faith as a means by which we might rise above the lowly, helpless condition it believed ours to be. There is a sense in which the Roman Catholic doctrine of infallibility, a doctrine accepted by faith, serves just such a purpose. The circumstances under which this extraordinary teaching was first promulgated are instructive. On December 8, 1864, Pius IX issued, without conciliar support, the dogma of the Immaculate Conception. On the same day he issued the encyclical *Quanta Cura* with a *Syllabus errorum* appended to it, in which he censured the "errors" of pantheism, naturalism, nationalism, indifferentism, socialism, communism, and so on. He also made extraordinary claims of temporal authority and power for the papacy and denounced freedom of conscience, of worship, and of tolerance.

The encyclical was aimed at the liberals among the Catholics who were growing powerful at the time. A great controversy ensued within the church and a Vatican Council was summoned to settle it. The Council went to the heart of the matter. Rather than debate the doctrine of the Immaculate Conception or the Syllabus of Errors, the Council adopted and proclaimed the dogma of (the pope's) papal infallibility when he speaks *ex cathedra* in matters of faith and morals. That settled it. If the pope could not be wrong, there was nothing to debate, and the doctrine of the Immaculate Conception and the Syllabus of Errors were allowed to stand.

While neither Protestantism nor Judaism holds doctrines comparable to that of papal infallibility, both, in their major divisions, have essentially the same stance. Both proclaim officially, as does Rome, that through faith human limitations can be overcome in the field of religion.

Within all three groups however, there is great dissent from this view, and in widely varying degrees, among clergy and laity alike. For example, a noted Roman Catholic scholar, commenting on this problem, said: "Infallible statements of Christian realities are not possible . . .; I am required to hold what intellectual honesty demands. . . . In the end I will stand before God, not before the Vatican."

Despite such signs of change, of which there are an increasing number today, it is still an open question as to how far these changes will go. Organized religion continues to be centered in the importance of believing, of having faith. Ecclesiastics today are not accustomed to ask: *How do you know the truth whereof you speak?* They ask rather: *What do you profess? To what truth do you bear witness?* The critical mind takes an opposite position. It is as interested in the credentials of knowledge as in knowledge itself. For the critical mind, alleged knowledge is only opinion unless its foundations have been checked and are known to be dependable.

Here then is the basic issue between the critical and the ecclesiastical way in religion. The ecclesiastical tradition insists that the knowledge it holds through faith is true knowledge, and that it is backed by all the credentials anyone could ask. The critical tradition, on the other hand, holds that the knowledge the ecclesiastical mind supposes itself to possess cannot withstand critical examination. Which is right? Which can make the more persuasive case?

1. Creeds

In chapter 4 we saw how believing came to take a central place in the religions of the West. We saw that making belief central also made central the question of which beliefs were "right" and which were not. The pressing need for clear, self-consistent statements of accepted beliefs then become paramount and resulted in the establishment of what is called "tradition" in Judaism and Islam, and of the creeds in Christianity. From the start, all three religions have been concerned not with how we know the truth and how we can be sure it *is* the truth: they have been concerned with persuading people to accept the truths that religion (theirs) gives us. They have attempted to explain how the God they worship has acted in human history with regard to that truth. Above all, they have been concerned with the importance of believing that the events recorded in their Sacred Scriptures were true—that they had really occurred, and that those events had transformed our human condition. For Christianity and Islam that meant, in particular, the transformation of our prospects in life after death as well as in the life we are given to live here on Earth.

Each of these religions sought to reduce its beliefs to a simple formula, a declaration of faith to be made by the believer. Judaism has the Shemah—"Hear O Israel the Lord our God is one." The Christians have the Apostles Creed, the Nicene Creed, and, in recent times, a wide variety of other formulas and credos. Islam, as the first of its Five Pillars, has the Kalimah, or profession of faith: "There is no God but Allah and Muhammad is his messenger."

But no creed, statement of faith, or set of principles, however lengthy or concise, ever quite does the job. The best of them seldom succeed in saying what a particular individual really believes. The best of them represent a compromise between many points of view; yet, the chance that any such compromise will state exactly what any particular individual happens to think is remote. Human thought is too complex and the shades of meaning in words too varied.

Over and beyond the question of whether it is possible to reduce religious belief to exact language lies the fact of obsolescence. Let us suppose for a moment that a satisfactory creed could be drawn up. How long would it last? Learned orthodox clergymen, believers in the use of creeds, have, in some instances, pointed out that in the nature of things a creed is already obsolescent when it is adopted. Inevitably, it represents the thought of the past, not that of the present, and certainly not that of the future. Any attempted statement of truth inevitably becomes archaic with the passage of time. The older the creed, the more obsolete it is likely to be. At last the day comes when it no longer conveys any real meaning to the worshiper unless it is explained in contemporary language or recast in contemporary language and concepts.

We have already reviewed at some length the manner in which creed making, creed using, and the idea of "right belief" became dominant in Christianity. In Judaism the accumulated thought and practice of the ages played the same role. Central in Judaism has been the "Halakah," which means "the Law." The word can equally well be translated "the Way." It is considered by many to be the essence of Judaism since it regulates Jewish life, ranging from lofty ethical principles to dietary rules. In Judaism the Law or the Way is seen as the means by which Jews, now dispersed throughout the world, and in the Jewish homeland as well, keep their covenant with the Lord of Israel. It is all spelled out in the Old Testament. And yet, because it has been interpreted in so many ways by respected thinkers, the Halakah has also often been the most divisive force in Judaism, each body of interpreters feeling quite certain that theirs was the one true interpretation.

In Islam the idea of "right belief" based upon revelation reaches its ultimate point of development. The Qur'an is held by Muslims to be the record of God's direct revelation to Muhammad, in fact to contain *in toto* the very words that God spoke to the Prophet. While Muhammad wrote nothing himself, his report of what he heard is regarded as having been accurately recorded by his close associates soon after his death. The record, it is said, was assembled from "scraps of parchment and leather, tablets of stone, ribs of palm branches, camel's shoulder blades and ribs, pieces of board, and the breasts of men." This last phrase refers to the tradition of learning by rote in the East, relied upon for accuracy since ancient times.

In the end, a panel of experts determined what was and what was not to be included in the body of Muslim sacred writings, and in what form it should appear. So deeply and completely did the followers of Muhammad believe in the validity of the very words of his revelation that they have held from the beginning that the Qur'an is untranslatable. Even the attempt would be blasphemous, and in any event would be impossible. They have insisted that, since God spoke to Muhammad in Arabic, in that language and in those literal words alone his message must ever remain.

We saw in part II that the idea of "right belief" in Christianity, Judaism, and Islam meant the suppression and virtual disappearance of the critical way in all three religions. Each demanded conformity from its adherents. Each required overt assent to the prevailing tenets of the religion and each strove to control, by various means, the expression of dissent. In this undertaking each was extraordinarily successful. As a result, in particular in Christianity, credalism is with us still.

Today, in Christianity, for example, the Nicene Creed continues to be used in Catholic and in many Protestant churches. The Apostles Creed is used in a large number of Protestant churches. Judging these archaic, however, some churches have developed new creeds or "statements of faith," using more modern concepts and language. An example is the Statement of Faith adopted in 1959 by the United Church of Christ when it was formed by the merger of the Congregational-Christian Churches and the Evangelical and Reformed Churches. It reads:

> We believe in God, the Eternal Spirit, Father of our Lord Jesus Christ and our Father, and to his deeds we testify:
>
> He calls the worlds into being,
> creates man in his own image
> and sets before him the ways of life and death.
>
> He seeks in holy love to save all people from aimlessness and sin.
>
> He judges men and nations by his righteous will
> declared through prophets and apostles.
>
> In Jesus Christ, the man of Nazareth, our crucified and risen Lord,
> he has come to us
> and shared our common lot,
> conquering sin and death
> and reconciling the world to himself.
>
> He bestows upon us his Holy Spirit,
> creating and renewing the Church of Jesus Christ,
> binding in covenant faithful people of all ages, tongues, and races.
>
> He calls us into his Church
> to accept the cost and joy of discipleship,
> to be his servants in the service of men,
> to proclaim the gospel to all the world
> and resist the powers of evil,
> to share in Christ's baptism and eat at his table,
> to join him in his passion and victory.
>
> He promises to all who trust him
> forgiveness of sins and fullness of grace,
> courage in the struggle for justice and peace,
> his presence in trial and rejoicing,
> and eternal life in his kingdom which has no end.
>
> Blessing and honor, glory and power be unto him. Amen.

Here is a direct and honest attempt to get over the obstacles that ancient creeds present to the modern mind. The United Church of Christ makes it clear that it is not a creed in the strict sense, but a "statement of faith" that is widely accepted as a modern interpretation of Christianity. Members of the United Church are said to be free in their decisions with regard to it. But does it solve the problem faced by the critical mind? It surely bears witness to Christian preoccupation with believing. Consider what it says. To do that we have first to translate it from its orotund phraseology into language that is a little more precise. The result of such an effort might read:

> *We believe that God exists. We hold that he is spiritual, not corporeal, in nature. We believe that he has always existed and always will. We believe too that God is the Father of Jesus Christ who, in turn, is our "Lord." This is a metaphor. It means that God's relationship to Jesus is like that of father and son. In the same metaphorical sense, God is a father to all of us. He cares for us, guides us, and helps us through the problems and trials of life.*

Mothers usually do these things to an even more conspicuous degree than do fathers. Why God is not also a mother in the metaphorical sense, the creed does not say. Here the creed runs into the problem all of us face today as we try to desexualize our language, a problem I have faced in writing this book. The language of the United Church of Christ creed involves this problem in an acute form. If God is a father in a metaphorical sense, he is also a mother in the same sense and a creed, because it seeks total truth, surely ought to say so. But it does not because people were not usually aware of the sexism in language a generation ago when the statement was drawn up.

To continue, in an attempt to make clear to ourselves what the United Church of Christ statement of faith means, it seems to say:

> *We believe that God intervenes in human history, and we now together list some of the things God does. Out of nothing he creates the planets and the stars. Using himself as a model, he creates man, whose destiny is to be born, to live, and then to die.*
>
> *Moved by love, God tries to prevent men from doing wrong and from living a life that is without purpose.*
>
> *God has special emissaries here on earth, his apostles and prophets. They have told us, correctly, that God is righteous. God is also a cosmic judge, and he pronounces judgment on individual men and upon nations as well, according to their merits.*

Need the translation be carried further? Confronted with statements like the foregoing, the critical mind is not enlightened. Assuming the desirability of a creed, how is this one superior to the Apostles' or Nicene Creed? How is our thinking clarified by saying that God "calls the worlds into being," rather than that he is "maker of heaven and earth"? The older language is far more explicit. Is there a gain in substituting vagueness for clarity? What is intended here? If we say God "calls the worlds into being," are we making an article of religious faith out of the present scientific theory of cosmic evolution?

The purpose of the foregoing analysis is not to discredit this "statement of faith," but to show the problems involved in the creed-making process itself. The United Church of Christ Statement of Faith was painstakingly worked out in the late 1950s and adopted only after the most thoroughgoing study and debate. It is as conscientious an attempt at creed drafting as one could ask and probably could not be improved upon. For the critical mind, however, far from being a vehicle for the expression of a true and heartfelt religion, it is instead an obstacle to the very purpose it was intended to serve.

The difficulties that creeds of any kind involve are sometimes overcome when a clergyman has explained what he believes to be the true meaning of the words. But for many conscientious people, and many of those who get around to formal affiliation with a church are conscientious, the problem is still there when they are asked to rise and recite the creed aloud with the congregation on Sunday morning. If they stop to think about the meaning of the words they are saying, even with all the explanations and interpretations of the clergy in mind, many of them find they still only half understand what they are saying, half believe it, or perhaps they hardly believe it at all.

Two generations ago a liberal churchman reached this conclusion and said so plainly. "Creeds, like miracles, once held to be supports of religious faith, have now become burdens upon it," he wrote. "A free church can have no creed. . . . It is well known that there has never been uniformity of belief in all the points of any creed, and it should be evident that such agreement is psychologically impossible. The attempt to enforce belief in creeds leads to divisions and throws doubt upon more important features of the faith. . . . The profession of any traditional creed in our day weakens religion, and weakens the character of religious people."

Apparently, it is a problem that just will not go away. In 1977 the two great divisions of the Presbyterian Church in the United States, attempting to unite, foundered upon this question. For the Presbyterian it was in essence: could the Westminster Confession of 1648 be broadened, perhaps replaced, or must it be adhered to as written?

A young churchman of my acquaintance found himself struggling with these problems in connection with the Prayer of General Confession used in many Protestant churches. Repeating it with the congregation Sunday after Sunday and realizing that neither he nor the congregation really meant what they were saying, he printed the following revision in the order of service one Sunday and led the congregation in its use. A few were mildly displeased; most were delighted. This is his revision. I have italicized his insertions.

> Almighty and most merciful Father, we have erred and strayed from thy ways like lost sheep. We have followed too much the devices and desires of our own hearts, *sort of.* We *perhaps* have offended against

> thy holy laws. We have left undone *a little bit of* some of those things which we ought to have done, and we have done some of those things which we ought not to have done. But thou, O Lord, have mercy upon us, *even if we don't need it.* Spare thou those, O God, who confess their faults, *but don't let them off too easily.* Restore thou those who are *pathetically gloomy,* penitent *creatures,* according to thy promises declared unto mankind in Christ Jesus our Lord. And grant, O most merciful Father, *while you are at it,* that we may hereafter live a godly, righteous, and sober life, to the glory of thy holy name. Amen.

The reason for this sort of thing is plain. Creeds, even when they settle theological arguments at the time they are drawn up, grow archaic. As Tennyson said, "Time makes ancient good uncouth." The need for revision and updating is ever present if a creed is to reflect the inner thoughts of the worshiper who recites it. Apparently a creed really adequate to its own purposes is an impossibility.

2. Revising and Interpreting Religious Belief

One reason the problem of the creeds is acute is that they are backed by an enormous and impressive literature. The creeds have been expounded and defended by the greatest churchmen—Augustine and Ambrose, Anselm and Aquinas, no less than by the leaders of our own time. Yet the very age and stature of the older writings is a part of the problem. They, no less than the original creeds, were written from an intellectual background and from a cultural milieu far different from ours. Their words, like those of the creeds, have to be interpreted in order to be understood and made acceptable to the contemporary mind.

Secondly, because the creeds are so ancient, they have acquired a special sanctity and are now surrounded with so many tender associations, that few want to give them up, and there is great reluctance even to attempt a revision. Instead, the approach is now usually to show how the old words may still be kept, while they are interpreted symbolically with the stress laid upon their inner and deeper message rather than their literal meaning.

Since the turn of the century, thinkers in the ecclesiastical tradition have tended increasingly to argue that the ancient beliefs of organized religion in the West, despite the archaic form in which they are often cast, are, nevertheless, quite acceptable to the contemporary mind: that while they cannot really be proved, they cannot be *dis*proved either. You *can* believe if you *want* to, they say. It may be difficult; it may take some effort on your part, but it can be done.

The visitor to a theological library is sure to be impressed by the prodigious effort in this direction that has been expended down the years by those who center religion in belief. The sheer volume of publications dedicated to the proposition that you *can* believe if you *want* to, explaining what the "right" beliefs are, and trying to make them consistent with modern knowledge, is itself almost beyond belief. And the end has not come. New titles on what to believe and how to believe it are still appearing. Here is a very small sample list:

1895 A. J. Balfour, *Foundations of Belief*
1899 Wm. Newton Clarke, *Can I Believe in God the Father?*
1915 G. T. Ladd, *What Should I Believe?*
1926 Charles Gore, *Can We Then Believe?*
1938 J. S. Whale, *The Right to Believe*
1948 Vergilius Ferm, *What Can We Believe?*
1958 Gerald Kennedy, *I Believe*
1961 Norman Pittenger, *The Pathway to Believing*
1967 Leslie Paul, *Alternatives to Christian Belief*
1972 Helmut Thielicke, *How to Believe Again*
1974 Richard L. Purtill, *Reason to Believe*
1976 Randolph C. Miller, *This We Can Believe*
1977 James C. Suggs, ed., *This We Believe*

In 1976 a leading Protestant evangelical publishing house began issuing a number of books advertised as a "new series that affirms old beliefs." Titles already in print or projected include:

I Believe in the Resurrection of Jesus
I Believe in the Holy Spirit
I Believe in the Revelation
I Believe in the Creation
I Believe in Prayer
I Believe in the Historical Jesus
I Believe in Man
I Believe in the Church

All this effort is lost on the critical mind, however, since none of it addresses the fundamental critical question: *How do you know?* In a moment of anger Sigmund Freud once wrote, "Where questions of religion are concerned, people are guilty of every possible sort of dishonesty and intellectual misdemeanor." He was answering the argument that you can still believe if you want to; that no one has ever *dis*proved the claims of religious faith. He was answering the question: why should one *not* believe, since the teachings of religion have so much on their side—tradition, the agreement of mankind, and all the consolations they offer?

"Why not indeed?" Freud demanded to know indignantly. "Do not let us deceive ourselves that arguments like these take us along the road of correct thinking. If ever there was a case of a lame excuse, we have it here. Ignorance is ignorance; no right to believe anything can be derived from it."

As we saw in chapter 2, believing for the sake of believing has by no means died out. Millions, inside religion and outside of it, seem to be far more willing to believe than to think. There are today, for example, people who are ready to believe that plants can be made to grow better by sweet talk than by sound horticultural methods. Laborious experiments have shown that moisture and carbon dioxide in the breath are the causative factors. In fact, as an aid to plant growth in these experiments, swearing proved quite as effective as prayer. But no matter: the belief continues.

True believers are not dissuaded by tedious *dis*proof of their ideas. Believers in the Sasquatch, the Abominable Snowman, the Loch Ness Monster and what not else apparently hold to these things merely because they want to. Bible scholars themselves have had to deal with this phenomenon. As an example, the late 1960s and 70s found them attempting to refute a theory that Canaanites of Bible times had made their way to the New World. The belief was supported by alleged Canaanitic inscriptions on stone found in various parts of North and South America. Careful technical rebuttal by scholars of established reputation did little to dissuade the believers. They angrily rejected the disproofs as a conspiracy by the religious "establishment" to conceal the "truth" from the public.

One of the most acute observers of the contemporary religious scene, Martin E. Marty, details the struggle of belief with unbelief in American religion. Beginning with his *New Shape of American Religion,* which appeared in 1958, Marty has published a series of books dealing with dissenters, schismatics, and unbelievers of the past century or more. Because of his extraordinarily wide reading, his books are not merely thoroughly documented, but his notes and bibliographies give the reader a sense of the sweep of modern unbelief and the mass of writing on the subject, both lay and clerical. Typical of such writing is a series of books that began in 1961 with *The Future of Unbelief* by Gerhard Szczeny. This was followed in 1965 with *Belief and Unbelief* by Michael Novak. *The Future of Belief* by Leslie Dewart came a year later, and *The Future of Belief Debate* finished the succession in 1969 with a summary of the conflicting views as seen in book reviews.

If, however, we turn from the writings of the believers to the unbelievers they are so much concerned about, we make a surprising discovery. The so-called unbeliever is not concerned about his unbelief at all. Often he would not even think of himself in that manner. There are two errors into which present-day writers on unbelief almost invariably fall. In the first place, they seem to think that the unbeliever suffers great anguish because he can no longer accept the beliefs of his church. Quite the opposite is the case. A number have no feelings at all about their supposed "unbelief." Many more enjoy a sense of relief and freedom from bondage. They will tell you quite frankly they are glad to have rid themselves of a restricting thought-structure they think is invalid.

Leslie Stephen, writing in an autobiographical vein, observed with regard to his becoming an agnostic, "I did not feel that the solid ground was giving way beneath my feet, but rather that I was being relieved of a cumberous burden. I was not discovering that my creed was false, but that I never really believed it." In the same vein a contemporary writer exclaims, "What a miracle is reason! Free of fear, deceit, habit, guilt and confinement, free of all the hazards that institutional anxiety and scriptural pseudo-security have put in the way of fully creative humanism, theology stands here as did mathematics at the invention of zero; with a range of possibilities opening on infinity."

The second error of most believers writing about the "unbeliever" today is their failure to see how deeply the so-called unbeliever believes; their failure to recognize that he is an unbeliever because of his *positive* beliefs. Few churchmen seem to be clear that the unbeliever rejects a number of the central allegations of the Judeo-Christian tradition because he holds a set of basic concepts inconsistent with those allegations. The repudiation of the concept of miracles, taken literally, is an example of rejection based on positive conviction. The "unbeliever" can find no evidence that divine intervention occurs in his world. All the evidence he can find points the other way: to a non-miraculous world. Hence his profoundly positive belief that it is in such a world, one that is non-miraculous (in the sense of direct divine intervention), that he lives.

The Judeo-Christian believer does not usually seem to see that what he calls "unbelief" is like the word gentile. It is a negative concept. You do not define it by what it is but by what it is not. The gentile and the unbeliever are both individuals who fall outside the defining group: in the first instance the Jews; in the second, those who hold to the central tenets of the Judeo-Christian tradition.

3. Heresy

Nowhere is the erosion of the ecclesiastical way in religion more in evidence than in contemporary attitudes toward heresy. Once a dread word, a name feared and denied by everyone, "heretic" today is often claimed as a badge of honor. As early as the eighteenth century Gottfried Arnold suggested that the heretics had made a positive rather than a negative contribution to the church. In 1884 a Boston minister published a popular series of sermons which he called *Some Heretics of Yesterday*. In it he took the then quite radical step of approving them all. By the early twentieth century we find the English Roman Catholic writer, Gilbert K. Chesterton, observing derisively that when a man declares he is a heretic he is apt to look around for applause. By 1924 the American Quaker Rufus Jones had published a book entitled *The Church's Debt to Heretics.* In it he stated quite flatly, "Today the charge of heresy means little. Who nowadays cannot be heard to say from time to time, 'You know I'm a bit of a heretic myself,' while, as Chesterton observed, looking around self-consciously for approval, provided he does not carry the matter too far." A contemporary philosopher thinks of himself as a heretic merely because he is committed to the quest for honesty: so broad has the definition of heresy now become.

From time to time even today churchmen are heard defending the heretic as if the idea were new to them. A volume published within the last decade declares that a heretic does not hate Jesus, despise the church, or corrupt the youth, nor is the heretic a troublemaker, arrogant, or think himself infallible. These are labeled false accusations. The heretic is described as one who, within the fold, deviates from accepted doctrine. He challenges a closed system of orthodoxy, the author concludes, and he is usually a saint and pays a great price for his heresy. Open affirmation is at the heart of heresy, this writer says; hence most heretics are genuinely Christian and legitimately Protestant. Another declares that Christianity has been "renewed" by heretics, a variation on the familiar theme noted above, that the church, when it accepts doctrines formerly denounced as iniquitous, says it is "enriched" by them.

A more accurate view defines the heretic as someone who loses in a power struggle in the Church. There is no denying it. It is now clear that heresy has actually often been the original form of a Christian doctrine. Later, when the doctrine had been more carefully thought through, and the earlier form abandoned, those who still clung to the older version were declared to be heretics. The most famous instance is, of course, the Arian doctrine of the nature of God and Christ, which, at the Council of Nicaea, was replaced by the more complex and intricate Athanasian doctrine of the Trinity. Before the Council, Arian views were quite as respectable and quite as orthodox as those of Athanasius. Once the Council had made its decision, however, the followers of Arius were declared heretical and their views declared anathema. Then, lest there be any ambiguity on the matter, the Council appended to the creed it adopted an explicit rejection of the views of the defeated party, which it listed *seriatim.*

Heresy once meant something more than the expression of a new idea. A typical older definition ran: the heretic is characterized by "obstinate adherence to opinions arbitrarily chosen in defiance of accepted ecclesiastical teaching and interpretation." The key words here are the last ones, *in defiance of accepted ecclesiastical teaching and interpretation.* Words like "obstinate" and "arbitrarily" are merely pejorative addenda.

To understand the concept "heresy" we need to understand that it implies something quite different from the thoughtful dissent or the appropriate innovation that romantic writers of today are wont to assign to it. Heresy was once an appallingly ugly word. Ostracism, disgrace, imprisonment, torture, even death were the heretic's lot. The heretic was a deviationist. Someone was required to determine that he was deviant, and in the culture of the West that agency was the Church.

The institutional basis for the doctrine of heresy was worked out in antiquity. None stated it better than one Vincent of Lerins in his *Commonitorium,* published in A.D. 434. What, he asks, is the guiding principle by which the true Catholic faith can be distinguished from heresy? And he answers: first, we turn to the authority of God's law and then to the tradition of the Catholic Church. That, of course, is not the end of the matter. It is rather the beginning. How are we to know what God's law is, and how are we to determine what the tradition of the Church is? Vincent's answer is worth our attention: The canon of Scripture is complete, he asserts, but because of its profound character all men do not always interpret it in the same way. Furthermore, the interpretations of earlier scholars are often explained in different ways later on, so much so that it seems possible to extract from Scripture as many opinions as there are men. Because of the opportunity for error in so complex a process, Vincent continues, there is great need for the laying down of rules for the exposition of what the Prophets and Apostles have said, and he spells them out as follows:

"In the Catholic Church we take the greatest care to hold that which has been believed everywhere, always, and by all. That it is truly and properly 'Catholic,' is shown by the very force and meaning of the word [Catholic] which comprehends everything almost universally. We shall hold to this rule if we follow *universality* [i.e., ecumenicity], *antiquity,* and *consent* [Italics mine]. We shall follow *universality* if we acknowledge that one Faith to be true, which the whole Church throughout the world, confesses. [We shall follow] *Antiquity,* if we in no wise depart from those interpretations which it is clear that our ancestors and fathers proclaimed; [And we shall follow consent] if, in antiquity, we keep following the definitions and opinions of all, or certainly nearly all, bishops and doctors alike."

Vincent does not say what we are to do should we, individually and personally, having followed his procedures to the end, come out with answers different from those officially promulgated by the Church. But he does not need to. The Church has already answered the question for him, and by implication he accepts it. Although he seems to be describing here what the individual is to do, he is really describing what the Church does. The Church, he is saying, follows the above procedures and when, by following them, it has determined what the truth of the matter is, then let the individual "take this as to be held by him without the slightest hesitation."

As Vincent makes clear, who is and who is not a heretic is an institutional matter. Without a church or an equivalent body to establish an orthodoxy, there can be no heresy. A heretic is one who is not willing to be bound by an orthodoxy because he disagrees with certain of its teachings. Heresy, as the Greek derivation of the word makes clear, is an individual matter. A heretic is one who makes a personal choice of religious doctrines of which his church disapproves. "Orthodoxy," on the other hand, is a Church matter. It means "right opinion" as determined by the Church. There can be no "right" opinion in the absence of an authority by which its rightness is established. Heretics are people who hold beliefs the Church finds erroneous.

Can an institution establish opinions that are "right"? Those of the ecclesiastical way in religion usually say that it can: that an institution has both the capacity and the authority to do so.

But what happens to the idea of "right" belief when two religious institutions hold conflicting views as to what is and is not "right"? This is the situation with Judaism, Christianity, and Islam. How are we to choose between the claim of each that it holds beliefs that are "right," when those claims differ from one another? Shall some superinstitution be asked to say which is really "right"? If so, how are we to set up such a superinstitution? And who shall decide the many questions that would follow from such an effort? And who within a given religion is to decide among conflicting beliefs within that religion? In Christianity, for example, who is to say whether the Catholics or the Protestants hold the "right" beliefs? Among the conflicting views in Protestantism which beliefs are "right"? And again, who shall say?

The self-contradiction that lies at the heart of any doctrine of heresy or "right belief" comes into very sharp focus for us when we view it through the eyes of someone who stands outside our own tradition. There, our perception is unclouded by the beliefs and ideas that are so much a part of us that we are scarcely aware of their presence. An obscure scroll dating to the third century A.D. called the *Poimandres* records the prophecy of an Egyptian whose name is lost to us. Apparently he had, or thought he had, a revelation of what seemed to him to be all truth. At the conclusion of his vision a voice he had been hearing asked: "Now why do you delay? Will you not, as having received all, become a guide to those who are worthy, in order that the race of humanity may, through your agency, be delivered by God?"

Following this direct divine command, the Egyptian prophet thereupon announced to men the beauty and piety of knowledge. He advised them against drunkenness and sloth and called them to repentance as the only sure road to immortality. "Some of them mocked and stood aside," he continues, "while others cast themselves before my feet and begged to be taught. I made them rise up and become a guide to the race, teaching them the doctrine, how and in what way they should be saved. And when it was evening and the rays of the sun began to sink wholly I bade them offer thanks to God; and when they had finished their thanksgiving they turned each to his own bed."

Quite clearly the Egyptian believed as sincerely as any of the prophets that he had had a vision that God wanted him to convey to man. Why, then, do the utterances of this noble man rest in forgotten scrolls while, let us say, the fantasies of Ezekiel are remembered, debated, and pondered even today? Why was not the Egyptian's vision as valid and as authoritative as that of Ezekiel, Isaiah, or anyone else? One conclusion seems possible. The prophets of Israel became part of a great religious tradition. They spoke out of it, and in turn they helped to mold it. Eventually their words became a part of the sacred literature of their tradition, and so their words remain today. The Egyptian seer, on the other hand, belonged to no organized religious tradition, spoke for none, and was subsequently adopted by none. His words were neither persuasive nor startling enough to enable him to start a tradition of his own. Among the reasons, no doubt, was the fact that by the year A.D. 300 when he spoke, the pathway of prophecy was well worn. The lonely Egyptian had seen nothing and he had said nothing that by that time had not been seen, heard, and reported many times before.

Was he a true prophet? Apparently few believed it during his lifetime and none has since. Yet his words glow. They lack neither power nor beauty, neither nobility nor moral elevation. They carry with them the kind of basic moral authority we perceive in ethical utterances generally. What they lack is institutional support. They lack believers, not in their worth but in the man who spoke them. They lack, in short, the one single thing that establishes a person as a prophet: belief by a continuing group of followers that the alleged prophet did in fact commune directly with God and did in fact convey accurately to men what God had said. "Right belief" for those followers consists in believing that such communion took place.

A recent study of Protestant liberalism in the United States tells the story of David Swing, a liberal Presbyterian preacher who was charged with heresy in 1874. He was not preaching the Westminster Confession, it was asserted, and he rejected the theory that the Confession must be accepted word for word. However, nearly a century later his insistence that the Confession need not be held to word for word was accepted by the Presbyterians almost in Swing's own words. When the Confession of 1647 was rewritten and adopted by the United Presbyterian Church in the United States in 1967, it contained traditional language but at its heart, and repeated throughout, was the assertion "that doctrines are products of culture and must respond to cultural change. . . . In every age the Church has expressed its witness in words and deeds as the need of the time required. . . . Confessions and declarations are subordinate standards. . . . No one type of confession is exclusively valid, no one statement is irreformable."

"Right" belief, then, is not necessarily determined by its truth, its moral elevation, or by its special religious quality. A belief becomes "right" when an institution claims to have the authority to declare it be so. "Heresy", unless the word is to lose all meaning, is a set of doctrines contrary to those previously declared "right." Present attempts to show that opinions once branded "heresy" were not heresy at all, but were really building blocks of the true faith, reveal the great inroads the critical tradition has made into the ecclesiastical way in religion.

4. Faith

Beneath the question of how you decide which beliefs are "right" lies the more fundamental question: How do you know any of them are? How can you be sure that any body of belief, however carefully considered, is valid? The answer to that question given by those of the ecclesiastical way is fundamental: We know these things by faith.

"Faith" is one of the half-dozen great religious concepts, often ranked with "God," "love," "truth," and "salvation." But what is faith? A question like this throws us back upon definitions again, and if we are to answer it we face the necessity of again sorting through word meanings. More than a generation ago an English thinker tried to give the word "faith" a very special meaning. He wanted to make it mean an exploratory venture into the realm of the things people hope for, but which are as yet unknown. There is much support for his views. George Santayana spoke of faith as "the soul's invincible surmise" and a contemporary educator wrote: "Beyond the intellectual quest there is another where one steps out on the venture of faith." Typical dictionary definitions equate faith with belief, trust, confidence, and more specifically, belief in God and in revelation. John Locke defined faith as "the assent of the mind to the truth of a proposition or statement for which there is not complete evidence." Locke and the dictionaries as well have an excellent authority on which to rely: the Epistle to the Hebrews, where it is written, "Faith is the assurance of things hoped for, the conviction of things not seen."

Religious leaders, however, have often argued that the true meaning of faith is trust. "Faith is always *fiducia* [trust] rather than *assensus* [assent]," writes one representative of the ecclesiastical tradition. "It is the God-given decision to live confidently on the promises of God that are declared to men in certain events in human history." However, the author of this bit of counsel seems not to realize that, when he turns faith into trust, he has not solved the problem for the religious seeker. He has only pushed it one step further back. He appears to be asking the worshiper to trust God. What he is really asking is that the worshiper trust the Church's account of "certain events in human history." He is asking, further, that the worshiper trust the interpretation of those events the Church has built upon it.

John A. T. Robinson, apparently in full retreat from his earlier *Honest to God* approach, in 1977 called for trust rather than inquiry into matters of religious faith. In a book published that year, he asked rhetorically, *Can We*

Trust the New Testament? and answered that committed Christians can. They have nothing to fear but truth, he said, and the truth is Christ. Scholarship strengthens faith but it provides no guarantees: consequently the Christian walks by faith, not by sight. "In [God] have I trusted," he concludes. "Let me never be confounded."

Some contemporary theologians would cut the Gordian knot by simply asserting that faith *is* knowledge. If you have faith, they say, then you really know. Faith is a way of knowing. But for many thoughtful people the result of such a formula is not enlightenment, but increased befuddlement. For most of us, to say that faith is knowledge amounts to little more than a new definition of an old word, the meaning of which we had supposed we already understood. In common parlance "faith" is the opposite of knowledge. Here the critical mind would ask: what is to be gained by redefining the one to make its meaning the same as the other?

Faith is a precious word to most of us. We tend to apply it to the beliefs we approve and associate with religion. When we call for a return to faith we mean faith in those verities by which we have always lived. "Having faith" thus tends to be seen as a virtue in and of itself. Obviously it is not—as the world saw so clearly in the case of National Socialism in Germany during the 1930s and '40s. Apparently we humans can be misled into putting our faith in evil principles as well as good ones. In their heyday the Nazis were able to secure the confidence of the youth and a large proportion of the adults in Germany, and the world still shudders at the result.

Beneath the plea to "have faith" forever lurks the question of the critical way: *How do you know?* How can we be sure that we and our churches, too, are not naive? What test are we to apply by which we can avoid putting our trust in propositions that will not stand up under sharp scrutiny? Certainly the record of the churches at this point is not very reassuring. Church history in the West shows all too clearly that organized religion has invited belief in doctrines which, later on, were quietly abandoned, as when Copernicus's view of the universe after fierce opposition was allowed without fanfare to replace the Ptolemaic view. In the end the distinction between faith as trust, and faith as assent, disappears. Both trust and assent are required in every act of faith. Faith requires that we trust the authority of the institution that invites us to believe and that, of course, means we assent to its teachings as well.

Once this is understood, once it becomes clear that an invitation to faith is an invitation to assent to the teaching of a church, we can see why the problem is so difficult for so many of us. What we are really being asked to do is to put our faith, not in God, but in human beings, specifically religious authorities. As a source for one's faith and in support of it, one's attention is directed to holy books wherein the record of God's "mighty acts" is to be found. In Christianity this is the Bible, in Judaism the Old Testament, and in Islam the Qur'an.

The sacred writings of Judaism, Christianity, and Islam all assert that they are divine in origin. The book of Leviticus, for example, begins: "The Lord called Moses and spoke to him saying, 'Speak to the people of Israel and say to them . . .'" The book that follows purports to be a transcript of the very words God then spoke to Moses. The book's concluding lines are: "These are the commandments which the Lord commanded Moses for the people of Israel on Mount Sinai."

The same claim is made in the New Testament. The Revelation of John begins "The revelation of Jesus Christ which God gave him. He made it known by sending his angel to his servant John who bore witness . . . even to all that he saw." The supposed revelation is then set forth at length.

Book IX of the Qur'an declares itself to be "A proclamation from God and his Messenger unto mankind." Book XIII declares at the outset: "That which has been sent down to thee from thy Lord is the truth, but most men do not believe."

For the believer, the fact that the Scriptures themselves say they are of divine origin is sufficient. For the critical mind it is not. Ever alert to the possibility of error, not to speak of deceit, the critical mind is in no way persuaded by such self-serving declarations. If lines like these are self-authenticating, then any writing becomes divine in origin if the author is bold enough to make such a claim for it. Whatever credence we give to one such claim cannot, with any pretense to logic, be withheld from every other. To be specific, we cannot take a claim to revelation found in the Bible at face value and deny such a claim when found in the Qur'an, the Book of Mormon, or any other writing.

To put your faith in God because of the Scriptural record of his character and activities, you have first to believe in the validity of the human experiences of the divine which the Scriptures report. You have then to believe in the veracity of those who claimed to have had such experiences. Following that, you must go on to believe in the trustworthiness of the Scribe who wrote the story down, whether at first or second hand. And beyond that, you have to believe that the transcript that has come down to our time is a full and accurate copy of the ancient original. That is a lot of believing to ask anyone to do without very solid evidence to support it.

How far the Christian churches go in inviting such belief can be seen in a statement made by Cardinal Newman: "From the time I became a Catholic," he wrote, "I have no further history of my religious opinions to narrate." From that time on, Newman said, he believed unquestioningly what his Church required of him. If at any point he was unsuccessful in his effort, he revealed his failure to no one. This is true *fiducia,* genuine trust. It is also credulity, and we should not allow the prominence of the man to obscure the fact.

In his attitude toward Christian dogma Cardinal Newman was not guilty of an abject surrender that was without precedent in the history of the

Church. There was ample precedent for his attitude, both in theology and biography. Tertullian, one of the early Church Fathers, while pondering the Incarnation, found he could accept it for the very reason that the doctrine seemed to him to be inappropriate for the deity. "*Credo quia ineptum,*" he wrote. With obvious justification Tertullian's words are often translated: "I believe because it is impossible." Saint Augustine, two centuries later, declared, "You will not understand unless you believe." In other words, if you find that Christian teachings don't seem to make very good sense to you, believe them anyway by sheer force of will. In that way your intellectual problems will be solved and you will be able to understand. A millennium later, Anselm, still struggling with the problem of both believing and understanding the complex body of doctrine the Church had developed by the eleventh century, sharpened Augustine's aphorism to read, "I believe in order that I may understand, not I understand in order that I may believe." We could hardly ask for a plainer declaration of credulity as a basic teaching of the Church.

In order to grasp the full import of this line of argument let us remove it from its Christian context where our personal convictions may distract us from what is really being said, and take an example of believing from a faith that is foreign to us. Since 1853 archeologists in Mesopotamia from time to time have been turning up clay bowls inscribed in concentric circles in the Aramaic language. These bowls are about the size of our cereal or soup bowls and date to the first three centuries of our era. The inscriptions on them are incantations against evil spirits. No two are alike. Each was evidently designed for the owner of the bowl who, having had it inscribed, thereupon placed it in his home as a shield from harm.

Because the bowls are of common clay and not very well made or carefully inscribed it is clear that they were used by the common people. How did such a practice develop? To explain it—to understand it—we need only recall that a belief in evil spirits was pervasive in the Graeco-Roman world at the beginning of the Christian era. A corresponding belief held that incantations were an effective defense against such spirits. This belief, in turn, was supported by an almost magical trust in the power of words, especially when set down in writing.

Given such a belief structure, what could have seemed more logical to a simple householder in late classical times, especially in Mesopotamia where Babylonian influence was strong, than to provide his home with a bowl on which were inscribed incantations known to be effective against unseen malevolence? As you and I might go to a doctor trained in the art of inoculation against disease, so he resorted to a magician trained in the art of fending off evil spirits. The Mesopotamian householder's actions followed upon a basic belief in a world of evil spirits. Ours follow upon a basic belief in a world of viruses. Given those basic beliefs, the actions of each make sense.

By the story of the Aramaic Magical Incantation Bowls I do not mean to suggest either directly or indirectly, that the beliefs of Anselm, Augustine, or Tertullian were anything but the noblest one might hold. The point is simply that once you accept a basic article of faith, then you accept and you understand the belief structure that rests upon it. If you place yourself within *any* belief structure, be it good or bad, well-founded or ill-founded, everything else then falls into place; one belief flows from another and you understand. It all makes sense.

The danger lurking in this approach is of course immediately obvious. We humans know from sad and often shocking experience that we can be dead wrong in our basic beliefs. It is this tragic fact that causes the critical mind to reject Anselm's argument. If we are asked to accept a belief in order that we may understand the belief structure that rests upon it, how are we to know whether it is good or evil unless we first examine it? Just as the critical mind would ask our Mesopotamian householder why he believed in evil spirits, so the critical mind would ask Christians or Jews, Muslims or Ba'hais why they believe as they do. The critical mind thinks that nothing is more important than to begin, not by believing but by thinking; not by proclaiming but by inquiring, and not by accepting but by testing. For the critical mind, Anselm had things exactly backwards. He said, "I believe in order that I may understand." Those who follow the critical way in religion would say instead, "I strive to understand in order that I may believe."

Today few defenders of the faith quote Tertullian, Augustine, and Anselm. Nevertheless, even in the face of the now-pervasive critical tradition, exhortations to believe continue. I omit the more bizarre aspects of this tendency as we see them in today's charismatics, evangelicals, and the like. But mainline churchmen are saying the same thing. The language is more sophisticated but the message is the same.

A negative but powerful impetus to the acceptance of traditional faith is given by a Jewish writer with the argument that the Nazi holocaust was the direct result of the process of secularization and rationalization that marks Western culture. He argues further that, for this same reason, Western culture as a whole is now heading in the same direction in which Nazism took Germany and that nothing we can do can stop or change it. The same writer, subsequently re-emphasizing his position and making it even more uncompromising, reaffirms his conviction that "those believing Jews and Christians who affirm that God acts decisively in history and most decisively in the history of Israel have no choice but to interpret the Holocaust as God's just chastisement of a sinful Israel. . . . The biblical theology of covenant and election [can] be maintained only if [we are] to regard Hitler and the SS as the prophets regarded Nebuchadnezzar—that is as unknowing agents of God's purposes in history."

He here makes the tragic mistake so common among the defenders of ancient faith. When a culture finds its ancient formulations of faith untenable, as increasingly Western culture does today, the alternative might be a descent to the lowest instincts within us, as this writer suggests. But not necessarily. An alternative would be a reformulation of the faith in concepts more congenial to the later stages of a culture. We cannot scare people back into the faith of their fathers. People believe because they are persuaded, not because they are afraid.

Still another approach is that of Jürgen Moltmann, who emphasizes the ancient Christian doctrine that God himself suffers and that he does so for us. Moltmann's reasoning inevitably becomes complex as he tries to explain how this is so within the Christian doctrine of the Trinity, where God is both one and three, both separate and inseparable in His three persons. To all of this the critical mind can only ask whether its effect is to enhance or to destroy belief, to explain or to obfuscate religious thought, to elicit trust or confusion in religion. Moltmann seems to be very close to Tertullian's resolve to believe because it is inept or absurd or impossible.

13

Revelation

Religious belief—"faith," based on the idea of revelation, and central in the ecclesiastical tradition—is not proved; it is proclaimed. It derives its status not from its power to persuade but from the authority of those who proclaim it. The churchmen have devoted untold hours and mountains of writing to demonstrating its validity, but as far as the critical mind is concerned, even after two thousand years of effort, the fundamental question remains unanswered: the doctrine of revelation remains an assertion, the truth of which is not borne out by the checking, questioning, and testing process. It is not that anybody has succeeded in *dis*proving the doctrine; it is the other way around. The revelations that the churchmen allege have not been established in the manner that the Western mind has followed in working out nearly all of its most basic ideas.

There is nothing whatever novel in my saying this. In effect, Pyrrho of Elis said it more than two thousand years ago. So did Cicero a little later and so did Montaigne. Thomas Paine, closer to our time, was more explicit. In his *Age of Reason* (1794), Paine wrote: "Revelation, when applied to religion, means something communicated immediately from God to man. No one will deny or dispute the power of the Almighty to make such a communication, if he pleases. But admitting, for the sake of a case, that something has been revealed to a certain person, and not revealed to any other person, it is revelation to that person only. When he tells it to a second person, a second to a third, a third to a fourth, and so on, it ceases to be a revelation to all those persons. It is revelation to the first person only, and hearsay to every other, and consequently they are not obliged to believe it." Courts of law have long since declared hearsay evidence to be unreliable and therefore inadmissible.

It is unnecessary to review the story of the vilification heaped upon Paine because of *The Age of Reason.* Most people are now aware that, although he has long been thought an atheist and a corrupter of morals, the allegation is false. The excoriation he suffered during his lifetime, and the shadow of impiety that still clings to his name, is but one more lamentable instance of the manner in which the Christian clergy as well as the laity down the centuries have sought, even by defamation of character, to destroy their critics. Paine clearly stated his purpose in writing *The Age of Reason.* In the face of the "superstition, false systems of government and false theology" that he felt were present in his time, Paine wrote, he said, in order that we not "lose sight of morality, of humanity and of theology that is true." He was not, as his critics alleged, trying to destroy religion. He was trying to implement the critical way in religion. He failed, not because his argument was invalid, but because he so infuriated those of the ecclesiastical way that what he actually said was never considered.

I introduce this discussion of revelation with a reference to *The Age of Reason* not only to give Paine the recognition he so seldom gets, but also to show how long his argument has been with us and how little effect it has had on organized religion. In the books on revelation now being produced, where do we even yet see a discussion of the problem he raises? Yet the point is crucial. Unless there is some way to deal with it, Paine's words stand. The doctrine of revelation on which Judaism, Christianity, and Islam all rest disintegrates as soon as we ask the central question of the critical way in religion: *How do you know?*

The idea of revelation is so familiar to us and so much a part of human culture generally that most of us are not aware that we hold it. We simply take it for granted. We neither question nor examine it. We believe in revelation as we believe in the alternation of night and day. Yet the concept is an extraordinary one. It is not simple, but complex. At least two major propositions are implicit in it, each of which is extraordinary in itself. The first concerns the existence of God; the second, his activity on earth. We need to take a hard look at both.

1. The Existence of God

When the word "revelation" is taken in its traditional and generally understood meaning, God is the active agent in the transaction. He is the revealer. While this seems so obvious as not to require statement, it is worth our noticing, nevertheless. To believe in revelation is to assert that God *is*: that he exists. This, too, is a proposition most people take for granted. Opinion surveys in the United States, for example, have repeatedly shown that a very high percentage of the people believe in the existence of God. To be sure, there has been a decided shift in the polls recently, but this may be only a minor fluctuation in a situation which, over all, remains stable.

When we try to determine what these figures mean we discover that the consensus, examined closely, generally turns out to be an agreement on words, not meaning. Opinion divides into a thousand fragments as soon as we begin to probe into what people are thinking when they say they believe in God. Among Christians and Jews alike, ideas of God stretch all the way from that of an almighty yet personal, loving, heavenly father to very hazy concepts of God as a force or power, as an ideal, the ground of being, the very heart of things, even God beyond God.

A formula popular at the moment is that of a "God Within." Because ecology is very much on people's minds it is suggested that "A truly ecological view of the world has religious overtones. . . . An ethical attitude in the scientific study of nature readily leads us to a theology of the earth." No doubt. But the question gnaws at us: what is really being said here? One of the more preposterous definitions I have come across asserts that God is "the creative and redemptive potentials in reality that are in the process of being actualized in concrete manifestations." Whatever this means it certainly does not mean the God of Abraham, Isaac, and Jacob, nor the God of Jesus Christ, nor even the God of the Enlightenment, nor even the God of any of the Modernists. The "God Within" is equally remote from traditional concepts, even though the Old Testament reports that God spoke to Elijah with a still, small voice. It was neither "relationships in complex systems" nor an "experience of harmony" that spoke to Elijah, but Yahweh, God of Israel, who, as the Old Testament makes clear, was a powerful, jealous, sometimes vengeful Person.

The *coup de grâce* was administered to writing like this in a forgotten book published almost a hundred years ago. In 1879 James Martineau, an English Unitarian clergyman, wrote: "Abstractions . . . cannot persuade us to bow down and worship them. . . . Will then the Benedicte swell with the same tones of joy, when it has to sing—'Bless the *Eternal Law,* all ye its works; bless the Eternal Law, O my synthesis of organs?' Will the contrition which now cries—'Blot out my transgressions, Cast me not away, A broken heart Thou dost not despise,' pour out its sorrows to a deaf ideal, and shed its passionate tears on an abstraction that cannot wipe them away? . . . Will any Crucified one lose the bitterness of Death in crying, *'O Stream of Tendency!'* Will any Heaven open and any Vision come, when he exclaims, *'Great Ensemble of Humanity,* receive me?'"

This was Spinoza's problem. The thoughtful Dutch Jew of the seventeenth century was both philosopher and mystic, both thinker and believer. He never managed to reconcile his feeling for the God of his fathers and the great Unity he perceived in all things as a mathematician. Thomas Hobbes, the Englishman, declared that Spinoza's position amounted to atheism. The Jewish community in Amsterdam apparently agreed. Spinoza was excommunicated for his "evil opinions." Concludes one student of Spinoza: his "intellectual love of God can only be maintained by devices which reduce his God to a legerdemain of words."

The gulf that lies between faith and inquiry is nowhere more evident than in human attempts to delineate the nature of the divine. The problem is accentuated by the ever-present tendency of our thought-concepts—including those about God—to grow obsolete. As our knowledge and understanding in all fields increase we outgrow our gods and have to fashion new ones to take their place. But this process is very unsettling. It introduces uncertainty into an area—ultimate reality—of which we had always believed certainty to be the essence. Often the modifying process renders the old gods altogether unrecognizable. The gods that have grown obsolete were not invented and thrust upon the gullible. They are holdovers from an earlier time, the ghosts of a presence once vital and strong but now gone forever.

Since ancient times philosophers and churchmen have been trying to "prove" the existence of God. Many of these proofs are still repeated today: for example, that the very age of the idea of God proves its truth. But the age of an idea—even our ideas about God—tells us nothing about its validity. From the dawn of human thought down to the time of the Renaissance (a few ancient Greek thinkers excepted), people everywhere simply took it for granted that the earth is flat. Probably no concept is older, and none is more demonstrably invalid. Yet even today, theologians argue that God must exist because the idea has been with us from the beginning.

A second ancient "proof" of the existence of God, frequently heard today, is the argument from design. How else, it is asked, are we to account for the wonders of the natural world, including man, his mind, and his ideals? Some great Being, it is argued, must have put it all together. A popular magazine prints the following adage: "The best reply to an atheist is to give him a good dinner and ask him if he believes there is a cook."

The argument from design is, at best, only an analogy. The existence of a watch does indeed indicate the existence of a watchmaker, but the analogy does not necessarily hold with an elephant or the solar system. We can explain the origin of the elephant through biological evolution and the origin of the solar system through the birth of our sun. But this is far from proving the existence of a designer or manufacturer of either. A contemporary student of meteorology observes, "To some the awful beauty of Nature is evidence of a creator. To me it is evidence that Nature is awfully beautiful."

A great many theologians, among them Albertus Magnus and Augustine, remind us that since God is ineffable, he can only be known by faith. How do we know what that faith is? As we noted in the previous chapter, it lies in the keeping of the Church, they say. And how does the Church know? Because God revealed it to those from whom the Church holds its knowledge and authority. This has been and continues to be the central Catholic position, although not all Catholics hold it today. The argument, of course, is circular. Knowledge of the content and meaning of revelation comes from God to the Church. The Church knows the truth of its teachings about revelation because the authority given to the Church by God endows it with that power. Such reasoning, when examined objectively, persuades only those who want to be persuaded.

The difficulty with an argument like this is not merely logical, it is also practical. As we also noted in the previous chapter, it opens to anyone of any persuasion the opportunity to claim divine origin for his teachings, and divine origin for the institution based upon them. Fascists as well as Christians may do so. If the Judeo-Christian claim is valid on the ground of the authority of that tradition, so would theirs be also. What one may claim, all may claim. It all degenerates into nothing more than a shouting match, the conclusion of which is determined not by persuasion but by force.

A quite different approach to the God-idea is that of modern anthropology. The story of human development since paleolithic times seems to indicate that ideas of the divine grew out of primitive attempts to organize and understand experience. Early human conceptions were animistic. Primitive people thought of their world as filled with spirits. They believed that spirits dwelt in all objects, animate and inanimate, including themselves. Gradually the concept of spirits in persons and things grew more abstract. This line of thinking culminated in ideas of the divine that have evolved in the "higher" religions, including Christianity, Judaism, and Islam. This story, retold in uncounted books on the philosophy of religion, readily accounts for the presence of ideas of the divine in man's thinking. In no way, however, does it establish their objective reality.

Sigmund Freud stated the principle in psychological terms. "Religious ideas are born of man's need to make his helplessness tolerable," he wrote. "Hence religion is an entirely subjective phenomenon. It altogether lacks the objective validity the priesthoods of the various religions claim for it. The teachings of the religions are derived from man's memory of his helplessness as a child. A second motive force in the development of religious ideas was the urge to do something about social justice." All would perhaps agree on this proposition, but not all would agree with what Freud derives from it. He continues, "Man creates the gods whom he dreads, yet he entrusts them with his protection."

Students of animal behavior bear out Freud's surmise. They find in the God-concept the prototype of the male authority figure who can be observed all the way from seals through the anthropoid apes into primitive human society, not to speak of its contemporary forms. The emergence of the idea of a heavenly father reflects our tendency and need, derived from an ancient and long-forgotten past, to submit to a powerful leader. Through him, it seems, we achieved social unity, the comfort of companionship, mutual cooperation, and the protection any such society requires. In a behavioral sense our present-day religious ceremonies—say the students of animal behavior—consist in the coming together of people to perform, in groups, acts that are symbolically submissive to a dominant father figure. Prostration, kneeling, bowing the head—all these, they say—seem clearly to be vestiges of actions designed to appease a dominant individual.

Advocates of the women's liberation movement are today making the same point, although their approach is different. The Judeo-Christian tradition, they say, is suffused with the idea of male superiority and male dominance. Evidence from the history of religions bears them out. El, the earliest known Semitic deity, and hence standing at the beginning of the Judeo-Christian tradition, was a father figure. Like Kronos for the Greeks, he was the father of gods and men. Yahweh, who succeeded him, was also a father figure. Both El and Yahweh symbolized mythically the patriarchal structure of early Semitic society. Why, the feminists ask, should we consider sacrosanct a tradition that demeans one group of people (women) and puts others (men) in authority over them? Do not such traditions (Christianity and Judaism) raise profound questions about the ethical level of such teachings?

Because the God-concept in Judaism, Christianity, and Islam is so totally male in all its aspects, and intricately a part of the concept of male dominance that has imbued Western culture, many an advocate of "women's liberation" has had serious doubts about the deity that traditional doctrines of revelation have laid before us. One feminist, with candor almost totally lacking in theological writing and in secular writing until very recently, declared, "I feel the term 'God' itself is no longer useful." It is a charge the ecclesiastical way in religion has not yet been able to answer.

While the churchmen say we have positive, dependable knowledge of God, the critical mind asks how such knowledge is possible. Have not the churchmen got things backward? Xenophanes suggested long ago that it is man who creates God, not the other way around. Recall his prophetic words: "If cattle or lions had hands . . . and could practice works of art as men do they would . . . give them bodies like their own . . . horses like horses, cattle like cattle."

Even today that is a startling statement. People still draw attention to themselves when they suggest such an idea, despite the fact that over a century ago Ludwig Feuerbach restated the principle about as flatly as anyone can. "The substance and object of religion is altogether human," he wrote. "Divine wisdom is human wisdom; the secret of theology is anthropology. . . . The consciousness of God is nothing else than the consciousness of the species. . . . There is no other essence which man can believe in, love and adore as the *absolute* than the essence of human nature itself. . . . God is the nature of man regarded objectively. Love to man must be no derivative love; it must be original. *Homo homini Deus est* (Man is God to man)," he concluded in a Latin aphorism.

In grappling with the concept of Deity we are trying to get our hands on one of the most fundamental ideas of which the human mind can conceive. We are trying to reach, in the physical, mental, moral, aesthetic and spiritual sense, the ultimate. It is the most difficult problem with which theology has to deal. As the active agent in revelation, the God-concept is the single foundation stone upon which the several thought-structures of the several religions have been built. The ability of theology to explain God's nature as a revealer and to persuade people that he exists, and that he actively reveals truth to the creatures of Earth, becomes crucial. As things now stand the case has not been made. The central dogma from which the doctrine of revelation is derived—the existence of God in any but the vaguest and most abstract sense—will not bear the scrutiny to which the modern mind is accustomed to subject its thinking in all other areas of experience.

Do those who follow the critical way in religion believe in God? Asked such a question, most of them would reply: It all depends on what you mean by the term "God." Some might say directly: I have given up using the term in the interest of clarity and honesty in communication, yet my beliefs about the fundamentals of our existence seem to me little different from those that are popular today in ecclesiastical circles. Others of a critical turn of mind might reply unhesitatingly: Belief in God is the cornerstone of my thought structure.

There is no reason why the meaning of the term "God" cannot evolve and change as do the meanings of other words. In Whitehead's thought this happened. Questions about belief in God have to do with the most fundamental concepts by which we seek to order our lives and understand the universe. When it becomes clear which of the many possible concepts of deity a questioner has in mind then answers to questions about belief in God can more easily be given.

2. Mysticism

We began this chapter with two questions. The first, Does God exist? immediately became: What kind of deity do you have in mind? We now come to the second question: If God (of whatever nature) exists, does he reveal himself and his will on the human scene? If so, how does he do it, and more importantly, how can we be sure that reports and experiences of revelation are what we think they are? We approach these questions mindful of the abundant evidence of human error, human gullibility, and human deceit reviewed in chapter 2.

There is a sense in which all these questions become one, since many understand God more as an experience than as a being; that is, not as a divine Super-Person, who exists objectively, but as One who is known subjectively, as One who acts upon us. In such a concept, being and doing are the same. Such an understanding of the meaning of revelation comes very close to mysticism. One writer says, for example, that we "discern God by deep involved intuitions, by an apprehension of the wonder and meaning of the given structure of things." Another writes of "the apprehension of God as the unseen Person dealing with him." The key words here are "intuition" and "apprehension."

Many people believe that mystical experience offers objective evidence for the existence of God. Sometimes these experiences are very general. People sense the presence of God in a sunset, in an act of self-sacrifice, or in a garden. The following is typical:

> Down in the meadow spread with dew
> I saw the Very God
> Look from a flower's limpid blue
> Child of a starveling sod.

Theologians have long since identified such experiences as "mystical," and a vast literature deals with this material. First, there are the writings of the mystics themselves. There is, further, the history of mysticism and of the great movements founded upon such experiences. The psychology by which they are to be explained has enjoyed extended attention in recent years, and it is a subject upon which theologians never tire of writing. But in it all a question persists for those of critical temper: how does the mystic know that "God" is the source of the mystical experience? Further, how do we get from subjective experience to objective reality?

Almost anyone will concede that mystical experiences are totally vivid and real to those who have them. We can grant that a mystic had a clear vision of God and still wonder whether or not he saw anything but the images of his own mind. We can grant that he heard what seemed to him to be God's voice, and that he wrote down the very words he heard, and still suspect that the mystic was only hearing the echoes of his own thoughts. How did he *know* that Almighty God had appeared and spoken to him? How do *we* know? These are the questions mysticism has to answer before it can escape from the problem of human error.

The idea of mystical experience involves a second problem: How does it deal with the fact of cultural conditioning? We have seen the role that such conditioning plays in the area of belief. Can it be any different with mystical experience? Recall Isaiah's vision in the temple. According to him, he "saw" God. But it is worth noting that the God he saw appeared in the form in which Semitic culture in the fertile crescent was accustomed to envision him in Isaiah's time.

Isaiah saw God "sitting upon a throne high and lifted up," as kings and gods alike were supposed to do at that time. "Above him stood the seraphim; each had six wings." In recent times stone statues of creatures like these, dating from that period, have been recovered in abundance in Mesopotamia.

But Prince Siddhartha in India, who subsequently became the Buddha, saw none of the winged creatures that adorned the temples of Assyria and Babylonia. Seated under the sacred Bo tree he saw, or rather sensed, enlightenment, an understanding of the problem of human suffering and how it was to be dealt with, characteristic of the Indian outlook on life. The Christian mystics, in their turn, saw visions of Christ, often as he hung on the cross, and with such a sense of vividness and immediacy, stigmata appeared on their hands and feet. The Virgin Mary, in particular, during the Middle Ages and later, tended to appear in the blue robe in which she was depicted in the statuary and stained glass windows of the Church. And so we must ask the mystics: Is God, in his communications with men, confined to the mind-set of his communicants? Does not the cultural conditioning of the mystical experience suggest that, like dreams, these experiences are more subjective than objective?

A third problem with which mysticism must deal is that of the drug-induced mystical experience. We have already noted in Part I that narcotics can produce vividly real experiences we know to be imaginary. We know too that drugs can produce experiences of a deeply religious character. The use of "sacred plants" such as mushrooms to induce psychic experience goes back at least three thousand years. The practice of using peyote cactus for this purpose by American Indians is familiar to many readers. Many argue that this practice is valid. We are, they say, such earthbound creatures that we can reach out and touch the infinite only with the aid of mind-expanding drugs.

What is the truth? Do we ever succeed in touching the Infinite, the Eternal, the Ultimately Spiritual, through drugs? A researcher addressed this question on Good Friday, in an experiment with theological students in a basement chapel. The service from the main auditorium upstairs was piped in to them. Half were given a strong drug. The other half were given placebos. Only the experimenter knew who had which. The subjects given the drug scored significantly higher in mystical experiences than the others. As religion is today thought of in more general terms, so their experiences too were general in character. One subject, for example, "felt a deep union with God," but his experience, as he described it, was clearly related to the Protestant form of worship to which he was accustomed and which was going on in the chapel above at the time.

"I remember feeling a profound sense of sorrow that there was no priest or minister at the altar," he reported. "I had a tremendous urge to go up on the altar and minister the services. But I had this sense of unworthiness, and I crawled under the pews and tried to get away. Finally I carried my Bible to the altar and then tried to preach. The only words I mumbled were 'peace, peace.' I felt I was communicating beyond words."

Recent experiments with Eastern mystics indicate that physiological changes take place in the body of the mystic during deep trancelike states of meditation. Yogis in India have long been known to perform phenomenal feats under these circumstances. It has been said that they can slow the heartbeat, and survive for extended periods in airtight pits, and also in extreme cold without food. They can continue for extended periods in distorted bodily positions. Yogis can reduce their rate of metabolism. In one experiment it was found that during meditation ten monks were able to reduce their oxygen intake by 20 percent and their carbon dioxide output by the same amount. It has also been shown that meditation slows the electrical activity of the brain as registered on an electroencephalograph. Experiments carried out by psychologists have confirmed an earlier surmise, that the beatific visions of the saints were, like those of drug-users, accompanied by changes in the chemistry of the human body.

Our question is, what do those experiences mean? Christianity and Judaism assert that Moses talked with God on Mount Sinai and that Isaiah saw God and heard him speak in the temple. But for the critical mind the old question rises: *How do you know?* Contemporary writers, echoing Pascal, say that we discover God through intuition. "The heart has its reasons which reason knows not of," they remind us. But the question persists: is it God that intuition or the "heart" discovers?

For those who say it is, the problem still persists. How does the heart "know" when our other faculties are uncertain? To believe something very deeply does not make it true. To repeat what has been said above, we can be very, very confident and be very, very wrong, both at the same time. The heart is said to "know" its true love, and there too "has its reasons which reason knows not of." But how often that same heart is later broken when what it supposed itself to "know" turns out to have been false. For the critical mind it is as important in religion as in love to know the difference between subjective confidence and objective validity.

To raise questions like these means to some people to reject poetry, fantasy, and mysticism. A contemporary writer says, for example: "Our fact-obsessed era has taught us to be cautious: always check impulsive visions against hard data. Secularism erodes the religious metaphors within which fantasy can roam." His is the familiar theological error, that truth can somehow be attained if we will only throw away our canons of judgment and cease to be troubled by the hard data of life.

The validity of the critical approach to mystical experience is thrown into sharp relief by today's mainline churchmen. Faced as they are by the contemporary widespread gospel of unreason they find themselves asking the evangelicals the very question that critical minds have for so long been asking them: *How do you know?* How can you be so sure of the truth you proclaim? On what besides your own self-assertion does it rest?

One such writer condemned "the theology of fantasy" that followed the religion of secularism of the 1960s. The theologians "stumbled into the fairyland of magic and mysticism and then formed a new reality principle . . . that was immune to the . . . assaults of theology's critics." But, he charged, "the peril in a 'theology of fantasy' is that fantasy can take itself too seriously, can make serious business out of not being serious. History shows that 'mystic, crystal revelations' . . . tend to degenerate into absurd orthodoxies simply because 'mystic revelations' allow no reality . . . testing." The case for the critical way in religion was never stated more clearly.

A stern critical approach to the problem of truth in no way implies that imagination, fantasy, or mystical experience is to be given up. The critical mind does not deplore fantasy, mystery, poetry, or myth. All it deplores is the failure to distinguish between fact and fantasy. The need to do so gave rise to the critical tradition and one of the basic reasons for its continuance is that religion down the ages has not made that hard choice.

3. What Revelation Means

As with arguments in support of belief in God, those in support of revelation often turn on the meaning of words. Here, as with the question of the existence of God, theologians have attempted to solve the problem by giving the old term new meaning. And as always, questions rise in the critical mind. When you change the meaning of a familiar word, what are you doing? Are you gaining clarity? Are you gaining in your ability to communicate? Are you not, instead, running the risk of deceiving others, perhaps even yourself? Do you not risk seeming to say something that people would like to hear, while in fact you are saying something they would find quite disturbing if they really understood it?

No theological term has been subject to more interpretation than "revelation." Many writers say, for example, that revelation is simply God's self-disclosure, his revelation of himself in history. "Revelation is not the miraculous one-way intrusion of the divine into the mundane," a liberal Jewish theologican asserts. "It is rather the result of progressive interaction between man and God. Whenever a human being reaches out to grasp a truth that has never been comprehended before . . . or to create or appreciate a higher dimension of beauty . . . or to achieve a loftier level of ethical conduct . . . there and then God has revealed Himself to man again."

What is really being said here? Apparently that revelation is now to be redefined as discovery. But why? What do we gain by doing so? As things now stand, the two terms "revelation" and "discovery" are clear and distinct in their contrasting meanings. There is no gain, only obfuscation and confusion, in redefining them so that they have the same meaning. Why not keep both terms? Then we shall know that to speak of "discovery" carries no theological assumptions whatever, while, as before, to speak of "revelation" involves the claim of divine intervention in the human world.

H. Richard Niebuhr, more than anyone else, established the pattern of dealing with these questions in his *Meaning of Revelation,* published in 1941 and still widely read. He began by saying flatly that theology for Christians must begin in Christian history. It must begin with revelation and must ask what revelation means for Christians. It means something that has happened to us. And what was that? It was, said Niebuhr, God disclosing himself in history. This disclosure comes about in two ways: God reveals *himself* in Christ, and the prophets reveal truths *about* God.

Those of critical temper can only reply to such statements by asking again: "*How do you know?* I do not doubt in any way the vividness of the experiences you report. I ask only for some evidence beyond your own statement that your experiences represent the reality you say they do. Not questioning at the moment the history on which you rely, I am forced to ask: how can anyone be sure your interpretation of it is valid? Aware of human fallibility as I am, I need more than your very firm conviction in order to be persuaded myself."

Those who have wrestled with the Christian doctrine of the Resurrection have followed a similar line of reasoning. They urge us to look past the details of the Resurrection story in Christianity and try to see its "inner meaning." Do not, they counsel us, get hung up on the question of bodily resurrection: look, rather, to the record of how the primitive church *felt* about the experience; look at the profound conviction the first Christians developed out of that experience. "The Resurrection is an event of history because it was primarily an experience of revolutionary hope," writes one scholar. "Something did happen in Jerusalem a few days after the Crucifixion. . . . We are certain the disciples had a life-changing experience of hope on that first Easter."

No one would deny what the writer says, provided the Bible record be taken at face value. But, the critical mind asks: What does that very vivid and deeply moving experience of the disciples prove? Nothing more than that they had it, which is at best only a redundancy. The central question remains: does the experience of "revolutionary hope" on the part of the Disciples establish in any way that Jesus rose from the dead? If not, to use that experience to support an event in history is certainly misleading.

As I pointed out in connection with theological arguments that favor "having faith," we run the risk here of opening a veritable Pandora's box of evil in the realm of religion. If a religious experience can become an event in history because the experience was vivid, and a church with power and authority can be built upon it, then any kind of church, good or bad, can come forward and claim ecclesiastical status on the basis of an experience no one can verify. If we are to distinguish the valid from the invalid, the evil, or the merely tawdry, some standard more objective than that of an intense emotional feeling is required.

Thomas Aquinas was perfectly clear on the doctrine of revelation. For him it was a fundamental article of the Christian faith and required neither examination nor proof. He pointed out that scientists often do not argue in support of their most basic principles. Nor, he insisted, need the theologians. As scientists go on from their most basic principles to prove other things, so, he said, did he. However, Aquinas did not think it enough merely to equate theology with other sciences. After all, in the Middle Ages theology was regarded as the queen of the sciences. Accordingly, as Augustine had done nearly a thousand years before, Aquinas buttressed his assumption with the authority of the Church and let it go at that. The principles of authority are given by revelation, he said, "and hence should be believed on the authority of those to whom the revelation was made. . . . An argument from authority based on human reason is weak, but an argument from authority based on divine revelation is most efficacious."

When we analyze Aquinas's argument, we find that it comes down to nothing more than this: the Christian revelation establishes the authority of the Church and the authority of the Church in turn establishes the validity of the revelation on which that authority is based. In other words, he argues that the truths the Church teaches as divine revelation are to be accepted as divine revelation because that is what the Church says they are. Again, as with the argument for having faith in God, this argument is circular and carries nothing more than the "authority of self-assertion."

The Church, in theory, might claim to be of divine origin, and so to possess unique knowledge and unique power. On the record, unfortunately, it cannot. A sad and dreadful history shows that the religious institutions of men are as subject to human failing as are the institutions of government. In fact, in the past it has often been impossible to distinguish between the two. The same thing is true of the personnel that operate religious institutions. Many have been totally dedicated to human welfare. More have been dedicated first to the welfare of the institution, sincerely believing that to be paramount. Many, however, have put their own personal ambition first. Even today we are forced to admit that, across the board, the clergy are not demonstrably more holy than the laity they serve. Sanctity is not conferred by such titles as "Reverend," "Most Reverend," "My Lord Bishop," or "Your Holiness." These are plaudits to be won by an exemplary life. They cannot be conferred by sacred vows or by succession in office.

One problem with the doctrine of revelation is the conclusions to which its premises can lead. An example from a recent Islamic writing will give Christians and Jews perspective on this observation which is often hard to come by within one's own household of faith. In 1966 the then Vice President of the Islamic University of Medina wrote: "The Holy Koran, the Prophet's teachings, the majority of Islam's scientists, and the actual facts all prove that the earth is fixed and stable, spread out by God for his mankind. . . . Anyone who professed otherwise would utter . . . a charge of falsehood toward God, the Koran, and the Prophet."

Whether or not this statement is typical of current Islamic thought, its logic is plain. Given the premise from which the Vice President began—that the Qur'an is God's word revealed to the prophet Muhammad—he is driven to a conclusion that the modern mind has rejected since the days of Copernicus, namely, that the sun moves around the earth as Muhammad supposed. Otherwise, from the same premises he is driven to the conclusion, intolerable for him, that the Qur'an, God's Word, is in error.

The dean of the theological school of one of the world's greatest universities once said to me: "The intellectual approach to religion must be scientific, but in the realm of faith the standard is different. Faith involves both revelation and election. To hold any religious faith you must hold that it has been revealed, that the revelation has been given to you, and that therefore you are one of the elect." There you have in the clearest possible form an essential addendum to the doctrine of revelation. The idea of election is an integral part of it. The critical mind is forced to ask in reply: how is it possible to accept the conceit, even the arrogance, implicit in such an assertion?

Even if one accepts the existence of a personal God who intervenes in human affairs, how can one think that he or she has been singled out for so incredible a distinction? Are we ready to accept a doctrine of God that makes him someone who plays favorites? Apparently many of us are. The idea does not seem inconsistent with a valid concept of deity only because it is so much a part of our culture. It has been in the intellectual and religious air we have breathed since infancy. We take it for granted as we do the law of gravitation and the coming of night and day. But on reflection, the question comes back, gnawing at us, and will not go away: Who are we or who were our religious forebears that we should suppose ourselves to have been granted special status by the Almighty? A human sense of fairness, not to say a divine concern for one and all, would seem to require a less capricious distribution of divine justice, mercy, and love.

4. The Final Contradiction

Two generations ago the scholarly journalist Walter Lippmann called these questions the "acids of modernity." These, he said, had dissolved the "faith of our fathers." Writing on behalf of "those who do not find a principle of order in the belief that they are related to a supernatural power," Lippmann pointed the way for questioners and inquirers. "They must find some other principle which will give coherence and distinction to their lives," he wrote. That new principle he identified as "the religion of the spirit," and continued: "It does not depend on creeds and cosmologies. It has no vested interest in any particular truth. It seeks excellence wherever it may appear." What he was reaching toward was the critical way in religion.

Lippmann saw the religion of the spirit as slowly replacing the belief that we are related to a supernatural power. In this he was right. But he seems not to have seen that his religion of the spirit and many of his acids of modernity were one and the same. Like so many other writers, he saw that the old order was giving way and that a new one was taking its place. But apparently he did not see, or perhaps did not want to say, that the new order was itself the solvent of the old.

We have already reviewed many of the responses the churchmen have made as they have watched "the acids of modernity" eating their way into ancient religious thought and practice. Still another response has been to ask: Why need the critical way destroy the ecclesiastical way in religion? Cannot belief, faith, and revelation stand together with questing, testing, and reconceptualizing? Are not both necessary? Are not both valid? Does not organized religion today constantly speculate, constantly test its speculations, and constantly check on the accuracy and validity of those speculations? The two modes of reaching religious truth, revelation and inquiry, have always been used together. Have they not for centuries lodged comfortably side by side with no sense of disjunction or conflict?

The answer to these questions is both yes and no. While, in truth, both assumptions have long been made in the ecclesiastical tradition, for the critical mind they cannot stand together. As we have seen, the reason is: the doctrine of revelation, the central tenet of the ecclesiastical tradition, asks, in effect, to be excepted from the testing process. In the ecclesiastical tradition, the idea of revelation is the place where you start. It does not require testing. In fact, any testing of the idea would be inappropriate if not meaningless since the truth in revelation is not known or understood through testing but through faith.

Revelation is a double-barreled concept, so to speak. It makes two assertions: it asserts a particular "truth," as for example, Isaiah's prophecy that Yahweh would destroy Israel unless the people mended their ways. But Isaiah's message to Israel contained a more basic "truth": that his prophecy was not human in origin but divine. Both of these assumptions underlay Isaiah's words as they are reported to us in the Bible.

Thus the basic assumption of the critical tradition not merely undercuts the basic assumption of the ecclesiastical tradition, it directly contradicts that assumption. If, as the critical mind asserts, truth can only be arrived at through the testing, questing process, the critical mind can never make the assumption on which the ecclesiastical way in religion rests. It can never accept the dogma of revelation or any dogma that rests on it. For the critical mind, these propositions must be submitted to the testing process like any other proposition. They must be examined to see how well they stand up under close scrutiny.

There is, of course, no reason why an alleged revelation cannot be so examined and accepted if it meets the critical test. The Roman Catholic Church does this constantly as claims to visions, miracles, and the like are made by its constituents. The problem comes, not with claims to particular revelations which are examined in this manner, but with the fundamental assumption of the ecclesiastical tradition that divine revelation to humanity can and does occur. The critical mind can find no persuasive evidence that this is so.

Flashes of insight come to us. The critical mind often experiences such flashes and has no problem with them. Stunning feats of imagination cause no problem either. Such insights and imaginings may turn out to be profound formulations of truth, and this too poses no problem. The problem arises when someone asserts that these imaginings and insights are true, particularly those recorded in "official" texts because they are regarded by the faithful as divine in origin. The problem rises when the ecclesiastical mind claims to know by faith that these insights and imaginings were in fact revelations from God. On this point the two traditions divide. On this point no reconciliation is possible. If the one is true the other is not and vice versa.

This fundamental contradiction has been the source of untold difficulty in the ecclesiastical tradition. Because organized religion in the West has employed both modes of thinking, its thinkers have had to wrestle with the problem of the cut-off point as we saw in chapter 1 where the distinction between modifying and thoroughgoing liberals was made. Where does reason stop and faith begin? Where do we leave off the more secular practice of questing and testing and enter the sacred precincts of acceptance of revelation of faith?

As with so many questions Thomas Aquinas cast into final form the explanation still given today by the Roman Catholic Church, and in other traditions as well. Truth is attainable by reason as well as by revelation, he said. Some truths are attainable in both ways and of course, some only through revelation. But these truths are not contradictory. They are simply two equally valid ways of reaching the same goal. On the other hand, Aquinas said, truths that can be reached only through revelation are so ineffable they can be arrived at in no other way. These truths are not *un*reasonable. Because of our finitude we may not be able to grasp them in their entirety, but that does not make them unreasonable. It only means, he concluded, that they are beyond the reach of reason alone.

But Aquinas never resolved the problem of the cut-off point between the use of faith and reason. Protestantism and Judaism have done no better. "The only way to enter the orbit of faith is to enter it," asserts a contemporary Jewish writer. A Protestant argues that we should not look *at* the Bible. We can only understand it by standing *within* it, by reading it with personal involvement. We can do this, he says, because as Christians we believe that the Bible is unique. "It is the Christian claim that the perspective set forth in the Bible has been provided by God through his own self-revelation."

These statements are typical of Protestant, Catholic, and Jewish opinions, but they leave unanswered the critical question: How do you know when to stop thinking and enter the orbit of faith? If you know, what is the criterion by which you decide?

In distinguishing between "modifying" and "thoroughgoing-liberals" we noted the cut-off point beyond which modifying-liberals were unwilling to continue modifying traditional doctrine. At that point they "stepped out on the venture of faith." The same principle applies with the use or non-use of the doctrine of revelation in the ecclesiastical tradition.

Present-day writers like to quote Paul's statement, "We have this treasure in earthen vessels." The earthen vessels that break, wear out, and are cast away are the doctrines and practices the writer thinks should be disposed of. The "treasure" these vessels hold is the central teaching of the church as the writer understands it, the enduring permanent truth of Christianity.

But the problem of the cut-off point remains. Once the questioning, testing, speculating process has begun, by what standard do you give it up? A contemporary theologian, once a believer, later, by his own admission an unbeliever, found his answer to this question in the Christian community and in its ancient hallowed traditions—in short, in the church. The creeds, he wrote, are not "statements of what really happened or will happen but . . . statements about . . . my tradition. To recite the creed is to recall my heritage, my roots. . . . Membership in a community united by a common symbolic paradigm [is what is wanted;] being part of a community of faith." As with all those who, at a given point, cease to inquire and "enter the orbit of faith," his is the ancient position of the believer, a position older than that of Augustine, Aquinas, and so many of the churchmen. Like them, he resolves the problem of the cut-off point with the authority and discipline of the church. In doing so, he attempts to save his own integrity by asserting that his choice of a community of faith to which to submit was freely made.

To all of this the critical mind as of old raises a single question. If the process of inquiry, of questing, testing, and reformulating is valid enough to enter upon, and valid enough to bring a believer to the point of clear and openly acknowledged unbelief in certain ancient dogmas, on what ground can the questing, testing, reformulating process then be given up and replaced by accepting the articles of faith in a particular religious tradition? On what ground can so important an undertaking be given into the hands of an ecclesiastical or any other kind of authority?

Today mainline churchmen in all faiths test and speculate in all fields and they do so very widely in the field of religion. On what ground can they stop their questing and testing at a particular point and say, "Here we enter the community of faith. Beyond this point our questions are no longer answered by the testing, questing process. Hereafter they are answered by the authority of the community of faith we choose to enter."

Can the holiness of a community of faith save it from error or from venality? The historical record shows the opposite. In fact, the critical way in religion arose because of the human frailties various households of faith have exhibited.

Such is the final contradiction between the ecclesiastical and the critical way in religion. A cut-off point where thinking stops and faith begins is impossible for the critical way in religion. The essence of the critical way is to continue the questioning process until the question *How do you know?* can only be answered: I do not know. In the critical tradition to say: "I know by faith" is not such an answer, for it leaves unanswered the further question: How do you know that what you believe yourself to know by faith is valid? Thus the process of inquiry begins again, and when it does, we have moved from the ecclesiastical back to the critical way in religion.

PART IV

The Critical Way

We come now to the deposit of "faith" that results from the critical process. Is there any, or does the critical way require that all conceptual formulations be kept in perpetual suspension? What, if any, are the teachings of the critical way in religion? What beliefs, if any, does it hold?

To answer questions like these we have first to remember that the critical mind shies away from the word "faith" unless it is defined with sufficient precision so that we know what we are talking about. People ask: What is your faith? but they mean: What are the official doctrines of your church? Or they may mean: What are the principles by which you live? The critical mind prefers words like "commitment," "axiom," "principle," "hypothesis," and "concept." These words suggest that you may hold in your heart convictions quite different from the official faith of your church. They suggest also that the passion with which you hold a belief has no bearing on its validity.

All of us, of course, live by some sort of faith, whether good or evil, accurate or faulty. For this reason, getting our faith into language is of the utmost importance. Critically minded people are not exempt from this requirement, although some of them seem to think they are. Ultimate certainty may be denied to us but that fact does not require us to hold everything in abeyance. In any case, life does not permit us to. It is simply not possible to wait until all the evidence is in before choosing a course of action for living.

Our formulations of truth, then, and our commitments to principles of action as well must be stated, written out. Then we will know what they are. Then we can examine them, think about them, and test them in order to be sure that the words say what we mean and not something else. And we can, of course, change them if they don't convey what we intend.

To require that our commitments and formulations be cast into language is not, as many fear, to fall back into dogma. The difference lies in the manner in which our commitments are held. In the critical tradition our principles are formulations only. They may seem to us to be as certain as the law of gravitation or the coming of the dawn, but they are always subject to review, correction, restatement, even abandonment, if a better formulation can be found.

But can we live by such a philosophy? We have now to consider what principles might emerge through the testing, questing process and whether or not it is possible to live our lives in accordance with them.

14

Despair, Hope, and Resolve

A thought structure as basic as that of Christianity, Judaism, and Islam cannot be questioned without serious consequences. We have seen that such questioning is now very widespread, especially in Christianity, and we have seen that the answers offered by the ecclesiastical mind, numerous and carefully thought out as they are, do not meet the questions. The resulting problem for critically minded people is far more serious than most church leaders seem to be willing to believe. They write and speak as if the problem was "secularism," "materialism," or even animosity toward religion itself. When critical questions are raised they are apt to sigh heavily and say: "We've heard all that before." They need to ask *why* they have heard it all before and why they keep on hearing it. They seem not to see the pervasiveness of the problem, or the increasing frustration of critical minds when their questions are turned aside rather than answered. Above all, church leaders fail to see that the sense of disillusionment and ennui that marks so much thought in our time is due in no small part to their own failure to take critical questions seriously.

1. The Ebb Tide of Faith

How far are the growth of the critical way in religion and the increasing disillusionment of our time interrelated? Many would answer: Very closely. Matthew Arnold is generally regarded as having caught this feeling in a vivid metaphor. In his poem "Dover Beach," written nearly a century and a half ago, he reflected as he watched the receding tide:

The Sea of Faith
  was once, too, at the full. . . .
But now I only hear
  Its melancholy long withdrawing roar.

Those who quote the poem as evidence of loss of faith among the Victorians do not always notice that Arnold pinpointed the reason exactly. He continued:

. . . The world which seems
  to lie before us like a land of dreams
So various, so beautiful, so new
  Hath really neither joy nor love nor light
Nor certitude, nor peace, nor help for pain.

The key word here is *certitude,* as we can see if we turn to Arnold's earlier contemporary and fellow-countryman Thomas Carlyle. In his *Sartor Resartus* he had written:

"Thus has the bewildered wanderer to stand . . . shouting question after question into the Sibyl-cone of Destiny and receiving no Answer but an Echo. . . . No Pillar of Cloud by day and no Pillar of Fire by night any longer guides the Pilgrim. To such lengths has the spirit of Inquiry carried him. . . . To me the universe was all void. . . . It was one huge immeasurable Steam engine, rolling on in its dead indifference, to grind me limb from limb. O, the vast gloomy, solitary Golgotha, and Mill of Death."

Accompanying expressions like these, there were others that hardly fitted the doctrine of progress we are accustomed to associate with our immediate ancestors. At least as far back as the eighteenth century we can see evidence that not everyone thought everything was steadily getting better. Recall the engravings of William Hogarth, with their harsh depiction of the seamier side of life, or Jean Millet's sensitive, nineteenth-century paintings that remind us of the tedium and suffering that life brings to so many. Victor Hugo and Charles Dickens did the same with their novels.

In our time artistic expression of this kind, if not this quality, seems to have become the rule rather than the exception. In 1942, during the German occupation of France, Albert Camus published the *Myth of Sisyphus.* The ancient, mythical Greek king, forever condemned to roll uphill a great stone that always rolled down again on reaching the top, symbolized for Camus the human race itself. Life, he was saying, is meaningless. Every gain is a loss and nothing is ever accomplished. Jean-Paul Sartre in his *Nausea* offers us a picture of the world that makes him sick. We have the hopeless picture of life given by Franz Kafka in *The Trial* and *The Castle*; we have T. S. Eliot's "hollow men," and a mass of latter-day writing, typified by Ionesco's *The Bald Soprano.* Behind these works lies a host of lesser writings that feed on their own gloom and that seem to take a kind of sinister joy in laying before us the absurdity of life and the degradation and evil we see among our fellow creatures and our helplessness to do anything about it. In contemporary novels, drama, and the cinema, a yet more vicious picture of the human creature is set before us.

The dismal view of human nature taken by the artistic and literary community has been nourished by a parallel phenomenon among newsmen and the media. Beginning in the early twentieth century and accelerating to a crescendo in our own time, we have been nearly overwhelmed by exposés of corruption, thievery, extortion, and indifference to human suffering of every kind, at all levels of society and in virtually all of its aspects. A disheartened academic has laid it down with quite unacademic dogmatism: "This civilization, already so far overtaken by barbarism, is at an end, and nothing we do will put it back together again."

The result of all this writing, and the depiction of these themes in painting and sculpture, on the screen and on the stage, is now widely reinforced by television. Daily, its cameras scour the earth for tragedy, disaster, evildoing, and suffering to serve up to the viewer at breakfast, during the evening meal, and on retiring. Confronted by such a mountain of evidence of our own venality, gullibility, incompetence, and indifference to human misery, we are filled with dismay. Worse still, the enormity and pervasiveness of it all, at every level of society and among all sorts of people, leaves us feeling utterly helpless. The prospect is chilling. We have reached a stage in the world's history where world government is essential to world survival; yet, we have little hope of achieving it and, as yet, little or no control over the kind of government we are to have should we achieve it. Time is running out, and in the meanwhile, we may pollute the earth to the point of uninhabitability or populate it to the point of mutual starvation.

We are equally helpless in other profoundly important ways. Guerilla-type warfare carried on by any group organized for any purpose, whether noble or mean, grows apace, and we have no power to stop that either. Private crime against both people and property, with no motive other than personal gain or a kind of private vengeance, also spreads and we seem to be without the means to stop that. Slowly, as individuals and as peoples, we are retreating behind locks and barricades; slowly, we are surrounding ourselves with armed guards whose task it is to protect the innocent from those who would maim or kill them for political purposes, private gain, or merely out of insensate rage. Slowly but surely we are giving up our freedom as people down the ages have done in order to achieve security.

A deadly parallel between contemporary Western culture and ancient Rome is now discernible. In this area, an arresting piece of writing comes to us from the pen of Gilbert Murray, the British classicist. His words are startling, not only because he was writing about Rome rather than about our own time, but also because he was writing in the heyday of optimism that dominated Western thought just before the outbreak of World War I. Murray wrote:

> Anyone who turns from the great writers of classical Athens, say Sophocles or Aristotle, to those of the Christian era, must be conscious of a great difference in tone. There is a change in the whole relation of the writer to the world about him. The new quality is not specifically Christian; it is just as marked in the Gnostics and Mithras-worshippers as in the Gospels and the Apocalypse, in Julian and Plotinus, as in Gregory and Jerome. It is hard to describe. It is a rise of asceticism, of mysticism, in a sense, of pessimism; a loss of self-confidence, of hope in this life and of faith in normal human effort; a despair of patient inquiry, a cry for infallible revelation; an indifference to the welfare of the state, a conversion of the soul to God. It is an atmosphere in which the aim of the good man is not so much to live justly, to help the society to which he belongs and enjoy the esteem of his fellow creatures; but rather, by means of a burning faith, by contempt for the world and its standards, by ecstasy, suffering, and martyrdom, to be granted pardon for unspeakable unworthiness, his immeasurable sins. There is an intensifying of certain spiritual emotions; an increase of sensitiveness, a failure of nerve.

The foregoing parallels with our own time are frightening because they have emerged since Murray wrote. He cannot, therefore, be accused of seeing the past in terms of the present, for the present he so vividly describes in terms of the past had not yet come about when he penned the above words in 1908. The parallels are the more alarming because they suggest that the disintegration of the Graeco-Roman world sets before us a general outline of the perhaps inevitable disintegration of our own.

Many of the implications of modern scientific thought reinforce our dour outlook on life. The young philosopher Bertrand Russell saw this as early as 1903 when he wrote:

"The life of man is a long march through the night, surrounded by invisible foes, tortured by weariness and pain, toward a goal that few can hope to reach, and where none may tarry long. Brief and powerless is man's life; on him and all his race the slow sure doom falls pitiless and dark. Blind to good and evil, reckless of destruction, omnipotent matter rolls on its relentless way. Man, condemned today to lose his dearest, tomorrow himself to pass through the gate of darkness." All he could say was that man "nevertheless preserves a mind free from the wanton tyranny that rules his outward life . . . proudly defiant to sustain alone the world his own ideals have fashioned despite the trampling march of unconscious power."

Today the cosmologists tell us that the sun will eventually burn itself out and, long before that, all life on this planet will have perished in cosmic cold. That event is so far distant the possibility should not depress us. But it does, nevertheless, and we are further dismayed when we learn that one day the universe as a whole may end in eternal frozen darkness.

Of course these predictions may be invalid. Science has changed its basic outlook more than once in the past. But many people, in particular those whose religious background has taught them to look for certainty, emphasize the fact that science itself today concedes its own uncertainty about its own first principles. A Cambridge University scientist has proposed a principle of ignorance to match Heisenberg's principle of uncertainty, on the ground that some things are in principle unknowable.

Heisenberg's Principle states that at the atomic level events simply cannot be observed with certainty. A second principle known as "the overthrow of parity" or "the collapse of symmetry" provides an occasion for yet further dismay. It used to be held that any conceivable experiment in atomic physics watched by one observer directly and by a second observer in a mirror would look the same. Neither observer, by the data before him, would be able to say whether he was seeing directly or looking into a mirror. In the language of quantum mechanics this is called "parity." It can be shown mathematically that a world marked by parity is one that is symmetrical. In such a world, right and left are identical and, when interchanged, result in no change whatever. That principle, too, has now been overthrown. Experiments have shown that there is a difference between right and left at the atomic level; in other words, a difference between right and left that is asymmetrical. A contemporary theoretical physicist writes: "It therefore seems that Einstein was doubly wrong when he said, 'God does not play dice with the world.' Consideration of particle emission from black holes would seem to suggest that God not only plays dice but also sometimes throws them where they cannot be seen."

The discovery of "anti-matter," the current debate as to whether time must always move forward, and doubt as to whether the fundamental laws of the universe are the same everywhere—all these further accentuate the contemporary uncertainty of science. For many religious traditionalists the implication is clear. Since both science and religion are uncertain, they would argue, it must follow that religion is the equal of science in science's own sphere. They would insist further that in the religious realm where, through faith, religion enjoys a certainty science can never claim, religion is superior to science.

Nevertheless, to concede as we must that we cannot be totally and finally certain about anything is not nearly as drastic as it sounds. Human ignorance about fundamental things is not growing. Where once we were sure, we are not now ignorant. The difference is not between what we know and what we don't know. The difference is between what we once thought we knew and what we are now not quite so sure of. Now we know that we don't know as much as we once supposed.

Western culture, taken as a whole, and much of world culture as well, has no trouble with this state of affairs. We have long since grasped the principle of ever-widening knowledge, accompanied by the continual exposure of former misconceptions and mistakes. We might wish to be more certain than we are, especially in the fundamentals of life, but since we cannot be, we readily accept the apparent loss for the greater gain.

2. Tearing Down and Building Up

Any attempt to improve the existing order implies criticism of it, modification of it, and sometimes the destruction and replacement of at least a part of it. For this reason from the beginning the critical tradition has suffered from the charge of negativism. For the same reason, those who like nothing so much as to pull things down, who exult in the crash and rising dust of destruction, sometimes seek respectability in the critical tradition. But they are soon frustrated, for the purpose of the critical mind is not to destroy but to build. Its basic thrust is not a release for the cantankerous, support for the cynic, or satisfaction for the nihilist, but opportunity for the idealist seeking to make things better than they are. The critical tradition criticizes in order to correct. It finds fault in order to improve; it destroys in order to build; it exposes error in order to move toward truth. Thales gave little if any attention to shortcomings in the cosmology of Homer and Hesiod. He simply offered the Greeks a new and, as it seemed to him, a better way of thinking about the nature of things. Did he realize that his speculations were an implicit denial of the Homeric pantheon and of the powers of the Olympic gods? Who can now say? In any case, the conflict was implicit, and only awaited the insight and boldness of Xenophanes to put it into language.

The priestly editors of the Old Testament attempted to do the same with the ancient Hebrew myths of creation. Bible scholars have shown that in Genesis there are two stories of man's beginnings. Much the older of the two begins in the second chapter where we read: "These are the generations of the heavens and of the earth when they were created, in the day that the Lord God made the earth and the heavens, And every plant of the field before it was in the earth, and every herb of the field before it grew; for the Lord God had not caused it to rain upon the earth, and there was not a man to till the ground, But there went up a mist from the earth, and watered the whole face of the ground, and the Lord God formed man of the dust of the ground, and breathed into his nostrils the breath of life; and man became a living soul."

This familiar story—as it continues on with the creation of Eden, the creation of woman, the temptation by the serpent, and the expulsion of Adam and Eve from Paradise—was far too primitive to satisfy the more sophisticated minds of the fifth century B.C., when most scholars agree that Genesis I was written. Whence they got or how they contrived the story of the creation of the world and of man in six days is a question with which we need not be concerned. Our purpose is to see that, as Thales believed he saw more deeply into cosmological questions than had Homer, so the priestly editors of Genesis thought they saw more deeply into the beginning of things than had the author of Genesis II and III. Each offered a new explanation that he or they thought did the job better than the old.

There is no evidence that the priestly compilers of Genesis sensed any discrepancy between the first and second chapters that could not readily be reconciled. In fact, they compiled the ancient and sacred writings of Israel in so skillful a manner and with such consistency of detail that it was not until the nineteenth century, with the development of the documentary hypothesis, that Bible scholars were able to begin the identification of the earlier sources from which the Bible we have today was compiled. In some instances, even today, after years of minute study and debate, all that scholars can offer is an educated guess. Genesis, most scholars now agree, is like a patchwork quilt into which much very old material has been set intact, to which much new material has been added, and the whole sewn together with such artistry as to make a single piece more lovely than any of its parts.

Because the critical way is often destructive to traditional doctrines and dogmas, defenders of the ecclesiastical way tend to suspect that its true purpose is not the improvement of religion but its destruction. Vincent of Lerins, for example, whose efforts to establish orthodoxy we have already noted, laid it down back in Augustine's time that the heretic "is a man of pride and malice—a wolf in sheep's clothing, a serpent in the garden, Satan's secret emissary on earth." Baruch de Spinoza, as we have seen, was excommunicated from the Jewish community in Amsterdam because of his "evil opinions" and of the "abominable heresies practiced and taught by him." The language of the decree indicates the revulsion of feeling that his thought aroused. It concluded, "Cursed be he by day and cursed be he by night. Cursed be he in sleeping and cursed be he in waking. The Lord shall not pardon him . . . and we warn you that none may speak with him by word of mouth, nor by writing, nor show any favor to him, nor be under one roof with him . . . nor read any paper composed or written by him."

Likewise, in Christianity, as late as the Enlightenment, we noted how often it was assumed that any questioning or criticism of Christian teaching was a result not of sincere searching for the truth but of hatred of the church. "Skeptics," "unbelievers," and "deists" alike were thought to be moved by hostility toward religion rather than a desire to improve it. In 1864, when Pope Pius IX issued his famous bull *Quanta cura,* he characterized liberals inside and outside the Roman Church, quite apart from their moral character, as "evil men . . . who endeavored by their fallacious opinions and most wicked writings to subvert the foundations of Religion and

Civil Society, to remove from our midst all virtue and justice, to deprave the hearts and minds of all. . . ."

Even so sober and dispassionate a scholar as Peter Gay in his book on the *Enlightenment* speaks of "the passion against religion" of David Hume, although he makes the statement after praising the great Scottish thinker as a philosopher. One of the most recent instances to come to my attention is a lengthy review of Brand Blanshard's *Reason and Belief.* "Beneath the veneer of rationality in this champion of secularism" a reviewer thought he saw "a deepseated and oftentimes blinding prejudice." That is severe censure of a writer the reviewer first praises as "a paradigm of the professional philosopher." By way of contrast you will search Blanshard's writing in vain for a comparable allegation of low motives in those with whom *he* disagrees.

John Henry Newman, in the last century, often spoke in this vein. Critics of his faith, he asserted, entertained toward Catholic theologians a feeling not merely of contempt, but of absolute hatred. He spoke of a world "not of professed Catholics, but of inveterate, often bitter, commonly contemptuous Protestants."

The suspicion that those who oppose us are not altogether honorable in their motives is by no means confined to religion. I have met it as often among social reformers as theologians. Social action people, whether Christian, Jewish, or nonreligious, can become very angry when their views are opposed. An argument with them can quickly degenerate into accusations of low and hidden motives, both conscious and unconscious. So universal is this tendency that I have seen it exactly replicated in the environmental movement, where high-minded people can become very acrimonious while debating policies designed to preserve the environment, a goal devoutly pursued by both sides. Where we care very much, we humans too readily mistrust anyone who opposes us.

If we are to understand the critical way in religion, however, we must be clear that it does not always include the moral reformers. They are critics, to be sure, but they are generally critics of conduct, not of thought. For the most part, moral reformers are defenders of the thought-structure of their own as well as of an earlier time. Most moral reformers strive to bring the behavior of men and women back to a previously established norm. Usually they are not innovators.

The movements of moral reform that continually swept through the Church during the Middle Ages and on into the Reformation sought in virtually every instance to bring the clergy, and the laity as well, back to the high level of personal morality that was taught and presumably practiced in the early Church. Saint Francis of Assisi and Bernard of Clairvaux, two of the most famous of the great Catholic reformers, had no quarrel with the doctrines of the Church, either theological or moral. They took the validity of these teachings for granted and never questioned them. All their criticism was directed toward those who affirmed Christian morality but did not practice it. The same was true of many of the so-called heretical sects, such as the Albigensians and Waldensians. While in the end they taught certain heretical doctrines, their original impulse was not theological, it was moral. Their purpose was not to criticize doctrine but to return to the moral practices of New Testament times.

A second aspect of movements of moral reform that does not belong in the critical tradition has become apparent in our own time: the sense of exhilaration to be derived from a movement of moral protest. Such protest often provides the protester with a sense of elation that is derived from participation in a struggle far more than it derives from the moral righteousness of the cause in the name of which the protest is made. To cite a single example, one of the participants in the student uprising at Columbia University in 1968 reveals the feelings of invigoration he often derived from the violence of those protests. He wrote, "One of the curious side effects of the experience of violence, at least for me, is that it creates sexual hunger . . . the violence was liberating." Later, calling to see how a friend was feeling after having been attacked by the police, the author found his friend "strangely elated by the triumph of having had several stitches sewn in his scalp. He told me part of his head was shaved and he considered it his red badge of courage." Still later, he writes, reflecting on his own feelings and his frustration with a girl, "Violence was wanted. . . . I hungered for it. I wanted to fight in front of my chick. To prove myself." His was a very ancient urge, but it had nothing to do with moral protest.

Many of the great moral reformers of history, however, clearly belong in the critical tradition, even though their protest was more moral than theological. When Amos cried to the people of Samaria, "Woe to you who are at ease in Zion," he was, so far as we can now judge, introducing into the traditions of Israel a new and higher moral standard than had prevailed heretofore. Amos stood in the center of the critical tradition when he denounced those who "sell the righteous for silver and the needy for a pair of shoes" and those who "trample the head of the poor into the dust of the earth and turn aside the way of the afflicted." He was not merely demanding a higher standard of conduct of the Israelites; he was sharply upgrading the standard of conduct itself. Isaiah and Jeremiah, Hosea and Micah were doing the same thing. Their call for righteousness was not a summons to return to the old way from which the people had departed, although they often spoke as if it were. Theirs was a summons to a new and higher standard of morality that many peoples of the world are still trying to achieve.

In Jesus of Nazareth, as his words are recorded in the New Testament, we can see this principle dramatically illustrated. According to the account in Matthew's Gospel, his rejection of the older canons of Jewish law and the introduction of new canons with which to replace them is explicit. Addressing the multitudes on a Galilean hillside, he said: "Ye have heard that it hath been said by them of old time 'Thou shalt not kill . . . thou shalt not commit adultery . . . an eye for an eye and a tooth for a tooth . . . love thy neighbor and hate thine enemy. . . .'"

Then, in each instance, he gives his audience a new and, as he sees it, a higher and better way: Do not kill; but do not even be angry with your brothers. Do not commit adultery, but do not even look on a woman to lust after her. Not an eye for an eye and a tooth for a tooth, but turn the other cheek, go the second mile. "Love your enemies, bless them that curse you, do good to them that hate you and pray for them which despitefully use you and persecute you." These are ideals toward which millions have striven since, but which few if any have fully achieved. Whether we agree with them or not, whether we think such ideals can be achieved or not, Jesus' admonitions belong in the critical tradition because they reject the old way in order to make way for that which is newer and better. But, as we know from the Bible record, they were very unsettling in his time. As we also know, many of his teachings are still very unsettling today. They are all familiar but many of them, put into practice, would be exceedingly disruptive of current modes of behavior and thought. The critical tradition is by no means alone in its insistence on the nobility as well as the virtual unattainability of the Christian ethic.

To criticize the established order; to insist that things should be better than they are; above all, to question teachings that are said to come from Almighty God, and to suggest improvements upon them—the negative character of all of this has seldom been doubted by the ecclesiastical mind. Church people have frequently and vehemently denounced the critical-minded for presuming to question authority and teachings that are said to be divine in origin. They hold that the testing, questing process is arrogant and they call upon the questioners to admit their limitations, to cease striving to know what cannot be known, and to let their arrogance give way to humility.

Their demands are supported by the ancient and widely held doctrine of human helplessness, one that we noted in connection with Giannozzo Manetti and Innocent III. More recently Sören Kierkegaard, the Danish theologian, has given expression to it. He opened one of his books, *Purity of Heart,* with the following lines, of which he must have thought well, for he repeated them verbatim at the end of the volume: "Father in Heaven! What is a man without Thee! What is all that he knows, vast accumulation tho' it be, but a chipped fragment if he does not know Thee! What is all his striving, could it even encompass the world, but a half-finished work if he does not know Thee."

Kierkegaard's is a dominant theme in Christianity and can be traced at least as far back as Saint Augustine, whose *Confessions* amount to a thoroughgoing presentation of the helpless philosophy of life. In an illustrative passage early in the book, Augustine asks God to allow him to pray despite the fact that he, Augustine, is totally unworthy to do so, since, as a human being, he is nothing but dust and ashes. Continuing, he speaks of his "dying life" and "living death." It is his way of describing the misery of our human condition.

Augustine's, however, is not a counsel of despair. "Thy compassion [God's] will take me up," he writes, feeling that he can rely on God's mercy to lift him out of his helplessness. That is his basic philosophy: what we humans cannot do for ourselves, God will do for us. For those who believe it, this teaching provides comfort in the present and hope for the future.

What is the reason for the nearly universal attempt on the part of the more orthodox clergy in their preaching and through the liturgy of the churches they serve to convict the worshiper of his or her helplessness and sin? In sermon and prayer, in reading and unison recital, the clergy seem to be attempting to persuade the congregation of its worthlessness and of its helplessness as well. Supposing for the sake of argument that some, if not all, are really seeking subservience to the church on the part of the communicants, do they not see that they are encouraging subservience generally, the subservience of one person to another, subservience to existing economic and social structures, and finally subservience to the state also? Do they want that? I cannot believe it.

A contemporary drama critic made the same point reviewing a particularly vicious depiction of human activity. He wrote: "The thesis that man is irretrievably bad and corrupt is the essence of fascism. What sort of social institutions are to be built on that pessimistic view of man's nature?" He answered his own question plainly, unmistakably: "They will—they must, if logic prevails—be the repressive . . . distrustful, violent institutions of fascism."

There is evidence based on research to support his views. A study of eight hundred Protestant male theological students made in 1961 showed that the theologically conservative students were far more authoritarian in their life-philosophy than were the theologically liberal students. Conservatives tend to be submissive, liberals tend to be dominant, the study found. As an example, the conservatives tended to conform to parental attitudes far more than the liberals did. The attitude of the liberals was shown to be a direct outgrowth of the liberal teachings of the parents themselves. In other words, liberal parents tended to produce children with the capacity to think problems through for themselves rather than merely reflecting parental attitudes.

The idea of human depravity and helplessness is usually advanced by people of privilege—people who enjoy the good things of life, while millions live in poverty and the despair that poverty induces. Those who support it tend toward aristocratic structures. They advocate a hierarchy of persons within which each has his or her place, a hierarchy within which the less privileged do not presume to tell their "betters" what should or should not be done. Those in authority, especially church leaders, are presumed to know, according to this view, since their knowledge and authority is presumed to be divine in origin. The task of the people, accordingly, is to accept, to obey, and to conform.

As in so many other instances, there is a curious reversal of roles here between those of the critical and those of the ecclesiastical way. The ecclesiastical approach is generally considered to be positive because it offers doctrinal certainty and often quite rigid ethical precepts. The critical way, on the other hand, is castigated for its negations. Yet what could be more truly negative than the doctrine of human helplessness? And what could be more truly positive than insistence upon the right to inquire, explore, question, and to develop new concepts to replace those that have become inadequate? Lying at the heart of the critical way in religion is a conviction diametrically opposed to that of the ecclesiastical tradition: that we humans are weak but not totally so; helpless but not without some resources; limited but not without remarkable capacities as well.

Those who follow the critical way in religion hold not only that we *can* do something about human misery, but that we must. There is no evidence anywhere, they say, that any person or any outside force will save us: only wishful thinking makes us believe in divine intervention. So far as we can see, we are on our own in the universe. Evil, sloth, greed, and sin do indeed beset us, but all of these can be lessened and increasingly controlled if we will only give ourselves to the task.

Followers of the critical way hold that no matter how bad things are, something can be done to make them better. They believe that we humans are endowed with enormous capacities of a very wide range and variety on which we can call. It is far from saying that we can do anything we choose, but it is saying very directly that, because there is much that we seem to be able to do, we must, therefore, do what we can. We betray ourselves if we sit down and weep at our limitations, or worse still, relieve ourselves of the obligation to try, by proclaiming our helplessness and laying the blame for our condition upon society or upon whatever gods our society believes in.

From the beginning, alongside those who have expressed disgust with the human race, have stood those who have proclaimed its potential if not actual dignity. Until recently these have been few in number, yet they have urged us on in the face of powerful opposition. They have called upon men and women to make the most of the abilities that lie within them.

The great periods of growth and development in the history of the West seem to have been periods dominated by this philosophy: most notably ancient Greece, the Renaissance, and the Enlightenment. What shall we say of our own time? We can point to enormous achievements in a wide variety of areas. But we can also point to the horrors of World Wars I and II, the aftermath of each and the misery, worldwide, to be found nearly everywhere. We can point to the greater premeditated horrors of Belsen and Gulag. Obviously, we are too close to assess the character of our own time accurately, but it appears that, in retrospect, it too may turn out to have been a time of very great achievement, despite the shortcomings of which we are all so well aware.

A behavioral scientist of the present day, frequently denounced for his supposedly dehumanizing tendencies, concluded one of his most controversial books with the line, "We have yet to see what man can make of man." Of such stuff the critical philosophy is made. To say this is not to endorse either the techniques or the philosophy of behavioral science. It is instead to cite from an unexpected source a philosophy of life that denies the pervasive ecclesiastical doctrine of human helplessness.

It is here that we begin to state the "faith" of the critical way in religion. Its supposed negations are based upon a fundamental view of human nature, and it is positive, not negative, in character. We shall explore this principle at length in succeeding chapters. The point here is that, where the critical mind seems to be destructive, it is instead disposing of false or inadequate notions in order that better ones may take their place. Where it seems to be tearing down, it is clearing the way for building up.

The critical mind asks many questions but it is not skeptical. Doubt is not its hallmark. The dictionary associates "doubt" with terms like unbelief, uncertainty, distrust, and with phrases like lack of confidence, to consider unlikely, to be dubious about, and deliberate suspension of judgment. Implicit is the idea of dismissal and rejection of something previously asserted.

The attitude of the critical mind does neither. It does not begin by denying, by rejecting, or by considering unlikely the ideas that others hold. But neither does it begin by accepting them. The critical mind begins by taking a hard look at any doctrine or practice anyone may propose and by asking: How valid is it? The answer to that question determines the response of the critical mind. If dissimulation and error appear, those of the critical tradition look elsewhere for their answers. If, however, the testing process reveals consistency in concept and viewpoint, and if it leads to greater understanding of the world and our human condition, then the critical mind is at home and will follow that path as far as it will go.

15

The University

The ecclesiastical way in religion is institutionalized; the critical way is not. No difference between the two has had more far reaching consequences than this. The ecclesiastical way is nurtured, protected, taught, and propagated through its churches, temples, priests, ministers, and lay members. Vast wealth endows it. The political power of religion in the West and the East as well is beyond measure. The power of organized religion is often exercised openly and publicly, as it was by the Christian Church in the Middle Ages, as it has been by both Protestant and Catholic Churches since the Reformation, and as it attained expression conspicuously in Islam after the revolution of 1979 in Iran. But the indirect power and influence exercised by religion is greater, more subtle, and far more pervasive, because it is supported by a very widespread, intricately interrelated array of social structures that seek to perpetuate themselves no less than to serve the religious needs of the people. We can only guess at the degree to which the mind-set of the various cultures of the world is determined by organized religion.

In chapter 6 we saw the reemergence of the critical way in western Europe after its demise in the Graeco-Roman world a thousand years before. Because independent thinking is a threat to any established order, be it that of church or state, the critical way might have been crushed again in the twelfth or thirteenth century had it not been institutionalized in a new social structure, the university. Started by churchmen within the church, the medieval schools soon developed an identity of their own, and steadily moved outside the orbit of the church. Today most but not all of our great universities, even those that began within the church, are steadfastly and clearly independent of clerical control. Today the university ranks with government and religion among the most potent and pervasive of all social structures. It emerged with the critical way in religion as a part of the broad and inclusive cultural development in the West that scholars identify as the Medieval Reformation and Renaissance.

The conjunction of these two beginnings was no coincidence. The appearance of the university and the reappearance of the critical way in religion were two aspects of the same development. At that time the West seemed suddenly to realize that it possessed a considerable body of knowledge of which people were largely ignorant. By the time of the high Middle Ages, an extensive body of law had accumulated; medical knowledge (as then understood) was rapidly increasing; natural science, including astronomy and, of course, alchemy and astrology as well, were gaining devotees, while a study of the Church Fathers and of the writings of classical Greece and Rome was opening a whole new vista to the Western mind.

The relatively sudden realization that all this learning lay waiting for the student who would apply himself led in its turn to a sense of excitement in the learning process—in the mastery of languages, for example—by which such a treasure chest could be unlocked. Putting the various pieces together, as they became available, lent further excitement to the process. New manuscripts continually were discovered. Meanwhile, new ideas occurred to those who had begun thinking about the meaning of all they were learning. New questions arose. In this way the emerging universities and the critical way grew at the same time, each interacting with the other and each a part of the same development.

All this occurred nearly a thousand years ago, and in speaking of it, we must be careful not to translate our pattern of thought back into those far-distant days. Only the faint reawakening of the critical tradition can be discerned at that time. The medieval mind was far from asking the critical question, How do you know? particularly in religion. Nevertheless, the process which leads to that question was then reasserting itself, primarily in the university community, and its growth has been more or less steady ever since. Today it is not exaggeration to say the critical way is the university way and the university way is the critical way.

1. The University Tradition

The wealth, facilities, and prestige of our universities are today beyond measure. In uncounted ways, government, industry, philanthropy, even the churches, all turn to the university community for assistance. Over and beyond their educational function, our universities provide information and data of incalculable value to contemporary society. In payment for these services, to insure their continuance and to provide for their expansion, government, industry, philanthropy, the churches—every aspect and segment of contemporary society—contribute directly and indirectly to the ongoing university enterprise.

The bare statistics on the growth of institutions of higher learning in the United States tell something of the story. Beginning in the late nineteenth century and continuing on in the twentieth, the population of the United States trebled. During the same period the enrollment in our high and preparatory schools increased some ninety times and in our colleges some thirty times. High and preparatory school teachers increasingly came from the ranks of the college-trained. Leaders of thought—men like William James, Josiah Royce, George Santayana, and John Dewey—spent most of their time in university teaching. Previous leaders of thought had not done so. Today's intellectual leaders come almost exclusively from our universities, and we have been witnessing an accelerating movement of university men into high policy-making positions in government and business.

As we might expect, the rapidly increasing role of the university in Western culture, and more recently in the world as a whole, has in turn brought about a sudden widening of the critical way as a basic mode of thinking. Meanwhile its standards have risen sharply. Checking, testing, verifying; the constant call for newer, better, more adequate and accurate concepts; the demand for accuracy, reliability, and integrity in the amassing and purveying of knowledge—all these have steadily been heightened by the interacting of the forces within the contemporary university community.

If the university community is scrupulous in ferreting out inadequacy and error, it is ruthless in cases of dissimulation and deceit. The penalty for falsification of data or conclusions in academe is not a fine or imprisonment, but disgrace. Although dishonesty appears to be on the rise today, even in the supposedly sacrosanct realm of scholarship and research, there have been very few cases, and the reason is not hard to see. The practice of testing and questing that lies at the heart of the critical tradition soon exposes the would-be deceiver. Whoever is tempted to falsify in order to gain prestige knows that other investigators will sooner or later expose him.

A more common practice, because it is so difficult to pin down, is stretching one's conclusions in order to make a point that a closer, more scrupulous attention to the data would not permit. Yet here, too, the scholar must expect that any such distortions will be discovered by those who follow after, eager as their predecessors to make their own mark. In the critical or university tradition honesty is not merely the best policy, it is the only possible policy.

Nobody pretends that our universities completely attain so exalted an ideal, either across the board or in any particular academic community. No institution ever fully embodies its own ideal. Our churches and temples do not, and they never have. Neither do our universities, nor are they ever likely to. Like all human institutions, they are made up of human beings, beset by the faults and shortcomings we all know so well.

As a noted scholar reminded me on reading this section, academic people can be no less vain, greedy, and insecure than anyone else. They are, he said, no less subject to petty jealousy, deceit, and vindictiveness than anyone else and they can be as dogma-ridden as any churchman. There is no more discouraging aspect to be found in our institutions of higher learning than the tendency of the academic mind to bog down in trivia. The tendency is built right into the system itself. The demand for accuracy, the demand that a scholar consult all the sources, that he or she know a particular field completely, results in many a study, completely covering the subject in hand, fully documented, but of concern to almost nobody but its own author.

Over a century ago, Cardinal Newman seems to have foreseen the rise of the critical way to a position of dominance in the universities of the west. A convert to the Catholic faith and thereafter one of its most redoubtable defenders, Newman argued that the sciences have a much easier time of it than revelation because they offer "tangible facts, practical results, ever-growing discoveries and perpetual novelties which feed curiosity, sustain attention and stimulate expectation." Therefore, he continued, the sciences "look for the day when they shall have put down Religion, not by shutting its schools, but by emptying them; not by disputing its tenets but by the superior worth and persuasiveness of their own."

Cardinal Newman was quite wrong in supposing that the sciences—the university tradition, speaking more generally—would try in any way to "put down" religion. The academic community has never attacked the church. Most of our greatest universities happily house a graduate school of theology. Most have chapels and chaplains. Religious exercises on campus are common. Many faculty members are devout adherents of established churches and temples in our society. The teaching and practice of religion is central in some Protestant colleges and in most Catholic colleges. Throughout the Western world there is little overt argument and little strife between religion and education. On the surface, at least, all is harmony; all is peace.

Cardinal Newman was quite right, however, in his anticipation of what would happen as the university and the ecclesiastical traditions came up against each other. The day that he foresaw is here. Religiously oriented colleges and universities continue to diminish in number, and the influence of religion in virtually all of them continues to shrink. The critical tradition has now largely replaced the ecclesiastical tradition, not by disputing its tenets but exactly as Newman foresaw—"by the superior worth and persuasiveness of its own." Time has done its work. The thought-pattern of present-day Western society, and much of the East as well, is so imbued with the critical way that the defenses offered by the churches are no longer effective. Like the Maginot Line, they have not been breached; they have been made obsolete. Still manned by those who hold to the ecclesiastical way, the old defenses are now simply bypassed. They stand today as monuments to a past that is dead, irrelevant to the controversies they were designed to still.

The central role of the critical way in the university today, as compared with the former central role of the ecclesiastical way, is thrust into sharp relief in the theological schools that are associated with universities. For generations these schools, especially those that are Protestant, have been in a kind of limbo, halfway between the church and the academy, halfway between the ecclesiastical and the critical way in religion. In the past, little was said about this, at least publicly. Now, however, the question is openly debated. How can a theological school pursue its teaching program in strict adherence to scholarly standards without finding itself eventually asking *How do you know?* in matters of faith? How can it hold to the critical way without continuing to ask that question until the answer has to be: *I don't know,* an answer wholly contrary to faith, the essence of which is to *know,* to be certain where others are in doubt.

The result has been a kind of isolation from the main body of the academic community on the part of our theological schools. "It remains a discouraging fact," runs a typical theological school comment, "that the seminaries are not fully involved in the university world. Even the strongest schools of theology are not conspicuous in the intellectual life of the universities." The author goes on to lament this state of affairs and to complain that as a result young clergymen are not sufficiently involved in the intellectual stream of their time. Thus, he continues, "their preaching becomes arid." Many a sermon-weary churchgoer will sadly but readily agree with him. So, unfortunately, will leaders in other departments of our universities.

Another mainline clergyman, wrestling with the problems created by the critical study of the Scriptures, observed in 1977, "It is far past time to break the truly vicious circle in which the student comes to the seminary and undergoes what is called a crisis of faith; then he graduates and goes to a parish where he preaches the Bible as though he had never heard of critical methodology, thus preparing yet another generation to repeat the same process." Yet writers like these never seem to see that their own ambiguity of mind is the cause of the situation they deplore. In few if any theological schools is it made clear to the students that the critical method, if it is valid, must be pursued all the way to the end. The crisis of faith of which the above writer speaks is never resolved, and that is why it is a lamentable and ever-recurring phenomenon in our theological schools.

In a sermon delivered to the Harvard Divinity School as recently as 1961 a distinguished Bible scholar observed: "The old ideals of learning (critical and disinterested habits of thought, a willingness to follow wherever the truth may lead our minds) so eloquently sponsored by Oxford and Cambridge, Harvard and Yale—these remain alive only in nostalgic dreams." For the university idea of truth he proposed to substitute "truth as fidelity, faithfulness to an order . . . that was revealed in the forms of a particular history" that he describes as "the revelation of a new reality in Jesus Christ which requires decision and loyalty, commitment, faithfulness. . . ."

In the ensuing two decades, those four universities and uncounted colleges and universities everywhere have gone on pursuing the ideal the professor thought obsolete in 1961. His attempt to redefine "truth" did not change things. It only revealed the depth of the struggle within himself to maintain his status in the community of scholars to which his distinguished work as a biblical archeologist fully entitled him, and at the same time to hold to his deeply felt Christian faith. The root problem here is easily stated: while the university has made the critical way its own, even the better theological schools have done so only in part. Where matters of faith are concerned they abandon the critical for the ecclesiastical way. One of the foregoing writers concludes by exhorting theological faculty members not to retreat into privatism and pietism. He seems not to be aware that the critical tradition, now central in our universities, has left devotees of the ecclesiastical tradition with no other choice.

The dean of a noted theological school made a similar observation in 1976: "The attitudes that characterize worship and those that characterize the search for truth—the attitudes of the church and the university . . . are not always understood as compatible. . . . It appears to the church that the seminary often sells out to Athens; to the university, that the seminary is in bondage to Jerusalem." The dean concluded: "A person must get inside a religious tradition, love it and question it at the same time."

These words may, of course, mean two quite different things, depending on the tradition from which one speaks, a difference of which the theological community seems often to be quite unaware. In the ecclesiastical tradition those words mean: "Question your tradition, yes, but since you are within it and love it, you can not question its basic articles of faith without putting yourself outside of it." In the critical tradition these words mean: "To love your tradition, to be fully inside it, is to probe its tenets and its assumptions as far as possible; to leave *no* questions unasked and *no* assumptions unexamined."

The pervasive character of the critical tradition as it affects contemporary thought in and through our universities is evident in the recent marked trend toward courses *about* religion, taught by scholars who make no pretense either of religious belief or disbelief, but who approach the subject as they would anthropology or geology, psychology or art. This development can be seen in the recent increase in courses on death in our universities. Why is there an interest in death on the part of young adults, and why do they register for college courses on the subject? There is much speculation on this question in religious circles. The answer seems to be that students today, imbued as they are with the critical tradition, want exacting analyses of data rather than exhortations to faith. Feeling that the university will meet their needs better because of its critical approach, they turn to their teachers rather than to their clergymen for answers to life's most profound questions.

To illustrate: a course on "The Meanings of Death" was offered at Yale University in the spring of 1975 with the requirement that applicants submit a statement explaining why they wanted to take the course. One student wrote: "I have worked in the emergency room of a hospital, where death was the password and life slipped through one's fingers. The current philosophical and legal question of 'death with dignity' bears a special import to me: a close relative is slowly dying from cancer. I want to understand death in order to live more wisely."

Another wrote: "Since childhood I have been confronted with a host of bewildering deaths in my family and I am certain that it had a profound psychological effect on my maturation process. Left at age twelve with the suicide of a twenty-one-year-old brother, I have been dealt a series of such puzzling events and have been trying to put it all together ever since."

Most of the other statements were similar. Almost all were of the kind one would expect to find coming from students interested in religion. It seems clear that these students, like most others today, having rejected the ecclesiastical way in religion, have turned to the university in their search for answers to religious questions. They do this because it is in the critical, not the ecclesiastical, way that they find more adequate and convincing answers to their questions.

Historians and social analysts have been commenting for some time on the "secularization" of our institutions of higher learning. By this they mean a shift in commitment from traditional religious principles to those that are critical. However, few, except the churchmen, spell out the meaning of this shift for religion. They have been giving the matter increasing attention of late. Many have bluntly set the two in the juxtaposition in which they lie in the academic community, in particular in the theological schools. A typical comment runs: "There is an inherent incompatibility between Christian evangelicalism and the idea of a university." Another announced the emergence of a "university theology" and charged that such a theology does not address the doubts and questions of faith raised by the community of faith, but concerns itself instead with the doubts and questions of those who ignore traditional faith. A series of letters to the editor in a widely read church weekly made the same point, especially with regard to theological schools. The letters were nearly unanimous in arguing that in theological school, at least, scholarship and the critical method should give way to the claims of faith.

Among the churchmen who see the fundamental conflict between the critical way and the ecclesiastical way as it comes to a head in the university community, a few are willing to state it clearly while holding that the claims of faith must in no way impair the integrity of scholarship. Jaroslav Pelikan, former Dean of the Graduate School of Arts and Sciences at Yale, a devout churchman and a front-rank scholar in the history of Christian thought, stated flatly in 1965 that research should be "free from distortion stemming from particular confessional stances." He called for a "commitment to scholarship" and added "the prime need of theology today is for a careful and conscientious study of the sources without paralyzing concentration on presuppositions or a premature formulation of conclusions."

Martin E. Marty, Associate Dean of the Chicago Divinity School, is equally clear about the commitment of the scholar to scholarship quite apart from his confessional status. Reflecting on the joint meetings of the American Academy of Religion, the Society of Biblical Literature, and the Society for the Scientific Study of Religion in 1974, he noted that the agenda showed little concern for religious beliefs and practices. "These are 'academic' and 'scientific' gatherings," he continued, "and the participants as a rule pay little attention to organized religion." After consulting the agenda for the 1975 gatherings, Marty concluded that religion can and should be studied and taught by the same standard as any other subject. "It is unfair to the humanities character of religious studies to expect the classroom to do what the chapel ought to do," he asserted. "Religious studies are worthy of being pursued as interesting subjects without having to carry the burden of being the main or only locus for value and meanings on campus, although they should be free to point toward values if they wish."

Such statements by churchmen are the exception rather than the rule, however. Most of those who teach religion in the university community are content to live by university standards, which are those of the critical way in religion, without ever raising the issue of the relation between scholarship and faith. But the issue remains—it will not go away. And while it remains, traditional faith must continue to erode under it, as has been the case since the university as an institution in human society first came into being.

2. Charles Sanders Peirce

The close connection between the university community and the cultural nonreligious community and the manner in which they interact is seen in a remarkable American thinker of the second half of the nineteenth century, Charles S. Peirce. Not an academic, Peirce was, however, throughout his life closely associated with the academic community. His father was a distinguished professor of mathematics and astronomy at Harvard. His brother was also a Harvard professor and mathematician.

For thirty years Peirce served on the staff of the United States Coastal Survey, in the end becoming superintendent. All the while he was also a member of a Cambridge circle of intellectuals intimately associated with Harvard—including, among others, Chauncey Wright, John Fisk, Oliver Wendell Holmes, Jr., and William James. They called themselves The Metaphysical Club and wrestled with questions like the one Pyrrho of Elis had put to the Western mind more than two thousand years before; the question Descartes, Hume, and Kant had all asked and had failed to answer satisfactorily; the question of the critical way in religion: *How can we be certain?*

Although Peirce is generally regarded as one of the most original minds of his time, his importance to the development of religious thought—in fact, of human thought generally—is only just beginning to be recognized. He was the father of pragmatism, and both William James and John Dewey stand in his debt. Why is he important in religion? For the ecclesiastical tradition he is not, but for the critical way in religion he is fundamental. C. S. Peirce asked in religion, as in all things, the question the critical tradition must always ask: How certain are we of the things we say we believe? On what evidence does that certainty rest? In short, Peirce came fully and completely to terms with the fact of human fallibility, and concluded that in the end we must learn to live with probabilities, since no ultimate certainty is possible.

Trying to analyze the problem, he concluded that we try to attain certainty in four different ways:

1. *Tenacity*: We doggedly hold to the opinions and beliefs that appeal to us.
2. *Authority*: We accept what someone else tells us is true because we think that the individual or the institution for which he speaks is in a position to know.
3. *A priori perceptions*: We first rid our minds of all possible error; then we hold to the clear and distinct ideas that are left.
4. *Science*: We first recognize the inescapable fact of human error. All our "truths" then become hypotheses. A hypothesis, by definition, is always subject to correction, enlargement, improvement, or abandonment.

Peirce found serious flaws in the first three ways of trying to deal with our human fallibility and concluded that the fourth was the only valid way. It is this that gives him a central role in the critical tradition. His is a fully articulate statement of the position taken by those of the critical way in religion.

Of course, no one can stop there, and Peirce did not. In an attempt to find a way through human fallibility to something dependable, he moved into logic and is credited with laying the foundation for the logic of relations, the instrument for the logical analysis of mathematics. He labored on probability theory and the logic of scientific methodology. In an attempt to distinguish between beliefs that are really believed and those that are held as opinions only, Peirce worked out the foundations for the viewpoint that later came to be known as "pragmatism."

Defining pragmatism very strictly, he coined the word "pragmaticism" to distinguish his concept from the looser usage of his better-known friend William James. Pragmatism or pragmaticism is normally associated with practicality, but Peirce made it clear that for him the concept was more logical than practical. His definition read: "In order to ascertain the meaning of an intellectual conception one should consider what practical consequences might conceivably result by necessity from the truth of that conception; and the sum of these consequences will constitute the entire meaning of the conception."

What do these words mean? A simple translation often given is that pragmatism is roughly equivalent to empiricism, the doctrine that truth is determined by experience, in short the scientific method. Another simplification runs: the meaning of a proposition is its logical (or physical) consequences. Whether or not we find these ideas useful today is of secondary importance. Of primary importance, however, is our indebtedness to Peirce for his stern insistence that nothing be taken for granted—that every concept, before it is accepted for use, be examined and tested to the uttermost in order to determine what, if any, validity it may have. That is the critical way, in religion and in life.

Not surprisingly, Peirce found Descartes' thinking very congenial. Like his seventeenth-century French predecessor, Peirce tried scrupulously to rid his mind of all preconceptions and all error. But, he disagreed with Descartes' conclusions on the ground that the great French empiricist had not followed his own method far enough; Immanuel Kant had shown that. Peirce gave Kant credit for raising all the relevant philosophical problems still lurking in Descartes' thought, but he insisted that Kant had not succeeded in answering them either. Kant believed that there are self-evident ideas from which reliable synthetic judgments can be derived. Peirce felt that there was a dangerous subjectivism in this point of view. When thoroughly tested the assumption that there are self-evident ideas breaks down, he said. Peirce argued that doubt enters when you say anything is self-evident because ideas that are self-evident to one person are not always self-evident to everyone else. Thereupon inquiry replaces the certainty that self-evident ideas were supposed to provide.

As with Descartes and Kant, Peirce is important more for the probing nature of his questions than for the answers he himself was able to offer. The sheer originality of mind his writings reveal continues to astonish those who read his works. With one accord they echo and re-echo the lamentation that even today Peirce's work is so little known, so costly to purchase, and so hard to come by. His collected works, when you can find a set, are very expensive.

Peirce is a kind of connecting figure in the critical tradition. He embodies in his own person the critical way as it has gained clarity and force in the academic community and as it is steadily gaining a corresponding force and clarity in Western culture more generally. He is important because of his critical approach to thought but also because of his belief in creativity. Peirce coined the word "musement" to designate the mental-spiritual mood he found most productive and which he also greatly enjoyed himself. He described it as a state of free, unrestrained speculation when the mind engages in pure play. This is a very apt description of the creative aspect of the critical way. Few thinkers in history have described it better or exhibited it more fully than this eccentric nineteenth-century American genius, who, so far as we know, took little if any interest in organized religion.

3. Cambridge University

It is risky to single out a particular university to illustrate the role of academia in world culture today. Any one of a hundred would do well enough to underscore the common qualities of our higher institutions of learning. Without intending any reflection upon any other of the world's leading universities, I have chosen Cambridge because it supremely illustrates the role of the critical tradition in the pursuit of knowledge and the development of thought. To select a moment or a person to mark the emergence of the special qualities that Cambridge has exhibited is, again, risky. Nevertheless, at England's growing assembly of scholars on the banks of the River Cam, certain men clearly were pivotal. We shall not be entirely arbitrary if we begin with Erasmus. It is now not possible to gauge with precision his influence on Cambridge in his time, but considering his enormous prestige in contemporary Europe in his lifetime it can hardly have been less at Cambridge. In part II we noted his insistence on the right of free inquiry and his role in the development of the critical tradition in Western thought.

The value placed upon freedom at Cambridge is illustrated by the fact that the university, in the seventeenth century, sided with Oliver Cromwell and Parliament against the king. Certainly Cambridge boasts no more influential and pivotal figure than Sir Isaac Newton, Lucasian Professor of Mathematics from 1673 to 1702. Truly scientific in temper, Newton accelerated the growing practice at Cambridge of asking the hard questions and demanding hard answers. By the eighteenth century, mathematics and science had gained a pre-eminent place there. Open and free discussion prevailed to a remarkable degree and continued to advance as the years went on.

The measure of a university is, above all, its faculty. More than anyone or anything else they give a particular academic community its particular character. They are, of course, influenced by the traditions of the university they serve, a factor that is important both in their own selection of a school and in the school's selection of them from among many candidates. At Cambridge both factors played a part. The faculty who were drawn there were by no means unaware of the spirit of the place. They thought of themselves as the inheritors of a great tradition; as participators in it but also as molders of it, clarifying and establishing it for the generations who would come after them.

Leslie Stephen, laying down the canons of judgment that guided him in the writing of his *English Thought in the 18th Century,* has no difficulty stating them. Early in his history he does so and his canons are those of the critical way. His description is at the same time a summary of the intellectual tradition that prevailed at Cambridge in the second half of the nineteenth century—a tradition that he sought to exemplify in his own work. He writes,

> Even the brutes have some implicit recognition of the simplest sequences of events; and in the lowest human intellect there are the rudiments of scientific knowledge. But these rudiments are strangely distorted by innumerable errors. In other words, before we know, we are naturally prompted to guess. We must lay down postulates before we arrive at axioms. Most of these, we must suppose, will possess an element of truth. A belief which brought a man into too direct collision with facts would soon disappear along with the believer. An erroneous postulate, however, may survive, if not so mischievous as to be fatal to the agent. Others may stand the test of verification by experience, and may finally take their place as accepted and ultimate truths. The greater number, perhaps, will be materially modified, or will gradually disappear, leaving behind them a residuum of truth. Thus the progress of the intellect necessarily involves a conflict. It implies destruction as correlative to growth. The history of thought is in great part a history of the gradual emancipation of the mind from the errors spontaneously generated by its first childlike attempts at speculation.

In 1970 an anthology of the *Cambridge Review* appeared, containing, according to the editor, a representative collection of the authors and thought-patterns that had characterized Cambridge University since the founding of the *Review* ninety years before. The essays "exhibit the common qualities that might be identified with the Cambridge mind," says the editor, describing them as: "a rigor of logical analysis; an uncompromising exercise of skeptical inquiry; a commitment to verification rather than imaginative construction." These characteristics are not exclusive to Cambridge, he continues, but "faithfulness to its canons has led Cambridge scholars to be perhaps especially guarded when faced with metaphysical systems and unusual propositions." At Cambridge, "exposing the grandiose" was "refined into an art . . . because pretentious dogma so often conceals the commonplace or the false."

Alfred North Whitehead, in offhand remarks to his classes, revealed a profound sense of indebtedness to Cambridge. The intellectual climate that prevailed there, he said, played a fundamental role in the development of his own mental outlook and in the shaping of his philosophy. Whitehead was equally clear about the influence of the academic community upon the wider reaches of thought. "The mentality of an epoch," he wrote, echoing Stephen, "springs from the view of the world which is dominant in the educated sections of the communities in question." These words appear in the introductory paragraphs to *Science and the Modern World,* in which the author lays down the principles on which his own thought is built.

True to the spirit of openness, inquiry, testing, and continually reassessing what you think you know, Whitehead spoke of the danger that the university could become an established authority. "Knowledge does not keep any better than fish," he warned. "It must come to the students, as it were, just drawn out of the sea and with the freshness of its immediate importance." The atmosphere of even a great university can become too rarefied, he insisted. "What saved me for civilization," he once remarked, "were two things . . . a student discussion club and being taken out of Cambridge and plunged into the University of London for fifteen years. It stirred me about among all sorts of people. Added to that was my experience in the university senate," where again he came up against a wide variety of personalities in an urban academic community, and the problems in which they became involved.

Bertrand Russell, who with Whitehead produced the great *Principia Mathematica* while both were at Cambridge, said in his *Autobiography*: "The one habit of thought of real value that I acquired [at Cambridge] was intellectual honesty. This virtue certainly existed not only among my friends, but among my teachers. I cannot remember any instance of a teacher resenting it when one of his pupils showed him to be in error, though I can remember quite a number of occasions on which pupils succeeded in performing this feat."

Like Whitehead, Russell also speaks of his indebtedness to a student discussion group known as "The Apostles." Its basic characteristic, to which both pay glowing tribute, was that of discussion—fully open, fully free, where any question might be asked, any answer given, and any opinion offered, however wild, improbable, or even sacrilegious it might seem. All that was asked of the participants was that each have truth as his goal and integrity as his standard. What was valuable to the students, evidently, was the practice which is the essence of the critical way, the practice of questing and testing, and of human interchange; the clash of mind with mind in the course of which all of the participants move together toward clearer understanding and more adequate concepts of what the truth is taken to be.

One further and quite different example must suffice. In 1939 E. M. Forster, the British novelist, published a pamphlet entitled, "What I Believe." It was one of a series by a number of writers, published as World War II broke upon the world. It was a time when there was much soul searching among the democracies. "I do not believe in Belief," Forster wrote, as any Cantabrigian of that period might have. Then he continued, "But this is an age of faith," meaning the Nazis, Fascists, and Communists who at that time commanded the passionate loyalty of millions as against the seeming lassitude of those who professed democratic principles. "Tolerance, good temper and sympathy," Forster continued, "they are what really matter . . . my law gives me Erasmus and Montaigne, not Moses and Saint Paul." Summing up his views he concluded: "So two cheers for Democracy: one because it admits variety and two because it permits criticism."

A student of Forster's work observed, regarding this essay, "His intellectual views remain today [1962] what they were when he was at Cambridge in 1897." And we might add: Forster, in his distrust of "Belief," in his love of tolerance, of good temper, of human understanding, and in the high estimate he put upon the freedom to criticize—in all this he represented the best of the Cambridge tradition and the ideal toward which the academic community still aspires today.

The cluster of pioneering thinkers that was to be found at Cambridge in the late nineteenth and early twentieth centuries demonstrates the influence that a great university can have on the minds of its faculty, and also the way in which these scholars, in their turn, helped to establish more firmly the mood of inquiry, testing, and speculation that prevailed there. A list of Cambridge luminaries would include, in addition to Erasmus, Newton, Stephen, Whitehead, Russell, and Forster:

John Milton, poet
George Gordon, Lord Byron, poet
Thomas Babington Macaulay, historian and essayist
Charles Darwin, naturalist
Alfred Lord Tennyson, poet
Frederic W. Maitland, jurist
Jane Harrison, classicist
F. M. Cornford, philosopher and classicist
G. E. Moore, philosopher
J. B. Bury, historian
George Trevelyan, historian

A visiting professor of history from the United States said of his stay at Cambridge: "It would be difficult for me to analyze the feelings of spiritual and intellectual freedom that I felt there. I came to appreciate deeply the atmosphere of tolerance and of regard for the simple human decencies as well as for civilization. Cambridge will continue to mean for me kind hearts, free minds, a place where human lives are made richer."

Members of academe continually remind us, as we have noted, that their community is beset by dogmatists, small minds, self-seeking pseudo-intellectuals protecting a principality of thought they happen to control, and scholars high principled enough in scholarship but lacking in integrity elsewhere. All this is lamentably true. Nevertheless, the university today is the critical tradition institutionalized, as the church is the ecclesiastical tradition institutionalized. No institution ever perfectly embodies its own ideal. Few, in fact, come close. Yet the force and power of the critical ideal shapes the policy of all our higher institutions of learning. It guides the thought and behavior of the members of academe while they in their turn maintain and foster the critical standards demanded of them as members of the academic community. Thus the critical tradition, born in ancient Greece, emerging again in the Middle Ages, nurtured in the growing universities of the West, and in turn nurturing them, is, in our day, the university tradition as well.

16

Fundamentals

The critical tradition in the religion of the West is but an aspect of Western culture as a whole. The universities, not the churches, are its guardians and proponents. Their faculties are its teachers and practitioners. Their students are its converts and missionaries. But the practice of questing and testing is not confined to the academic community. It is now the dominant way of life in the West and, despite obvious exceptions, is apparently on the way to becoming the way of life for humanity the world around.

There are problems, of course, and they are very great—problems of the scope one would expect to find when fundamental changes are taking place. To ask *How do you know?* and to keep asking it is to enter upon an infinite regress. It is to pursue the questioning process until there is no longer any answer to give, until you have to say: I saw it or felt it or heard it or can demonstrate it. Yet anyone aware of his or her own fallibility knows how feeble such an answer may be, for even *that* may be in error. The speaker may not have seen what he thought he saw, or heard what he thought he heard, or felt what he thought he felt. Once we concede the fact of human fallibility we can never again claim the certitude so characteristic of organized religion. This would include self-serving allegations by our churches and temples that God has spoken through their prophets and saints, their Sacred Scriptures and liturgy, and, in some sense, still speaks so today.

The result is an attitude toward knowledge, old in most areas of life but new in religion. Now we can see that all supposed knowledge, religious knowledge included, rests in the end on assumptions, postulates, or axioms. These assumptions are not arbitrarily chosen. We do not adopt fundamental principles because they are to our liking. We adopt them because we must. They assert themselves. They are not made; they are found. They are not contrived; they are discovered. Basic assumptions emerge because human thought and ingenuity cannot devise anything more basic. They are postulates, hypotheses; in the language of mathematics, they are axioms. In the language of religion, they are articles of faith.

1. The Self

With what axiom does the critical mind begin? What is the most basic assumption we can make? René Descartes began such an inquiry with the now famous assertion: "I think, therefore I am." A contemporary biologist, speculating on the same theme, wrote: "I am a human being, whatever that may be. I speak for all of us. I speak as an individual unique in a universe beyond my understanding. I am hemmed in by limitations of sense and mind and body, of place and time and circumstance. I am like a man journeying through a forest, aware of occasional glints of light overhead, with recollections of the long trail I have already traveled and conscious of wider spaces ahead. I want to see more clearly where I have been and where I am going, and above all, I want to know why I am where I am and why I am traveling at all."

A contemporary theologian has stated this point of view in more philosophical terms. He speaks of the "functional ultimacy" of the human being. It is another way of saying that each of us, in his life-philosophy and in his religion, begins with himself or herself. That is not where we come out: we do not conclude with the self. But it is there, of necessity, that we start.

The ecclesiastical mind has a question for those who would begin with the self and the experience of that self rather than with the teachings of organized religion: Is not your point of departure just as much an article of faith as any of ours? Does your reluctance to call your view "belief" or "faith" change the reality in any way?

Superficially it might seem that to begin with ourselves is, in reality, an article of faith, but there is a fundamental difference between the two points of view. To rely upon our thoughts, sensations, and experiences after we have carefully checked them against the thoughts, sensations, and experiences of others is far from asserting that we *believe* in them in the way that the devout Christian *believes* in salvation through the blood of Christ or the devout Muslim *believes* that Muhammad was *the* prophet of Allah. In the one case, we accept on faith the teaching of a religion; in the other we adopt a method of organizing experience—*our experience*—because it seems to us, and to great numbers of people we respect, the best way to go about it.

No group of people, organized or unorganized, is trying to persuade us to accept and live by such an axiom. To be sure, vast numbers who themselves have adopted the critical way advocate our doing the same, and they will gladly tell us *why*. But terms like "proselytizing," "evangelizing," "missionary work"—the methods by which organized religion has sought converts to its various systems of faith—do not apply to those who have adopted the critical way in religion.

The persuasive force in the idea of beginning with the self rather than with articles of faith is seen in the doctrine of miracles that organized religion quite generally supports. The natural world presents us with a picture we readily accept—one that is ordered, reliable, and self-consistent. The results we obtain from close scrutiny of natural phenomena usually stand up under severe and repeated testing by people of widely varied tastes and purposes, who are widely dispersed geographically and often culturally as well. The idea of an ordered universe may be, and indeed is, checked uncounted times, and ordinarily with the same result.

On the other hand the miraculous world-picture offered to us by the religions is hard to believe in because it requires endless (and never very satisfactory) explanation. The idea that miracles interrupt the natural order cannot be confirmed in any consistent manner.

The case for a miraculous universe is not made when we exclaim with Walt Whitman:

> Why, who makes much of a miracle?
> As to me, I know of nothing else but miracles.
> To me every hour of the light and dark is a miracle.
> Every cubic inch of space is a miracle.
> Every square yard of the surface of the earth. . . .
> What stranger miracles are there?

We know what the poet means. Our thoughts and feelings are his. But we know too, as he himself said, that his metaphors were never meant to be taken as a theological argument. They were intended to direct our attention to the wonder of all life and experience, a wonder that is akin to worship, if it is not, in fact, worship itself.

Superficially also it might seem that the critical tradition is not different from traditional religion in that both invite us to trust evidence developed by other people. Yet here too the difference is fundamental. In the ecclesiastical tradition we are asked to have faith in what religious people say: that God exists, that he is omniscient and omnipotent, that he has revealed himself to the people of earth, that he cares for us, and will answer our prayers. The critical tradition does not ask us to put our faith in anything anyone has said. It asks only that we accept what seems believable to us, regardless of who says it and regardless of the authority with which he or she speaks. The critical tradition says in effect:

Do not accept anything anyone says just because he holds a high office in church, state, academe, or anywhere else. Accept what you accept because it is persuasive to you even though the person who would persuade you may be very lowly. Do not accept what someone says because a wise or a holy man is supposed to have said it, or because it comes out of a holy book of some religion. Of course, the fact that a saying comes from a holy man, a holy book, or a holy temple should not stand in the way of your accepting it. You need only remember not to allow alleged holiness to dull your critical judgment.

We cannot, of course, investigate everything for ourselves. We must rely on one another in uncounted ways, both secular and religious. We go to the doctor, for example. He diagnoses our ailments, prescribes a remedy, and in full trust we follow his directions because we have faith in him as a person and in the validity of the medical knowledge of which he makes use in telling us what to do. We go to the astronomer and ask him about celestial phenomena. Out of his knowledge we learn about galaxies and quasars, black holes, and charmed quarks. We believe what he tells us because we have faith in him as a person also and faith as well in the knowledge he possesses and which in turn is derived from the body of knowledge the science of astronomy has accumulated.

Then, if we believe in the body of knowledge the astronomers have built up and the body of knowledge medicine has established, why are we not entitled to do so with the body of knowledge the theologians have built up? For one fundamental reason. Because all the other bodies of knowledge we have amassed are thought to be just that: bodies of knowledge about some area of life and experience, painstakingly put together through diligent investigation, through the scrupulous elimination of errors made in the past, coupled with the continual re-examination and correction of the total corpus in the present.

The doctor doesn't worry about your beliefs when you go to see him. He leaves that up to you. He will diagnose and prescribe. If you don't believe him and would rather not do as he says, you are free to make that choice. Neither are the astronomers nor the experts in other areas of knowledge concerned with your private beliefs. You may take what they say or leave it, as you wish.

In medicine you do not put your faith in what Hippocrates wrote; you put your faith in the entire medical enterprise that has developed since his time and is a living, self-correcting organ of human knowledge today. In astronomy you do the same. You do not put your faith in what Copernicus wrote but in the living body of contemporary astronomy. But in the Judeo-Christian tradition you are asked to put your faith in what Moses wrote or in what someone wrote in his name. In Christianity you are asked to put your faith in what the Gospel writers set down and in what Paul wrote to the churches he founded, not the literal language necessarily, but the intent at all levels. In Islam you put your faith in the truth of the Qur'an.

George Bernard Shaw, with burning indignation, observed in this connection: "Let the churches ask themselves why there is no revolt against the dogmas of mathematics though there is one against the dogmas of religion. It is not that the mathematical dogmas are more comprehensible. The law of inverse squares is as incomprehensible to the common man as the Athanasian Creed. But no student of science has yet been taught that specific gravity consists in the belief that Archimedes jumped out of his bath and ran naked through the streets of Syracuse shouting Eureka, Eureka, or that the Law of Inverse Squares must be discarded if anyone can prove that Newton was never in an orchard in his life. . . . In mathematics and physics, the faith is still kept pure, and you may take the law and leave the legends without a suspicion of heresy. . . ."

In the religions there is corporate consensus, to be sure, just as there is corporate consensus in medicine and astronomy. But there is a profound difference as to how that consensus is achieved. In the ecclesiastical tradition the sayings and writings of a particular individual or individuals—Moses, Isaiah, Jesus, Paul, Muhammad—are definitive. Consensus is achieved on this point. In medicine neither the writings of Hippocrates nor those of anyone else are taken to be definitive. Consensus in medicine is centered instead in the validity of the total growing body of medical knowledge. This includes the *invalidity* of most of Hippocrates' writings. Unlike the consensus in religion, that in medicine, astronomy, or any other body of knowledge is not static. What is taken to be valid in Hippocrates in one generation may be rejected altogether in the next. Corporate consensus is the goal in both religion and medicine. The difference lies in what the doctors and the theologians agree upon and in the manner in which these agreements are held during the period of their currency.

The critical position stands midway between that of the ecclesiastic and that of the skeptic. The one tries to overcome our ultimate uncertainty by a declaration of faith. The other tries to overcome it by asserting that we can never know anything, that we are not merely uncertain, we are doomed to permanent ignorance in basic matters. We cannot prove that either the skeptic or the ecclesiastic is right or wrong. But the absence of proof does not compel us to accept either position. Where proof is lacking, the inability to offer disproof proves nothing. The claims of the skeptic and those of the ecclesiastic are rejected by the critical mind for the same reason. Neither bears up under critical examination. In the end, neither has an answer to the question: *How do you know?* How do you know that what you say is true?

Essentially, then, in the critical way in religion we begin with ourselves. We begin with the fundamental assumption that in some sense we can trust human experience. We begin by assuming that what we think of as knowledge is in fact knowledge, at least to some degree, and not just a construct of our own minds. We do not forget what David Hume showed us: that in the end we do not *know*. But neither do we forget that Hume also said that when he left his closet he left his philosophical doubts behind him. He found they did not carry much weight when he returned to the real world of joy and pain, love and hate, beauty and ugliness, good and evil. We find meaning in the words of William James who affirmed in the face of ultimate uncertainty that this life is a real fight, among other reasons because it feels like a real fight, and because it is more plausible on all the evidence, than to assume, as we might, that it is all a chimera, all a mirage, all a bad dream.

2. Getting Outside of Ourselves

Starting with the self, as we must, seeking to order our experiences in some fashion, yet keenly aware of our liability to err, what do we do? We seek corroboration. We seek it from other selves who face the same problem we face. As with our first step—beginning with the self—we take the second step, not because we choose it among several alternatives, but because we must. How else are we to overcome our fallibility? How else are we to test our experiences and the thoughts we derive from them? How else are we to get outside ourselves?

Repeating what we do, to see if the same result will follow, is a form of corroboration, but it is not enough, for we can never be certain that we are not repeating the same error each time we test our conclusions. The same mistake can be made by unnumbered people unnumbered times, as, for example, during the long centuries when it was supposed that the sun rose and set while the earth stood still. The experience was repeated daily, but that very repetition only served to confirm rather than expose the error.

The goal, then, is to obtain objectivity on our experiences, and the means is corroboration through the experience of others. But is that sufficient? Can we in this way achieve the certainty we seek, the certainty organized religion believes itself to possess? Apparently not: at least not in the opinion of Percy W. Bridgman, Nobel laureate in physics. The reasons he gives are persuasive.

In 1956 Bridgman was one of the honorees at a conference sponsored by the American Academy of Arts and Sciences. He was also one of the speakers. Toward the end of his very brief paper he declared that objectivity in any basic sense is impossible. The problem is, he said, that for any observation there has to be an observer and "we are that observer."

Bridgman illustrated his point by reminding his audience of the problem of the observed and the observer as it becomes evident in the quantum theory: "For the purposes of quantum theory, the observer is highly specialized. He is essentially the measuring instrument. A detailed examination of the unavoidable reaction between instrument and object of measurement provides the justification for the Heisenberg Principle of Indeterminism."

Moving out of the field of his specialty to the topic of the conference, Bridgman then went on to generalize. "While it is clearly very difficult to separate the observer and the observed in atomic physics," he said, "it is no less difficult to do so in science generally and in the humanities as well. In a very real sense it is more difficult in the familiar and common sense areas of life because then we tend not to see that a problem exists. We cannot have information without acquiring that information by some method. The story is not complete until we have told both what we know and how we know it. To do this we have to get away from ourselves. This is something the human race has been trying to do ever since it started philosophizing or worshipping."

Then, as if he had set out to state the position of the critical tradition, Bridgman said, "Religion is the field above all others where the need to do this is the greatest and where the practice is least observed. The beings and principles which are the concern of religion are beings and principles external to us and independent of us." He was insisting on a point long central in the critical tradition but which the religions tend to gloss over or ignore—that the data of religion, even though sacred in character and sacred in origin, are like all data and all knowledge caught in the interrelationship of the observer and the observed. In order to reach the certainty that religion claims, Bridgman pointed out, the observer who does the observing has to get outside himself. But this is impossible in religion, as in science, the humanities, or anything else. There are certain things, he said, we cannot do with our minds.

Bridgman illustrated his point with a mathematical principle known as Godel's theorem: "It is a consequence of this theorem that mathematics can never prove that mathematics is free from internal self-contradictions. Out of this experience, mathematicians and logicians have acquired a new insight—the insight that there are some things that neither they nor anyone else can do with their minds. . . . The most devastating point is the realization that the human mind can never have certainty either by logical or metaphysical or mystical methods. . . . Godel's theorem cuts the Gordian knot with the insight that 'certainty' is an illegitimate concept. . . . There are things a system cannot do with itself." This, Bridgman asserted, might well be the first law of mental dynamics: that we cannot get away from ourselves; true objectivity is impossible in ultimate matters since we ourselves are the observers of what we observe.

Religion, Bridgman concluded, is the field of human concern in which we have most obviously moved beyond the bounds of validity. It is the field above all others in which we are trying to do something with our minds that cannot be done. In religion we have declared that we are certain. But the certainty we claim is unattainable. In religion, where we most need to get outside ourselves in order to establish the authority of our beliefs, we are doomed to fail. Our failure is not due to anything peculiar about religion; it is due to the fact that we have come up against a principle applicable in all fields, but unfortunately in religion least acknowledged and understood.

Nowhere have I seen a clearer statement of the central problem of contemporary religion: the candid acknowledgment that we do not know what the theologians have so long claimed to know. Bridgman adds a new dimension to this insight. He not only says we do not know what we think we know in religion but we *cannot* know what the theologians say we know. The certainty they claim is denied to us because we cannot get outside ourselves. Since we are the observers, we are locked in by the system of the observer and the observed.

It was the end of the line of reasoning that had begun more than two thousand years before. The conclusion to which Pyrrho of Elis had been driven was right. In the ultimate sense, we cannot *know*; we can only surmise, feel, intuit. "The presumption of objectivity is man's darkest heresy," Bridgman observed later. "It is the nature of knowledge to be subject to uncertainty."

3. Science

Science is the system of thought and practice we have devised in an attempt to overcome our human limitations to seek corroboration, to gain such objectivity as we may, and to be as error-free as possible. It is by no means a perfect system. The scientists themselves, Bridgman among them, have been very clear on that point. They face their limitations realistically, and thus far have successfully resisted the very human urge to deny them by adopting some variation of the doctrine of infallibility.

William James once said, borrowing a phrase from C. S. Peirce, "I have to forge every statement in the teeth of irreducible and stubborn facts." Whitehead once cited these words as the essence of modern science. "Science is marked," he wrote, "by a vehement and passionate interest in the relation of general principles to irreducible and stubborn facts." The nature of the critical tradition could hardly be stated more succinctly. To say it the other way around, if a datum can be discovered that appears to contradict a conclusion already reached, that conclusion is then abandoned or at least modified, unless a re-examination of it proves the datum itself to have been invalid. The essence of the process is the questing, followed by testing, the unflinching approach to hard data that asks no quarter, gives none, and never permits hope or desire to color the result that follows.

There have been many attempts to describe and define science. One of the better formulations comes from the pen of the twentieth-century chemist, James Bryant Conant, who served as president of Harvard. In science, he observed, new concepts arise from observation and experiment. These concepts in turn lead to new experiments; these in turn lead to new observations; these then lead to yet newer concepts, and so on. "The test of a new idea," he wrote, "is therefore not only its success in correlating the then known facts but much more its success or failure in stimulating further experimentation and observation which is fruitful. This dynamic quality of science viewed not as a practical undertaking but as development of conceptual schemes seems to me to be close to the heart of the best definition."

Copernicus' placing the sun at the center of the solar system is perhaps the supreme example of Conant's definition. When Copernicus began his work, Ptolemy's great *Syntaxis,* an astonishingly comprehensive text on astronomy, enjoyed unparalleled prestige and authority owing both to its age and its completeness. To gain a measure of Copernicus' genius and the boldness of his thought, we need to remember that when he wrote, Ptolemy's work had been the authoritative text in astronomy for thirteen hundred years.

During this period, however, and in particular during the Renaissance, many commentaries had been written on Ptolemy's work as new data came in. Refinements on the original had been made in order to accommodate the new data to the old system. The result was an increasingly complex system, far removed from the majestic simplicity of Ptolemy's original work.

In Book I Ptolemy had written, "In seeking to explain phenomena, we should choose the simplest possible hypothesis, provided it is not contradicted in any important respect by observation." Copernicus, a thoroughgoing student of Ptolemy as well as of other ancient authors, had made this principle his own. He had no trouble with the Ptolemaic concept of rotating, transparent, spherical shells supposed at that time to bear the sun and the stars around the earth. What bothered Copernicus was the degree of complexity the Ptolemaic system had developed by the sixteenth century. By that time it required eighty-four spheres to explain the known astronomical data. Even that was not quite enough. To account for everything satisfactorily, some intellectual dishonesty was also necessary. Ptolemy himself had been guilty on this score. "A certain resentment against this type of sleight of hand," observed one scholar, "seems to have given Copernicus a special urge to change the system."

Copernicus saw that to reduce all this complexity to a simple, easily understood system, with no fudging of the facts, he had only to assume that the sun and not the earth was at the center of the planetary system. That was his revolutionary conceptual scheme. "Who indeed in this most magnificent temple would put the light in another or a better place?" Copernicus exclaimed rhetorically. He grows lyrical as he continues, "There the sun can illumine the whole of it. Therefore it is not improperly that some people call the sun the lamp of the world, others its mind, others its ruler. Trismegistus calls it the visible God, Sophocles' Electra, the All-Seeing. Thus assuredly, as residing in the royal see, the Sun governs the surrounding family of stars."

Copernicus' revolutionary achievement, then, was not the discovery that the sun is the center of the planetary system. Ptolemy himself had considered that hypothesis and had rejected it on the ground that it did not account for the astronomical data he possessed at that time and because it did not square with Aristotelian metaphysics, which he felt must also be taken into account. Some seventy-five years before Copernicus' time, Nicholas of Cusa had raised the possibility that the Sun and not the Earth was the astronomical center of things. But it was Copernicus and not Nicholas who overturned the mind of the West because Copernicus, through detailed mathematical computations, was able to show that the heliocentric concept was simple, graceful, and uncomplicated, while the Ptolemaic concept was complex, clumsy, and unable to encompass the data it sought to explain. Copernicus' greatness lay in his abandoning—in effect, destroying—an old concept, by assembling all the known data under a new one by which every detail was more easily understood. Perhaps his greatest achievement lay in his break with Aristotelian metaphysics on which the Ptolemaic system was based. Without such a break, the Copernican system would have been impossible.

The theory of plate tectonics is a contemporary example of similar scientific reconceptualizing. Geologists now believe that the continents float about on the earth's surface much as logs might jostle one another in a mill pond. Hardly more than a decade ago Alfred Wegener, to whom more than anyone else we owe the development of the theory of plate tectonics, was greeted with derision in scientific circles. Again, the idea itself was not new. A clear statement of it can be found at least as far back as 1756. What was new with Wegener was that the concept, at first a wild guess, became at his hands the simple explanation of an increasingly complex and seemingly inconsistent mass of data. When the spreading of the ocean floor at the mid-ocean ridges at last was demonstrated, the theory of plate tectonics became, in the eyes of the geophysicists, the "concept that unifies the main features of the earth's surface and their history better than any other concept in the geological sciences." Most recently, the theory has been further confirmed by satellite photos from space.

The abuse and derision that Wegener endured through most of his life show that the guardians and practitioners of the discipline of science can be no less rigid, no less dogmatic, and no less self-righteous than the theologians. Despite its severe standards of accuracy and adaptability, there is no reason to think science will not grow more rigid, more doctrinaire, and more self-righteous as its thought and practice grow older and the sanctity of age and tradition are added to its already impressive credentials.

Time lays its stultifying hand on all human institutions, and science can scarcely be expected to escape. The history of science shows that clearly enough already. Luigi Galvani felt the ridicule of his colleagues during his pioneering work on electricity in the late eighteenth century. Louis Pasteur met the same thing at the hands of the French Academy in the nineteenth century when he tried to lecture on his discoveries in bacteriology. It is the price science has to pay for its increasing institutionalization; the price it has to pay because it is subject to the stupidities, the jealousies, the pride, and self-seeking of the human animal.

A current theory advances the novel idea that markings on bones two to three thousand years older than Egypt's hieroglyphs are notations and not primitive art. Again the old argument is repeated. The doubters scoff and the scoffers meet the evidence not with argument but with derision. Meanwhile, evidence continues to accumulate that these notations (if that is what they are) may have antecedents as old as the Ice Age. Is the theory sound? It may well be since it is based not only on markings on ancient bones but also upon the concept of "time factored" process in the hard sciences. All processes develop at measurable or estimable rates or periodicities. So too, this theory holds, human notation developed.

Science today is threatened by its own growing body of rules, practices, and hierarchical structures. Secondly, it is threatened by its rapidly increasing involvement with government, in particular in socialist countries. Ironically, however, its greatest threat comes from the university, the institution that houses and nurtures most of its activities and personnel; the institution in human society that came into existence as a result of the re-emergence of the critical spirit in the culture of the West. The impact of size and age upon the commitment of the university to total, unbiased, unhampered, objective freedom of inquiry cannot yet be measured. We still do not know whether today's great universities, beset as they are by ever-increasing size, wealth, power, prestige, and authority, will be able to maintain the truly objective critical spirit and practice in which they grew to their present status and to which, in principle, they are totally committed.

Over and beyond the problems faced by the critical spirit because of the institutionalization of science and because of the burgeoning size and authority of our universities, there is yet another: How does the critical way distinguish itself from science? If science is marked by the determination to forge every general principle in the teeth of stubborn fact, and if the same may be said for the critical way in religion; if, as Conant asserted, science is the development of ever-more adequate conceptual schemes, and the critical way is also, is there any difference between the two? Is the critical way in religion scientism? When you come right down to it, does not the critical way usually adopt the scientific dogmas of a particular age?

The answer to that question is both yes and no, as we shall see in the next section. The critical way in religion accepts the working cosmic structure that science has built up, but it does not do so in a dogmatic sense, any more than science does. With most Christians, for example, it is a dogma that in the person of Jesus, God came down to earth and dwelt among men in human flesh as the Christ. That dogma does not change. In science the laws of motion and gravity laid down by Isaac Newton are not dogmas. They were accepted as working principles until modified, if not altogether abandoned, by subsequent thinkers.

"Scientism" is the word for a too-great reliance on science by religious people, whereby the formulations of science are treated like the dogmas of religion. The eighteenth-century Deists, for example, followed the critical way in their efforts to rid Christianity of teachings that had been rendered archaic by the discoveries of science up to that time. Many Deists, however, went further and attempted to construct a theology based upon eighteenth-century science, assuming, apparently, that it was as permanent and unchanging as the dogmas of religion. To the degree that they did so they departed from the critical tradition. Auguste Comte attempted a theological world-view based on nineteenth-century science. Herbert Spencer did the same with the doctrine of evolution. Each of these theologies, however true it may have seemed at the time it was put forth, soon lost its persuasive power. Each was time-bound, too closely tied to the particularities of the thought of its day.

The scientists themselves are the first to point out that they can be wrong even when they are quite confident of being right. Their views can be in error even when they are based upon careful observation and experiment. It has recently been learned, for example, that the famous carbon-14 test for dating ancient organic material gave erroneous results even when the rather large margin of error the method required was taken into account. The discovery came as a result of a discrepancy in dating that appeared between carbon-14 results and quite dependable historical records from ancient Egypt. The fact of the discrepancy was pinned down by counting the growth rings in the bristlecone pines of California. These trees, the longest-lived entities of which we know at present, yield an exact dating system going back more than seven thousand years. A comparison of the two dating systems showed that the carbon-14 system underestimates the age of living things and that the error accelerates as we go farther back in time. As a result of this discovery, supposedly certain dating based upon carbon-14 tests has now to be revised backward, in some cases by many hundreds of years.

While the method of science and the critical way in religion are one and the same, except for the religious dimension of the latter, it is quite the opposite with science and the ecclesiastical way. For a century there has been talk about "the war between science and religion," and ever since the appearance of Andrew D. White's book of that title, writers have been busy "reconciling" the two. The literature on this subject is enormous. But it is all in vain if by such reconciling we mean squaring the critical with the ecclesiastical way in religion; if by it we mean reconciling the doctrine of revelation with the practice of questioning and testing. True reconciliation can take place only when our religious leaders recognize the degree to which the method of investigation, followed by the framing of new concepts, has permeated contemporary culture and has begun to permeate religion as well.

Charles H. Townes, a recipient of the Nobel Prize in physics, once suggested that religious beliefs should "be viewed as working hypotheses, tested and validated by experience. To some this may seem a secular and even an abhorrent view," he continued. "But I see no reason why acceptance of religion on this basis should be objectionable. The validity of religious ideas must be and has been tested and judged through the ages by societies and by individual experience. Is there any need for [religious teachings] to be more absolute than the law of gravity? The latter is a working hypothesis whose basis and permanency we do not know. But on our belief in it, as well as on many other complex scientific hypotheses, we risk our lives daily."

Here is a clear statement of the critical way in religion as it relates to our human limitations. After all, it is possible that sense-experience gives us an impression of what reality is that is not merely partial, but distorted, even erroneous. If we humans were constituted differently we would have a quite different set of sense-impressions of ourselves and of our world as well. Such is the measure of our finitude. Such are the limitations under which we labor. Nevertheless, when all this has been said—and organized religion is very fond of saying it—we can make use of the scientific method and we can follow the critical way in religion in an attempt to carry the process of inquiry as far as possible. We can ferret out mistakes and misconceptions in the ideas we already have and we can formulate new and more adequate concepts in the never-ending attempt to come as near to understanding the nature of reality as we are able.

A step toward objectifying human knowledge was taken a generation ago when Hans Berger found that by attaching electric wires to the head of a man, he could measure electrical impulses in the brain. These "brain waves" were recorded on a revolving drum. The importance of his discovery has since been acknowledged and hundreds of thousands of brain-wave readings have been made. Scientists say these results constitute man's first objective view of the workings of his own brain.

In the same period in which Hans Berger conducted his experiments, electronic calculators, radar, and television sets made their appearance. Their method of operation suggested analogies to what happens in the brain. So far these analogies are guesses only. No one pretends to know the truth of the matter. The one thing of which we are certain is that the brain waves now being recorded on charts in laboratories all over the world tell us something positive and reliable about how the human brain works. The new science of ethology is steadily accumulating data on behavior, both animal and human. All of this material can be corroborated. All of it is verifiable in the sense that the experiments are repeatable.

Reliance upon our human faculties then is not wholly an act of faith. It means reliance upon the sort of thing that Berger began and others have continued since his time. It means that, among other things, we are prepared to regard the human creature as a biological entity whose brain has the electrical impulses our charts indicate. It means that we are expectantly awaiting such explanations of the charts as may be offered. We are not going to be blindly credulous, but we hold ourselves ready to accept a theory that can stand up under the severest testing and that is able at the same time to take all the known data into account. Specifically it means that, lacking anything better, we are ready to think of the human brain as operating in some such fashion as a computer, the principles of which we are beginning to understand.

To identify the critical way in religion so closely with science may suggest that it is a kind of latter-day rationalism. To be sure, the critical mind is a rational mind. But it is not "rationalist." The critical way in religion does not rely on reason alone. Intellectual history, from the time of the Sophists in Athens on, offers too many instances of reason going up a blind alley, ending in paradox or even in error. For the critical way in religion, reason is an important but not the sole guide: it is one of several instruments we use in our effort to achieve adequacy and validity in the concepts by which we seek to understand life and experience.

To put the question another way: Is the critical way a religion at all? In answer we might say: the critical way is not so much a religion as it is a way of dealing with religion. It is not so much a body of doctrine as a way of deciding which doctrines to accept and which to reject. The critical way is not a form of worship. It has no rituals of its own, no ceremonies, and no mysticism to which it lays any special claim. It is not a way of myth making, a way of dealing with myths others have made, nor is it a way of developing and assessing the true role that ritual, myth, and ceremonial can play. It is a way in religion of testing the validity of any system of myths and any mystical experience religion may bring to us.

A final question follows. If the method of criticism is to be so strictly applied to religion—any religion—does it not act as a solvent? Is not the "religious" part of the religion thereby dissolved? No, the critical way in religion merely dissolves the false certainty upon which traditional religion has so long rested. What remains is often more religious than ever. When our thoughts and emotions are pointed toward the highest of which we can conceive; when we turn to the moral and spiritual side of our nature, however defined; when we seek an understanding of the most profound questions it is possible to ask, the presence or absence of the critical tradition does not affect our religiosity. It does not affect the quality or the power of our religious feelings. It affects their adequacy and validity.

The critical way in religion makes no attempt to reconcile religion and science. None is necessary when religion is approached according to the critical way. Science, and religion that is critical in character, follow a common path, and there is no distinction between them in the way they go about it.

Both ask hard-nosed questions at every point. Both formulate and reformulate answers in a never-ending attempt to attain the most adequate concepts. At the start both set clearly before themselves the over-arching facts of human fallibility, gullibility, and our readiness to deceive one another. With J. Robert Oppenheimer, both would say, "the hallmark of science [and of the critical way in religion] is the refinement of techniques by which to eliminate errors." And with Conant they would add: "Its goal is to evolve ever more adequate conceptual schemes," by which to understand and interpret human experience.

4. Knowledge

If critical thinking is the means we have developed by which to overcome our human fallibility, what positive, reliable knowledge does it yield to us? If science is the technique the critical mind has evolved by which to achieve this goal, what does it tell us? As we all know, it would require the contents of several libraries, plus all the current scientific periodicals, and, from time to time, even the daily papers to answer this question. The findings of science are not only enormous, rapidly broadening and changing, but new findings are being reported all the time and new concepts are constantly being developed through which to correlate and explain it all.

What can we be said to know with some confidence as a result of this prodigious effort? The body of knowledge we now possess, A.D. 1980, tells us that we are living in a universe apparently limitless in time and space. Some ten, twenty, twenty-five billion years ago perhaps, an incredible cosmic explosion took place. As a result of it, the part of the universe we are at present able to observe—perhaps the universe as a whole—began flying apart in all directions at something approaching the speed of light. So far as we can judge, this "flying apart" is still taking place.

Among the entities that eventually resulted from that explosion was a galaxy of some one hundred billion stars, one hundred thousand light-years across, shaped like a pinwheel and revolving like one. Part way out from the center of that star mass was a single star, our sun. Eventually around that star, our sun, a set of planets began to revolve. Our earth was one of them. On the earth, currently estimated to be about four billion years old, life appeared perhaps three billion years ago, and after evolving until only a million years old (perhaps two, maybe even more than three million) produced a creature we today recognize as human, biologically very like ourselves. Notions as to when and where this human appearance occurred are now in a state of flux owing to discoveries being made in East Africa and elsewhere. We are today rapidly filling in details in the story of this creature's later development, from the first use of stone implements, through the invention and widespread making of pottery, down to the introduction of bronze, copper, gold, and iron.

We are, for example, only now beginning to understand how writing was invented. It had always been supposed that it evolved from primitive drawings of objects, like people, animals, the sun, rivers, etc. These drawings, it was thought, gradually became more abstract until, at last, writing, as distinguished from notation and numbering, eventually made its appearance.

Apparently the process was quite different. As is so often the case, necessity seems to have been the mother of the invention of writing. The necessity of keeping records, specifically records of commercial transactions in the course of trade, seems to have been the impetus. Archeological evidence from Western Asia dating to the ninth century B.C. reveals the following story:

1. Since very early times pebbles have been used as counters: i.e., five pebbles stood for five sheep, five ears of corn, or five arrows.
2. Small clay spheres were substituted for pebbles.
3. Clay tokens of differing shapes appeared: e.g., discs, cylinders, and cones as well as spheres. They designated different objects.
4. The clay tokens were in enclosed hollow clay cases, known as bullae, for security in transport. These bullae served as bills of lading. They were broken open on receipt, and the contents noted on the arrival of the goods they accompanied.
5. A two-dimensional portrayal of the tokens within was inscribed on the outside of the bulla so that the contents could be determined without breaking it open.
6. The hollow bulla with its contents noted on the exterior and its tokens enclosed within gave way to a clay tablet (at first curved to resemble a bulla) designating the contents a bulla would have contained, *but without the confirming tokens* formerly enclosed inside.
7. Writing can be said to have been invented at this point: when the pebbles or clay tokens were seen to be unnecessary because a record of those that would have been used was inscribed on a flat clay tablet that served quite as well. The convex profile of the earliest tablets descended directly from the curved surface of the bullae they replaced.

More than a generation ago the Egyptologist James Henry Breasted sought to pinpoint the time when moral values first became real in man's growing consciousness. He felt he could locate it through the literature the Egyptians left behind them. "For several hundred thousand years the Age of Material Conquest had gone on," he wrote, "but yesterday, as it were, through the dust of an engrossing conflict our Father Man began to catch but faintly the glory of the moral vision and to hear a new voice within. . . . It was interfused of love of home, of wife and children, of love of friends, and love of neighbors, of love of the poor, lonely and oppressed, of love of country and veneration of the Sovereign."

The more we learn about ourselves the further back our origin seems to recede. The discoveries in the Olduvai Gorge in East Africa, made by Louis S. B. Leakey during the 1960s, dated human origin back some 1,750,000 years. Discoveries in the same gorge made since that time by Leakey's wife Mary and by his son Richard have already moved that date back to 3,750,000 years ago. More recent discoveries appear to have pushed that date even further back. Who can now guess where and when the date of our human origin will be fixed—if ever?

The same regression in dating appears as we seek to date the awakening of man's moral sense. Where Breasted, only a generation ago, dated it around 2000 B.C., some writers today would push the beginnings of a moral sense back into the animal kingdom. On the other hand, others would date our awakening to a sense of our own selfhood somewhere between the two latest ice ages.

In what sense can this account of the origin of the universe and of the development of life on this planet be said to be true? We don't know. In a very real sense the story is a myth like the familiar ancient biblical attempt to explain by narrative the origin and development of natural phenomena. Our contemporary scientific world view is not a fabrication, as the myths of primitive people appear to us to be, but who is to say how much it may look like a fabrication five or ten thousand years from now, if people are still around to read and reflect on it?

A new picture of the human creature is emerging today, not out of our striving to be better, nor out of utopian dreaming, nor out of some ancient theology, but out of a study of ourselves by ourselves, conducted according to the most exacting standards possible. The results are neither certain nor final. All we can say of them is that they are growing, that they are capable of withstanding the most thoroughgoing tests, and that almost daily the resulting picture becomes ever clearer, ever more self-consistent, and ever more persuasive. Apparently it represents, albeit in a limited fashion, a picture of the reality we are seeking when we speak of the pursuit of knowledge.

It is not only the experts, the scientists and technicians, the biologists, paleontologists, and anthropologists who see things this way. Increasingly the rank and file of thoughtful men and women see the body of knowledge we have been accumulating through the questing and testing process as adequate to their needs. They are not distressed, they are not unsure of themselves, and they do not feel "lost." Contemporary culture may not provide them with the certainty organized religion has offered down the centuries, but they count that a gain, not a loss, because they have ceased to believe that the dogmas of organized religion were as certain as their churches and temples claimed.

Two collections of personal belief gathered before and during World War II amply illustrate the point. These individual credos were set down by citizens of a democracy at a time when the widespread success of dictatorship was raising questions about the validity of the democratic way in the minds of thoughtful people. Among these personal credos, only those written by exponents of the ecclesiastical tradition cast their beliefs in the language of traditional theology. The rest wrote as if such belief systems did not exist. Most said they had never before attempted a statement of personal belief and found the exercise difficult but very rewarding. One wrote: "It surprises me to find out in how many areas of life I have doubts and unanswered questions rather than beliefs. It surprises me even more to find that, in many of these areas, a change from doubts and questions to beliefs would feel to me like a change for the worse, not for the better."

The body of knowledge we possess today is not alone "scientific." It consists in the totality of the experience of the human race, collated by the several cultures to be found on our planet. All these cultures by no means agree about what "knowledge" is. Elements within the several cultures are also in sharp disagreement with one another as to what should be accepted as knowledge and what should be dismissed as error or nonsense. Yet still the principle is not invalidated. For us all, wherever we are, what we are ready to accept as knowledge consists in such elements of worldwide knowledge as make sense to us, together with such insights as we ourselves may bring to it all.

In civilization, even when it is primitive, one of the largest areas of experience comes to us out of the body of knowledge built up by the civilization of which we are a part and all those that have preceded it. Thus, to begin with the self, its sensations and experiences, its thoughts and its concepts, is also to begin with the music and poetry, the drama and literature, the art and science of the culture to which we belong. It is to begin with such history, philosophy, technology, and psychology as may be available to us. It is to be aware that we are influenced by the understanding and practice of government, politics, law, industry, commerce, and religion that prevails in our place and time; and also by anything we may learn of the knowledge and practice of social structures other than our own.

The more we look at the vast body of knowledge, experience, and understanding the human race in its many aspects has accumulated, the more it somehow seems to fit together. All of the arts and all of the sciences interact and corroborate one another. The data, incomplete as they are, tend to support rather than contradict one another. Experience continually supports the accumulating body of scientific knowledge. Thus we have every reason to trust, step by step, the picture of the universe that science is constructing. We are reassured by the readiness, even the eagerness, of the scientists to check every datum and to test every generalization in order to be as certain as possible that the principles in current use are as sound as they seemed to be when first stated.

Out of the totality of human experience has emerged the principle of ultimate unity and harmony in all things. No one can prove it. Uncounted instances of disharmony and conflict can be cited. Nevertheless, on the assumption that ultimately all things somehow are interconnected and fit together, the body of knowledge that is ours today was built up. It was the basic assumption from which Thales and Anaximander worked, even though it was more implicit than explicit in their thinking. Heraclitus put it into words: "Those who speak with sense must rely on what is common to all, as a city must rely on its law and with much greater reliance. For all the laws of men are nourished by one law." And again: "This world-order did none of gods or men make, but it always was and is and shall be." In Heraclitus we see for the first time the principle of a comprehensive unity in all things exhibited in the thinking of a single individual. It was this assumption that led Copernicus to his revolutionary discovery, as he struggled to make sense of the intricacies into which the Ptolemaic system had grown by the sixteenth century. Einstein did the same with the complexities of the Newtonian universe. His conviction, that a simple unifying principle could explain space, time, mass, energy, and gravitation, drove him on to the concept of relativity as we understand it today.

Rabindranath Tagore has written:

> The same stream of life that runs through my veins night and day
> runs through the world and dances in rhythmic measures
> It is the same life that shouts in joy through the dust of the earth in
> numberless blades of grass and breaks into tumultuous waves
> of leaves and flowers.
> I feel my limbs are made glorious by the touch of this world of life.
> And my pride is from the life-throb of ages dancing in my blood
> at this moment.

The more we learn about the universe the more impressed we are with the order it exhibits, the regularity of its motions, the design that underlies it, and the almost infinite variety and variability it exhibits at the same time. All this could, of course, be a gigantic deception. There are those who argue that the design we think we see in the universe is only the design we impose upon it with our own minds. They contend that the regularity and order we think we see are but a reflection of the rationality by which we seek to understand it. Maybe, we concede; and yet we feel there is very little risk in assuming that the regularities, the patterns, and the consistencies we seem to see are real. The ever-accumulating, mutually self-supporting evidence that lies all about us leaves us with no other alternative.

The new science of ecology is based on this principle. In the biological world everything interacts with everything else. "The cosmos," writes René Dubos, "is a gigantic organism evolving according to laws which are valid everywhere and therefore generate a universal harmony. The fundamental law of ecology, it is often said, is that everything is relevant to everything else." Fred Hoyle, the astronomer, adds: "The behavior of [cosmic] physical systems is a compound of certain basic laws and of an interaction with the universe in the large."

It will readily be seen that the two assumptions are one. To rely upon the self in concert with other selves is to rely upon the universe of which we are a part; and to trust the universe is to trust ourselves who are an integral part of it. Never completely, of course; we learned long since that the concept of a mechanistic universe, where everything proceeds according to a predetermined plan, continually breaks down. The universe is not, so far as the human mind is concerned, to be pinned down to any kind of inflexible order, and any final demonstration of an ultimate harmony in all things remains as elusive as ever.

Nevertheless, our experience of the world and of ourselves yields sufficient order and predictability to permit us to begin with a single axiom seen in two aspects—the universe and ourselves as sentient, thinking beings within it. We begin, too, with a far greater sense of certainty in these axioms and in the knowledge built upon them than can be found in the articles of traditional religious faith. These axioms are not threatened by skepticism. They stand upon their own feet. The entire belief system and the body of knowledge derived from it does its own persuading and invites its own acceptance. The content grows and changes. The basic principles may be modified, perhaps even replaced from time to time, but the structure remains intact and provides us with understanding and guidance sufficient for our needs.

17

The Tribunal of Truth

Anyone with sufficient imagination may lay down a set of axioms of his own choice and build upon them the structure that they require. Mathematicians have done this in geometry. Abandoning the axioms laid down by Euclid in classical times, they have developed non-Euclidian sets and have built perfectly cohesive and workable non-Euclidian geometric systems on them. Such geometric systems represent nothing we know in the real world, to be sure, but for mathematicians that is beside the point. They would insist that the Euclidian system is an equally arbitrary mental construct, and that nothing in the real world exactly corresponds to that, either.

But for the philosopher, scientist, and theologian, if not for the mathematician, it makes a very great difference from which axioms you take your departure. In theology and philosophy you are not developing an intellectual system in order to see where it leads and how well it can be made to work. Theology, philosophy, and science purport to tell us about ourselves and our world. It is their purpose to help us order and understand experience. They have the task of providing the bases for human conduct and for social organisms as well. For this reason it is meaningless for philosophers, theologians, and scientists to choose an arbitrary set of axioms and then to construct upon them the system of thought to which they lead. Philosophy, theology, and science must all frame axioms that suggest themselves because, insofar as one may judge, they delineate the fundamentals of life.

The critical tradition has rejected the axioms on which the Judeo-Christian and Islamic traditions are built because, desirable as they may seem to be, they do not commend themselves as being descriptive of reality. In their place the critical tradition offers a set of axioms as consonant with experience as possible. With the human creature and human fallibility as its starting point, the critical way in religion moves on to the universe and its regularity and to the need for freedom as the best way for us to deal with it all. But how does a system of thought built upon such axioms work? We say we must check and test our thoughts and experiences with those of others—but how? How do we achieve the corroboration required to eliminate error and gain as much objectivity as possible? Let us attempt an explanation through a metaphor.

1. The Council of Humanity

In the first book of the *Iliad* Homer describes a great debate. For nine fruitless years the Greek warriors had been encamped on the plain before the city of Troy, their ships drawn up on the shore behind them. As the *Iliad* opens, a plague is decimating the ranks of the Greeks and Achilles calls an assembly of the leaders of the expedition to see what is to be done. A debate ensues, which Homer describes in great detail. Early in the second book of the *Iliad* there comes a second debate that Homer also describes in impressive detail. Obviously, debate in council played an important role among the Greeks at the time of the Trojan War. Obviously, too, debate in council was a matter of interest and concern to their descendants, who loved to hear the Homeric epics recited.

We have seen how fundamental a role these poems played in the formation of Greek character. We have also seen how fundamental a role Greek civilization played in the formation of Western culture, and we have seen how fundamental a role Greek genius played in the birth and growth of the critical tradition. It cannot be an accident, then, that the most basic aspect of this tradition, the interchange of ideas, the impact of mind upon mind, played so conspicuous a role among our cultural ancestors.

Apparently, the Greeks of Homer's time and before made their decisions as we do in our democratic assemblies today and as the scientific community, in a broader sense, also does. They made their decisions by open debate in council where each in turn was heard and a decision was reached that amounted to a consensus. Neither Agamemnon nor Menelaus nor Achilles nor even the wily Odysseus could alone make a decision that all the rest of the Greeks felt bound to follow.

The assembly was apparently not an organized body, but rather, an informal gathering of the leaders of the Greek forces, and it gives us a clear picture of the origin of one of the greatest contributions made to human thought by the Greek mind. There, in the assembly of the Greeks on the Aegean shore, as Homer presents it to us in the *Iliad,* we see the beginnings of the Greek polis, the elected assembly of the representatives of the people, where issues were debated and resolved in a gathering of peers. Reason, not force; persuasion, not physical strength and skill, determined the outcome.

An important aspect of every such assembly is the self-control of the individual members. It was clearly present in the scenes depicted in the *Iliad* and it is no less apparent in the assembly of the Greek polis. Whoever spoke enjoyed the self-imposed silence of the other members in order that he might be heard. A thousand years later the principle of free debate in a self-disciplined assembly of the members of a community is clearly seen among the Essenes at Qumran. In their "Manual of Discipline," dating to the first century B.C., we read: "This is the procedure for a Session of the Many [the assembly of the members of the Essene community] . . . Let them sit each according to his rank, and equally let them interrogate with regard to judgment and for all manner of counsel and of any matter which concerns the Many, each bringing in knowledge to the Council of the Community. No man shall interrupt the words of his fellow before the other has finished speaking. Neither shall he speak before his proper order. . . . Each shall speak in his turn. And in the Session of the Many, no one shall speak any word which is not according to the pleasure of the Many, and at the request of the man who is the overseer of the Many."

In the intervening millennium a change has taken place, the importance of which we must not miss. Whereas the Greeks debated what action they should take, the Essenes seem to have debated questions of truth as well as policy. In the earliest Christian communities, which resembled Essene thought and structure in so many ways, we can see this principle even more clearly. The Book of the Acts of the Apostles tells how a dispute arose in the new Christian church that had been established at Antioch. As in the earliest Christian churches, the original constituency at Antioch had been Jewish. When Gentiles began to join, however, some of the original members insisted that, according to Jewish law, they must be circumcised; others thought it unnecessary.

Unable to resolve the question, the Antioch church sent a delegation to the then central and authoritative Christian church at Jerusalem for a ruling on the matter. A similar dispute ensued among the apostles and elders there, which they, like the people at Antioch, sought to resolve by debate in assembly. The debate in the Jerusalem church is reported at length in the Book of Acts. Its conclusion was a compromise: that the church at Antioch "should not trouble [with circumcision] those of the Gentiles who turn to God." The new Gentile members were, however, to conform to certain dietary requirements of Jewish law. They were to "abstain from the pollutions of idols, and from unchastity and from what is strangled and from blood." On hearing this we are told the people of Antioch "rejoiced at the exhortation" and so the matter was resolved. In the Council of Nicaea, as we have seen, an assembly of churchmen called together by Emperor Constantine in the year 325 A.D. addressed itself to questions that were purely theological in nature.

Ancient Greece and Israel do not provide the only examples of debate in an assembly of peers. The Roman senate is a conspicuous instance of the practice. But it is a far wider concept than that applicable to the world of classical antiquity: the free exchange of ideas in an assembly of peers for the purpose of reaching the soundest decision possible is in fact an elemental human practice and in this sense it is universal. We see it in the powwow of the American Indian and in the meeting of the chief with the elders of the tribe in primitive, ancient, and modern times. We see it in the meeting of the king and his council in all times and places. We see it in emperors, dictators, and autocrats of every sort as they consult their advisors, even though in the end they may make the final decision themselves.

We can see this principle on a smaller scale in nearly all walks of life today, never fully embodied, to be sure, but often present in remarkably varied contexts. We see it in commerce and industry, where the most elaborate means are devised to insure a thoroughgoing consideration of every new idea and of every relevant fact. We see it in science, where everyone who wishes to challenge a proposition advanced by anyone else is listened to intently, or should be, if true scientific principles are adhered to.

We see it in the academic community in all fields of research. We see it in government, too, never perfectly applied, of course, but always present as the ideal. Whoever has a relevant datum, an idea, or a plan brings it before the decision-making body of the group to which he belongs. If that body is wise, he is heard. His facts and his ideas are weighed, considered, and, if persuasive, are accepted; if not, they are rejected, but only after due deliberation.

Because none of us today has any stake whatever in the debate among the Greeks before the walls of Troy (as many do in the outcome of the debate at Nicaea) let us take that self-gathered and self-governing assembly as a metaphor for the truth-seeking process that is the essence of the critical way in religion. Let that loose-knit assembly symbolically represent the entire world and everyone in it. Let us think of this world assembly, so to speak, as something we might call the Council of Human Judgment. Now, just as any member of the Greek assembly who wished to might rise, speak, and be granted a hearing, so today anyone may bring whatever he wishes to say before the World Council of Human Judgment.

To continue the metaphor: anyone, at least in theory, may present views for consideration by the Council. Practically speaking, of course, just as in the Homeric assembly, it was the leaders who usually spoke; so it is in the Council of Humanity: there too only the leaders are heard most of the time, although occasionally an unknown voice rises from the crowd and is given a hearing.

There is already a vast body of truth or knowledge that has resulted from this process: science, law, medicine, psychology, art, drama, poetry, literature, history, economics, politics—any attempt to draw up a list would inevitably omit something important. How much of this deposit is truth or knowledge? How much is half-truth? And, how much is downright error?

No one can say. But we can say—and this is what is important—in the Council, whatever at any moment passes for knowledge or truth is constantly being debated, re-examined, and restated. As a result, what is accepted as knowledge is constantly growing and changing, while much that once passed for knowledge is modified, sloughed off, and discarded.

One of the most important sources of the data that come before the Council is the literature of the ages—those volumes we look upon as classics. Truth glows in such writings like nuggets of quartz in a granite ledge. Through the eyes of an earlier day we often perceive truth we otherwise might have missed—such is the mark of great literature, whether drama or poetry, philosophy, essays, biography, history, or novels.

As we have seen, a too-great reverence for ancient writing can be stultifying, but the greater danger lies in a neglect of these sources. Truth is seldom merely contemporary. It is too hard to come by, and too varied, to be formulated in a single lifetime. The latest idea, the current fad, the topic of the day, in all probability will prove to be a passing wisp of speculation, a seeming insight into deeper truth that is later known to have been only the polishing of a familiar surface corroded and dulled by the passage of time. How quickly the books most of us read, even the large "important" ones, fade from view and are forgotten. A check of the leading books of ten to twenty-five or fifty years ago shows why. Few of them got their sights above the immediate problems of their time. That is why they were successful then, and why they are forgotten now.

For this reason, the critical way in religion would place the Bible and the Sacred Scriptures of the religions of the world high on the list of the data the Council must consult. The Christian Bible, in its own right, is one of the greatest of the classics. No small part of its importance is due to the fact that it has informed so much of Western culture that no understanding of our culture is possible without it. The truths the Bible contains have been too often recited to require repetition here. Exponents of the critical tradition, despite their many and necessary criticisms of the Bible, need also to recognize and to emphasize the importance of the role it has played. Too often, on seeing the manifold shortcomings of the Bible and the exaggerated claims made for it, critics have leapt to the conclusion that it should be banned, banished, and forgotten. In the pursuit of truth they could not make a greater mistake.

The Council of Humanity needs only to remember that the Bible is a book like any other book: one to be considered on its own intrinsic merit, not by what the churchmen or the disillusioned have said about it. Take away the doctrinal baggage with which the Bible is encumbered in almost all our minds and you have a truly remarkable, insightful, and inspirational assembly of writings in which the dross and the more revolting passages can be understood for what they are—authentic instances of the standards and practices of another time.

The more broadly we conceive the Council of Humanity, the nearer we shall come to grasping the concept. Its dimensions are not merely lateral; they are vertical as well. The participants in its decisions are not merely all living men and women. All the preceding generations, who have left behind them a record we can read and ponder, are to be included. The vertical dimension is the dimension of history. As our techniques of data-recovery and accessibility improve, the participation of past thinkers will also increase and the relevance of what they have said will be seen more easily. As we have already learned to read the hieroglyphs of the Egyptians and the cuneiform of the Sumerians; as we are now learning to read the Mayan language of Central America and Linear A and B of ancient Crete, so tomorrow we shall doubtless know more about the meaning of monuments like Stonehenge and other similar stone circles in Britain. Whoever would advance an idea must expect it to be measured by everything that is being said today everywhere, and everything said in the past as well.

There is, of course, no Council of Human Judgment, no Tribunal of Truth, and there never will be. It is only a metaphor, used as metaphors are: to communicate an idea. The Council exists nowhere; it sits nowhere, and has no personnel. No one comes before it, and it hands down no decisions or decrees. The Council is a metaphor that points to a fundamental aspect of human life: that people have always exchanged knowledge, ideas, feelings, and experiences with one another. They have always sought advice from one another. They do this because they know they dare not trust themselves alone.

We can see the Council principle operating at its best in the scientific community today. At the moment, that particular community seems to be remarkably free from the extraneous considerations that bend men's judgment to lesser aims. That is why the moon shots were successful. Incredibly complex as the preparations were; astronomical as was the possibility of fatal error; success came again and again, because of the total dedication of all the participants in the project and the totally free atmosphere in which they sought to eliminate all possible errors.

Another instance in which we can see the Council principle now operating is in the multitude of voluntary associations, both secular and religious, with which American life is replete today. Many of these associations are small, fluid, intensely interpersonal, and utterly free in the exchange of ideas that takes place within them. Not answerable to the demands of pressure groups and not motivated by the self-seeking of the members so common in politics, many of them are able to achieve a very high degree of objectivity. Organized around a set of ideals in which the members believe, they pursue these ideals with zeal, but also with a sense of fair play. The attitude of the members toward one another and toward those outside their organization is both respectful and charitable.

The right to form voluntary associations, the right to unite with like-minded people for a common purpose, is one of the most essential elements in any doctrine of freedom. Freedom of thought, even freedom of speech, can be quite an empty exercise if, in the mass society of today, what we say goes unnoticed. The right to join with others of like mind and gain a hearing thus becomes one of the most essential ingredients in the kind of freedom that makes the Council of Humanity real. No one has insisted upon this point more emphatically than James Luther Adams of the Harvard Divinity School. He wrote, "The crucial question [regarding freedom] is whether there is freedom of association, freedom of citizens to organize a group to promote an idea or a cause and particularly to promote a cause that may be in conflict with policies of the establishment, in short, the freedom to organize dissent."

There are also great dangers to freedom in the voluntary association. An association dedicated to truth seeking is an asset to the Council. An association organized for narrow ends, interested in its own welfare and willing to twist and pervert language to its own special purposes, is a liability to the Council. How much of the material provided by such a group is propaganda? How are we to tell? Sifting the valid from the invalid is in any case a time-consuming and an irritating operation.

Whether a voluntary association advances or impedes the truth-seeking process is, unfortunately, not merely a matter of noble motive. High-principled people can become quite doctrinaire and anything but objective in outlook. They are not always free from personal ambition and they can be quite uncharitable towards those who, for valid reasons, may disagree with and oppose them. Such persons do not, of course, serve the purpose of the Council of Human Judgment. The metaphorical Council is totally dispassionate, totally selfless, always respectful of disagreement, always more eager for valid criticism than for praise. That is one reason why the Council is not a reality but only a metaphor.

One of the most difficult problems the Council of Humanity faces, even when we think of it as a metaphor, is that of communication. In a small group—like the assembly of the Greeks before Troy, of the apostles and elders of the first-century church at Jerusalem, or of today's small voluntary associations—there is no problem. Every member of the group who wishes to may be present and be heard at its deliberations in assembly. Not so when the group is large and when the assembly is of necessity a representative one. Thomas Jefferson was still wrestling with this very concrete question even after he had finished his two terms as President of the United States. In 1816 he wrote from Monticello: "This corporeal globe and everything upon it belong to its present corporeal inhabitants, during their generation. They alone have a right to direct what is the concern of themselves . . . but how to collect their voice? This is the real difficulty."

Jefferson did not solve the problem satisfactorily, nor has anyone since that time. For us today its resolution is far more difficult. How, in the mass society of the twentieth century, and in the far larger society that we foresee in the twenty-first, is one single voice to be heard in the Council of Human Judgment? It is a question of fundamental importance, one for which there is no answer at the moment. Some means for the communication of ideas in the mass society must be found. Without it there is no true freedom, and without full freedom there is no true Council. If none but the politicians, writers, and members of the news media, educators, industrial and religious leaders can be heard, the Council will be but a sorry shadow of the instrument it must be if it is to discern truth and determine sound policy.

It would be utterly impossible for us to manage the volume of data we are now accumulating were it not for the computer. Even with it, some are predicting that we shall soon drown in it all. But there is no reason to be discouraged. Just as the computer has come along now when we should be utterly lost without it, so there is good reason to think new technologies will be devised in the future to resolve the problems that future technologies will create.

The analogy of the Council to a court of law, of course, suggests itself. The analogy is useful but cannot be pressed too far. The common law of the Anglo-Saxon tradition provides the best analogy. Attempting to pinpoint the uniqueness of that particular legal system, Oliver Wendell Holmes took issue with those who think of law as a logical construct in which everything falls easily into place. "The life of the Anglo-American common law has not been logic," he wrote; "it has been experience." It is exactly so with the critical tradition. Often it has seemed to be quite illogical. The judgments rendered by the Council of Humanity are multiple and varied; often they are inconsistent and even contradictory. Sometimes they are simply foolish. History records uncounted opinions popularly and vehemently held in one age and as emphatically discredited and rejected in the next. In the Council of Humanity the rendering of judgment is a process, rather than always a straight-line development.

Holmes, in his description of the growth, development, and use of the common law in ordering the affairs of men, came as close as anyone has to delineating the role of the Council of Human Judgment in human affairs. The analogy is particularly apt because of the cumulative aspect of Anglo-Saxon jurisprudence. Individual cases are not decided in accordance with rigid rules or abstract concepts. They are decided in accordance with the accumulated wisdom in that particular area suggested by the line of preceding cases most nearly like the one before the court. The earlier cases are not binding; they are, rather, a guide. The judges may reject or overturn the decision of an earlier court if for any reason it seems to be faulty.

Roscoe Pound, former Dean of the Harvard Law School, believed that the spirit of the common law is its essence. It lies in "the habit of the common law judges of applying to the cause in hand the judicial experiences of the past." The result, he said, is a body of tradition, which the judges may gradually change but which is above king and commoner, parliament and prelate. Sir Coke, Pound reminds us, once confronted his king with the proposition that even the king is under the law. The Council of Humanity enjoys and makes use of the deposit of wisdom accumulated down through the ages. None of it, whether derived from church or state, from the academy or through the arts, is looked upon as impervious to change; yet everyone is subject to it, kings and commoners, churchmen and scientists, artists, prophets, criminals, and fools. In general we know what the Council agrees to. We know until someone changes it, but that is always happening.

The analogy to the common law and its courts can be carried no further. The body of knowledge established by the Council of Humanity is more like a boiling cauldron than the relatively more fixed principles of Anglo-Saxon jurisprudence and the mass of statute law added to it. But to this point the analogy holds. It suggests, as it is intended to do, how knowledge is acquired in the critical tradition, how it is held, how it expands, is modified and—in more instances than we might think—eventually abandoned altogether.

2. The Goal of Truth

Since one of the chief goals of the Council of Human Judgment is truth, I have also called it the Tribunal of Truth. Here again, face to face with something elemental, we could easily sink into the mire of definition and consume all the space that remains trying to extricate ourselves from it. What is truth? It is, said Einstein, "what stands the test of experience." Whitehead said, "Truth is the conformation of Appearance to Reality." Einstein and Whitehead propose to take nothing for granted but experience. That will be our criterion or definition also. Such a position follows inevitably from the conclusion we reached in the chapter on axioms—that there are a certain few elemental things we must assume since there is no way to get beneath them to anything more elemental. In the critical tradition we assume that we can know something about ourselves and about our world. The nearer our knowledge comes to the reality it is intended to represent, the closer it comes to being true.

There is no ideal or goal or principle higher than truth. "A man can live a long time with injustice," observes a modern writer, "but he cannot long live with untruth." "It does not matter whether a man believes in God," remarked Erich Fromm. "It matters whether he thinks truth." At the deepest level the horror in the future foreseen by George Orwell in his *1984* is the all-enveloping falsity of the world Big Brother constructed.

We owe our concept of truth to the Greeks. It was one of the three fundamentals in their highly complex triad of truth, beauty, and goodness. All three concepts were ideals, intimately interrelated, but elusive, always to be sought after, never wholly achieved. Despite the claims of the churchmen to know truth by revelation, the Greek view dominates Western culture today and much of the world as well. It is the ultimate commitment of the critical way, its ultimate concern, and its final goal.

That would mean for some thinkers that the critical way defines God as truth, in the way that others define God as love, as intelligence, or as power. Does the word "God" gain in meaning if it is said to equal "truth"? I think not. Neither do we gain in understanding if "truth" is said to be the God of the critical way. Let people define God as they think best, but if they seek the essence of the critical way, they will find it in the concept "truth" more than in any other concept of the divine. If some thinkers find divinity in a concept of truth, surely no one will object. People have long believed truth to be an aspect of divinity. But in the critical tradition it is truth, not divinity, that is the goal, and truth remains the goal whether or not it is held to be an aspect of the divine nature.

In the critical tradition formulations of truth are never final. Thus they can be said to be "true" only in the sense that they are the best formulations of knowledge we can make at any given time. Statements about the nature of things that emerge in the critical tradition are the best statements we can fashion about the really real, the ultimately true. They reach toward the truth we seek. They yield a partial if not a total understanding of it. In the critical way, truth is not a destination; it is a way station. It is a point we reach and eventually pass beyond in what appears to be an endless journey. John Milton, in his "Areopagitica," wrote: if the waters of truth "flow not in a perpetual progression, they sicken into a muddy pool of conformity and tradition."

In the Tribunal of Truth, the clash of contending "truths" provides the assurance that what we conclude comes as close to the ultimate truth as possible. The clash gives the process its vitality. It is the instrument by which we come as close to truth as we can. "In a democracy," Robert Maynard Hutchins wrote, "controversy is an end in itself. A civilization in which there is not a continuous controversy about important issues, speculative and practical, is on the way to totalitarianism and death." Justice Oliver Wendell Holmes put it a little differently. "The ultimate good desired is better reached by free trade in ideas," he wrote in a dissenting legal opinion in 1919. "The best test of truth is the power of the thought to get itself accepted in the competition of the market." William Ellery Channing, in a Boston sermon on slavery in the early nineteenth century, anticipated John Stuart Mill by several years by declaring that truth "is aided most by the opposition of those who can give the full strength of the argument on the side of error." Then he added: "When I hear a man complaining that some cause which he has at heart will be put back for years by a speech or a book,

I suspect that his attachment to it is prejudiced and that he has no consciousness of standing on a rock."

Possible citations in support of this proposition are legion. Bronowski and Mazlish concluded their study of *The Western Intellectual Tradition* by observing that "those societies are most creative and progressive which safeguard the expression of new ideas." Two generations earlier, J. B. Bury, surveying European intellectual history toward the end of a brilliant life of scholarship, had written: "If the history of civilization has any lesson to teach it is this: there is one supreme condition of mental and moral progress which it is completely within the power of man himself to secure, and that is perfect liberty of thought and discussion. The establishment of this liberty may be considered the most valuable achievement of modern civilization, and as a condition of social progress it should be deemed fundamental."

We gain some measure of the towering figure of Socrates, or perhaps of Plato, the biographer of his mind and spirit, when we realize that in the course of formulating these principles we are following a path they first hewed out of the jungle of human thought. The central role of free and open discussion in arriving at truth is clearly stated in the *Apology* where Plato notes Socrates' description of himself as a gadfly and as one who seeks truth by asking questions that expose the ignorance of the wise. Socrates, we recall, said at his trial that he could not remain silent even though he were to be condemned to death. He could not refrain from probing about in search of the truth. If we can believe Plato's account, Socrates gladly paid with his life the price the Athenian assembly exacted of him for asserting and for living by the principle that truth, if it is to be known, must be spoken and it must be heard by those who seek to know what it is.

Such questionings and probings are not necessarily constructive, however. In the critical way, whether in religion, science, or any other avenue of human endeavor and activity, the purpose of the questioning process must be to expose inconsistency, folly, and error. Often that is not the purpose of questioning. Today, as in ancient Greece with the Sophists, people may ask questions, not to elicit truth, but to embarrass an opponent. They enter a debate, not to exchange ideas but to create turmoil; in effect, to obstruct the exchange of ideas. Their purpose is not to sharpen concepts but to prevent their being considered. They are not trying to establish the truth but rather to obscure it. They precipitate an uproar in which valid ideas that might otherwise be persuasive are not even considered because they cannot be heard.

This tactic gained very wide currency in Germany during the Nazi controversies of the late 1920s and in the United States during the student demonstrations of the late 1960s. There is no development of ideas, no honing of truth, when such tactics are used. Controversy is creative only when ideas of which we disapprove are examined dispassionately. Controversy has a place in the Tribunal of Truth only when persuasion is its method and truth is its goal.

Ideas cannot be sharpened in a forum if either party to the debate seeks victory rather than understanding, glory rather than truth. As Socrates observes in Plato's *Phaedo*: "The partisan, when he is engaged in a dispute, cares nothing about the rights of the question, but is anxious only to convince his hearers of his own opinions." There is no place for the partisan in the Tribunal of Truth. It does not carry on adversary proceedings. The degree to which a participant seeks to win in debate disqualifies him from a place in the Tribunal of Truth.

At least since Averroës' time, the churchmen have sought to protect official dogma from inquiry and contention by the doctrine of two truths, the truth with which reason deals and the truth which lies in the province of faith. The one is said to be the result of thought and experience: the other comes from divine revelation. Both are equally valid, so the argument goes, and in the end they are essentially one and the same. Any inconsistency is apparent, not real, and is due to the very evident limitations that circumscribe our ability to understand ultimate things. According to this doctrine, the methods of religion do not deal with scientific conclusions and the methods of religion cannot be expected to yield the truths science holds.

The distinction here is not merely one of method, it is also one of result. The result is not one truth but two, consistent, it is hoped, with each other but not necessarily so, at least as far as our human powers of understanding are concerned. The problem and the argument that accompanies it persists. Contemporary writers still assert that the truths known by faith and held by faith are of a different order than those attained by reason, experience, or science. Such truths, they hold, go beyond literal scientific truth to a more profound truth.

One writer put it this way: "The most important change in religious understanding in recent centuries is an awareness that religious truths are made up, not of propositions but of symbols." But if we substitute symbols for propositions, the critical mind would ask, do we gain in clarity of understanding? Do we not then have to ask what the symbols symbolize, and will not that have to be stated in propositions? There is no gain in such a formula, only the further complication of a question that is already complicated enough.

A related set of ideas concerns the concept "paradox," of which the neo-orthodox made much in the 1930s and 1940s. Life is filled with it, they pointed out, filled with inconsistencies and ambiguities. Try as we will, we can't sort all these things out. The most profound questions forever remain unanswered, or such answers as we are able to give turn out to be inconsistent with one another. A contemporary proponent of the paradox idea solves the problem by repeating that "there are different *kinds* of truth. Theological truth differs from other kinds. A true statement is usually understood to be one which corresponds to what is the case or that which is internally self-consistent and coherent with other truths. But a theological statement cannot tell us what is the case for the subject of theology is God and my finite, contingent intellect cannot precisely comprehend what is infinite and necessary. . . ." He follows with the usual argument that our conceptualizations concerning God must inevitably be inadequate. Hence, in the realm of the divine we end in paradox and inconsistency.

The critical mind reacts in a manner exactly opposite. Confronted by inconsistency, incomprehensibility, and paradox, the critical mind does not kneel as if at the altar of truth. For the inquiring mind a seeming inconsistency is not a point of arrival: it is a point of departure. It is an indication not that the journey is over but that it has just begun, at least that there is farther still to go.

In effect the ecclesiastical way seems to be willing not merely to settle for ambiguity in the most basic areas of life but to assert that in ultimate matters ambiguity is a kind of self-validating principle. The critical mind believes no greater mistake can be made. To find truth in paradox, as religion has so often done in the past, is to give permanence to inadequacy and to come to rest only part way along the road.

We have already noted at a number of points the importance of clarity of language for the critical way in religion. Such clarity is, of course, never completely attainable. It is one of the goals toward which we forever move but never attain. Our concepts at the deepest level always will be inadequate and vague because they are reaching toward yet more profound concepts we are still trying to formulate. But we are not thereby excused from the requirement that we seek the utmost in clarity in every idea we express with everything we have to give.

Percy Bridgman, at the meeting of the American Academy of Arts and Sciences referred to earlier, spoke of the problem of vocabulary. We must, he said, give the most careful attention to the meaning of words. Philosophers have done so by developing the concept of "operational" meanings. In order really to know the meaning of a term, we must be able to describe what we do when we use it. This is its operational meaning. Bridgman conceded that there might well be a better way to get at word-meanings, but that was not his point. His point was that in order to know the meaning of any word we have first to establish a criterion according to which we make our choices among all possible meanings. The criterion is the basic assumption we make, the axiom with which we begin.

Bridgman thereupon took his departure from the world of physics and of science as well and said, "I believe that very few terms of harmonistic—as distinguished from scientific—import have been subjected to an analysis for meaning as articulate as this." The critical mind would agree and add that theology is one of the worst offenders in this regard. There are innumerable examples of fuzzy word-meanings in the language of religion to which we might turn. We have already noted the introduction of new meanings into words that once were clear and unambiguous, the most conspicuous instance being the term "God," which has been given so many meanings it now has no dependable meaning at all. In former times "God" meant a person, almighty in power, of whom man is the image. God was not "love" or "creativity," the "force for good," the "ground of being," or even the "unmoved mover." Those whom the church called "unbelievers" sought to stretch the meaning of the word "God" and to widen the meaning of theological concepts generally, in order to adjust them to the widening horizons of the human mind. But for centuries the Church would have none of it. Theological language was kept clear, distinct, and as exact as possible.

Today we face a curious reversal of these roles as we have noted. Today it is the churchmen who are permissive and latitudinarian in their use of ancient theological terms, while the "unbelievers" insist upon the importance of saying what you mean and meaning what you say, especially when it comes to a profession of faith made at the altar of the God you worship. They want neither to distort language nor to perjure themselves, especially in religion. They would argue that if a creed has constantly to be interpreted in order to be useful, sharp attention needs to be given to what is actually being communicated. A creed may have value as a symbol; it may be comforting when used as a part of the liturgy of a church; the music of its words may be precious because they are poetic in character and hallowed by tradition; but, if the words of a creed or liturgy do not say what they mean, then for the critically minded worshiper, it cannot serve a religious purpose. At best, it is a form, the obvious meaning of which is to be ignored. At worst, it amounts to a deception. A creed that says one thing yet is interpreted to mean something else can become not a vehicle for, but rather an obstacle to, worship because it may require the worshiper to affirm what he actually disbelieves.

"Perhaps all living is just learning the meaning of words," wrote a contemporary observer of our manners and morals. "Not the sesquipedalians that we look up in the dictionary, but the big one-syllable basic words that are fully defined only in the lexicon of experience: 'work and play,' 'joy and pain,' 'peace,' 'love,' 'life,' itself—and 'death,' its silent inevitable companion. Their meanings, alas! we master too late to employ completely. The learning is all."

On the other hand, the multiple meanings of words play an important role in man's pursuit of truth. To seek out the clearest and most precise meaning possible for words rules out neither poetry nor myth, neither narrative nor drama. When we are seeking to express a new idea for which there is no word, when we are feeling after concepts never before envisioned or understood, or when we reach toward the abstract, we make use of such language as is available. We may resort to similes, metaphors, or myths. We may use analogies and allegories, or simply extend the meaning of a familiar term, in an attempt to grasp a new idea and make it real.

When Barbara Ward coined the phrase "Spaceship Earth" she was quite consciously reaching toward a new idea by using an analogy to one that was already familiar and understood. No spaceship had been built at the time, but science fiction had already filled the skies with them, and they were already on the drawing boards of Russian and American scientists. People knew what they were when, in 1965, Barbara Ward wrote: "In the last few decades, mankind has been overcome by the most fateful change in its entire history. Modern science and technology have created so close a network of communication, transport, economic interdependence—and potential nuclear destruction—that planet Earth, on its journey through infinity, has acquired the intimacy, the fellowship, and the vulnerability of a spaceship."

Since Barbara Ward penned those words American astronauts have beheld our planet from the moon. Through the lenses of their cameras we have seen how very like a spaceship we are. We have seen the beautiful blue sphere that is our home rising from the surface of the moon, as we have so often beheld the sunrise and moonrise from earth. We know now that our earth is a spaceship little different essentially from those in which we have sent our astronauts to the moon. These ships have to be self-contained and everything that occurs within them affects everything else. Specifically, whatever wastes, whatever poisons each produces remain on board. This is the new meaning of ecology as we have come to understand it in our time. We, the citizens of Earth, are all on the same voyage and we are making that voyage together in the *same* vehicle. We must learn to get along with one another and with the demands of our planet or we shall all perish together.

So, the truth moves forward, our horizons widen, and so, we learn. So knowledge increases and we understand more clearly, never completely, yet enough for our purposes.

3. Can the Critical Way Be Institutionalized?

In using language like the "Tribunal of Truth" or "Council of Human Judgment" we need constantly to remind ourselves that this concept is a metaphor only. The Council exists nowhere: it is a tribunal in the conceptual sense only. We need to transform the metaphor from an idea of which we approve into a reality by which to live. That means some kind of structure, a social institution. In religion it means a church or its equivalent.

For many people accustomed to organized religion, the fact of organization is no problem. For many who follow the critical way in religion there is a problem and it is very grave. They want to know how a religion of the type they find real can be organized. They are concerned that even the best of religious structures would eventually extinguish the critical spirit, because of the stultifying tendency that eventually seems to overcome almost every social structure.

As we might expect, Whitehead has dealt with the numbing effect of organization upon religion. Religious ideas become "enshrined in modes of worship, in popular religious literature, and in art," he observed. Religions cannot do without such representations (I am paraphrasing), but if they are allowed to become dominant, then they become idols. Idolatry is the result of static dogmas. Our task is to handle popular forms of religious thought, maintaining their full reference to their primary sources and, at the same time, keeping them in touch with the best current critical thought.

How this is to be done Whitehead did not say. It remains one of the most central questions of the critical way in religion. Supposing such an institution could be designed, how could it be protected from the shortcomings and follies to which all institutions are subject, because fallible, gullible, and sometimes venal human beings operate them?

The question of institutionalizing the critical way in religion has come up many times in the preceding pages. We explored it at length in connection with the development of the university. We saw that the concept "heresy" is essentially institutional in character. In order to know who is and who is not a heretic, there has to be an organization to establish an orthodoxy from which the heretic, as an organization member, chooses to depart. Unless he first belongs he is not a heretic, he is merely an unbeliever. In the critical way in religion there can be no heresy because, in it, there can be no orthodoxy to modify or change.

If the critical way in religion is to be transformed from a tradition in Western culture into an institution capable of nurturing and expanding the critical way, it will inevitably become involved in all the tendencies toward rigidity with which human institutions, by their very nature, are beset. Unfortunately, high motives do not save the church from the evils of bureaucracy. The self-seeking, venal, sometimes corrupt aspects of human nature that find expression in other social structures do so in the church also.

The problems indigenous to bureaucracy have been described in many ways. A popularizer recently identified one of them and named it for himself "The Peter Principle." It holds that: *In a hierarchy every employee tends to rise to his level of incompetence.* Members of any institutional structure ride up the organizational escalator until they reach a post just above the level of their competence. Having attained so high a position, they thereafter devote more time to maintaining themselves at that level than to discharging their duties. Their goal shifts from service to security, from performance to job holding. Organized religion has never been free from the operation of this principle, nor is it ever likely to be. Nor can the critical way in religion expect to be free of it. Noble origins and noble aims are no safeguard against the overarching need for the individual to find and hold a place in the larger economic and social structures within the society to which he or she belongs.

"Parkinson's Law" is similar. It holds that: *Work expands to meet the time available for its completion.* Earlier, Dom Virgil George Michel formulated what he called the "Iron Law of Oligarchy." Freely rendered it reads: the larger the organization, the more completely do its workings become encumbered by bureaucratic controls. Yet other such principles could easily be invented—doubtless many have been, all of them illustrating the general principle: when you organize any human activity, be it industry, labor, government, education, or religion, into the structure you build will crawl the weak, the incompetent, the venal, and the personally ambitious, all of them ready, and some of them eager, to bend the structure to their own private purposes.

Martin Marty is among the few mainline churchmen who have recognized and openly acknowledged the problems that beset a church because it is an organized human institution. He writes: "If you wish to propagate something new [in religion] you cannot avoid becoming somehow corrupt. . . . New movements are given a little time in which to be fluid, inchoate, inexpensive. Then they take on the problems the rest of us have. Life between God and Mammon afflicts them too. To them we [the leaders of the established churches] say, Welcome to the Club."

We saw in the chapters on Belief and Faith that Christianity has tried to institutionalize religious thought, with marked success in medieval times but with steadily decreasing success since the Renaissance and Reformation. It was in reaction to this effort that the critical tradition arose and grew strong. Any attempt to institutionalize the critical way must start from the premise that human thought cannot be institutionalized in such a manner. What now needs institutionalizing in the church is the full opportunity for freedom of thought.

If we were to choose the most difficult of all the problems the churches face as institutions it would undoubtedly be the problem of prophecy—not the foretelling of the future, but prophecy in the tradition of ancient Israel. It is the problem of the social critic and the problem of the heretic. How is an organization to deal with those who denounce it even as they proclaim their loyalty to its most basic principles? Amos and Isaiah, Micah and Jeremiah live with us still because of the prophetic quality of their words. Yet how they troubled Israel! It was the same with Jesus of Nazareth and with the prophetic voices in Western culture since ancient times, some of whom we noted in Part II. How is organized religion to guarantee a hearing to such people without undercutting its own power and authority?

In order to gauge the full impact of such a question, we must turn it around. Let us suppose that we find our church—or society itself—wanting in some way that appears to us to be of great importance. Let us suppose further that to voice our thoughts publicly might seriously damage the very institution we desire to improve. Would we speak? Suppose, as in Socrates' case, the body politic regards what we are saying as blasphemous and deleterious to the formation of good character in the young. Do we hold our peace or do we speak? If we speak contrary to the laws of the state or the canons of good taste, by what authority do we do so?

Socrates, we recall, said he spoke out of the wisdom the oracle at Delphi declared he possessed. Later, on trial for his life, he went much further. Offered life in exile if he would agree to stop teaching, we recall that he replied, "Men of Athens, I shall obey God rather than you, and while I have life and strength I shall never cease from the practice and teaching of philosophy. I shall continue my teaching. This is the command of God." We need to understand what Socrates is saying here. He is not saying, as Isaiah and Jeremiah did, "Thus saith the Lord." He is not saying that he speaks the words of God to men. He is saying simply that God commands him to say to men what it seems to him that he should say. Even in this declaration Socrates is not thinking in the terms that are so familiar to us from the Judeo-Christian tradition. He is not thinking of a personal God directing him to do as he does. To be sure, he speaks of his "daemon," the meaning of which has been extensively debated. It means simply that, in the concepts and language of our time, he is speaking about conscience, an inner voice, or the voice of God in the soul of man. In speaking of his daemon, Socrates was saying that he felt compelled to speak the truth as he saw and understood it, and that he felt the compulsion despite the laws and the sense of good taste of the people of Athens.

The prophets of Israel did the same, even though they described what they did in different language. They expressed their thought in Israelitic rather than Greek concepts, but they, too, spoke out of a sense of inner compulsion. They were not free to speak, but they felt they had a mission: to utter the truth that had come to them regardless of the consequences; and they were heard because the Israelites believed that they were in fact God's messengers here on earth.

Jesus of Nazareth, John Wyclif, John Hus, and Martin Luther all spoke from the same inner sense of compulsion. Faustus Socinus, Francis David, and Galileo Galilei had the same motivation. So too did the men of the Enlightenment in the seventeenth and eighteenth centuries, and the Bible critics of the nineteenth century. All alike said aloud what they felt they must say and stood ready to take the consequences. The urge to speak the truth as one sees it is as old as the critical tradition itself and that urge lies at its heart. "The voice of the intellect is a soft one," wrote Sigmund Freud, "but it does not rest until it has gained a hearing."

Those who have testified to the urge within us to speak what we feel we must are without number. Nevertheless, there are still more who exercised the right without claiming it, because no one challenged them, and it never occurred to them to formulate the principle. They simply saw an error and sought to correct it, or they worked out a better explanation of things than their culture offered and proffered it instead. The authors of Genesis I did not ask permission to write a preface to the ancient holy books of Israel. Thales did not set forth the reasons why he speculated on the origin of things rather than repeating the myths of Homer. Once the hold of the Church on the minds of men was broken, neither Newton nor Einstein, neither Pasteur nor Darwin, nor James Frazer asked leave of anyone to say what they said or to defend their right to say it. By what authority did they speak? Einstein said, "I put my trust in my intuition." Perhaps without realizing it he was echoing Heraclitus, who had said more than two thousand years earlier, "I inquired of myself."

This question can be put in a very much wider context. By what authority have the poets spoken—Aeschylus or Euripides, Shakespeare or Goethe? By what right have the philosophers spoken—Plato or Aristotle, Descartes or Hume? By what right have the artists created—Praxiteles or Rembrandt, Michelangelo or Hiroshige? Or the world's great religious leaders—by what right have they spoken? Confucius, Lao-tzu, Siddhartha, Muhammad, Mohandas Gandhi, or the leaders of the Judeo-Christian tradition?

"Under all forms of the state and in all periods of their history, the preservation of the proper balance between private judgment and constitutional authority has proved the deepest and most perplexing of all political problems," wrote a profound student of government. He added, "No political philosopher has ever dared set up permanent markers bounding the respective fields of liberty and authority, and none need even try."

For the critical mind the voice of prophecy is the central problem of all organized religion. How is a church to be built with the power to endure if it is required to give a public hearing to anyone and everyone who wants to criticize it? Even when criticism is potentially destructive, must it be permitted? Cannot the long-term health and high purpose of the church be weighed in the balances against disruptive and destructive commentary?

Yet, for the critical mind there is but one option open. The voice of the would-be prophet must be heard, for the sake of the prophet and for the sake of the church as well. In the end there can be but one authority for the individual—the self. Whatever seems to us to be real and true past all doubting remains so, though all the world denies it, but with this all-important proviso—that we have first checked out every conceivable opposing argument, and every last contradictory datum.

The critical mind, criticizing the church, does so with the same claim to authority made by the artist and writer, the mystic, the philosopher, the scientist, and the dreamer. None can deny the validity of these insights to those who have them, but the world divides on the question of what we are to do with such persons. The critical way says we can best find out whose experience is valid, and whose is not, by giving any and all of them a hearing. This is the function of the Council. Through that device, ideas however novel and strange are given utterance. Those that are valid slowly gain acceptance, while the flaws in those that are not are slowly exposed.

The voice of the would-be prophet must be heard for the sake of the church and also for the sake of the truth itself. This is the basic principle by which the Tribunal of Truth operates. A full public hearing for all is the only guarantee we have that what passes for truth at any given time comes as close to the truth as possible. History affords us too many examples of those who were silenced, ignored, or denounced in their own time, only to be acclaimed as heroes by a later generation. Obviously the Council principle is basically democratic since it requires that each individual be given full opportunity for self-expression and since it requires a structure with these guarantees built into it.

But democracy in the Church, as in the State, is a very fragile thing. Like a candle in the night, political democracy flickered briefly into light in ancient Greece and went out. It appeared again in a religious context in the assembly of the Essenes at Qumran and in the earliest Christian churches. From then on it is hard to say when and where democracy was present, if at all, but we can clearly identify it in sectarian Christianity in the early Reformation period and before. The signing of the Mayflower Compact in 1620 by a group of English Separatists called Pilgrims is perhaps as clear an instance as we could cite of the formation of a religious and political democratic structure.

For at least five centuries since the Reformation period, sectarian Christianity has been struggling with democratic forms of church structure in which the full participation of all the members in all aspects of church government and doctrine has been sought. These experiments in turn have been schools for political and social democracy. They have shown the West how the full participation of members in a group can be organized; tyranny controlled; criticism, innovation, and creativity nurtured. We saw in §1 of this chapter of the manner in which voluntary organizations, in particular in the United States, have done the same. Each has learned from the experience of the rest what mechanisms are best calculated to involve group members to the greatest degree, and what mechanisms can at the same time prevent a predatory leader from subverting the structure to his private purposes.

The experimenting and learning are still going on. Ruler and people, boss and workers, chief and warriors have been so much a part of human society for so long, we cannot expect so profound a change in our ways to come about very rapidly. Instinctively we think in terms of master and servant, governor and governed. It still requires an effort on our part to think of social organisms being operated according to decisions in which all who wish to may play a part. We still tend to think in the old patterns, among other reasons because it is often difficult to follow a path of action if very many people play a part in deciding how it is to be carried out. Nevertheless, this is and must remain the goal.

A feminist writer, pointing to the deep-lying pattern of male dominance in our culture, argues that the women's movement has at last exposed the basically hierarchical structure of human society. Women have had to probe more deeply into this problem than have men, she asserts, because they have been so peculiarly victimized by it. For the most part, she says, these hierarchical structures are unseen, and unacknowledged, but they are none the less pervasive and none the less degrading. The feminist movement of our time is becoming a powerful ally in the age-old struggle to guarantee equality of opportunity and equality of participation in the human decision-making process.

Unfortunately, institutions, including churches, seem to have a built-in inability to reform themselves. It has been said that this single fact was responsible above all others, perhaps almost alone, for the Protestant Reformation. The medieval church was quite simply unable to reform itself. Movements of moral reform, like the monastic movement, had been allowed to grow but were soon absorbed with no lasting effect upon the Church. Intellectual movements of reform on the other hand were ruthlessly crushed.

A prior question would be: need the critical way in religion be organized at all? Some would answer emphatically, "No: I can be more religious looking at a sunset, or sailing my boat, or walking through the woods than ever I can in church." But this point of view completely overlooks the social aspects of religion and the strength we derive from worship in community, the mutual sharing and celebration of our hopes, aspirations, and basic beliefs. All these are enhanced by mutual sharing. Courage and fortitude, high moral purpose, and self-sacrifice for a greater good than our own are stirred and strengthened within us by membership and participation in a community of like minded people.

Some form of religious institution appears to be inescapable. The earliest records of *Homo sapiens* indicate that we have been religious from the beginning. Even if we should decide that we would be better off without churches and temples, priests, rituals, moral codes, and declarations of belief, we are not likely to rid ourselves of them very soon. Most people think it would be a mistake to try: that if we were to give up the church, a malevolent substitute might well grow up to fill the vacuum. The universal and ancient lineage of organized religion indicates a basic human need that organized religion evolved to meet. The question is not whether to continue organized religious structures, but how best to carry them on: how to enable them to provide for the religious aspirations of our time.

If religion is to continue to be a reality in the lives of people, it must be nurtured like any other human activity, whether it be art, music or poetry, science, literature or drama. The church is as necessary to religion as the university is to thought, research, and education. Both require structure and discipline, governors and participants, authority and economic resources. To make use of these means and to achieve these ends the institution is essential. That is the definition of the church or temple—religion institutionalized. To be either, the church or temple requires no special set of beliefs or worship, hierarchy, structure, or government. It is the presence of religion that makes such an institution a church.

And what is religion? It is our attempt as human beings to grasp the meaning of our own existence and that of the universe in which we dwell. To no less a degree it is our attempt to relate to other human beings, to see that their needs are the same as ours, and to meet them in so far as we are able. Religion is also the communal celebration of these feelings, hopes, and aspirations.

A reading of history indicates that the critical mind has no choice but to build an institution within which to embody and nurture its ideals. Anyone can work out an elaborate and seemingly valid theory as Plato did in the *Republic.* And as with Plato, whose theories of the state failed in practice, the validity of a thought system can only be known when it is tested in practice, possibly not even then, but certainly not without embodiment in an institution.

The crucial role of religious institutions in human development is seen in the number of structures now serving Western society that were born within the church. Subsequently these structures grew to sufficient strength and importance to establish themselves independently. The practice of medicine and the creation of hospitals in Western society grew out of the church. We saw in chapter 15 how the university as a separate educational movement was born in the Church. The movement of organized philanthropy, so characteristic of the United States and prominent in other countries as well, originated in the Church. Who is to say that many more institutions of great benefit to human welfare will not originate among people who are organized to serve the highest ends we know?

The critical way in religion does not seek to establish a new religion; it does not seek to establish yet another church or temple, yet another competitor in an already overcrowded field. The critical way seeks, rather, to become a recognized tradition *in* religion, wherever religion is found. It seeks not to weaken but to strengthen existing religious structures. The critical tradition in religion is not itself a religion; it is a way of being religious—a way of going about providing a religion that meets the intellectual and moral as well as the spiritual needs of people.

It is the thesis of this study that there is a critical tradition in the religion of the West that can be traced from early Greek civilization down to the present. In the sense that such a tradition exists, it can be said to have been institutionalized. As such it has clearly identifiable teachings and clearly identifiable exemplars. Most of these thinkers had some sense of belonging to a tradition. They were aware, at least to some degree, of their antecedents and of the principles they all held in common. In reading the life stories of thinkers in the critical tradition, I have been impressed with the sense of indebtedness the members felt toward kindred spirits who preceded them, often centuries before.

We have seen again and again how the reading of earlier authors influenced the thought of those who lived in a much later time. Perhaps the most conspicuous instance of direct influence leaping over centuries of time is that of Aristotle and Plato and the impact of their writings on the mind of medieval Europe some fifteen hundred years later and on our own time as well. Influence equally direct occurs, of course, between living people, usually from an older teacher to a younger pupil. Influence of this sort has been traced in the early development of Thomas Jefferson, among others. At age nine he was placed in a school run by a Scottish clergyman, the Reverend William Douglas, where he was well grounded in Latin, Greek, and French, skills for which Jefferson said later, "I thank him [Douglas] on my knees."

A clergyman of Huguenot descent, Reverend James Maury, added to Jefferson's classical background, but also introduced him to liberal principles of religion and government, in particular to the idea that the power of the clergy should be separated from the authority of the state, a concept that became central in Jefferson's later thought. The young Jefferson acquired from Maury another characteristic conspicuous in his later years, a love of learning. Dr. William Small, another Scotsman, also played a definitive role in forming the thought and character of the author of the American Declaration of Independence. Jefferson's biographer writes: "This gentleman, the single non-clergyman on the faculty [of the College of William and Mary while Jefferson was a student there] had been swept up in the enlightened thought of the age. His teaching was rational and scientific rather than religious and didactic and he gave this cast to Jefferson's mind. . . . Jefferson continued in his company after leaving the College and commencing the study of law."

The direct molding of the thought and character of Thomas Jefferson by his teachers and others can be duplicated in uncounted instances, and it raises a very interesting question for a tradition we have said might be fully institutionalized. In the light of the fundamental role played by Thomas Jefferson in fashioning the structure of the new United States of America and in determining its political ideals, would it not be desirable to establish institutions in which such ideals and practices could be nurtured and taught? Specifically, by analogy, does it not suggest that if we value the ideals of the critical way in religion we should organize a church in which to teach them and put them into practice?

A final question remains. When a religious institution is organized according to the principles advocated by the critical mind, what happens in worship? When people gather in a church of the critical way on a Sunday morning or at any other time, what procedure is followed and what is thought to be its significance?

The forms of worship in such churches would of course vary greatly since an open approach in comparison to a fixed set of rubrics encourages, indeed demands, experimentation and change. But the purposes sought, and the ideals given expression would be the same. Those who follow the critical way and those who follow the ecclesiastical way are often unable to see how close they are to each other in their standards of human conduct, their goals for human welfare, and their sense of the religious or spiritual dimension of life. Generally speaking, they differ from each other with regard to the means by which these goals are to be achieved, and not by the ends they have in view. For the ecclesiastical mind the way of tradition leads toward these goals; for the critical mind, tradition plays a lesser role: the emphasis is instead on open interchange and the development of concepts and structures more adequate to the purposes they are designed to serve.

How are we to account for the extraordinary mix of similarity and difference between what happens in worship for followers of the critical as against the ecclesiastical way? It is the strongest evidence we have of the inroads the critical way has made into organized religion. Religion at its best has always pointed humanity toward the highest goals of which we can conceive. At its best—and its best occurs more frequently than many suppose—religion still does so. Those of the critical way are saying: Because of the fatal flaw in the ecclesiastical way—the failure to apply standards of accuracy and reliability that prevail in almost every other aspect of contemporary life—the form of worship that the traditional churches offer is ineffective, often alienating for the critical mind.

Speculating, then—and speculating only—what might happen in a church on Sunday morning that would be effective for the critical mind? Superficially perhaps, not much that was different from what would happen in many churches or temples of the ecclesiastical way. Yet in most instances, that difference would be fundamental because the concept of what was happening would be fundamentally different.

A basic goal of the ecclesiastical way would be to comprehend whatever it is that is ultimate in the universe and in our lives. Here the critical and ecclesiastical ideal would be the same. The difference would come at the point where the nature of the ultimate was stated. The ecclesiastical mind would confidently, often dogmatically, identify the ultimate with a traditional concept of the deity, always being careful to make use of the divine Name. To be concrete and definite with regard to the deity is important, it would say. For the critical mind such definiteness would be an obstacle to worship, however, because it would mean speaking as if we had knowledge where knowledge is lacking.

Both forms of worship would be characterized by aspiration toward the highest. The difference would be the same as with the nature of the ultimate. The ecclesiastical mind would speak as if it knew for certain, out of its ancient tradition, what the highest is. The critical mind would speak as if we were in the process of determining what the highest is, and as if, in that determination, we still had a long way to go.

Both forms of worship would seek to instill hope into the worshiper, a conviction that the dreams we dream can be realized. Traditional religion grounds its hope in ancient theological structures. The critical mind, unconvinced that those theological structures are valid, grounds its hope in our human capacity to make things better.

Both forms of worship would help the worshiper achieve joy in living. Many who follow the ecclesiastical way, however, would be more likely to stress joy in the next life than in this one. The critical mind, on the contrary, lays all its emphasis on the satisfaction to be found in life as we know it here and now.

It will be said that too much emphasis on this life leads to self-indulgence and hedonism. The critical mind counters that the opposite is the case, as we shall see in the final chapter. Attention to this life means, if it means anything, not only attention to the self and the needs of the self, but also attention to other selves as well. It takes no argument to show that joy can not flow from a pattern of each for himself and herself with no concern for anyone else.

The underlying difference in outlook between the critical way and the ecclesiastical way could be illustrated through many more examples, but they would all add up to the basic difference we have been describing throughout this volume: the failure of the ecclesiastical mind to see that the critical mind is unpersuaded by ecclesiastical efforts to update ancient religion. Critically-minded people, like all people, can truly worship only when they believe in their hearts the teachings on which their worship is based. For the critical mind, the ecclesiastical case grows less persuasive as the years go on. As a result, its forms of worship diminish in value.

In church on Sunday morning, we seek, in community with other like-minded persons, a sense of meaning for our lives, and for the universe as well. We try to view our lives in the light of notions like eternity and infinity, omniscience and omnipotence. We try to view our lives against the values we hold, and to assess the worth of these values, since one of the highest values of all is the confidence that the values we value are generally valuable, judged by universal standards.

To conclude, the critical way in religion can be institutionalized. In the natural course of events it is more than likely to be. We humans have a way of institutionalizing the things we care about in order to protect them and nurture them. For this reason the critical way in religion gives promise of replacing present ecclesiastical structures or of replacing current ecclesiastical patterns of thought. Religion cannot remain outside the main currents of Western thought. Our need for religion is too great. But the need is always for a religion that is deeply believed, and for vast numbers of people today, that means the critical way in religion.

18

The Way Leads On

Human understanding rests upon a set of axioms or principles so elementary in character that we are unable to formulate anything simpler or more basic: this is the conclusion we reached in chapter 16. We noted two such axioms there: the self, and the universe around us. Are there only two? The Greek mind would have added at least three more—their famous trinity: truth, beauty, and goodness. We shall do the same, for in the intervening twenty centuries or more the human mind has not been able to penetrate more deeply into the nature of human experience.

We have already had much to say about truth. Seen as a concept, it turns out to be something like a mirage, ever shining before us, ever beckoning us on, but ever receding as we pursue it. However, in the pursuit, a vast body of what we think of as truth or knowledge is accumulated. None of it is regarded as final, although much of it may be relatively so. All of it is subject to later development, modification, or even elimination as our human understanding grows.

We can also compare our accumulation of knowledge or truth to a circle of light. Within it lies understanding of such sort as we have achieved. Beyond it lies ignorance of we know not what. As the perimeter of knowledge widens, so does the edge of ignorance. The more we learn, the more there is to learn. The more we know, the more we discover there is to know. The more knowledge we gather, the more we see how ignorant we are. George Santayana's lines come to mind:

> Our knowledge is a torch of smoky pine
> That lights the pathway but one step ahead
> Across a void of mystery and dread.

Isaac Newton remarked shortly before his death, "I do not know what I may appear to the world; but to myself I seem to have been only like a boy, playing on the seashore, and diverting myself in now and then finding a smoother pebble or a prettier shell than ordinary, whilst the great ocean of truth lay still all undiscovered before me."

Since the first speculations of Thales, the first questioning of religion by Xenophanes, and the first announcement of the Pyrrhonist view that all judgment in such matters must be suspended, has the West made any progress in its pursuit of knowledge? Summing up the long history of Western thought since that time a contemporary scholar concludes, "The basic problem at issue is that any proposition purporting to assert some knowledge about the world contains some claims which go beyond the merely empirical." We are back to the central question of the critical way in religion: of what basic knowledge can we be certain, and on what grounds does such alleged certainty rest?

1. In Search of the Beautiful

The question we are asking has to do with the status of the body of knowledge that the metaphorical Council of Humanity is developing. Although the Council rests its case upon axioms and not on certainties supposed to have been revealed; although from the critical point of view knowledge is a turbulent mass forever growing and changing, with the details often conflicting, sometimes regressing; although the body of knowledge the critical mind supposes itself to possess is marked by controversy and contention over its validity, is it really any less certain than the knowledge the religions claim to hold?

In order to be sure we have such questions in perspective, let us turn them around and ask them the other way. Are we not at least as confident that the stars are what the astronomers say they are as we are that God is what the religions say he is? What we ourselves suppose to know about the stars rests upon admitted assumptions; let us be clear about that. But are we not at least as confident of the findings of astronomy as we are of the findings of organized religion? Are we not equally confident that life has developed on this planet the way the biologists say it has, even though their findings, too, rest upon assumptions? Are not the certainties here at least equal to those of traditional religion? As a matter of fact, are not a great many of us far more confident of the findings of science than we are of the doctrines of traditional theology?

To gain further perspective on the degree of certainty attainable in the critical way in religion, let us turn to quite a different field, that of art. We find that it, too, rests ultimately on a few admitted assumptions. Kenneth Clark, the art historian, has put the matter succinctly. In 1971 the Cosmos

Club in Washington, D.C. conferred on him its annual award for outstanding contributions to science and the arts. Following the presentation Clark, in a short address, summed up his views on the role of art in human life.

"I believe in a central tradition of art," he said. "It begins in Egypt, reaches its first perfection in Greece, divides like the Empire into East and West, reaches a second perfection in Medieval France, and continues down to our own times. Because this tradition is never broken, because I can recognize certain formal and human values as persisting under a multiplicity of disguises, I cannot help giving them some absolute value."

In the remainder of his talk he explained what he meant by these words. It was not that the art of the West could claim absolute value. Other traditions also exhibit recognized values, he said. It was that he, a Westerner, found these values in his own experience as he studied the art of the West. The point upon which he was insisting was that neither he nor any other critic of art or historian of art had imposed his own values on those art objects. It was, he said, the other way around. Objects of art embodied and exhibited values that he, and others as well, were able to recognize.

Archibald MacLeish, a contemporary poet who also served as Librarian of Congress and as Assistant Secretary of State advanced the same view with regard to poetry. He argued that poetry spoke more clearly to us about the human condition than science, history, or philosophy. Confronted by the mystery of the universe, as we all are, the poet is a center of awareness and a center of receptivity. To convey his meaning MacLeish quoted a Chinese poet of the fourth century A.D., Lu Chi. It is the function of the poet, said this thoughtful Chinese, to "trap Heaven and Earth in the cage of form." How better could the purpose of the critical way be described? The poet must "struggle with the meaninglessness and silence of the world," Lu Chi continued, until he can "'know' the world, not by exegesis or demonstration or proofs, but directly, as a man knows apple in the mouth."

It is the same sense of immediacy that characterizes the rock paintings of the Ice Age peoples in France, Spain, and North Africa, especially the magnificent animal renderings found at Altamira in northwestern Spain. No one has to argue that these pictures are great art, and that they will remain so, regardless of the greatness of classical art in Greece, Renaissance art in Europe, or that of China and Japan in any of their several phases. If art, beauty, truth can ever be self-validating, they are in the drawings of bison and other animals in the Altamiran cave.

In the recognition of values in art objects we see the kind of decisions the Tribunal of Truth is constantly making. In such statements, as they echo our own thoughts and impressions, we find certitude sufficient for our needs. Many of us heard a similar echo of our own thoughts in the address given by Aleksandr Solzhenitsyn on receiving the Nobel Prize for Literature in 1970. "A work of art bears within itself its own confirmation," he said on that occasion. "Works steeped in truth and presenting it to us vividly alive will grasp us, will attract us to themselves with great power—and no one ever, even an age later, will presume to negate them. The Greeks joined beauty, truth and goodness in a kind of Trinity. If Truth and Good are crushed, perhaps the whimsical, unpredictable unexpected thing we call Beauty will move up and perform the work of all of them."

Solzhenitsyn was not the first to see truth in beauty. Long ago Plato had seen their close interconnection with each other and with goodness as well. In the *Symposium* he pays his tribute to beauty in lines that are rhapsodic: "The life which, above all others, a man should live is a life in the contemplation of beauty absolute. . . . If man had eyes to see the true beauty—the divine beauty, I mean, pure and clear and unalloyed . . . in that communion only, beholding beauty with the eye of the mind, he will be enabled to bring forth, not images of beauty but realities (for he has hold not of an image but of a reality) and bringing forth and nourishing true virtue to become the friend of God and be immortal, if mortal man may."

The initial perception of the mystical relationship between truth, beauty, and goodness was, of course, not Plato's. He merely cast into language—his own peculiar art—a discovery made by the genius of the Greek mind itself. The world has not yet seen the full implications of this concept. We accept and acclaim this contemporary perception of its meaning because it evokes within us a response we can recognize.

Through the reaction of mind upon mind and spirit upon spirit: through the reaction of the totality of the experience of each of us upon the totality of the experience of everyone else, we attain all the certainty that is to be had, whether with regard to truth or beauty or anything else. And that certainty is sufficient for our needs. If in this volume we had not been dealing with man's search for truth, we might have spoken of the Tribunal of Beauty or the Tribunal of the Good. The principle is the same, the purpose is the same, and in the end, if the project were carried far enough, the result would be the same. For, like Clark and Solzhenitsyn and Plato and countless others living and dead, I believe that as we move toward the most profound understanding of life, then truth, beauty, and goodness merge into a single concept, and as a unity they speak to each of us with their own sense of immediacy and inner compulsion.

I have chosen the concept beauty rather than truth through which to illustrate the kind of certitude the critical tradition offers in order to disengage what I am saying from theological controversy. It may not be possible, but that is the hope. Beauty is as real, as fundamental, as important, and as illusive as is truth. But those who are ever ready to do battle for their faith are not usually roused to action by a discussion of aesthetics. Few churches have attempted to declare with finality what beauty is, as so many have with truth and goodness. All people inside and outside the churches may join hand and heart in the untrammeled pursuit of the beautiful. Art has its dogmatists, to be sure, but no holy book of beauty delimits their judgment.

No ancient council is alleged to have established canons of beauty finally, for all time. No hierarchy of churchmen speaks on God's behalf in order that the world may know what beauty is. No missionaries go forth to persuade the world that salvation lies in their particular concept of beauty and that it had better be embraced.

It is the purpose of the critical tradition to persuade the religions to look upon truth and goodness as they now do beauty. If we are not dogmatic about the beautiful, why should we be about truth and goodness? We live in the midst of beauty. It is very precious to us, but we do not divide up into warring camps and lay anathemas upon one another because we cannot agree as to its ultimate nature. If beauty can speak to the human heart, so can goodness and so can truth. With beauty there is no orthodoxy, save in very narrow transient circles; there is only the beautiful and the ugly, each speaking in its own way, each commending itself or inviting its own rejection. So should it be with truth.

Goodness, truth, and beauty are not, of course, altogether apposite terms. For ordinary human intercourse, goodness is much more important than beauty. Truth is also. We order our lives with one another by these concepts. Nevertheless, the fundamental character of each remains the same. Despite their obvious differences, each speaks to us with an immediacy all its own that we recognize, and our understanding of each is in turn sharpened by the clash of mind upon mind and insight with insight.

Joseph Campbell believes that "It has actually been from one great variously inflected and developed literate world-heritage that *all* of the philosophies, theologies, mysticisms and sciences now in conflict in our lives derive." In advancing this thesis, he is pointing to the evidence he sees that there is a commonality of experience and conceptualization to be found in the human race.

After a study of the human attitudes underlying the thinking of Lao Tzu, Buddha, the Prophets, Socrates, Jesus, Spinoza, and the philosophers of the Enlightenment, Erich Fromm concluded that "There is a core of ideas and norms common to all of these teachings." There are significant differences between them, he conceded; nevertheless, he felt the common core he discerned could be stated as follows:

1. Man must strive to recognize the truth and can be fully human only to the extent to which he succeeds in this task.
2. He must be independent and free.
3. He must be an end in himself and not the means for any other person's purposes.
4. He must relate himself to his fellow men lovingly.
5. If he has no love, he is an empty shell even if all power, wealth, and intelligence were his.
6. Man must know the difference between good and evil.

7. He must learn to listen to the voice of his conscience and be able to follow it.

It is not important whether we agree with Fromm or Campbell or any of the great number of others who have attempted to state the commonality of thought and understanding in different religious groups. Such statements range all the way from attempts to distill the belief of "universal religion" to creeds drawn up by local Protestant churches in the United States uniting for worship in a community church. What is important is that today we are seeing increasing insistence that people need not be divided from one another by religion or philosophy. A basic commonality (not uniformity) is increasingly discerned among the religions that expresses itself when given a chance. I would argue that we can see this commonality of outlook in religion if we look not at the creeds and liturgies that divide us, but at our sense of the beautiful.

A word of caution needs to be added here. I do not mean to imply in any sense that the artist is always right, that artistic perceptions are always accurate, or that the conclusions the artist reaches are necessarily valid. They may be quite invalid. The artist is as likely as anybody to be dead wrong in what he sincerely believes to be beautiful or true. The human creature is not necessarily the monster that current novels, cinema, and drama depict. Nor are we the noble, kindly men and women prominent in popular literature before World War I. It is the business of art to depict the world as the artist sees it, as Theodore Dreiser and Somerset Maugham did when people were reading the novels of Mrs. Humphrey Ward. The critical mind has the obligation to examine whatever picture the artist chooses to present and then to assess its validity. Doing so, we find Shakespeare and Goethe perceptive and accurate. We unhesitatingly say the same for the great Greek dramatists Aeschylus, Sophocles, and Euripides, for Praxiteles and for the unknown designer-builder of the Parthenon.

We shall probably never know *the* beautiful, but meanwhile, we can know beauty in all its myriad forms. We shall recognize it, though we may not always agree on what it is. We shall enjoy the possession of beauty even while we differ in our understanding of it. So it will be with goodness and so it will be with truth. We do not require ultimate certainty to know when we stand in their presence. We do not need to agree upon the way we are to describe what we see or sense or feel or apprehend. It will be enough if, when beauty, truth, and goodness speak to us, we hear; and, hearing, seek to bring them into our lives, as far as we may.

2. Value

We have spoken of truth and beauty. A word has now to be said about the third aspect of the Greek "trinity," goodness. Since the time of

Socrates, Plato, and Aristotle the debate has gone on as to what goodness *is.* We are not likely to settle it in our time. For the critical way in religion, the significant thing is not a final determination of the question but the open and free debate by which we deepen our understanding of it. For the critical way in religion it is paramount that we relate our mutual experiences of good and evil to one another; that we sort out those experiences, and try to determine their meaning. It then becomes incumbent upon us to decide, in so far as we can through the clash of mind with mind and perception with perception, what is good, what is evil, what is partly good and partly evil, and how we are to tell the difference. These are not questions we can answer with finality. What is important is the deposit of knowledge and understanding that results from the answer-seeking process.

As with truth and beauty, no certainty results from the endeavor. But as with our pursuit of the other two goals, the fact that final certainty is denied us about what is good should be no occasion for dismay or for giving up. It is true that we yearn to know exactly what goodness is, and to know which of all the various competing goods is to be preferred above all others. Admittedly, in the realm of ethics and morals, such decisions are often crucial. Because we live, we must make moral decisions daily, and in many instances such decisions are irrevocable. Again and again, we need desperately to know what path to choose. Yet the need in no sense endows us with the capacity.

Let us begin then, not with what we would like to know about goodness, but with what we do know. Let us begin with the impulse toward goodness we feel in ourselves and perceive in others. We sense goodness as we sense beauty and truth. It speaks to us with the same quality of firsthand immediacy. No one has to tell us that there is goodness in sacrificing one's life for the welfare of someone else. In the welter of cross purposes and unsuspected motives in the midst of which we live, we may not always identify goodness even when it is staring at us straight in the face. But once we have seen through the distracting shadows that mar our vision, we have no trouble identifying goodness as something excellent in and of itself in what we then behold.

As an example I once helped to develop a neighborhood block project among the poor and dispossessed in Washington, D.C. Among the data we gathered in preparation for the project was the fact that the tenants who lived on the block felt quite hopeless about life. They saw little or no prospect of improving their lot, although nearly all of them desired to do so. With regard to their children, however, it was different. Almost all of them believed that the lot of their children could be improved, that for them the future held a promise of better things to come. The parents, almost without exception, were ready to do what they could to help, even though they expected little if any benefit personally.

The critical tradition does not despair at our human prospects. It would leave the myth of Sisyphus to those who find a realistic picture of humanity in it. It would leave the story of Eden, as Christianity has interpreted it, to those who find in the concept of our fallen state the clearest way of helping us to understand ourselves. In place of Sisyphus, Adam, Eve, and the serpent, the critical tradition would place the figure of Prometheus, who stole fire from heaven in order that our human lot on earth might be made better.

There is, to be sure, ample evidence that the human creature is corrupt and seems at times to be almost beyond the power of redemption. But we should be hardly accurate or complete in our appraisal of ourselves if we did not look at the evidence on the other side. There is more than enough to indicate that, despite our evil tendencies, we are as much like the bold and purposeful Prometheus as we are like the servile, trembling Adam.

If we cannot make the world a better place for ourselves, perhaps we can for our children or for our children's children. If our knowledge is incomplete, perhaps that of future generations will be less so because they can build on the knowledge we have sought and found. After all, we today are the benefactors of the inheritance we hold from Thales and Socrates, Jesus and Erasmus, and from Newton, Hume, and Einstein. It is enough to know that we have a chance to bequeath to posterity a better world than we have known and greater knowledge than we have enjoyed.

The Judeo-Christian tradition, despite the dismal picture it has often painted of the human creature, has throughout its history seen the summons to virtue as lying at the heart of human experience. The summons has been personalized in the figure of a deity who has been seen as the source of the impulse. It has been the same in Islam. There too, God or Allah, the cosmic ruler, has been looked upon as the source of the demand humanity feels that life be ordered in accordance with canons of virtue. It is no less true of all the "higher" religions. Scholars have found the so-called Golden Rule (Do as you would be done by) to be central in at least ten of the great world faiths.

We are now in the realm of value theory, one of the fields more recently identified and named by the philosophers. An extensive literature has already grown up on the topic. Many subdivisions have developed within it. Many new concepts have been added and many precise distinctions drawn. All alike point to the nearly universal fact of value-perception.

Rather than attempting a summary of any of the various essays in value theory, of which there are so many, here again perhaps personal testimony that can be generalized will serve us better. Early in my professional life as a minister, I was struck by the constantly repeated set of virtues attributed to the dead in our society. Whether attending a funeral service conducted by someone else or talking with the members of a bereaved family in the parish, in preparation for conducting a service myself, I realized that the pattern was the same. The virtues the minister or the bereaved family saw in the deceased varied from person to person, to be sure, yet the degree to which those virtues were repeated from person to person was striking. Soon the broad outlines of the value-pattern of urban Protestants in northeastern United States became clear to me. Clearer still was the fact that such a pattern existed; that these people had such values, that they could identify them, that at least to some degree they themselves sought to live by them, and that at the death of a beloved relative or friend they saw exemplified in that person's life a great many of the values they cherished.

Students of values have often sought data through questionnaires and personal interviews. To me their results are not always reliable. Under such circumstances the best of us cannot be sure we are saying what we really think or, rather, what we should like to think we think. With the bereaved, however, there is no such problem. As they pour out their grief to a clergyman, you learn at first hand and with no reason for doubting what they value in their fellow human beings.

As an example, in 1977 a pamphlet containing some forty pages of tributes to a beloved teacher came to my desk. On the title page was a line from the teacher's own words: "What matters more than anything else is integrity." Sprinkled through the tributes were phrases like: "great personality," "sense of humor," "affection" (that of his friends and associates for him), "friendly," "sincere," "reasonable," "gave good advice," "guidance," "kindness," "directness," "Man of convictions," "devotion to . . . institutions, persons, principles," "wisdom," "knowledge," "the humanity of the man," "concern," "high intellectual standards," "goal of excellence," "sense of duty," "served with devotion," "fair to all."

A parallel list from ancient Egypt enables us to gain some perspective on such a list of virtues. The Pyramid Texts of the early Egyptian Dynasties were accustomed to list on the doors of the tombs of the kings and nobles the good deeds they had performed during their lives. Typical lines read: "I gave bread to the hungry, clothing to the naked; I ferried him who had no boat. . . . I never oppressed anyone. . . . Never did I take the property of any man by violence, I was the doer of that which pleased all men." These long-dead kings and nobles also declared themselves innocent of certain wrongs, such as blasphemy, reviling the king, gossiping, giving vent to anger, as well as more serious crimes such as murder, stealing, cheating, lying, adultery, and temple robbing.

Those in the ecclesiastical tradition who think all is lost if there are no moral absolutes should ponder the human qualities admired by the Egyptians nearly five thousand years ago. How like our own they are. With so clear an indication of the power of moral principles to present themselves to the human mind consistently over so long a period of time and under such widely different circumstances, it would seem that the danger of stultification from immobility in such matters is far greater than the danger of social disintegration resulting from the view that moral values are not absolute. Give me the heartfelt funeral tributes of a people, from Pericles' "Ode to the Athenian Dead" to the lowliest tribute paid by a minister or priest or rabbi to a beloved parishioner, and I will list for you the true values of that community.

Arguments about whether values really exist, whether they are absolute, relative, or transient, often seem quite pointless. On the contrary, they are very useful in clarifying our thinking. The problem is, we expect too much of them. We expect certainty to result from them when certainty is not to be had. The question is not whether values are temporal or eternal, but whether any proposed value is or is not a value, how it relates to every other value we claim, how we are to pursue it, and what will happen if we do.

To illustrate, a value the critical way in religion sets above most is, as we have seen, that of free discussion. Only under such circumstances can all alleged values be thoroughly examined and tested in the light of one another. That is the essence of the critical way: to examine values as well as facts, moral principles as well as the data of experience. Einstein once remarked: "Ethical axioms are found and tested not very differently from the axioms of science."

The ethics a religion teaches must run the same risk as its metaphysics. After the experts have thought about them and have hammered them together into a self-consistent system, inevitably, it seems, they congeal. Later generations come to think of such moral precepts as holy, and therefore immutable. The critical way in religion would break this pattern. People have too little confidence in themselves. They dare not tamper with an ancient moral code lest it disintegrate in their hands. The critical mind insists that the risk has to be run, that it is not very great, and that the risk in testing moral precepts is nothing compared with the danger of stagnation from trying to keep ancient moral codes unchanged. Such codes, grown rigid, defeat the very values they were designed to protect.

Programs of value-education are now being introduced into the schools. Founded upon extensive research conducted by psychologists, these programs are not designed to instill particular values into the students, as a church might attempt to do. Their purpose is to aid the students in choosing among the multiple values available to them. For example, under the new system, students are not admonished to be honest. They are told neither that honesty has been one of the great values of Western culture, however little it may have been followed, nor are they told that "honesty is the best policy." They are not told that God requires honesty of us and will reward or punish us according to our conduct in this regard, nor are examples of honesty held up to them, like the story of George Washington and the cherry tree. Rather, they are invited to reason and to debate with one another incidents set before them in which the alternatives of honesty and dishonesty play a crucial role.

Skeptics argue that the art of choosing among possible values cannot be taught without, at the same time, instilling values into the students of which they (and perhaps the teachers also) are quite unaware. To a degree they are right. Certainly in an instruction system that involves assessing the worth of various choices, at least two values are being taught that should be openly acknowledged: the value of reasoning about which of several values is preferable, and the value of having a value-system of one's own. Experiments appear to show that as we grow older our ability to deal with value-systems increases, exactly as does our ability to deal with the principles of mathematics. In both cases, with values and with mathematics, the ability to reason cogently can be taught.

These new experiments and teaching methods provide another example of the increasing acceptance of the critical way in religion by the mind of the West. The method of value-reasoning and the assumptions implied in it are wholly consonant with the approach of the critical mind. With both, ethical principles are not given in advance, neither from Mount Sinai nor from the shores of the Sea of Galilee, nor from any other authority. In the critical tradition, ethical principles are sought in the open mind and heart of the individual who finds himself or herself alive in a world filled with other individuals having the same needs and desires, the same hopes and fears, the same joy, pain, sorrow, and sometimes ecstasy.

Starting with the self, as we do when we follow the critical way, we discover that all our hopes and fears, all our greed and will to dominate, and our fallibility as well, are to be found in varying degrees in everyone else. If we are honest with ourselves, one of the first things we acknowledge is that the impulses and urges and concerns we wish to express may with equal propriety be expressed by everyone else. We recognize further that our desire to take advantage of others and our fallibility are matched by their desire to take advantage of us and by their fallibility. Obviously some mutual adjustment of our various conflicting desires and impulses is going to have to be worked out.

Starting with ourselves then, we discover that, in addition to the greed and fallibility we share with all humanity, we also share with our fellow creatures impulses toward generosity, helpfulness, joyousness, beauty, truth, and love. We discover that we care very much for some of the people around us and that some of them care very much for us. We discover that our mutual caring creates a bond far deeper and stronger than the loving and caring with which we began. We discover in ourselves and in others both love and hate, both good and evil, both truth and error, as we move from the self that we are to the various selves around us. We discover companionship and the need for human society, despite all its problems.

We discover, too, that if we cannot control our predatory instincts or do not want to, the other selves around us will be very glad to do it for us. If we become too predatory in the pursuit of our wants we may find that as a necessary precaution those other selves will decide to lock us up. If, on the other hand, we are willing to exercise self-control in the light of the needs of our fellows, we are glad to join with them in curbing those who will not exercise such self-control and who are trying to aggrandize themselves at our expense. We are glad to be part of a structure that protects us from the avarice of others and enforces mutual cooperation and restraint where it is not given voluntarily.

This is the kind of picture of our world that emerges if we begin with the self we know, move out into the world about us, and try to see it in its entirety. An honest facing of the needs of the self leads us at once to the needs of others—those who are closest to us, whose needs we know and understand best, but also the needs of people in our community whom we do not know and those of the wide world as well. A realistic view of the whole will then lead us on to a concern for those yet unborn, those who will occupy our places after we are gone. They will have the same needs and desires we have, perhaps more. Their right to have their needs satisfied and their hopes fulfilled will be just as deep as ours. The obligation we have to them is no less than the obligation we have to those who are closest to us today.

I shall not be honest with myself, nor shall I be true to myself, unless I can see that this, too, is so. I am but one among billions living today. I am also one among an incredibly greater number yet to appear on this planet, and who knows where else. There is nothing I can ask for myself that I am not bound to ask for them also. To deny rights and opportunities to the generations yet unborn is to deny them to myself as well. This is the categorical imperative, stated some two hundred years ago as a philosophical principle by Immanuel Kant. It does not translate well into English but a rough approximation of his meaning might read: So act that the principles implied in your actions can become universal law. In familiar language it is the Golden Rule, common to all the great religions.

A value-system must not merely apply equally to all people everywhere; it must also be totally self-consistent. If, for example, we find two values in conflict with each other and we choose between them, we are saying at the same time, whether or not we get it into words, that the value we choose is the greater of the two and that the other is subordinate to it. If, for example, we support a policy that advances the welfare of our own nation but is detrimental to humanity, we thereby place a higher value on our own national welfare than we place on human welfare as a whole. If we pursue a policy that advances the welfare of our church, yet is detrimental to humanity as a whole, again we have placed a higher value on the group to which we belong than we have on humanity itself.

It should immediately be apparent that neither of these can be a true value, for neither can be applied universally. True values in this instance would be policies that advance the welfare of humanity, even against the presumed welfare of our particular nation or our particular church. It should be apparent also that in the long run, whatever seems to advance our nation or church at the expense of humanity, is bound in the end to prove detrimental, since our nation and our church is a part of the humanity we are ready to damage.

The categorical imperative does not, of course, lay its demands upon each individual in the same way or to the same degree. Those of the critical tradition are the first to point to the viciousness of some people, the callousness of others, and the self-centered character of most of us. Few individuals, if any, are completely attuned to the inner voice of value as it speaks its various language to us. Equally few individuals possess the capacity or the mind to see, or the heart to feel, the full effect of all that we do on the lives of those around us. For a clear mind and a full heart, the demand of the categorical imperative is total, but it is safe to say that almost no one is so endowed. As we see humanity today, ourselves included, our minds are beclouded with ignorance and our hearts encrusted with the concerns of self. The critical way is the way of those who would make the human mind as clear and the human heart as warm as possible.

3. The Ultimate

When we enter the debate on values, we soon discover that what we are really doing is setting up a value scale. How else do you decide whether heroism is better than cowardice? How do you know whether your welfare is of greater value than the welfare of someone else? In any attempt to answer such questions, we are driven to choose among several values. In the end we are driven to choose a supreme value by which all the others can be arranged and tested. What is it to be? To put the question in yet more elemental terms, what is ultimate? What is the very most basic concept of all—the one with which we begin and the one to which we must always return?

Down the ages, thinkers outside and inside the churches have identified the ultimate with God. As the source of all good, truth, beauty, and love, God has also often been declared to be identical with them. Increasingly, as our notions of the divine nature grow less anthropomorphic and more abstract, the idea of God has been transmuted into one or another of these concepts or into all of them taken together.

A contemporary philosopher, one of the leaders in the current "process philosophy" movement wrote, "God's goodness is the self in its purposes transcending the personal future and making itself a trustee for others." This is an elaborate way of making the point the critical mind insists on: that no value can be limited to the individual—to the self. A value, to be a value, must be universal. The statement is also an extreme example of the current practice of defining "God" in such a manner as to make everyone a believer. As we saw in chapter 13 there is no gain, only confusion, in such twisting of word meanings.

We reach the ultimate as quickly and inexorably through a study of the natural world as we do through the realm of human values. A modern philosopher of religion has capsuled this progression in the following paragraph: "The great astronomer Harlow Shapley, as he looks in his telescope or does his celestial mathematics mutters to himself 'All nature is God, all God is nature." He approaches this nature God however, not by traditional forms of worship but through his observations and calculations, which have become his sacrament. Few human beings have a conception of the immensity of the universe, or of the smallness of man in it, compared to Shapley's. But the *tremendum* has no terrors for him. He looks at it with quiet eyes, astonished, reverent, but unafraid."

In speaking of the ultimate I find almost irresistible the impulse to capitalize it as "the Ultimate." The divine Name, virtually everyone feels, is appropriately capitalized, if for no better reason than because it is a proper name. The writings of some modern philosophers—Whitehead in his *Adventures of Ideas* is a conspicuous example—carry the practice further. They capitalize terms in order to indicate that they are basic or ultimate in character. I have resisted this usage, however, on the ground that it involves a subtle and uncritical loading of the argument. The use of the capital in words like Beauty, Truth, Goodness, Universe, Ultimate inevitably adds stature to them. Otherwise, why use the capitals? So used, they indicate to the reader the dimension of the capitalized terms in the mind of the writer.

The critical mind demands to know what the introduction of capitals is intended to convey over and beyond the fact that the capitalized terms are fundamental. Critical standards would seem to require an explanation and a defense as well. Accordingly, here, in an attempt not to load the argument, but to allow it to stand on its own feet, capitals will not be used. If what I have ventured to call ultimate appears to be so, that should be enough.

What then is ultimate? Most of us, liberal and orthodox, churchly and secular, have long since outgrown the concept of God instilled into us as children. But we need to realize that to outgrow such a concept is not necessarily to give up belief in God. It does not follow that because the old gods have vanished there is no God at all. On the other hand, neither does it follow that there is.

As with most of us, my views on this question slowly evolved as I grew up. In theological school and in my early years in the ministry as this process continued, I took the position that one's concept of God could grow and change quite as legitimately as a scientist's conception of gravitation. Meanwhile, the name of the object did not change, only the understanding of its nature. And so, like many clergymen, well aware that my notion of the deity was undergoing radical transformation, I continued to speak and write about "God" with no sense of inconsistency or dissimulation.

Then one Sunday in 1954 I preached a sermon on the Devil. It was a historical account and an analysis of the Devil-idea that was being discussed at that time as a result of Whittaker Chambers' use of the concept in his book *Witness.* I pointed out the evil uses to which the Devil-idea had been put during the Middle Ages and since that time, and showed that damage could be done only when people believed that the Devil really existed. I argued for total disbelief in the Devil-idea, and concluded with the sentence, "Without human belief the Devil is dead."

The congregation printed the sermon. Proofing it, after it had been cast into type, I was startled by that last sentence, "Without human belief the Devil is dead," and the thought flashed through my mind: if the Devil exists only when people believe in him, the same thing is true of God. Then you don't believe in God either, I thought to myself. It was an unsettling idea at the time, but I didn't get up in the pulpit the next Sunday and announce the fact to the congregation. That would have delighted some of my parishioners, dismayed others, and confirmed the suspicions of the rest. Above all, it would have misled nearly everyone, for I had not suddenly "lost my faith," as they say in the mainline churches. No change whatever had occurred in my belief about God. The only change was in the clarity of my thinking about the use of the divine name. It was now apparent to me that my thinking about the ultimate was approaching the point beyond which evolution in the meaning of a word cannot go. Beyond that point, true communication breaks down and thereafter you are more apt than not to be misunderstood.

As with many people, my immediate answer to the question was neither linguistic nor theological, it was autobiographical. At first I continued to use the divine name, in particular in leading public worship where it is impossible to stop and explain what you mean. In worship the words you use have to stand upon their own and the divine name still seemed to me the best way of conveying my sense of the reality of the ultimate. Nevertheless, continuing to strive for the greatest possible clarity of speech, the fullest possible communication, and, at the same time, the most genuine and the most profound sense of worship in the public services I led, my use of the divine name slowly but steadily diminished until in the end I ceased to use it altogether. For some, of course, those for whom the name itself was important, there was a loss. For most, however, I found there was a gain. For them, worship without the use of the divine name freed them from the constant need to translate ancient theological language into living contemporary concepts of an ultimate nature.

In our culture one does not easily give up the use of the divine name, yet increasing numbers of people are doing so today, not out of skepticism or atheism, but out of profound religious conviction. Oddly enough, at the same time and perhaps for the same reason, the use of the divine name in profanity is rapidly spreading throughout all Western age, economic, and cultural groups. The sense that somehow the name itself is holy and fraught with meaning lies deep in our Western mentality. A glance at the Old Testament shows how important the Name was to the ancient Israelites. To them it was so sacred it could not be spoken and could be spelled only with consonants. "You shall not take the name of the Lord your God in vain" runs the third of the Ten Commandments. In Christianity, ceremonial acts are performed "in the name of the Father, Son and Holy Spirit," or "in the name of Jesus Christ our Lord." It is the same in Islam. Each book of the Qur'an begins with the formula "In the Name of God the Merciful, the Compassionate."

Here we are in danger of bogging down in linguistics on which there is already an extensive literature. At the moment such consensus as there is appears to do little more than indicate the scope of the problem. On the question of the use or non-use of the divine name we appear to be working at cross purposes. Half a century ago Walter Lippmann observed almost in passing: "It is a nice question whether the use of God's name is not misleading when it is applied by modernists to ideas so remote from the God men have worshipped." Like so many before me, I too, in my own experience, reached the same conclusion. The use or non-use of the divine name must remain a personal choice for each of us. So far as our beliefs are concerned, in the realm of the ultimate I find my own quite as strong as any and far stronger than the convictions of many who loudly proclaim their belief in God and as loudly denounce those whom they think are unbelievers.

The question "Do you believe in God?" sounds like a question of the most fundamental character. Once upon a time it was. For the critical mind it is so no longer. Today an affirmative answer can mean almost anything. For the critical mind, always insistent upon the fullest and most complete interchange of meanings possible, the follow-up question is now the important one: What *kind* of God do you believe in?

When someone proclaims his belief in God today the critical mind wants to know, for example, whether that God demands tolerance toward other religions or whether he (or she, or he/she, but hardly "it") calls for intolerance toward them. Does he demand suppression or destruction of competing faiths on the ground that they are "error" and are, therefore, dangerous to human welfare? Does he countenance the use of political power to prosper a particular church, or will he insist that all churches make it on their own with no assistance from the powers of the state? Does he require a full and complete integrity in everything his worshipers do? Would he, for example, go so far as to condemn his people for dissimulation, even when that dissimulation was on his own behalf? Does he demand that his church and the clergy that serve him devote themselves to the cause of all humanity, even when to do so may cause that church and its clergy to suffer temporarily?

The critical mind and spirit, like the ecclesiastical mind and spirit, worships or commits itself to that which it conceives to be ultimate. For the critical mind those ultimates cannot be personified in any way. There is no basis on which to do so. For the critical mind, the ultimates are concepts or principles like truth, beauty, and goodness, and the quality in these concepts that makes them not merely abstract principles but also moral and spiritual imperatives as well.

Some would add love to the list, overlooking the fact that it is part of goodness as the Greeks conceived of it. I would also include in any concept of the ultimate: confidence (but not faith) in the trustworthiness of our human experiences when checked against the experiences of others; the basic fact of order and consistency in the universe; the demand that a total integrity characterize all our thoughts and actions; the absolute necessity for freedom for each of us, but always limited by the right of everyone else to an equal degree of freedom; a full recognition of the demand laid on each of us that we look upon our neighbors as having every requirement that we have, and as having as good a right to have those requirements met as we do.

To declare that the critical mind worships deities that really are concepts or principles or values is not very novel. Nor is there anything startling in a list of such ultimates. They are all old and familiar friends as the gods we worship must always be. Such a list might include the following abstractions: truth and virtue, beauty and justice, mercy and loving kindness, liberty and honor. There are, of course, many more. I do not pretend that the list is complete, but these should be enough to make the concept of the ultimate clear.

To some it may seem a little odd to suggest that we look upon our ethical principles as gods. But here again we shall not be the first. The Greeks personified abstract principles in exquisite human form. Who cannot call to mind the figure of Olympian Zeus or Athene, Apollo, Aphrodite, or Hermes? Today we do not hesitate to set up similar statues. Liberty, cast in human form, guards the harbor of New York City; Justice sits atop the Supreme Court in Washington; and another image of Liberty stands atop the Capitol. Everywhere you go in this country you find statues of Truth and Freedom, Justice and Mercy, Honor and Sacrifice adorning our public buildings. That this is so speaks well of us.

These, then, are my gods. They are gods in the sense that they are both in the world and beyond it: abstract yet very real, unseen yet a tremendous force in my life, and spiritual in the sense that they possess my mind, consume my heart, and lead me to better things than I have known before. I worship these entities, in the sense that commands issue from them which I must obey. The vision of truth demands that I be truthful and seek the truth in every aspect of my life. It is the same with beauty and goodness, the same with justice and mercy, the same with tenderness and love. I may be false to these commands, as anyone may be false to the gods he or she worships, but I cannot do it without a sense of wrongdoing. In religious language, I cannot be false to any of these principles without a sense of sin. To the best of my ability, I must be loyal to virtue or I am disloyal to myself.

Let me say this in another way, for the point is fundamental. To see truth is to see falsehood and to reject it. To see beauty is to see ugliness and reject that. To see virtue is to see vice and reject that also. To recognize high principles is to recognize the ills they are set against. To see the two in juxtaposition is to be required to choose between them. The element of command makes itself felt when you realize that virtue is desirable, that evil is to be avoided, and that you are required to choose between them.

This, I believe, is what the Psalmist meant when he cried:

> Whither shall I go from thy Spirit?
> Whither shall I flee from thy presence?
> If I ascend to heaven thou art there!
> If I make my bed in Sheol thou art there!
> If I take the wings of the morning and dwell in the
> uttermost parts of the sea,
> Even there shall thy hand lead me, and thy right hand
> shall hold me.

While a personal God is the source of the summons to virtue in Judaism, Christianity, and Islam, the sense of urgency that characterizes the summons is not necessarily personal. Most of us think of God as personal because we were brought up to do so. We were told that the voice of conscience was God's voice speaking within us, drawing us into the path of right, even as he spoke with a still, small voice to Elijah on Mount Carmel. We were taught to enlist God's assistance through prayer in our efforts to follow the path of virtue. We were told that he would hear our prayers and that when he thought it best he would answer them. We may continue to believe these teachings and to personalize the impulses they generate in us if we wish. That is up to us. But we need to notice that the impulse is just as strong whether or not we personalize it. In fact, for many of us, the impulse to virtue is stronger if we think of it as emanating not from a celestial governor, but from our own recognition of the intrinsic worth of the ideal itself.

Once you have caught the vision of virtue—of the ideal of goodness as a goal for your life; of the ideal of truth by which to understand it; and of beauty to enhance it; once you have seen that every need you have is matched by parallel needs in your fellow creatures—you are no longer free. The vision will not let you go. It consumes you and galvanizes all your actions. You may choose not to obey the summons, but you disobey it at your peril. To hear it and to fail to heed it is to leave yourself feeling unclean, unworthy, guilty. This is what Francis Thompson was trying to say through the powerful imagery of his poem "The Hound of Heaven." He wrote:

> I fled Him, down the nights and down the days;
> I fled Him, down the arches of the years;
> I fled Him, down the labyrinthine ways
> Of my own mind; and in the mist of tears

I hid from Him, and under running laughter,
Up vistaed hopes I sped;
And shot, precipitated,
Adown Titanic glooms of chasmed fears,
From those strong Feet that followed,
followed after.

No doubt he took the image of the feet from Second Isaiah: "How beautiful upon the mountains are the feet of him that bringeth good tidings." Perhaps he fashioned the pursuit down labyrinthine ways and on up vistaed hopes from the universe that astronomy has revealed to us. But no matter. It was the flight he gave us: the hopeless, helpless, headlong flight; and the pursuit, so gentle, so tender yet so insistent, so all-pervasive, and so utterly inescapable.

You may make his poem as personal or as abstract as you wish. Its truth is not affected. The imagery remains exact. The vision of virtue is as demanding today as it was in Francis Thompson's time. Once you have caught that vision, the idea of God upon his throne surrounded by all the angels in Heaven does not make your sense of obligation one whit more compelling. Once you have caught that vision, your perception of love (and of its opposite, hate), your sense of the need for love, and the need to destroy hate, is alone enough. Such is the power of virtue. No decree, even one that is divine in origin, can make it more demanding.

Few if any of us are ever completely seized by such a vision and the critical mind is not. Let me reiterate and underscore that point: there is no blind optimism in the critical way in religion. Quite the opposite. Its view of humanity is stonily realistic. The critic is among the first to point to human frailty and evil. Many of us are able to live our lives impervious to the needs of those around us. Too many seem to be willing to live their lives at the expense of others. Yet many people become highly sensitized to human needs, to the demands of truth and to the call of beauty. The summons remains, constant and unfailing. It is our response that changes, not always for the better, and yet not always for the worse.

In the end, as a final answer to all the questions we have been asking, do we find God standing behind all life and experience, all knowledge and hope? This is the age-old assertion of religion. Do we then, in the end, find God binding us and the world and our ideals into one great metaphysical Reality which he himself created, which he himself *is,* and which he also directs and controls?

How easy it would be to answer "yes." How easy to allow our yearnings, given form by a cherished tradition, to dictate our thoughts in the most fundamental area of our lives. How easy to allow hope rising out of a hallowed past to answer our questions.

For myself I can answer this question best through a recent and very vivid personal experience. The astronomers now think they have located the center of the galaxy to which Earth and the Sun belong. It has long since been determined that the Milky Way is "our" galaxy seen as if set on edge. There has been general agreement also that our galaxy probably looks like the great spiral nebula Messier 31 or M 31 in the constellation Andromeda. But there was much speculation about the location of its center. The evidence seemed to point to a position at the southern end of the Milky Way, as it is seen in the northern hemisphere, and it had been surmised that the galactic center lay in the constellation Sagittarius. But until 1979 the evidence was indirect.

Early that year Eric J. Chaisson of the Harvard-Smithsonian Center for Astrophysics and Louis Rodriguez, a graduate student from Mexico, published their conclusion that the center was a black hole, as had been suspected, and that it was indeed in the constellation Sagittarius. The direct evidence on which Chaisson and Rodriguez based their findings consisted in radio waves that can travel through cosmic dust. A dense cloud of such dust had obscured the galactic center from visual telescopes. Learning this, initially from the *New York Times,* and later having it spelled out at length in the *Scientific American,* my favorite "theological" publication, I went out one clear night in June to "see" the center of our galaxy. I was hardly the first to gaze at the star-filled sky in wonder and in awe. It was by no means the first time I myself had done so.

As I had done many times before, I first located myself, standing on Earth in the northern hemisphere, looking up at the night sky. Next I envisioned Earth in our planetary system with the Sun at its center. Then came the moment of discovery. Gazing at the Milky Way, which indicates the plane of our galaxy, dropping my eyes to Sagittarius, its center, for the first time I saw as I understood, and understood as I saw, Earth's home in a great spiral nebula, where our Sun is one star among billions, in a universe where galaxies seem small.

The surge of emotion that overwhelmed me at that moment would be regarded by many as a religious experience. It was so intense, many traditionalists might have felt and would not have hesitated to say that in it, God had spoken personally and directly to them.

Was my personal experience of discovery of the universe in which I dwell "religious"? To me it was, profoundly so. But its religious quality would be diminished, not enhanced, by an attempt to cast it in traditional theological language or to relate it to one of the many thought structures theology has built. The critical mind seeks truth and understanding. Under the stars that night, it seemed to me that I achieved both.

The same thing happened more than a decade earlier when some black friends and I talked late into the night about the disintegration of the civil rights movement then in progress, and the black withdrawal from white society that followed. They made me see the problem from their point of view. Through them I saw it, felt it, and understood it for the first time, and with it came the same sense of power, the same sense of discovery, the same sense of truth, the same religious quality I felt alone under the stars eleven years later.

I have no quarrel with those who find God in profound experiences that can only be described as religious. It is our task to understand all experience and to interpret it as best we can. My only quarrel is with those who insist upon interpreting *my* experience through *their* theology, or who insist that I must accept their theological interpretation of their own experiences. The critical mind objects in particular to the human habit of accepting at face value ancient interpretations of religious experience. These are of necessity cast in the thought patterns and imagery of ancient times, a pattern and imagery that to the modern mind is usually archaic, often bizarre, and occasionally false. The critical mind objects to the ecclesiastical habit of accepting these ancient accounts as more valid and more authoritative than, let us say, the findings of Chaisson and Rodriguez, indicating that a black hole lies at the center of our galaxy.

Those who follow the critical way in religion make two demands: first, that we cease to think that ancient accounts of religious experience are more valid and more authoritative than modern accounts; second, that religious experience seen and felt in contemporary imagery and thought patterns be understood to have no less validity and no less authority than if couched in the traditional concepts and language of theology.

The problem of casting religious thought and experience into language is no different for the critical way in religion than it is for Judaism, Christianity, Islam, or any other religion. It is a dual one and is set by two questions: 1. What is your concept of the ultimate? For you does the ultimate mean a Cosmic Person, a Force, an Ideal, the really Real, whatever is ultimate, or what? 2. In what sense does your concept of the ultimate correspond to something demonstrable when compared with something you hope for or desire but cannot establish with any degree of objectivity? For the critical way in religion, these two questions are as inescapable as they are for the most orthodox members of the established religions.

To answer them according to the critical tradition, let me resort to a metaphor familiar in the ecclesiastical tradition. The Book of Genesis tells the story of Jacob wrestling with a man in the night. Jacob does not know who the man is. As the dawn breaks Jacob asks the man his name and he replies: "You have striven with God and with men and have prevailed."

For uncounted Christians and Jews this story has symbolized the age-long human attempt to come to grips with the Divine, however we may conceive it; so it is for me also. But an important part of the story does not fit, the final clause "and have prevailed." Few in the critical tradition, after attempting to grasp the nature of the ultimate, have ever felt that they prevailed. More often the process of questing, followed by sharp testing, results in a feeling not of victory but of defeat because the task is quite literally impossible to accomplish.

In order to convey what happens in such a struggle according to critical standards, let me resort to a second metaphor—also taken from the Jacob cycle in Genesis. According to this second story, Jacob lay down one night and dreamed that he saw a ladder extending up to heaven from the place where he lay. The symbolism of the story, as it has been used countless times since, is nowhere seen more vividly than in an old Negro spiritual that opens with the following lines:

> We are climbing Jacob's ladder
> Soldiers of the cross.
> Every rung goes higher, higher
> Soldiers of the cross.

In the metaphor of a ladder reaching upward, but with its feet firmly planted on the earth where we dwell, we have a symbol that points to the central concept of the critical way in religion. In a *ladder,* do I say? Yes. At any rate, not in a Person, no matter how many superlatives like Almighty, All-knowing, All-wise we may summon to our aid in an attempt to delineate the concept; not in a Power or Force, whether or not we add qualifiers like Creating, Sustaining, Transforming, or any other; not in the Holy, the Ineffable, the Mysterious, or the Wholly Other; not in the Infinite or Eternal; not in the King of Kings, Lord of Lords, the Heavenly Father, or the Creator; not in the Unmoved Mover, the Principle of Concretion, the Ground of Being, or the God Beyond God or simply the Ultimate; not in any of these, nor in a host of other concepts with which the works of theology and philosophy are filled; but in a ladder, of which

> Every rung goes higher, higher. . . .

I began by saying that the symbol of the path is the best means by which to indicate the essential character of the critical way in religion. The symbol of the ladder sharpens the concept. It suggests that the path we follow in religion leads upward: to broader understanding, to greater comprehension, to nobler and more generous attitudes toward one another, and to a greater spiritual dimension for the whole. But I return to the symbol of the path lest any dogma of evolutionary progress creep in. For the critical mind believes only that we *may,* not that we surely *will,* move toward nobler actions, a more profound experience of beauty, and a better understanding of truth.

If the life of humanity here on earth is like a pathway, so, too, is the life of each of us: sometimes rough and sometimes smooth, sometimes steep and sometimes level. Sometimes it runs downhill. Often it is rocky, stormy, dangerous, and cold. Sometimes it is treacherous. But always, as we go along, the way unfolds before us, as does a road that we have never traveled, a mountain path that we have never followed, or a wilderness trail that we have never seen before. If it be the critical way we are following, always we will stop and check, lest we fall into error, lest someone deceive us, lest we deceive ourselves, and, above all, lest we injure or impede someone else along the way.

The way may end abruptly. It may extend on indefinitely. We never know. What we do know is that the way leads on, and that it is there for us to follow, out of yesterday, through today, and into tomorrow. And as we go along, there whispers in the inward ear the summons: to knowledge and virtue, to love and beauty, to truth and high adventure. Some do not even hear; some hear but do not heed or do not understand; but some hear very clearly, and heeding, press on.

Whence comes the summons? Why do we feel its compulsion? Again, we do not know. We only know that for some the summons grows ever more insistent and ever more inescapable. It does not bring them to their knees; it does not fling them prostrate on the ground; rather, the summons to truth and beauty, to justice and love, to goodness and high adventure, stands them up upon their feet, glad that they live and glad to respond, insofar as they are able.

NOTES

The following notes give the references for the quotations in the text and direct the reader to the principal sources I have consulted. With one or two exceptions, Bible quotations are from the *Revised Standard Version.* The abbreviation MAC stands for *Man Against the Church,* Beacon Press, which I published in 1954; EAC stands for *The Essenes and Christianity,* Harper & Brothers, which I published in 1957; FAF stands for *The Fourth American Faith,* Harper & Row, which I published in 1964. References to these volumes indicate further development and documentation of the point being made in the text of the present volume.

Page Line

PART I

DIVINE TRUTH AND HUMAN ERROR

2 17 Isaiah 6: 1–8.

19 *The Book of Mormon*: An Account Written by the Hand of Mormon Upon Plates Taken from The Plates Nephi Translated by Joseph Smith Jun. Salt Lake City: The Deseret Book Co., 1962. The first paragraph contains these words: "Written by way of commandment and also by the spirit of prophecy and revelation."

3 5 Baumer, Franklin L. *Religion and the Rise of Scepticism.* New York: Harcourt, Brace & World, Inc., 1960, p. 31.

CHAPTER 1

THE CRITICAL WAY IN RELIGION

1. The Critical Way and the Ecclesiastical Way

6 15 Hesiod. *Works and Days.* Trans. by Samuel Butler in *Collected Essays.* London: Jonathan Cape, 1925, vol. II, p. 319.

Page	*Line*	
6	16	Kirk, G. S. and Raven, T. E. *The Presocratic Philosophers.* Cambridge: Cambridge University Press, 1971, p. 266.
	18	Genesis 24:56.
	18	Amos 8:14.
	18	Jeremiah 10:2, 10:23, 12:1, 21:8, 21:38–39.
	18	Psalms 119:1, 3, 5.
	18	Isaiah 40:3.
	21	Burrows, Millar. *The Dead Sea Scrolls.* New York: The Viking Press, 1955, p. 384.
	21	Acts 9:2, 19:9, 23; 22:4; 24:14, 22.
	21	Niebuhr, H. Richard. *The Meaning of Revelation.* New York: The Macmillan Co., 1960, p. 139, quotes Augustine: Christ as the way.
7	35	Green, Alberto R. W. *The Role of Human Sacrifice in the Ancient Near East.* Missoula, Montana: Scholars Press, 1975, pp. 145, 153, 197.
8	1	Breasted, James H. *Dawn of Conscience.* New York: Charles Scribner's Sons, 1933, p. 178.
	7	"In this Issue." *Christian Century,* Sept. 15, 1976, p. 746.
	37	News item: *Christian Century,* Feb. 24, 1971, p. 247.
9	31	Milton, John. Quoted by Roland Bainton in "The Religious Foundations of Freedom." *Christian Century,* Jan. 26, 1955, p. 108.
	32	Lovejoy, Arthur O. *The Great Chain of Being.* New York: Harper & Brothers, 1960, p. 293.
	33	Whitehead, Alfred North. *Science and The Modern World.* New York: The Macmillan Co., 1925, p. 259.
10	13	Boyd, Malcolm. "Night Comes for the Archbishop." *Christian Century,* April 10, 1974, p. 390.
11	27	Bishop Butler, the great eighteenth-century defender of orthodoxy against deism, argued in his *Analogy of Religion* that Christianity, like anything else, rests in the end on probabilities. See, Peter Gay. *The Enlightenment.* New York: Vintage Books, 1968, p. 376.
12	25	Many of the works cited in these notes deal extensively with one or more of the basic elements in the critical way in religion. The following, at the points indicated, come closer to identifying the critical way as a long continuing *tradition* in Western thought and culture.

Baumer, Franklin, L. op. cit., pp. 4, 21, and 22.

Bronowski, J. and Mazlish, Bruce. *The Western Intellectual Tradition.* New York: Harper & Bros., 1960, pp. 491 ff.

Brotherston, Bruce W. *A Philosophy for Liberalism.* Boston: Beacon Press, 1934, pp. 11 ff.

Bury, J. B. *History of Freedom of Thought.* New York: Henry Holt & Co., 1913, pp. 18, 19, 240.

Cassirer, Ernst. *The Philosophy of the Enlightenment.* Boston: Beacon Press, 1955, pp. 135 ff.

Coates, Willson H., White, Hayden V., and Schapiro, J. Salwyn. *The Emergence of Liberal Humanism.* New York: McGraw Hill, 1966, vol. I, p. vi.

Coates, Willson H. and White, Hayden V. *The Ordeal of Liberal Humanism.* New York: McGraw Hill, 1970, Vol. II, pp. 3 ff.

Cornford, F. M. *From Religion to Philosophy: A Study in the Origins of Western Speculation.* New York: Harper & Bros., 1957, pp. v, vi.

Draper, John William. *History of the Conflict Between Religion and Science.* New York: Grosset and Dunlap, 1874.

Dunham, Barrows. *Heroes and Heretics.* New York: Alfred A. Knopf, 1963, pp. vii and viii.

Page Line

Edman, Irwin. *Fountainheads of Freedom.* New York: Reynal and Hitchcock, 1941, pp. 3 and 190 ff.
Frankel, Charles. *The Case for Modern Man.* New York: Harper & Bros., 1956, pp. 208–9.
Murray, Gilbert. *Stoic, Christian and Humanist.* Boston: Beacon Press, 1950, p. 162.
Orton, William Aylott. *The Liberal Tradition.* New Haven: Yale University Press, 1945, pp. 1, 19 ff.
Popkin, Richard H. *The History of Scepticism.* New York: Harper & Row, 1964, pp. ix ff.
Popper, Karl R. *Conjectures and Reflections.* New York: Harper & Row, 1963, pp. 150, 151.
Robertson, John MacKinnon. *A Short History of Freethought, Ancient & Modern.* Second Edition, Revised. New York: G. P. Putnam's Sons, 1906.
Rokeach, Milton. *The Open and Closed Mind.* New York: Basic Books, 1960, p. 391.
Schapiro, J. Salwyn. *Liberalism: Its Meaning and History.* New York: Van Nostrand, Reinhold Co., 1958, pp. 9 ff.
Skinner, Clarence R. *Liberalism Faces the Future.* New York: The Macmillan Co., pp. 2 ff.
Smith, Homer W. *Man and His Gods.* New York: Grosset & Dunlap, 1952.
Whitehead, Alfred North, op. cit., p. 3.
———. *Adventures of Ideas.* New York: The Macmillan Co., 1933, pp. 12 & 13.

11 39 Richert, William O. *Partisans of Freedom: A Study in American Anarchism.* Bowling Green: Bowling Green University Popular Press, 1976. He holds that free thought, libertarianism, anarchy, deism, the Enlightenment, etc., are all virtually one and the same.

13 7 MAC, pp. 207 ff.

2. Criticism in the Ecclesiastical Tradition

13 37 I Cor. 1:10.
39 I Cor. 13.

14 6 Gaustad, Edwin Scott. *Dissent in American Religion.* Chicago: University of Chicago Press, 1973, p. 6.
11 Berton, Pierre. *The Comfortable Pew.* Philadelphia: J. B. Lippincott Co., 1965.
11 Berger, Peter S. *The Noise of Solemn Assemblies.* New York: Doubleday, 1961.
12 Winter, Gibson. *The Suburban Captivity of the Churches.* New York: The Macmillan Co., 1962.
19 *Newsweek,* Jan. 3, 1966, p. 37.
37 Cauthen, Kenneth. *The Impact of American Religious Liberalism.* New York: Harper & Row, 1962, Chaps. 3–10.

15 42 See "Results of Gallup Poll," *Journal of Current Social Issues,* Vol. 14, no. 2 (Spring 1977), pp. 1 and 53 ff. Gallup's questions reveal the presence of an implicit religious belief structure in the lay mind of the West.

17 11 Mead, Frank S. *Handbook of Denominations.* Sixth ed. Nashville: Abingdon Press, 1975.

Page *Line*

17 16 McLean, Milton, D. "Religious World Views." *Motive Magazine.* Orientation Issue, 1961, pp. 24 & 25 contains a chart similar to mine but with a slightly different arrangement of church groups.

24 Rosten, Leo. *Religions of America.* New York: Simon & Schuster, 1975.

18 6 Frost, Edward A. "Masters of the Temple." *Journal of the Liberal Ministry,* Winter, 1974, p. 3.

16 Cauthen, Kenneth, op. cit., pp. 5 ff.

3. THE CRITICAL WAY AND LIBERALISM

19 24 Hutchison, William R. "How Radical Is the New Religious Radicalism?" American University, Washington, D.C.: 1968, Second Annual Distinguished Faculty Lecture, p. 11.

24 Schapiro, J. Salwyn, op. cit., p. 9 also supports the centrality of freedom in liberalism.

34 See Sidney Hook, *Commentary,* Jan. 1980, pp. 46–47.

21 15 Ames, Edward Scribner. In Vergilius Ferm, *Contemporary American Theology.* New York: Round Table Press, Inc., 1933, vol. II, p. 10.

21 Ibid., p. 11.

32 Fosdick, Harry Emerson. *The Living of These Days.* New York: Harper & Bros., 1956, p. 52.

———. *The Modern Use of the Bible.* New York: The Macmillan Co., 1924, pp. 121 ff.

41 Parker, Theodore. *The Transient and Permanent in Christianity.* Centenary Edition, ed. by G. W. Cooke. Boston: American Unitarian Assn., 1908, vol. IV, p. 1.

22 24 Berton, Pierre, op. cit., p. xvi.

27 Winter, Gibson, op. cit., p. 194.

CHAPTER 2

HUMAN FALLIBILITY

24 9 Jastrow, Joseph. *The Story of Human Error.* New York: D. Appleton-Century Co., Inc., 1936, p. 2.

1. THE PROBLEM OF ERROR

25 3 Kirk, G. S. and Raven, J. E., op. cit., p. 197.

17 Cameron, Norman. *The Psychology of Behavioral Disorders.* Boston: Houghton Mifflin, 1947, pp. 403, 412, 415.

26 36 Heron, Woodburn. "The Pathology of Boredom." *Scientific American,* Jan. 1957, p. 52.

38 "Science and the Citizen." *Scientific American,* April 1974, p. 51.

27 11 Wallace, Robert Keith. "The Physiological Effects of Transcendental Meditation." *Science,* March 27, 1970.

25 ———. "The Physiology of Meditation." *Scientific American,* Feb. 1972, p. 85.

25 Gregory, R. L. and Gombrich, E. H., eds. *Illusion in Nature and Art.* New York: Charles Scribner's Sons, 1974.

28 23 Cantrill, Hadley, ed. *The Morning Notes of Adelbert Ames, Jr.* New Brunswick: Rutgers University Press, 1960, pp. v ff.

23 Ames, Adelbert, Jr. "Visual Perception and the Rotating Trapezoidal Window." *Psychological Monographs,* 65, no. 7 (1951).

32 Wittreich, Warren J. "Visual Perception and Personality." *Scientific American,* April, 1959, p. 56.

Page	*Line*	
28	39	Parducci, Allen. "The Relativism of Absolute Judgments." *Scientific American,* December, 1968, p. 84.
29	3	"Can the Mind Learn to Control a Painful Illness?" *Massachusetts General Hospital News,* 33, no. 5 (June–August 1974), p. 1.
	9	Buckhout, Robert. "Eyewitness Testimony." *Scientific American,* Dec. 1974, p. 23.
29	42	Johnson, Wendell. *People in Quandaries: The Semantics of Personal Adjustment.* New York: Harper & Row, 1946, pp. 11, 17.
30	9	Peterson, W. Wesley. "Error-correcting Codes." *Scientific American,* Feb. 1962, p. 96.
	26	Bonner, John Tyler. *The Ideas of Biology.* New York: Harper & Row, 1962.
31	3	Bronowski, J. *The Ascent of Man.* Boston: Little Brown & Co., 1973, p. 353.
	3	Ibid., pp. 358, 360.

2. Our Credulity

Page	*Line*	
31	26	Gardner, Martin. *In the Name of Science.* New York: Putnam & Sons, 1952.
33	6	Shepard, Odell. *The Lore of the Unicorn.* London: Allen & Unwin, 1930.
	8	Rose, H. J. *Religion in Greece and Rome.* New York: Harper & Bros., 1959, pp. 262 ff.
	20	Hawkins, Gerald S. *Stonehenge Decoded.* New York: Dell Publishing Co., 1965.
	33	Murray, Gilbert. *Five Stages of Greek Religion.* Boston: Beacon Press, 1951, pp. 143–4.
	37	Burckhardt, Jacob. *The Civilization of Renaissance Italy.* New York: Harper & Bros., 1958, vol. II. pt. VI, chap. iv.
	38	Ibid., p. 492.
	41	Thorndike, Lynn. *A History of Magic and Experimental Science.* New York: Columbia University Press, 1958.
34	2	Murray, Gilbert, op. cit., p. 132.
	34	"The Atom." *Time* Magazine, April 12, 1954, p. 23.
35	19	Freud, Sigmund. *Future of an Illusion.* Ed. by James Strachey. Garden City: Anchor Books, 1964, pp. 48, 49.
	42	Menzel, Donald. *Flying Saucers.* Cambridge: Harvard University Press, 1953, p. viii.
36	9	"UFOs." *Canusa Newsletter,* no. 3, Feb. 1979, p. 2.
	11	Hynek, J. Allen and Vallee, Jacques. *The Edge of Reality.* New York: Henry Regnery and Co., 1976.
	11	Jacobs, David Michael. *The UFO Controversy in America.* Bloomington: Indiana University Press, 1975.
	11	"Reports of UFO Sightings Appear to Rise With the Curtain." *New York Times,* Dec. 9, 1977. This tells how reports of UFO sightings began to pour into government offices on the release of two motion pictures, *Star Wars* and *Close Encounters of the Third Kind.*
	24	Gardner, Martin. *Fads and Fallacies in the Name of Science.* New York: Dover Publications, Inc., 1957, p. 67.
	27	Cohn, Norman. *Europe's Inner Demons.* New York: Basic Books, 1975.
	27	Trevor-Roper, H. R. *The Crisis of the Seventeenth Century.* New York: Harper & Row, 1967, pp. 90 ff.
	27	Garcon, Maurice and Vinchou, Jean. *The Devil.* New York: E. P. Dutton & Co., Inc., 1930, Chaps. 7, 8.
38	6	Miller, Perry. *The New England Mind from Colony to Province.* Cambridge: Harvard University Press, 1953, p. 198.

Page	*Line*	
39	6	Caporael, Linuda. *Science,* April 2, 1976, pp. 21-26.

3. The Will to Deceive

39	30	Psalms 52:1-3.
	31	Psalms 59:12.
	32	Proverbs 13:5.
	34	Proverbs 20:17.
	40	Romans 16:17, 18.
40	2	II Thes. 2:9 ff.
	3	Eph. 4:25.
	5	Col. 3:9.
	6	Rev. 21:8.
	9	Gen. 26:1-11.
	14	Gen. 27:28, 29.
	14	Gen. 29: 15 ff.
	14	Gen. 31:20, 26-28, 34-35.
	22	*The Interpreter's Bible.* Nashville: Abingdon Press, 1952. vol. I, pp. 668, 715, 689.
41	16	*Biblical Archeologist,* vol. XIV, no. 4, Dec. 1951, p. 85.
	29	Rose, H. J. *Religion in Greece and Rome.* New York: Harper & Bros., 1959, p. 128.
	34	Milbourne, Christopher. *The Illustrated History of Magic.* New York: Thomas Y. Crowell Co., 1974, p. 8.
	34	Williams, Walter G. *The Prophets, Pioneers to Christianity.* Nashville: Abingdon Press, 1956, p. 141.
	40	Bettenson, Henry, ed. *Documents of the Christian Church.* New York: Oxford University Press, 1947, p. 137.
42	35	Coleman, Christopher B. *The Treatise of Lorenzo Valla on the Donation of Constantine.* New Haven: Yale University Press, 1922, p. 25.
	36	Ibid, p. 23.
43	2	Burckhardt, Jacob. *Civilization of the Renaissance in Italy.* New York: Harper & Bros., 1929, vol. II, pp. 446, 449.
	19	Marjoe, Gortner. *Newsweek* Magazine, July 31, 1972, p. 62.
	34	"Mexican Pilgrims Flock to the Shrine of the Virgin of Guadalupe." *New York Times,* Dec. 4, 1969.
44	3	Barmash, Isadore. *The World Is Full of It.* New York: Dell Publishing Co., Inc., 1974.
	5	Arnau, Frank. *The Art of the Faker.* Trans. by J. Maxwell Brownjohn. Boston: Little, Brown & Co., 1961.
	5	Kurz, Otto. *Fakes: A Handbook for Collectors & Students.* London: Farber & Farber, Ltd., 1948.
	15	Cromwell, Oliver. In Wilbur Cortez Abbott, *The Writings and Speeches of Oliver Cromwell.* London: Oxford University Press, 1937, vol. II, p. 303.
	17	Whitehead, Alfred North. *Science and the Modern World.* p. 24.
	32	Stephen, Leslie. *An Agnostic's Apology and Other Essays.* London: Smith, Elder & Co., 1893, p. 379.

Page Line

PART II

THE CRITICAL TRADITION IN THE RELIGION OF THE WEST

48 2 Newman, John Henry. *The Idea of a University.* London: Longmans Green & Co., 1921, p. 383.

CHAPTER 3

THE CRITICAL TRADITION IS BORN

49 4 Jaspers, Karl. *The Origin and Goal of History.* London: Routledge and Kegan Paul, Ltd., 1953, Chap. 1.

4 Muller, Herbert J. *Freedom in the Ancient World.* New York: Harper & Bros., 1961, pp. 106 ff., 149.

1. Insight in Ionia

49 23 Jaeger, Werner. *Paideia: The Ideals of Greek Culture.* Trans. by Gilbert Highet. 2nd ed. New York: Oxford University Press, 1945, vol. I, Bk. I.

50 6 Guthrie, W. K. C. *The Greeks and their Gods.* Boston: Beacon Press, 1950, Chaps. 4–5.

35 Kirk, G. S. and Raven, J. E., op. cit., p. 73.

35 Popper, Karl. *Conjectures and Refutations.* New York: Basic Books, 1962, pp. 150–152.

44 Jaeger, Werner, op. cit., vol. I, pp. 156 ff.

51 7 Kirk and Raven, op. cit., pp. 143 ff.

28 Cornford, F. M., op. cit., p. 122.

40 Genesis 2, 3, 11:6–9.

52 23 Doblhofer, Ernst. *Voices in Stone*: the Decipherment of Ancient Scripts and Writings. Trans. by Mervyn Savill. New York: Viking, 1961.

28 Gordon, Cyrus. *Before the Bible:* the Common Background of Greek and Hebrew Civilizations. New York: Harper & Row, 1962, pp. 9, 207 ff.

28 McCarter, P. Kyle. "The Early Diffusion of the Alphabet." *Biblical Archeologist,* Sept. 1974, p. 62.

28 Gordon, Cyrus. "The Minoan Bridge." *Christianity Today,* March 15, 1963, p. 575.

2. The New Philosophy and the Old Religion

53 28 Jaeger, Werner, op. cit., vol. I, p. 70.

28 Popper, Karl R., op. cit., pp. 236 ff.

54 6 Xenophanes. *Fragments.* In M. C. Nahm, *Selections from Early Greek Philosophy.* New York: Appleton Century Crafts, 1947, p. 109.

29 Murray, Gilbert. *Euripides and his Age.* New York: Henry Holt, 1913, p. 50.

34 Jaeger, Werner, op. cit., vol. I, p. 339.

34 Cornford, F. M., op. cit., p. 126.

41 *Cambridge Ancient History.* New York: The Macmillan Company, 1927, vol. V, p. 379.

55 12 Grene, David and Lattimore, Richmond, eds. *The Complete Greek Tragedies.* Chicago: University of Chicago Press, 1959, vol. III, p. 333.

12 Jaeger, Werner, op. cit., vol. I, pp. 332 ff., 357.

Page Line

55 32 Jowett, B. *The Dialogues of Plato: The Republic.* New York: Random House, 1937, pp. 377, 378, 382, 383.

56 10 Hamilton, Edith. *The Greek Way.* New York: New American Library, 1948, pp. 6, 34, 35.

36 Hippocrates. *The Sacred Disease.* Trans. by W. H. S. Jones. London: William Heinemann, 1923, vol. II, p. 139.

3. SOCRATES

57 11 Cornford, F. M. *Before and After Socrates.* Cambridge: Cambridge University Press, 1932, p. 54.

14 Eliot, Alexander. *Socrates.* New York: Crown Publishers, 1967, p. 59.

14 Dickinson, G. Lowes. *The Greek View of Life.* New York: McClure Phillips & Co., 1905, p. 153.

15 Jaeger, Werner, op. cit., vol. I, pp. 338–9.

17 ———, vol. II, pp. 75–6.

28 Cornford, F. M., op. cit., p. 28.

30 Jowett, B., op. cit., vol. I, p. 420.

32 Cornford, F. M., op. cit., pp. 1, 29 ff.

58 3 ———, pp. 46–7.

3 Robinson, C. E. *Hellas.* Boston: Beacon Press, 1955, pp. 136 ff.

8 Jaeger, Werner, op. cit., vol. II, p. 63.

8 Taylor, A. E. *Socrates.* Boston: Beacon Press, 1951, pp. 139 ff.

59 3 Bury, J. B. *A History of the Freedom of Thought.* pp. 33, 34.

17 Jowett, B., op. cit., vol. I, p. 412.

21 Jaeger, W., op. cit., vol. I, pp. 55 ff.

CHAPTER 4

"RIGHT" BELIEF

61 17 Jowett, B., op. cit., vol. I, p. 864.

1. TRUE AND FALSE PROPHETS IN ISRAEL

62 4 Ward, James M. *Amos & Isaiah, Prophets of the Word of God.* Nashville: Abingdon Press, 1969, p. 18.

4 Mays, James Luther. *Amos: A Commentary.* Philadelphia: Westminster Press, 1969, p. 4.

13 Amos 3:3, 4, 6.

21 Isaiah 1:2, 10, 24; 2:1; 8:1.

24 Jeremiah 1:9.

30 Jeremiah 36.

63 3 Amos 7:10.

9 Jeremiah 5:30, 31; 14:4; 23:25, 26, 30–32.

18 "Deuteronomist." I am assuming here the views of most scholars as to the origin, date, and authorship of Deuteronomy. See, Chamberlin, Roy and Feldman, Herman. *The Dartmouth Bible.* Boston: Houghton Mifflin Co., 1961, p. 149.

36 Deuteronomy 12:29–13:18.

64 7 Matthew 24:5 ff.

Page *Line*

64 13 Acts 13:6–12.
22 Revelation 16:13, 19:20, 20:10.

2. THE ESSENES AND THE NEW COVENANT

66 4 Isaiah 40:1, 3, 4.
17 Isaiah 54:11.
30 Isaiah, 60:1.
37 Isaiah 65:17.
67 23 EAC, Chaps. 3 & 4.
29 Genesis 9:12–17.
29 Genesis 17:1–21.
35 Jeremiah 31:31, 33.
41 EAC, pp. 110 ff., 130 ff.
68 4 EAC, pp. 22, 82.

3. CHRISTIANITY: "UNLESS YE BELIEVE . . ."

68 30 EAC, Chaps. 16 & 17.
69 8 Mark 1:14.
23 Mark 5:36, 34.
25 Mark 9:23.
32 Mark 11:23.
42 John 1:6.
70 24 John 20:25, 27–30.
37 Revelation 21:8.
71 4 Bindley, T. Herbert. *The Oecumenical Documents of Faith.* Rev. ed. F. W. Green. London: Methuen and Co., 1950, p. 1.
7 Kelly, J. N. D. *Early Christian Creeds.* London: Longmans Green and Co., 1950, p. 13.
10 Riddle, Donald W. *The Martyrs.* Chicago: University of Chicago Press, 1931.
10 EAC, pp. 82-83.
15 Kelley, J. N. D., op. cit., p. 5.
73 24 Lecky, William Edward Hartpole. *History of European Morals.* New York: D. Appleton & Co., 1869, vol. II, chap. iv, pp. 206–12.
35 Kelly, J. N. D. *Jerome.* New York: Harper & Row, 1975, pp. 52, 255.
74 21 Bettenson, Henry, ed., op. cit., p. 36.

CHAPTER 5

DEFENDERS OF THE FAITH

1. INTERPRETATION AND ALLEGORY

77 30 Rose, H. J., op. cit., chap. 5.
40 Jaeger, Werner, op. cit., vol. I, p. 347.
78 5 Hatch, Edwin. *Influence of Greek Ideas on Christianity.* New York: Harper & Bros., 1957, pp. 58, 60.
16 Cornford, F. M. *Greek Religious Thought.* Boston: Beacon Press, 1950, p. 132.
18 Hatch, Edwin, op. cit., p. 62.

Page *Line*

78 20 See B. Jowett, op. cit., vol. II, p. 715, where Plato discusses this question in the *Lesser Hippias,* vol. II, p. 715.

44 Wolfson, Harry Austryn. *Philo.* Cambridge: Harvard University Press, 1948, vol. I, p. 115.

79 15 Galatians 4:21–31.

18 I Cor. 15.

18 Romans 5:14.

25 Songs of Songs 1:2.

31 Pope, Marvin H. *Song of Songs: A New Translation with Introduction and Commentary.* New York: Doubleday, 1977.

41 Wolfson, Harry Austryn. *The Philosophy of the Church Fathers.* Cambridge: Harvard University Press, 1956, vol. I, pp. 24 ff.

44 Hanson, R. P. C. *Allegory and Event.* Richmond: John Knox Press, 1959, pt. I, pp. 233 ff.

80 10 Sallustius. *Concerning the Gods and the Universe.* Ed. by Arthur Darby Nock. Cambridge: Harvard University Press, 1926, pp. xcvii, ff.

16 Murray, Gilbert. *The Five Stages of Greek Religion,* chap. 5, and app.

32 Gilkey, Langdon. "Biblical Symbols in a Science Culture." In Ralph Burhoe, ed., *Science & Human Values in the 21st Century.* Philadelphia: Westminster Press, 1971, p. 72.

32 Gilkey, Langdon. *Religion and the Scientific Future.* New York: Harper & Row, 1970, pp. 6 ff.

34 Cochrane, Charles N. *Christianity & Classical Culture.* London: Oxford University Press, 1940, chap. vii.

81 7 Wolfson, H. A. *Philosophy of the Church Fathers.* Cambridge: Harvard University Press, 1964, vol. I, pp. 73 ff.

40 Murray Gilbert, op. cit., p. 74.

82 6 Fletcher, Angus. *Allegory.* Ithaca: Cornell University Press, 1964, pp. 2–13.

6 Berger, Harry, Jr. *The Allegorical Temper.* New Haven: Yale University Press, 1957, p. 3.

2. SAINT AUGUSTINE

82 38 Knowles, David. *The Evolution of Medieval Thought.* New York: Vintage Books, Random House, 1962, chap. 3.

83 5 Kristeller, Paul Oskar. *Renaissance Thought.* New York: Harper Torchbooks, 1961, p. 76.

5 Simpson, W. J. Sparrow. *St. Augustine's Episcopate.* New York: The Macmillan Co., 1945.

5 ———. *St. Augustine's Conversion.* New York: The Macmillan Co., 1930, p. 65.

13 Gilson, Etienne. *The Christian Philosophy of Saint Augustine.* Trans. by L. E. M. Lynch. New York: Random House, 1960, pp. 229 ff.

15 II Corinthians 3:6.

20 Augustine. *Confessions.* Trans. by E. B. Pusey. London: J.M. Dent & Sons, Ltd., 1907.

32 Augustine. *Anti-Manichaean Writings.* In Philip Schaff, ed., *Nicene and Post-Nicene Fathers of the Christian Church.* New York: Christian Literature Co., 1887, vol. IV, p. 41.

85 5 Augustine. *Anti Donatist Writings,* ibid., vol. IV, p. 411.

Page	*Line*	
85	15	Luke 14:16.
	21	Frend, W. H. C. *The Donatist Church.* Oxford: Clarendon Press, 1952.
	22	Augustine. "On the Grace of Christ and On Original Sin." In Philip Schaff, op. cit., vol. V, p. 217.
	22	Ibid., "On Nature and Grace," p. 121.
	22	Ibid., "On Grace and Free Will," p. 443.
86	13	Cyprian. *De Catholicae Ecclesiae Unitate.* Quoted in Bettenson, op. cit., p. 102.
	32	Jones, R. M. *The Church's Debt to Heretics.* New York: George H. Doran Co., 1924, p. 124.
	40	Bettenson, Henry, op. cit., p. 76.
	40	Pelagius. *Pro Libero Arbitrio, ap. Augustine, De Gratia Christi.* Quoted in Henry Bettenson, op. cit., p. 75.
87	18	Nock, Arthur Darby. *Conversion.* London: Oxford University Press, 1933, p. 14.
	18	Jordan, Wilbur K. *Development of Religious Toleration in England.* Cambridge: Harvard University Press, 1932, vol. I, p. 375.
		Pelagius. *Pro Libero Arbitrio, ap. Augustine, De Gratia Christi.* Quoted in Henry Bettenson, op. cit., p. 75.
87	29	Bailey, Cyril. *Lucretius on the Nature of Things.* Oxford: Clarendon Press, 1921, pp. 5–23.
	29	Bury, J. B., op. cit., p. 40.
88	27	Ruffini, Francesco. *Religious Liberty.* New York: G. P. Putnam's Sons, 1912, p. 25.

CHAPTER 6

THE REBIRTH OF THE CRITICAL TRADITION IN EUROPE

90	13	Leff, Gordon. *Medieval Thought.* Baltimore: Penguin Books, 1958, p. 57.

1. The Slender Thread

90	23	Knowles, David, op. cit., pp. 52 ff.
91	19	Highet, Gilbert. *The Classical Tradition: Greek and Roman Influences on Western Literature.* New York: Oxford University Press, 1950, pp. 41 ff.
92	23	Fremantle, Anne. *The Age of Belief.* New York: New American Library, 1954, pp. 54 ff.
	29	Knowles, David, op. cit., p. 93.
	29	Leff, Gordon, op. cit., p. 90.
	36	Bensusan, S. L. *Titian.* London: T. C. and E. C. Jack, p.

2. The Universities Emerge

93	11	Thompson, J. W. and Johnson, E. N. *Medieval Europe.* New York: W. W. Norton & Co., Inc., 1937, pp. 724 ff.
94	16	Leff, Gordon, op. cit., p. 55.
	32	Duckett, Eleanor Shipley. *Alcuin, Friend of Charlemagne.* New York: The Macmillan Co., 1951, pp. 85 ff.
	32	Walker, G. S. M. *The Growing Storm.* Grand Rapids: Wm. B. Eerdmans Publishing Co., 1961, pp. 42 ff.
	32	Leff, Gordon, op. cit., pp. 52 ff. and 59 ff.
	32	Easton, Stewart C. and Wieruszowski, Helen. *The Era of Charlemagne.* Princeton: D. Van Nostrand Co., Inc., 1961, p. 99.

Page Line

94 32 Knowles, David., op. cit., p. 71.
43 Easton, Stewart C. and Wieruszowski, Helen, op. cit., p. 98.
43 Leff, Gordon, op. cit., pp. 33, 62–73, 95.
43 *Cambridge Medieval History*. New York: The Macmillan Company, 1926, vol. V, pp. 784 ff.
44 Copleston, F. C. *Medieval Philosophy*. London: Methuen & Co., 1952, pp. 28 ff.
95 10 Fremantle, Anne. *The Age of Belief*, pp. 79 ff.
18 Taylor, Henry Osborn. *The Medieval Mind*. London: Macmillan Co., Ltd., 1911, vol. I, p. 230.
38 Ibid., p. 303.
42 Quoted in Thompson-Johnson, op. cit., p. 692.

3. THE CRITICAL TRADITION IN THE MIDDLE AGES

97 2 Haskins, Charles H. *The Renaissance of the Twelfth Century*. Cleveland: Meridian Books, World Publishing Co., 1957, pp. 368 ff.
2 ——. *The Rise of the Universities*. New York: Henry Holt & Co., 1923, esp. chap. i.
12 Cohn, Norman. *The Pursuit of the Millennium*. London: Secker & Warburg, 1957, p. xiii.
12 Bainton, Roland H. *The Medieval Church*. Princeton: D. Van Nostrand Co., Inc., 1962, pp. 33 ff.
98 11 Kristeller, Paul Oskar, op. cit., pp. 27–46.
11 *Cambridge Medieval History*, vol. V, p. 811.
11 Haskins, Charles H. *The Renaissance of the Twelfth Century*, p. 278.
99 6 Leff, Gordon, op. cit., p. 176.
6 Knowles, David, op. cit., pp. 199, 216, 279, 280.
6 Leff, Gordon, op. cit., p. 246.
6 Haskins, Charles H. *Studies in Medieval Science*. Cambridge: Harvard University Press, 1924, p. 40.

4. IBN-RUSHD (AVERROËS)

100 4 Peters, Francis E. *Aristotle and the Arabs*. New York: New York University Press, 1968.
4 Hitti, Philip K. *Islam and the West*. Princeton: D. Van Nostrand Co., Inc., 1962, pp. 72, 73, 74.
4 Wolfson, H. A. *Philo*. Cambridge: Cambridge University Press, 1947, p. 158.
4 Peters, Francis E., op. cit., pp. 215 ff.
7 Hitti, Philip K. *History of the Arabs*. London: The Macmillan Co., 1963, p. 582.
19 Watt, William Montgomery. *Muslim Intellectual: A Study of Al-Ghazali*. Edinburgh: Edinburgh University Press, 1963, pp. 172 ff.
34 Sweetman, James Windrow. *Islam & Christian Theology*. London: Lutterworth Press, 1967, Part II, Vol. II, p. 190.
34 Watt, William Montgomery. *Islamic Philosophy & Theology*. Edinburgh: Edinburgh University Press, 1962, pp. 139 ff.
40 De Boer, T. J. *The History of Philosophy in Islam*. Trans. by Edmund R. Jones. New York: Dover Publications, Inc., 1967, pp. 187 ff., 197–8.
101 29 Hitti, Philip K., op. cit., p. 584.
30 De Boer, T. J., op. cit., p. 209.

Page Line

CHAPTER 7

THE RENAISSANCE

103 14 Nelson, Benjamin and Trinkhaus, Charles. In Jacob Burkhardt, *The Civilization of the Renaissance in Italy.* New York: Harper & Bros., 1958, vol. I, Introduction pp. 3, 8.

17 Ibid., p. 4. Scholars now generally agree that Burckhardt's concept was original and essentially valid.

21 Kristeller, Paul O. *Renaissance Thought,* pp. 92–96 and 153; the debate on Burckhardt.

1. Medieval Pioneers

104 19 Dunham, Barrows. *Heroes and Heretics,* p. 3.

19 Beck, H. F. "Monotheism in Akhenaton and the Second Isaiah." Ph.D. thesis, Boston University, 1954.

24 Leff, Gordon. *Heresy in the Later Middle Ages.* Manchester: Manchester University Press, 1967, p. 1.

105 1 Taylor, H. O., op. cit., vol. II, p. 305.

6 Haskins, Charles H. *Renaissance of the Twelfth Century,* p. 354.

10 Bainton, Roland H. *The Medieval Church,* p. 57.

10 *Cambridge Medieval History,* vol. V, pp. 797 ff.

24 Gilson, Etienne. *The Christian Philosophy of St. Thomas Aquinas.* Trans. by L. K. Shook. New York: Random House, 1956, pp. 9 ff.

32 Baumer, Franklin L., op. cit., p. 80.

106 22 Greenway, G. W. *Arnold of Brescia.* Cambridge: Cambridge University Press, 1931.

44 Leff, Gordon, op. cit., pp. 185, 187.

107 21 Knowles, David, op. cit., pp. 281, 282, 283.

35 Bacon, Roger. Quoted in J. W. Thompson and E. N. Johnson, op. cit., p. 717.

2. Freedom of Speech

109 27 Siegel, Jerrold E. *Rhetoric & Philosophy in Renaissance Humanism.* Princeton: Princeton University Press, 1968, pp. 3, 5.

27 Kristeller, Paul Oskar. *Eight Philosophers of the Italian Renaissance.* Palo Alto: Stanford University Press, 1964, chap. 1.

33 Murchland, Bernard. *Two Views of Man.* New York: Frederick Ungar Publishing Co., 1966, p. viii.

110 7 McGrade, Arthur Stephen. *The Political Thought of William of Ockham.* Cambridge: Cambridge University Press, 1974.

7 Ockham, William of. *The Power & Dignity of the Pope.* C. K. Brampton, ed. Oxford: Oxford University Press, 1927.

13 Munz, Peter. *The Place of Hooker in the History of Thought.* London: Routledge & Kegan Paul, Ltd., 1952, pp. 93 ff.

24 Ruffini, Francesco, op. cit., pt. 2, chaps. 9–10.

41 Fremantle, Anne. *The Age of Belief,* p. 201.

111 2 Knowles, David, op. cit., p. 319.

112 4 Leff, Gordon, op. cit., p. 291.

Page	*Line*	
111	28	McFarlane, K. B. *Origins of Religious Dissent in England.* New York: Collier Books, 1966.
112	6	Schwarze, W. N. *John Hus.* New York: Fleming Revell, 1955, pp. 55, 64.
	16	Kaminsky, Howard. *History of the Hussite Revolution.* Berkeley: University of California Press, 1967.

3. THE CRITICAL WAY IN THE RENAISSANCE

112	36	*Cambridge Medieval History,* vol. II, p. 586.
113	7	Siegel, Jerrold. *Rhetoric & Philosophy in Renaissance.* Princeton: Princeton University Press, 1968, pp. 137 ff.
	24	Coates, W. H., et al. *Emergence of Liberal Humanism.* New York: McGraw Hill, 1966, pp. 18 ff.
	31	Bainton, Roland H. *The Medieval Church,* p. 183.
114	4	Kristeller, Paul Oskar. *Eight Philosophers of the Italian Renaissance,* p. 32.
	14	Janson, H. W. and Janson, Dora Jane. *The Story of Painting.* New York: Harry N. Abrams, Inc., pp. 50 ff.
	23	Kristeller, Paul Oskar. *Renaissance Concepts of Man.* New York: Harper & Row, 1972, p. 60.
	27	Ibid., p. 61.
	32	Ibid., p. 132.
	32	Cassirer, Ernst. *The Philosophy of the Enlightenment.* Boston: Beacon Press, 1955, p. 137.
115	27	Kristeller, Paul Oskar, op. cit., p. 136.

4. THE DIGNITY OF MAN

116	11	Trinkaus, Charles. *In Our Image and Likeness*: Humanity and Divinity in Italian Humanist Thought. Chicago: University of Chicago Press, 1970, pp. xiii ff.
	11	Kristeller, Paul Oskar. *Eight Philosophers of the Italian Renaissance.* pp. 3 ff.
	21	Job 3:1–16.
	40	Pope Innocent III. *On the Misery of Man.* In Bernard Murchland, op. cit., pp. 3, 4.
117	4	Gianozzo Manetti. *On the Dignity of Man.* Ibid., p. 6.
	14	Trinkhaus, Charles, op. cit., vol. 1, p. 230.
118	16	Pico della Mirandola, Giovanni. *Notes & Documents of The Dignity of Man.* Ed. by Elizabeth Livermore Forbes in *Journal of the History of Ideas,* June 1942, vol. III, no. 3, p. 348.
	44	Kristeller, Paul Oskar. *Renaissance Thought,* pp. 159 & 138.

CHAPTER 8

ERASMUS AND CASTELLIO

1. DESIDERIUS ERASMUS

119	18	Bainton, Roland H. *Erasmus of Christendom.* London: Collins, Fontana Library, 1972.
120	3	Erasmus, Desiderius. *The Praise of Folly.* Trans. by John Wilson and ed. by Hendrick Willem van Loon. New York: Walter J. Black, Inc., 1942.
122	3	Bainton, Roland H., op. cit., p. 168.

Page *Line*

122 17 Erasmus, Letter to Robert Guibé. Quoted in Preserved Smith. *Erasmus.* New York: Harper & Brothers, 1923, p. 115.

41 ———. Quoted in Roland H. Bainton, *Medieval Church,* p. 183.

44 ———. Quoted in Roland H. Bainton, *Erasmus of Christendom,* p. 216.

123 2 Ibid., p. 237.

3 Abelard. Quoted in H. O. Taylor, op. cit., vol. II, p. 380.

2. Sebastian Castellio

123 10 Bainton, Roland H. *The Travail of Religious Liberty.* Boston: Beacon Press, 1951, pp. 97 ff.

10 Jones, Rufus M. *Spiritual Reformers in the Sixteenth and Seventeenth Centuries.* Boston: Beacon Press, 1959, pp. 83–103.

10 Popkin, Richard H. *History of Scepticism.* New York: Harper Torchbooks, 1968, pp. 4 ff.

10 Williams, George H. *The Radical Reformation.* Philadelphia: Westminster Press, 1962, p. 627.

31 *Encyclopedia Britannica.* Chicago: Wm. Benton Publisher, 1958, vol. IV, p. 632.

124 44 Castellio, Sebastian. *Concerning Heretics.* Quoted in Earl Morse Wilbur, *A History of Unitarianism.* Cambridge: Harvard University Press, 1945, vol. I, p. 203.

125 13 Castellio, Sebastian, op. cit. Quoted in Stefan Sweig, *The Right to Heresy.* New York: The Viking Press, 1936, p. 161.

Even the tolerant and theologically liberal Minor Church in sixteenth-century Poland was forced to adopt a creed or statement of faith in order to end theological strife that threatened the very life of the movement.

See Williams, George H., op. cit., p. 703, and Wilbur, Earl Morse, op. cit., vol. I, p. 412.

127 8 Ozment, Steven E. *Mysticism and Dissent.* New Haven: Yale University Press, 1973, pp. 168 ff. He argues that Castellio was among the mystical theoreticians of dissent.

25 Jacquot, Jean. "Castellio's Influence in England." *London Times Literary Supplement,* July 27, 1951, p. 469.

35 Coates, W. H., et al., op. cit., p. 75.

35 Wilbur, E. M., op. cit., vol. I, p. 207.

35 Allen, J. W. *Political Thought in the Sixteenth Century.* London: Methuen & Co., Ltd., 1928, p. 101.

CHAPTER 9

THE ENLIGHTENMENT

1. Excitement and Change

129 17 Gay, Peter. *The Enlightenment.* New York: Alfred A. Knopf, 1966, pp. 130, 141.

131 7 Drake, Stillman. *Discoveries and Opinions of Galileo.* Trans., with an introduction. New York: Doubleday Anchor Books, 1957, p. 27.

131 25 Gay, Peter, op. cit., p. 132.

25 Popkin, Richard H. "The Skeptical Crisis and the Rise of Modern Philosophy." *Review of Metaphysics,* vol. VII, Dec. 1953, p. 2.

Page Line

2. Great Enlightenment Thinkers

132 15 Frame, Donald. *Montaigne*. New York: Harcourt Brace World, Inc., 1965.
35 Popkin, Richard H. *History of Skepticism,* p. xi.
133 13 Ibid., pp. 19, 55 56.
13 Blanchard Bates, ed. *Montaigne: Selected Essays.* New York: Modern Library, 1949, pp. xiv, xxii, xxiii.
27 Rée, Jonathan. *Descartes.* London: Allen Lane, Div. of Penguin Books, 1974, p. 157.
37 Popkin, Richard H. "Charron and Descartes: the Fruits of Systematic Doubt." *The Journal of Philosophy,* vol. II, no. 25, Dec. 9, 1954, pp. 831 ff.
37 Popkin, Richard H. "The Skeptical Crisis and the Rise of Modern Philosophy, II," in *Review of Metaphysics,* vol. VII, no. 2, Dec. 1953, p. 307.
134 6 Descartes. *Selections.* Ed. by Ralph M. Eaton. New York: Charles Scribner's Sons, 1927, pp. 16, 29.
13 Ibid., p. xxxviii.
34 Gay, Peter, op. cit., p. 295.
135 11 Cassirer, Ernst. *The Philosophy of the Enlightenment.* pp. 160 ff.
17 Bronowski, J. and Mazlish, B. *The Western Intellectual Tradition,* p. 241.
136 17 Beller, E. A. and Lee, M. DuP., Jr., eds. *Selections from Bayle's Dictionary.* Princeton: Princeton University Press, 1952, pp. 203–4.
20 Robinson, Howard. *Bayle, the Sceptic.* New York: Columbia University Press, 1931, pp. 246 ff.
28 Gay, Peter, op. cit., pp. 385–399.
28 Baumer, F. L. *Religion and the Rise of Scepticism,* p. 23.
138 3 Maurois, André. In *Candide,* by Voltaire. Trans. by Lowell Bair. New York: Bantam Books, 1959, p. 4.
35 Popkin, Richard H. "David Hume and the Pyrrhonian Controversy." *Review of Metaphysics,* vol. VI, no. 1, Sept. 1952, pp. 65, 81.
35 ———. "David Hume: His Pyrrhonism and his Critique of Pyrrhonism." *Philosophical Quarterly,* vol. I, 1950–51, pp. 103, 183.
35 Hume, David. *Essays Literary Moral and Political.* London: Alex. Murray & Son, 1870, p. 331.
35 ———. *Treatise of Human Nature.* In Charles W. Handel, Jr., ed. *Hume Selections.* New York: Charles Scribner's Sons, 1927, book I, Part IV, Conclusion, p. 97.
138 4 Gay, Peter, op. cit., p. 3.

CHAPTER 10

THE LEGACY OF THE ENLIGHTENMENT

1. The Power of the Christian Church

140 17 Stephen, Leslie. *History of English Thought in the Eighteenth Century.* New York: G. P. Putnam's Sons, 1902, vol. I, p. 87.
141 2 McLachlan, H. *The Religious Opinions of Milton, Locke and Newton.* Manchester: Manchester University Press, 1941, p. 130.
8 Manuel, Frank E. *The Religion of Isaac Newton.* Oxford: Clarendon Press, 1976.
23 McLachlan, H., op. cit., p. 200.
23 Milton, John. "Areopagitica." "As good almost kill a man as kill a good book. . . . We should be wary . . . how we spill that seasonal life of a man preserved and stored up in books. [In suppressing books we] slay an immortality rather than a life." Quoted in Crane Brinton. *Age of Reason Reader.* New York: Viking Press, 1956, p. 135.

Page Line

141 23 McLachlan, H., op. cit., pp. 22 ff.

29 Rukeyser, Muriel. *The Traces of Thomas Hariot.* New York: Random House, 1971.

142 2 Franklin, Benjamin. Letter to Ezra Stiles, quoted in Crane Brinton. *Age of Reason Reader,* p. 378.

33 Reimarus, Herman Samuel. Quoted in Peter Gay, *Deism: An Anthology.* Princeton: D. Van Nostrand Co., Inc., 1968, p. 160.

2. THE CHURCHMEN COUNTERATTACK

143 7 Gay, Peter. *Deism: An Anthology,* p. 159.

26 Stephen, Leslie, op. cit., vol. I, p. 205.

144 15 Jordan, Wilbur K. *The Development of Religious Toleration in England,* vol. II, pp. 435–444.

23 Baumer, F. L., op. cit., p. 32.

37 Gay, Peter. *The Enlightenment,* p. ix.

3. THE ECCLESIASTICAL RETREAT

145 9 Frei, Hans W. "Religion in the Enlightenment." *Yale Alumni Magazine,* May, 1975, p. 22.

16 Cragg, Gerald R. *Reason and Authority in the 18th Century.* Cambridge: Cambridge University Press, 1964, p. 34.

146 8 Whitehead, Alfred North. *Science and the Modern World,* p. 271.

17 Ferguson, Wallace K. "The Church in a Changing World: A Contribution to the Interpretation of the Renaissance." *The American Historical Review,* vol. LIX, no. 1, Oct. 1953, p. 18.

27 Brown, Jerry Wayne. *The Rise of Biblical Criticism in America,* 1800–1870, the New England Scholars. Middletown, Conn.: Wesleyan University Press, 1969, pp. 153 ff. and 171 ff.

41 Strauss, David Friedrich. *The Life of Jesus Critically Examined.* Trans. by George Eliot. London: Swan Sonnenschein & Co., 1892.

41 Cromwell, Richard S. *David Friedrich Strauss and his Place in Modern Thought.* Fair Lawn, N.J.: R. E. Burdick, Inc., 1974.

147 4 Massey, J. A. "Lowered Sights." Review of R. S. Cromwell, op. cit., *Christian Century,* November 6, 1974, p. 1046.

34 Coates, W. H., et al., op. cit., pp. 150 ff.

34 Feuerbach, Ludwig. *The Essence of Christianity.* Trans. by George Eliot. New York: Harper and Brothers, 1957, p. 270.

42 Marx, Karl. "Critique of the Hegelian Philosophy of Right," in *Selected Essays.* Trans. by H. J. Stenning. London: Leonard Parsons, 1926, p. 12.

42 Tucker, Robert. *Philosophy and Myth in Karl Marx.* Cambridge: Cambridge University Press, 1961, pp. 21 ff.

42 Acton, H. B. *What Marx Really Said.* London: Macdonald, 1967, pp. 24 ff. and chap. 2.

24 Hume, David. *Enquiry Concerning Human Understanding.* Quoted in Crane Brinton, *Age of Reason Reader,* p. 394.

25 Voltaire. *Complete Romances.* New York: Walter J. Black Co., 1927, p. 501.

148 1 Wright, G. Ernest. *Biblical Archeology.* Philadelphia: Westminster Press, 1957, pp. 17 ff.

4 Glueck, Nelson. *Rivers in the Desert.* New York: Farrar, Strauss & Cudahy, 1959.

Page Line

148 14 Marty, Martin E. *The Infidel: Free Thought and American Religion.* Cleveland: World Publishing Co., 1961.

14 Ferm, Vergilius, ed. *Contemporary American Theology.* New York: Round Table Press, Inc., vol. I, 1932; Second Series, 1933.

14 Morrison, Charles Clayton. "How Their Minds Have Changed." *Christian Century,* Oct. 4, 1939–Nov. 1, 1939.

19 *The Cambridge Bible Commentary on the New English Bible, Genesis 1-11.* Commentary by R. H. Davidson. Cambridge: Cambridge University Press, 1973, p. 5.

26 FAF, p. 133.

4. THE CRITICAL WAY ENTERS ORGANIZED RELIGION

150 7 Gilkey, Langdon. *Religion and the Scientific Future,* pp. 9, 4.

18 Smith, R. G. *Secular Christianity.* New York: Harper & Row, 1966, p. 148.

21 Winter, Gibson. *The New Creation as Metropolis.* New York: The Macmillan Co., 1963, p. 45.

23 Indinopulos, Thomas A. *The Erosion of Faith.* Chicago: Quadrangle Books, 1971, p. ix.

29 Amos 5:24.

29 Matthew 19:21; 5:7, 44; 7:12.

32 Luke 10:29 ff.

151 2 Troeltsch, Ernst. *The Social Teachings of the Christian Churches.* Trans. by Olive Wyon. Vol. I. London: George Allen & Unwin, Ltd., 1931, pp. 303 ff.

15 Baumer, F. L., op. cit., p. 71.

34 Wright, Conrad. "*Fresh Responses to New Situations.*" Lecture before Visiting Committee and Faculty, Harvard Divinity School, Oct. 20, 1964, p. 4.

36 Peabody, Francis Greenwood. *Jesus Christ and the Social Question.* New York: The Macmillan Co., 1900.

40 Rauschenbush, Walter. *Christianity and the Social Crisis.* New York: The Macmillan Co., 1907, pp. xiii ff.

152 2 ———. *Christianizing the Social Order.* New York: The Macmillan Co., 1912.

2 Handy, Robert T. *The Social Gospel in America.* New York: Oxford University Press, 1966, p. 253.

12 Herberg, Will. *Protestant, Catholic, Jew.* Garden City, N.Y.: Doubleday & Company, 1955, pp. 85 ff.

17 Marty, Martin. "Protestantism Enters Third Phase". *Christian Century,* Jan. 18, 1961, p. 72.

17 FAF, pp. 42 ff.

29 Wilbur, Earl Morse, op. cit., pp. 275, 363.

35 Robinson, Robert. *Ecclesiastical Researches.* Cambridge: Francis Hodson, 1792, p. 598.

153 1 See "Catholic Anglican Dispute over Communion is Ended." *New York Times,* Dec. 31, 1971.

21 Maximus of Tyre, quoted in Gilbert Murray, *Five Stages of Greek Religion,* p. 77 n.

6 McLeod, N. Bruce. "Christian Muslim Dialogue: Toward a Wider Ecumenism." *Christian Century,* Oct. 18, 1972, p. 1044.

10 Baumer, Franklin L., op. cit., p. 102, The story of the "Three Rings" in Boccaccio (1313–75).

26 Cusa, Nicholas of. *De Pace Fidei.* In Roland H. Bainton. *The Medieval Church.* Princeton, N.J.: D. Van Nostrand Co., Inc., 1962, p. 179.

30 Gay, Peter, op. cit., p. 29.

42 Moffitt, John. "Christians and non-Christians: Confrontation and Beyond." *Christian Century,* April 4, 1973, p. 392.

Page	*Line*	
154	6	Cox, Harvey. *The Seduction of the Spirit.* New York: Simon & Schuster, 1973, p. 242.
	11	"Memorial Church Study." *Harvard Divinity Bulletin,* Dec. 1974, p. 6.
	19	Singer, Dorothea Waley. *Giordano Bruno, His Life and Thought.* With annotated translation of his work *On The Infinite Universe and Worlds.* New York: Henry Schuman, 1950, pp. 54 ff.
	35	"Eschatology: New Views on Heaven and Hell." *Time,* May 19, 1967, p. 44.

CHAPTER 11
MODERN TIMES

1. LIBERALISM AND MODERNISM

156	16	Liley, A. Leslie. *Modernism: A Record and Review.* New York: Charles Scribner's Sons, 1908.
157	7	*Houston Chronicle,* March 27, 1969.
	8	*New York Times,* April 4, 1969.
	9	*New York Times,* April 5, 1969.
	11	*New York Times,* October 28, 1974.
	12	*New York Times,* March 6, 1976.
	13	*Washington Post,* December 6, 1976.
	15	*New York Times,* December 31, 1976.
	26	Ferm, Vergilius, ed. *Contemporary American Theology.* New York: Round Table Press, Inc., 1932; and Second Series, 1933, vol. I.
	36	Horton, Walter Marshall. In Vergilius Ferm, op. cit., p. 179.
158	7	Horton, Walter Marshall. *Realistic Theology.* New York: Harper & Bros., 1934, p. 99.
	10	Averill, Lloyd J. *American Theology in the Liberal Tradition.* Philadelphia: Westminster Press, 1967.
	10	FAF, pp. 93 ff.
	21	Hutchison, William R. "Getting to Know Modernism." *Harvard Divinity Bulletin,* Winter 1969, p. 1.
		———. *The Modernist Impulse in American Protestantism.* Cambridge: Harvard University Press, 1976.
	35	FAF, Ch. 4, §§1, 2.
	35	Ahlstrom, Sidney. *Religious History of the American People.* New Haven: Yale University Press, 1972, pp. 932 ff.

2. THE DEAD SEA SCROLLS

159	24	EAC, p. 27.
	26	Sanders, James A. "The Dead Sea Scrolls—A Quarter Century of Study." *Biblical Archeologist,* vol. 36, no. 4, Dec. 1973, pp. 114 ff.
	37	Wilson, Edmund. *The Scrolls from the Dead Sea.* New York: Oxford University Press, 1955.
160	11	EAC, pp. 10, 169, 173.
	11	Burrows, Millar. *More Light on the Dead Sea Scrolls.* New York: The Viking Press, 1958, p. 39.
	18	Frank, Henry Thomas. *Bible Archeology and Faith.* Nashville: Abingdon Press, 1971, p. 339.
	24	James Charlesworth in *New York Times,* Feb. 2, 1978.
	28	La Sor, William. *The Dead Sea Scrolls and the New Testament.* Grand Rapids: Wm. B. Eerdmans Pub. Co., 1972, pp. 254 ff.
	32	Trever, John C. *The Untold Story of Qumran.* Westwood, N.J.: Fleming H. Revell Co., 1965, pp. 160 ff.
	34	Sanders, J. A., op. cit., p. 148; but see: Yadin, Yigael in *New York Times,* Nov. 13, 1977 and Milgrom, Jacob. "The Temple Scroll." *Biblical Archeologist,* Sept. 1978, p. 119, both of whom find close connections between the Essenes and primitive Christianity.

Page Line

3. DIETRICH BONHOEFFER

161 25 Bethge, Eberhard, ed. *Letters and Papers from Prison,* by Dietrich Bonhoeffer. Trans. by Reginald H. Fuller. New York: The Macmillan Co., 1953, pp. 7 ff. Originally published as *Prisoner for God.* London: S.C.M. Press, 1953; translated from the original German edition *Widerstand und Ergebung—Briefe und Aufzeichnungen aus der Haft.* München: Chr. Kaiser Verlag, 1951.

38 Ibid., p. 218.

162 12 Ibid., p. 219.

30 Ibid., pp. 217–8.

163 18 Ibid., p. 217.

31 Hamilton, William. "The Shape of Radical Theology." *Christian Century,* October 6, 1965, p. 1219.

4. THE DEATH OF GOD AND CHRISTIAN SECULARISM

164 13 Baumer, F. L., op. cit., pp. 128 ff.

18 Vahanian, Gabriel. *The Death of God.* New York: Braziller, 1961, p. xiii.

18 Hamilton, William. *The New Essence of Christianity.* New York: Association Press, 1961.

18 Van Buren, Paul. *The Secular Meaning of the Gospel.* New York: The Macmillan Co., 1963.

18 Altizer, Thomas J. J. and Hamilton, William. *Radical Theology—the Death of God.* New York: Bobbs Merrill, 1966.

18 Altizer, Thomas J. J. *The Gospel of Christian Atheism.* Philadelphia: Westminster Press, 1966.

21 Hamilton, William. "A Funny Thing Happened on the Way to the Library." *Christian Century,* April 12, 1967, p. 469.

25 Altizer, Thomas J. J. *The Self Embodiment of God.* New York: Harper & Row, 1977. A slim, seemingly incomprehensible book in which the divine name appears innumerable times on several pages.

31 Van Buren, Paul, quoted in *New York Times,* April 15, 1974.

31 Hamilton, William. "Finding a Voice, Shaping a Style." *Christian Century,* July 5–12, 1978, p. 682.

31 Vahanian, Gabriel. "God is Dead: Bake Better Bread." *Christian Century,* Sept. 27, 1978, p. 892.

165 24 Robinson, John A. T. *Honest to God.* Philadelphia: Westminster Press, 1963.

29 Edwards, David L., ed. *The Honest to God Debate.* Philadelphia: Westminster Press, 1963.

35 Clarke, O. Fielding. *For Christ's Sake.* Wallington: Religious Education Press, Ltd., 1963, p. 9.

166 1 Robinson, John A. T. "Our Image of Christ Must Change." *Christian Century,* March 21, 1973, p. 342; see also, Robinson. *The Human Face of God.* London: S.C.M. Press, 1973.

1 Hick, John, ed. *The Myth of God Incarnate.* London: S.C.M. Press, Ltd., 1977. Where contemporary churchmen publicly abandon or explain away traditional Christian beliefs that had been given up by Enlightenment thinkers two hundred years earlier.

1 Green, Michael, ed. *The Truth of God Incarnate.* Grand Rapids: Wm. B. Eerdmans Co., 1978. The inevitable orthodox answer.

8 Vahanian, Gabriel, op. cit., chap. 4, p. 60.

Page	Line	
166	10	Cox, Harvey. *The Secular City*. New York: The Macmillan Co., 1965.
	10	Callahan, Daniel, ed. *The Secular City Debate*. New York: The Macmillan Company, 1966.
	17	Cox, Harvey. "*The Secular City*—Ten Years Later." *Christian Century*, May 28, 1975, p. 544.
	25	Piepkorn, Arthur Carl. *Profiles in Belief*: The Religious Bodies of the United States and Canada. New York: Harper & Row, 1977, vol. I, pp. 192 ff.
	25	Miller, John H., ed. *Vatican II: An Interfaith Appraisal*. Notre Dame, Ind.: University of Notre Dame Press, 1966, pp. 3 ff.
	25	Regan, Richard J. *Conflict and Conscience*, Religious Freedom and the Second Vatican Council. New York: The Macmillan Co., 1967.
	27	Schlink, Edmund. *After the Council*, The Meaning of Vatican II for Protestantism and the Ecumenical Dialogue. Trans. by Herbert J. A. Bouman. Philadelphia: Fortress Press, 1968.
	27	McKenzie, John L. *The Roman Catholic Church*. New York: Holt Rinehart & Winston, 1969, pp. 123, 270.
	27	See Hardon, John A. *The Catholic Catechism*: a contemporary catechism of the teachings of the Catholic Church. New York: Doubleday & Co., Inc., 1975.
	27	*New York Times*, June 25, 28, 30; July 1, 4, 1977.
	31	Blau, Joseph. *Judaism in America*. Chicago: University of Chicago Press, 1976, pp. 57 ff. and p. 136.
	31	Borowitz, Eugene B. "Judaism in America Today." *Christian Century*, Nov. 8, 1978, p. 1066.
	34	Wine, Sherman T. "A Humanistic Rabbi's Viewpoint." *Humanistic Judaism*, vol. I. no. 1, June 1967, pp. 3, 7.
167	2	Margulis, Lynn. "Why I am Not a Humanistic Jew." *Humanistic Judaism*, Winter 1968, pp. 23, 24.

CONCLUSION

Page	Line	
169	9	Fowells, H. A., ed. *Silvics of Forest Trees of the United States*. Agricultural Handbook No. 271, Washington, D.C.: U.S. Department of Agriculture, Forest Service, 1965, p. 702.
170	33	Goodman, Saul L., ed. *The Faith of Secular Jews*. New York: KTAV Publishing House, 1976, p. xiii.
171	6	Channing, William Ellery. Quoted in John White Chadwick, *William Ellery Channing*. Boston: Houghton Mifflin Co., 1903, p. 339.
	9	*New York Times*, June 30, 1977.

PART III

THE ECCLESIASTICAL WAY AND HUMAN FALLIBILITY

CHAPTER 12

BELIEF AND FAITH

Page	Line	
174	12	*Quanta Cura*. Quoted in Ann Fremantle, *The Papal Encyclicals*. New York: New American Library, 1956, p. 135.
	31	Novak, Michael. "The Kung Case." *Christian Century*, March 26, 1975, p. 300.

Page	Line	
174	31	Kung, Hans. *Infallible? An Inquiry.* Trans. by Edward Quinn. Garden City, N.Y.: Doubleday, 1971.
		———. *The Church.* Trans. by Ray and Rosaleen Ockenden. New York: Sheed & Ward, 1967.
	31	Rynne, Xavier. "The Rebel and the Pope." *New York Times* Magazine, Oct. 12, 1975, p. 13; see also, Davis, Charles. *Temptations of Religion.* New York: Harper & Row, 1974.

1. Creeds

175	26	Deuteronomy 6:4.
	30	Arberry, Arthur J. *The Koran Interpreted.* London: Oxford University Press, 1964, p. ix.
176	36	Watt, W. Montgomery. *Companion to the Qur'an.* London: George Allen-Unwin, 1967, p. ix.
177	43	"United Church of Christ, Statement of Faith." *Christian Century,* July 22, 1959, p. 846.
179	28	Ames, E. S. In *Contemporary American Theology,* ed. by Vergilius Ferm, vol. II, p. 13.
180	9	Lovell, Maine, United Church of Christ, *Bulletin,* Nov. 16, 1975.
	13	Tennyson, Alfred Lord. *In Memoriam.* Part XCVI, Stanza 3.

2. Revising and Interpreting Religious Belief

180	35	Miller, Randolph C. *This We Can Believe.* New York: Hawthorn Books, 1976.
181	8	Balfour, A. J. *Foundations of Belief.* New York: Longmans Green & Co., 1895.
	9	Clarke, William Newton. *Can I Believe in God the Father.* New York: Charles Scribner's Sons, 1899.
	10	Ladd, George T. *What Should I Believe?* New York: Longmans Green & Co., 1915.
	11	Gore, Charles. *Can We Then Believe?* New York: Scribner's Sons, 1926.
	12	Whale, J. S. *The Right to Believe.* New York: Charles Scribner's Sons, 1938.
	13	Ferm, Vergilius. *What Can We Believe?* New York: Philosophical Library, 1948.
	14	Kennedy, Gerald. *I Believe.* Nashville: Abingdon Press, 1958.
	15	Pittenger, Norman. *The Pathway to Believing.* Indianapolis: Bobbs-Merrill & Co., 1961.
	16	Paul, Leslie. *Alternatives to Christian Belief.* Garden City: Doubleday & Co., 1967.
	17	Thielicke, Helmut. *How to Believe Again.* Trans. by H. George Anderson. Philadelphia: Fortress Press, 1972.
	18	Purtill, Richard L. *Reason to Believe.* Grand Rapids: William B. Eerdmans Publishing Company, 1974.
	19	Miller, R. C., op. cit.
	20	Suggs, James C., ed. *This We Believe.* St. Louis: The Bethany Press, 1977.
	24	Ladd, George Eldon. *I Believe in the Resurrection of Jesus.* Grand Rapids: William B. Eerdmans Publishing Co., 1976.
	39	Freud, Sigmund. *Future of an Illusion.* Ed. by James Strachey. Garden City: Doubleday and Co., 1964, p. 51.
	43	FAF, pp. 137–147.

Page Line

182 12 Galston, Arthur W. "Talking to Your Plants: A Yale Botanist Talks Back." *Yale Alumni Magazine,* Dec. 1975, p. 27.

19 McKusick, Marshall. "Canaanites in America: A New Scripture in Stone?" *Biblical Archeologist,* Summer 1979, vol. 42, no. 3, p. 137.

27 Marty, Martin E. *New Shape of American Religion.* New York: Harper and Bros., 1958.

———. *The Infidel.* Cleveland: World Publishing Co., 1961.

———. *Varieties of Unbelief.* New York: Holt, Rinehart & Winston, 1964.

33 Szczesny, Gerhard. *The Future of Unbelief.* Trans. by E. B. Garside, New York: Braziller, 1961.

34 Novak, Michael. *Belief and Unbelief.* New York: The Macmillan Company, 1965.

34 Dewart, Leslie. *The Future of Belief.* New York: Herder and Herder, 1966.

36 Baum, Gregory. *The Future of Belief Debate.* New York: Herder and Herder, 1968.

36 FAF, chap. 1.

183 13 Irion, Mary Jean. "Wrenching Free of the Patriarchal Past." Review of Mary Daly, *Beyond God the Father. Christian Century,* Jan. 16, 1974, p. 46.

183 8 Stephen, Leslie. *Some Early Impressions.* London: n.p., 1924, p. 70.

31 Marty, Martin. *The Infidel,* pp. 11 ff., gives the unbeliever his due as a believer.

3. HERESY

183 36 Hayakawa, S. I. *Modern Guide to Synonyms.* New York: Funk and Wagnalls Co., 1968, p. 270.

43 Herrick, S. E. *Some Heretics of Yesterday.* Boston: Houghton Mifflin & Co., 1884.

184 2 Chesterton, Gilbert K. *Heretics.* London and New York: John Lane Co., 1905, p. 12.

7 Jones, Rufus M. *The Church's Debt to Heretics.* New York: George H. Doran Co., 1924, p. 11.

9 Kaufmann, Walter. *The Faith of a Heretic.* Garden City: Doubleday & Co., 1961, p. 101.

19 Shriver, George H., ed. *American Religious Heretics.* Nashville: Abingdon Press, 1966, Introduction.

22 Hillerbrand, Hans J. *A Fellowship of Discontent.* New York: Harper & Row, 1967.

24 Matthews, Shailer. "Theology as Group Belief." In *Contemporary American Theology,* Vergilius Ferm, ed., Second Series, p. 172.

———. "Unrepentant Liberalism." *American Scholar,* Summer, 1938, p. 297.

25 Bauer, Walter; Kraft, Robert A.; and Krodel, Gerhard, eds. *Orthodoxy and Heresy in Earliest Christianity.* Philadelphia: Fortress Press, 1971, pp. xi ff.

36 Bettenson, Henry, op. cit., p. 36.

42 Thompson, J. W. and Johnson, E. N., op. cit., p. 620.

185 8 Morris, Rudolph E. *Fathers of the Church.* New York: Fathers of the Church, Inc., 1949, vol. VII.

32 Bettenson, Henry, op. cit., p. 117.

43 Dunham, Barrows. *Heroes and Heretics,* pp. 18 ff.

186 33 Nock, Arthur Darby. *Conversion,* p. 3.

Page Line

187 40 Hutchinson, William R. "How Radical is the New Religious Radicalism?" Second Annual Distinguished Faculty Lecture, American University, Washington, D.C.: 1968, pp. 20 ff.

43 Christie-Murray, David. *A History of Heresy*. London: New England Library, 1976, p. 226. He declares: "The greatest heresy may be the existence of any dogma at all."

4. FAITH

188 18 Tennant, F. R. *Nature of Belief*. London: Centenary Press, 1943, p. 102.

22 Santayana, George. *Poems*. London: Constable & Co. Ltd., 1922, p. 5.

24 Pusey, Nathan M. "Spiritual Odyssey." *Christian Century*, July 24, 1957, p. 889.

27 Locke, John. *Essay Concerning Human Understanding*. London: H. Woodfall, 1768, 16th ed., vol. II, bk. IV, chap. xviii, sec. 2, p. 309.

30 Hebrews 11:1.

32 Whale, J. S. op. cit., p. 109.

44 Robinson, John A. T. *Can We Trust the New Testament?* Grand Rapids: Wm. B. Eerdmans Pub. Co., 1977, pp. 133, 134.

190 7 Leviticus 1:1, 27:34.

11 Revelation 1:1.

15 Arberry, A. J., op. cit., pp. 179, 239.

38 Newman, John Henry. *Apologia Pro Vita Sua*. New York: Catholic Publishing House, 1864, p. 264.

191 3 "Incarnation": The doctrine that the divine and the human were united in the person of Jesus Christ.

4 Tertullian, "Credo quia ineptum," I am indebted to Roland Bainton for the exact wording of this quotation.

6 Tertullian. Quoted in Sigmund Freud. *Future of an Illusion*. New York: Doubleday & Co., Anchor Books, 1964; first published Vienna, 1927, p. 43.

7 Augustine. Quoted in J. W. Thompson and E. N. Johnson, op. cit., p. 696.

14 Anselm. Quoted in Ibid., p. 696.

14 Anselm. Quoted in John Morton. *Man, Science and God*. London: Collins, 1972, p. 234.

34 Isbell, Charles D. "The Story of the Aramaic Magical Incantation Bowls." *Biblical Archeologist*, Mar. 1978, p. 5.

192 32 Rubenstein, Richard. *The Cunning of History: Mass Death and the American Future*. New York: Harper & Row, 1976.

193 9 Moltmann, Jurgen. *The Crucified God*. New York: Harper & Row, 1975.

CHAPTER 13

REVELATION

194 24 Paine, Thomas. *Age of Reason*. Alburey Castle, ed. New York: Bobbs-Merrill Co., 1948, p. 5.

Ibid., p. 1.

1. THE EXISTENCE OF GOD

196 2 *Christian Century*, May 22, 1974, p. 559.

Page	*Line*	
196	2	*Washington Post,* Dec. 27, 1967.
	8	Bevan, Edwin. *Symbolism and Belief.* London: Allen & Unwin, 1938, p. 254.
	9	Powys, John Cowper. *Religion of a Sceptic.* New York: Dodd Mead & Co., 1925.
	14	Dubos, René. *A God Within.* New York: Charles Scribner's Sons, 1972, pp. 3–4.
	18	Miller, Randolph Crump. *The American Spirit in Theology.* Boston: Pilgrim Press, 1975.
	23	I Kings 19:13.
	38	Martineau, James. "Ideal Substitutes for God." Pamphlet No. 65, Boston: American Unitarian Ass'n., 1935, p. 20.
197	3	Feuer, Lewis Samuel. *Spinoza and the Rise of Liberalism.* Boston: Beacon Press, 1958, pp. 247–50.
	3	Ibid., p. 1.
	3	Spinoza, Benedict de. *Ethics.* Trans. by A. Boyle. London: J. M. Dent & Sons, Ltd., 1910.
	38	Scorer, Richard. *Clouds of the World.* Harrisburg, Pa.: Stackpole Books, 1972, p. 7.
	40	Jones, Rufus M. *Studies in Mystical Religion.* London: Macmillan Co., Ltd., 1923, pp. 219 ff.
	40	Ayer, A. J. *The Central Questions of Philosophy.* London: Weidenfeld-Nicholson, 1973, pp. 211 ff. Ayer says those who believe by faith, when pressed for detail and precision in their beliefs, take refuge in the ineffability of God.
198	14	FAF, pp. 155 ff. on the Authority of Self-Assertion.
	26	Haydon, A. Eustace. *Biography of the Gods.* New York: The Macmillan Co., 1941, pp. vii, 314 ff.
	36	Freud, Sigmund. *Future of an Illusion.* Garden City: Anchor Books, Doubleday & Co., Inc., 1964, pp. 24 ff.
199	5	Morris, Desmond. *The Naked Ape.* New York: McGraw Hill Book Co., 1967, p. 179.
	14	Pope, Marvin H. *El in the Ugaritic Texts.* Leiden: E.J. Brill, 1955.
	18	Daly, Mary. *Beyond God the Father.* Boston: Beacon Press, 1973.
	26	Washbourne, Penelope. "Authority as Idolatry: Feminine Theology and the Church." *Christian Century,* Oct. 29, 1975, p. 963.
	33	Xenophanes. In G. S. Kirk and J. E. Raven, *The Presocratic Philosophers,* pp. 168–9.
	43	Feuerbach, Ludwig. *The Essence of Christianity.* New York: Harper & Bros., 1957, p. 270.
200	23	Whitehead, Alfred North. *Science and the Modern World,* p. 250.

2. Mysticism

201	3	Gilkey, Langdon. "Biblical Symbols in a Scientific Culture." In Ralph W. Burhoe, ed., *Science and Human Values in the Twenty-first Century.* Philadelphia: Westminster Press, c. 1971, p. 97.
	5	Hick, John. *Faith and Knowledge.* Ithaca: Cornell University Press, 1957, pp. 128–9.
	14	Brown, Alice. In Caroline Miles Hill, ed., *World's Great Religious Poetry.* New York: The Macmillan Co., 1923, p. 220.
	41	Isaiah 6:1–8; see also, Ezekiel 1:4–6, 8, 10.
	44	Swain, Joseph W. *The Ancient World.* New York: Harper & Bros., 1950, vol. I, p. 182.

Page	*Line*	
201	44	Wright, G. Ernest. *Biblical Archeology.* Philadelphia: The Westminster Press, 1957, p. 137.
202	5	Muller, Max, ed. *Sacred Books of the East.* Oxford: Oxford University Press, 1879–1910, vol. 11, pp. 152–3.
	36	Pahnke, Walter N. "Drugs and Mysticism." Harvard Ph.D. Thesis, 1963, pp. 3, 5, 87 ff., 131 ff.
	36	Pahnke, Walter and Richards, William. "Implications of LSD and Experimental Mysticism." *Journal of Religion and Health,* vol. V, no. 3, Sept. 1966, pp. 191 ff.
203	12	Wallace, Robert K. and Benson, Robert T. "The Physiology of Meditation." *Scientific American,* Feb. 1972, p. 85.
	18	Pascal, Blaise. *Pensées.* Trans. by W. F. Trotter. New York: The Modern Library, 1941, chap. iv, no. 277, p. 95.
	33	Cox, Harvey. *The Feast of Fools.* Cambridge: Harvard University Press, 1969, p. 10; see also: ———. *The Seduction of the Spirit.* New York: Simon and Schuster, 1973.
204	6	Raschke, Carl. "The Fantasies of the New Theologians." *Christian Century,* March 15, 1974, pp. 535, 536.

3. What Revelation Means

204	36	Gittelsohn, Roland B. "Mature Religion and Mature Science." In Edwin P. Booth, ed., *Religion Ponders Science.* New York: Appleton Century, 1964, p. 57.
	44	See Pannenberg, Wolfhart, ed. *Revelation as History.* New York: The Macmillan Co., 1968.
205	4	Niebuhr, H. Richard. *The Meaning of Revelation.* New York: The Macmillan Co. 1941, p. 16, 30, 82, 93, 97, 101, 111.
	16	See also Miller, Randolph Crump. "Empiricism and Process Theology: God Is What God Does." *Christian Century,* March 24, 1976, p. 286.
	23	*The Common Catechism: A Book of Christian Faith.* Ed. by Johannes Feiner and Lukas Vischer. New York: Seabury Press, 1975.
	27	Messer, Donald E. in *Together,* quoted in *Context,* April 15, 1973, p. 1.
206	14	Aquinas, Thomas. Quoted in Thompson, J. W. and Johnson, E. N., op. cit., p. 712.
	22	See FAF, chap. v, §5, "The Authority of Self Assertion."
207	2	bin Baz, Sheik Abdel Aziz. Quoted in Theodosius Dobzhansky. "Evolution: Implications for Religion." *Christian Century,* July 7, 1967, p. 936.
	18	Wall, James M. "Eyes to See, Ears to Hear." *Christian Century,* Sept. 3–10, 1975, p. 750. Wall writes, "There is something terribly snobbish about the Christian faith although we don't like to admit it."

4. The Final Contradiction

208	2	Lippmann, Walter. *A Preface to Morals.* New York: The Macmillan Co., 1929, pp. 51, 326.
	32	Isaiah 24, 25; 6:9, 11.

Page	*Line*	
209	40	Cohen, Arthur. *The Natural and Supernatural Jew.* New York: Pantheon Books, 1962, pp. 243, 244, summarizing the thought of Abraham Joshua Heschel in *Man is Not Alone.*
210	2	Anderson, Bernard W. *The Unfolding Drama of the Bible.* New York: The Association Press, 1971, p. 10.
	2	Fackenheim, Emil L. *Encounters Between Judaism and Modern Philosophy.* New York: Basic Books, Inc., 1973.
	13	II Cor. 4:7.
	16	Gustafson, James M. *Treasure in Earthen Vessels.* New York: Harper Bros., 1961, p. ix; see also:
	16	Pike, James A. *A Time for Christian Candor.* New York: Harper & Row, 1964, the theme of which is "treasure in earthen vessels."
	32	Miller, Donald. "Returning to the Fold. Disbelief Within the Community of Faith." *Christian Century,* September 21, 1977, p. 811.

PART IV

THE CRITICAL WAY

CHAPTER 14

DESPAIR, HOPE, AND RESOLVE

1. The Ebb Tide of Faith

216	14	Arnold, Matthew. "Dover Beach." In W. H. Auden and Norman Holmes Pearson, eds. *Victorian and Edwardian Poets.* New York: The Viking Press, 1950, p. 210.
	25	Carlyle, Thomas. *Sartor Resartus.* 2nd ed. London: James Frazer, 1841, p. 193.
217	14	Sontag, Susan. "Culture as Elitist." *Salmagundi,* Fall–Winter, 1975–76, Skidmore College, reprinted in *New York Times,* Feb. 2, 1976.
	21	Spengler, Oswald. *The Decline of the West* (1918–1922). Trans. by C. F. Atkinson; republished New York: Alfred A. Knopf, 1970, is perhaps the best known exponent of the parallel between ancient Rome and the modern West.
218	20	Murray, Gilbert. *Five Stages of Greek Religion.* Boston: Beacon Press, 1951, p. 123.
	41	Russell, Bertrand. *Why I Am Not a Christian.* New York: Simon & Schuster, 1964, p. 115.
	44	*New York Times,* Nov. 2, 1975.
219	7	Gamow, George. "The Principle of Uncertainty." *Scientific American,* June 1958, p. 51.
	9	Hawking, Stephen. "The Quantum Mechanics of Black Holes." *Scientific American,* Jan. 1977, p. 40.
	27	Ibid., p. 40.
	27	Hook, Sidney, ed. *Determinism and Freedom in the Age of Modern Science.* London: Collier-Macmillan Ltd., 1961, p. 64. Percy Bridgman also faults Einstein for proclaiming that God does not throw dice.
	31	Bronowski, J. *The Ascent of Man.* pp. 364 ff.
	31	Morrison, Philip. "The Overthrow of Parity." *Scientific American,* April 1957, p. 45.

Page	*Line*	
219	31	Alfven, Hannes. *Antimatter in Cosmology.* Trans. by Rudy Feitner. Stockholm: The Royal Institute of Technology, 1966.
	31	Blatt, John M. "Time Reversal." *Scientific American,* Aug. 1956, p. 107.
	31	*New York Times,* Jan. 27, 1972.
	31	Layzer, David. "The Arrow of Time." *Scientific American,* Dec. 1975, p. 56.
	36	Barbour, Ian G. "Response to Strom: An Analysis." *Christian Century,* March 29, 1961, p. 383.

2. Tearing Down and Building Up

220	41	Genesis 2:4 ff.
221	2	Chamberlin, Roy B., and Feldman, Herman, eds. *The Dartmouth Bible.* Boston: Houghton Mifflin Co., 1961, p. 69.
	25	Vincent of Lerins: see chap 12, §3.
	27	Dunham, Barrows, op. cit., p. 168.
	35	Feuer, Lewis Samuel, op. cit., p. 1.
222	2	Pius IX, *Quanta Cura,* Dec. 8, 1864, quoted in Barrows Dunham, op. cit., p. 168.
	6	Gay, Peter, op. cit., p. 409.
	9	Drane, James F. "Prejudice Beneath a Rational Veneer." *The Review of Books on Religion,* vol. V, no. 2, p. 1, in a review of Brand Blanshard. *Reason and Belief.* New Haven: Yale University Press, 1975.
	17	Newman, John Henry. *The Idea of a University,* pp. 377, 390, 396.
	42	Jones, Rufus M. *Studies in Mystical Religion.* London: MacMillan & Co., Ltd., 1923, pp. 132, 150 ff.
223	22	Rader, Dotson. *I Ain't Marchin' Anymore.* New York: Paperback Library, 1969, pp. 37, 48, 153 ff.
	32	Amos 6:1; 2:6–7.
224	9	Matthew 5:7.
	38	Kierkegaard, Søren. *Purity of Heart Is to Will One Thing.* Translated by Douglas V. Steere. New York: Harper and Bros., 1938, pp. 31, 38.
225	6	Augustine, Saint. *Confessions.* Translated by E. B. Pusey. London: J. M. Dent & Sons, Ltd., 1907, Book I, §6.
	25	Hechinger, Fred M. "A Liberal Fights Back." *New York Times,* Feb. 13, 1972.
	35	Ranck, James G. "Religious Conservatism-Liberalism and Mental Health." *Pastoral Psychology,* March 1961, p. 34.
227	6	Skinner, B. F. *Beyond Freedom and Dignity.* New York: Alfred A. Knopf, 1972, p. 215.

CHAPTER 15

THE UNIVERSITY

228	21	Thompson, J. W. and Johnson, E. N. *Medieval Europe.* New York: W. W. Norton and Co., Inc., 1937, pp. 607, 687.
	21	Haskins, Charles H. *The Medieval Renaissance.* Cleveland: Meridian Books, World Publishing Co., 1957, p. vi.

1. The University Tradition

230	14	*General Education in a Free Society.* Report of Harvard University Committee. Cambridge: Harvard University, 1945, p. 7.

Page Line

230 14 Rudolph, Frederick. *The American College and University, a History.* New York: Alfred A. Knopf, 1962, pp. 264 ff., 329 ff., 417 ff.

14 Flexner, Abraham. *Universities.* London: Oxford University Press, 1930, pp. 188 ff.

14 Sontag, Frederick and Roth, John. *The American Religious Experience.* New York: Harper & Row, 1972, p. 99.

231 20 Newman, Cardinal John Henry. *The Idea of a University.* London: Longmans Green & Co., 1921, p. 403.

44 Marty, Martin. *The Modern Schism: Three Paths to the Secular.* London: SCM Press, 1969, p. 140.

232 23 Trotter, Thomas. "The Seminaries: Survival and Revival." *Christian Century,* Feb. 5–12, 1975, pp. 102–3.

30 Neuhaus, Richard J. "Freedom for Ministry." *Christian Century,* Feb. 2–9, 1977, p. 86.

44 Wright, G. Ernest. "Truth, Freedom or Slavery." *Harvard Divinity School Bulletin,* Jan. 1962, pp. 11–14.

233 12 Trotter, Thomas, op. cit.

30 Te Selle, Sallie McFague. "Between Athens and Jerusalem: the Seminary in Tension." *Christian Century,* Feb. 4–11, 1976, p. 89.

35 "Sharp Increase in Objective Study of Religion on College Campuses." *Time* Magazine, Feb. 4, 1966, p. 72.

234 20 "The Meanings of Death." *Yale Alumni Magazine.* April, 1975, pp. 12, 13.

29 Averill, Lloyd J. "Can Evangelism Survive in the Context of Free Inquiry?" *Christian Century,* October 22, 1975, p. 924.

33 Osborn, Robert T. "Jesus and Liberation Theology." *Christian Century,* March 10, 1976, p. 225.

37 "Readers Response." *Christian Century,* Nov. 19, 1975, pp. 1057 ff.

235 4 Pelikan, Jaroslav. "Tradition, Reformation and Development." *Christian Century,* Jan. 6, 1965, p. 8.

19 Marty, Martin. "American Protestant Theology Today." *Thought,* vol. XLI, no. 161, June 1966, p. 165.

———. "The Roots of Religious Revolution." *University of Chicago Magazine,* vol. LIX, no. 7, April 1967, p. 5.

———. "Religion as a Damn Interesting Subject." *Christian Century,* Oct. 22, 1975, p. 921.

———. "Capillary Action Between Religion's Two Cultures." *Christian Century,* Oct. 16, 1974, p. 950.

26 Lindbeck, George et al., eds. *University Divinity Schools*: a report on ecclesiastically independent theological education. New York: Rockefeller Foundation, 1976, p. 6, asserts that university theological schools must have freedom of thought; no dogmatic interference, no credal tests for faculty or students, and full freedom to sponsor theological education in as many traditions as they wish.

26 Bowden, Henry Warner. *Church History in the Age of Science*: Historiographical Patterns in the United States 1876–1918. Chapel Hill: University of North Carolina Press, 1971, deals with the same issue: should church history be written doctrinally or as part of general history?

2. Charles Sanders Peirce

236 3 Murphy, Murray G. *The Development of Peirce's Philosophy.* Cambridge: Harvard University Press, 1969, pp. 9 ff., 20 ff., 97 ff.

3 Davis, Wm. H. *Peirce's Epistemology.* The Hague: Martinus Nijhoff, 1972.

Page	Line	
236	6	*New York Times,* October 12, 1976.
	33	Sontag, Frederick and Roth, John, op. cit., pp. 103 ff.
	41	See Hartshorn, Charles and Weiss, Paul, eds. *Collected Papers of Charles S. Peirce.* Cambridge: Harvard University Press, 1931–1935, vol. V, ch. 6, pp. 15, 258, 281.
237	21	Peirce, Charles S. *Chance, Love and Logic.* Ed. with an introduction by Morris R. Cohen. New York: George Braziller, Inc., 1956, p. 1.
		Ibid., p. 308.
	21	Peirce, Charles S. *Chance, Love and Logic.* Edited by Morris R. Cohen. New York: George Braziller, Inc., 1956, p. 1.
	37	Mills, C. Wright. *Sociology and Pragmatism.* New York: Paine-Whitman Publishers, 1964.
	43	Gardner, Martin. "On Charles Sanders Peirce: Philosopher and Gamesman." *Scientific American,* July 1978, p. 18.

3. CAMBRIDGE UNIVERSITY

238	24	Flexner, Abraham. *Universities,* op. cit., pp. 265–302.
239	25	Stephen, Leslie. *English Thought in the Eighteenth Century.* 3rd ed. London: Smith Elder & Co., 1902, vol. I, p. 4.
		———. *Sketches from Cambridge* by "A Don." London: The Macmillan Co., 1865.
		———. *Some Early Impressions.* London: Leonard and Virginia Woolf, 1924.
239	39	Homberger, Eric, ed. *The Cambridge Mind.* London: Jonathan Cape, 1970, pp. 13 ff.
240	1	Price, Lucien. *Dialogues of Alfred North Whitehead.* New York: New American Library, 1956, pp. 11, 25, 42, 45, 193, 284.
240	3	Whitehead, Alfred North. *Science and the Modern World.* p. ix.
	9	———. *Aims of Education.* New York: The Macmillan Co., 1929, p. 147.
	16	Price, Lucien. *Dialogues.* p. 284.
	26	Russell, Bertrand. *Autobiography, 1872–1914.* Boston: Little, Brown & Co., 1975, p. 100.
	37	Ibid., p. 91.
241	6	Forster, E. M. *What I Believe.* Hogarth Sixpenny Pamphlets, No. 1, London: Hogarth Press, 1939, reprinted verbatim in *Two Cheers for Democracy.* New York: Harcourt Brace, 1951, p. 68.
	9	Crews, Frederick C. *E. M. Forster: The Perils of Humanism.* Princeton: Princeton University Press, 1962, pp. 3–10.
241	39	Dobie, J. Frank. "A Texan Teaches American History at Cambridge University." *National Geographic Magazine,* April 1946, p. 441.
	39	Bronowski, J. *A Sense of the Future*: Essays in Natural Philosophy. Cambridge, Mass.: The M.I.T. Press, 1977, p. 76. Bronowski says the standard of high liberal conscience set at Cambridge in the teens or twenties gave way, in the thirties, to a search for certainties with which to counter worldwide disasters like the crash of 1929 and the rise of fascism.
	39	Barswell, Noel. *Cambridge.* London: Blackie & Son, Ltd., pp. 36 ff.

CHAPTER 16

FUNDAMENTALS

1. THE SELF

244	20	Berrill, N. J. *Man's Emerging Mind.* Greenwich, Conn.: Fawcett Publications, Inc., 1955, p. 11.

Page *Line*

244 23 Jones, William R. "Theism and Religious Humanism: The Chasm Narrows." *Christian Century,* May 21, 1975, p. 520.

245 25 Whitman, Walt. *Leaves of Grass.* New York: Heritage Press, n.d., p. 349.

247 12 Shaw, George Bernard. *Prefaces.* London: Constable & Co., Ltd., 1934.

2. Getting Outside of Ourselves

248 34 *Daedalus,* Winter 1958, p. 6.

39 Bridgman, Percy W. "Quo Vadis." *Daedalus,* Winter 1958, p. 88.

249 21 Ibid., p. 89.

21 Ibid., p. 91.

34 Ibid., p. 90.

249 43 Bridgman, Percy W. "Determinism in Modern Science." In *Determinism and Freedom in the Age of Modern Science,* Sidney Hook, ed. London: Collier-MacMillan Ltd., 1961, pp. 71–75.

3. Science

250 30 Whitehead, Alfred North. *Science and the Modern World,* p. 3.

251 5 Conant, James Bryant. *On Understanding Science.* New York: New American Library, 1951, p. 37.

32 Butterfield, Herbert. *The Origins of Modern Science.* New York: The MacMillan Company, 1951, pp. 20 ff.

42 Copernicus, Nicolaus. *De Revolutionibus Orbium Coelestium,* I, 1, chap. x. Quoted in Alexandre Koyré. *From the Closed World to the Infinite Universe.* New York: Harper & Brothers, 1958, p. 33.

252 22 Calder, Nigel. *The Restless Earth.* New York: The Viking Press, 1972, pp. 42 ff.

31 Toksoz, M. Nafi. "The Subduction of the Lithosphere." *Scientific American,* Nov. 1975, p. 98.

31 Sullivan, Walter. *Continents in Motion*: the New Earth Debate. New York: McGraw-Hill Book Co., 1974.

31 *New York Times,* Dec. 18, 1975.

42 Ducasse, C. J. "The Guide of Life." *The Key Reporter,* Jan. 1958, p. 2.

253 14 Marshack, Alexander. *The Roots of Civilization.* New York: McGraw Hill Book Co., 1972, p. 9 ff.

Merton, Robert K. *The Sociology of Science.* Ed. by Norman W. Storer. Chicago: University of Chicago Press, 1973.

27 Conant, James Bryant, op. cit., p. 109.

27 Hixson, Joseph. *The Patchwork Mouse.* New York: Anchor Press, Doubleday, 1976, deals with growing deception in scientific circles relating to grants.

254 12 Baumer, Franklin L., op. cit., chap. 2.

13 Murray Gilbert. *Stoic, Christian, and Humanist.* Boston: Beacon Press, 1950, chap. 4.

13 Coates, W. H. et al. *Ordeal of Liberal Humanism.* New York: McGraw Hill, 1970, pp. 135, 139.

13 Andreski, Stanislav. *The Essential Comte.* Selected from *Cours de Philosophie Positive,* trans. by Margaret Clarke. London: Croom Helm, 1974, Introduction.

14 Peel, J. D. Y. *The Evolution of a Sociologist.* New York: Basic Books, 1971.

33 "The Bristlecone Correction." *Scientific American,* July 1970, p. 52.

39 White, Andrew D. *Warfare of Science with Theology in Christendom.* 2 vols. New York: D. Appleton & Co., 1896.

Page	*Line*	
255	12	Townes, Charles H. "The Convergence of Science and Religion." *The Technology Review,* May 1966, p. 41.
	32	Walter, W. Grey. "The Electrical Activity of the Brain." *Scientific American,* June 1954, p. 54.
	41	Feigenbaum, Edward A. and Feldman, Julian, eds. *Computers and Thought.* New York: McGraw-Hill Book Co., Inc., 1963.
257	7	Oppenheimer, J. R. *The Open Mind.* New York: Simon & Schuster, 1955, p. 93.
	8	Conant, James Bryant, op. cit., p. 117.

4. Knowledge

257	30	Saslaw, William C. and Jacobs, Kenneth C., eds. *The Emerging Universe.* Charlottesville: University Press of Virginia, 1972, p. 149.
	30	Davies, Paul. *The Runaway Universe.* New York: Harper & Row, 1978.
	30	Brown, Hanbury. *Man and the Stars.* New York: Oxford University Press, 1978.
	30	See Pierre Teilhard de Chardin, *The Phenomenon of Man.* Trans. by Bernard Wall. New York: Harper and Row, 1959, and other works by the same author: attempt of a French Catholic priest to transform the theory of evolution into a great philosophico-theological system.
258	2	Cloud, Preston. *A Short History of the Universe.* New Haven: Yale University Press, 1978.
	34	Schmandt-Besserat, Denise. "The Earliest Precursor of Writing." *Scientific American,* June, 1978, p. 50.
259	2	Breasted, James H. *The Dawn of Conscience.* New York: Charles Scribner's Sons, 1939, p. 409.
	10	Leakey, Richard E. and Lewin, Roger. *Origins.* New York: E. P. Dutton, 1977.
260	2	Fadiman, Clifton, ed. *I Believe.* New York: Simon & Schuster, 1931; 2nd ed., 1939.
	2	Murrow, Edward R. *This I Believe.* New York: Simon & Schuster, 1952, p. ix.
	14	Overstreet, Bonaro. In Edward R. Murrow, op. cit., p. 129.
261	15	Kirk, G. S., and Raven, T. E. *The Presocratic Philosophers.* pp. 199, 213, 214.
	31	Tagore, Rabindranath. *Collected Poems and Plays.* New York: The Macmillan Co., 1964, p. 26.
262	6	Dubos, René, op. cit., p. 15.
	8	Hoyle, Fred, and Narlikar, J. V. *Action at a Distance in Physics and Cosmology.* San Francisco: W. H. Freeman & Co., 1974.

CHAPTER 17

THE TRIBUNAL OF TRUTH

1. The Council of Humanity

264	22	Lattimore, Richmond. *The Iliad of Homer.* Chicago: University of Chicago Press, 1951, bk. I, pp. 59 ff.
265	3	McIlwain, C. H. *The Growth of Political Thought in the West.* New York: The Macmillan Company, 1932, pp. 3, 76.
	17	DuPont-Sommer, A. *The Jewish Sect of Qumran and the Essenes.* New York: Macmillan Company, 1955, p. 79.
	40	Acts 15:1–33.
267	23	Krutch, Joseph Wood. "In These Days Our Literature in All Its Might Came of Age." *New York Times Book Review,* Oct. 7, 1956.

Page	*Line*	
268	35	Pennock, J. Roland and Chapman, John W., eds. *Voluntary Associations.* New York: Atherton Press, 1969.
269	13	Adams, James Luther. *On Being Human—Religiously.* Boston: Beacon Press, 1976, p. 57.
	20	Robertson, D. B. *Voluntary Associations: A Study of Groups in Free Societies,* Essays in Honor of James Luther Adams. Richmond: John Knox Press, 1966.
	43	Koch, Adrienne and Peden, Williams, eds. *Life and Selected Writings of Thomas Jefferson.* New York: Modern Library Random House, 1944, p. 676.
270	25	Holmes, Oliver Wendell. *The Common Law.* Boston: Little, Brown & Co., 1943, p. 1.
271	5	Pound, Roscoe. *The Spirit of the Common Law.* Boston: Beacon Press, 1963, pp. 3, 61, 194.

2. The Goal of Truth

271	27	Einstein, Albert. In Philip Frank, *Relativity, a Richer Truth.* Boston: Beacon Press, 1950, Foreword, pp. v, vii.
	28	Whitehead, Alfred North. *Adventures of Ideas,* p. 309.
	39	Lukacs, John. *The Passing of the Modern Age.* New York: Harper & Row, 1972, p. 166.
	42	Orwell, George. *1984.* New York: New American Library, 1950.
272	27	Milton, John. Quoted in J. B. Bury, *History of Freedom of Thought,* p. 99.
	40	Mill, John Stuart. *On Liberty.* London: J. M. Dent & Sons, 1910, p. 79.
273	2	Channing, William Ellery. "On the Slavery Question." Boston: American Unitarian Association, 1875.
	6	Bronowski, J. and Mazlish, Bruce. *The Western Intellectual Tradition.* New York: Harper & Brothers, 1960, p. 501.
	13	Bury, J. B., op. cit., p. 239.
	26	See Chap. III, §3, p. 108a.
274	5	Jowett, B. *Dialogues of Plato.* New York: Random House, 1937, vol. I, p. 475.
	12	Leff, Gordon. *Medieval Thought*: St. Augustine to Ockham. Hammondsworth: Penguin Books, 1958, p. 229.
	28	Gilkey, Langdon. *Religion and the Scientific Future.* New York: Harper and Row, 1970.
	33	Greeley, Andrew. *Unsecular Man: The Persistence of Religion.* New York: Schocken Books, 1972.
	33	Montifiore, Hugh. *Christian Believing.* London: SPCK Press, 1975, p. 145.
275	39	Bridgman, Percy. "Quo Vadis." *Daedalus,* Winter, 1958, pp. 25 ff.
276	11	Meland, Bernard E. *Fallible Forms and Symbols.* Philadelphia: Fortress Press, 1976, p. xi.
	26	Mitchell, Basil, ed. *Faith and Logic: Oxford Essays in Philosophical Theology.* Boston: Beacon Press, 1958.
	32	Greenslet, Ferris. *Under the Bridge.* Boston: Houghton Mifflin Company, 1954.
277	10	Ward, Barbara. *Spaceship Earth.* New York: Columbia University Press, 1966, p. vii.

3. Can the Critical Way Be Institutionalized?

278	8	Whitehead, Alfred North. *Religion in the Making.* New York: The Macmillan Co., 1927, p. 147.
	32	Peter, Laurence J., and Hull, Raymond. *The Peter Principle.* New York: William Morrow and Co., 1969, p. 7.

Page Line

279 2 Parkinson, C. Northcote. *Parkinson's Law.* Boston: Houghton Mifflin Co., 1957, p. 2.

19 Marty, Martin E. "God and Mammon Department: Holy Spirit Division." *Christian Century,* Nov. 15, 1972, p. 1171.

280 5 Jowett, B., op. cit., *Apology,* p. 404.

9 Ibid., p. 412.

38 Freud, Sigmund. *The Future of an Illusion.* p. 87.

281 7 Einstein, Albert. Quoted in Fritz Kahn. *Design of the Universe.* Crown Publishers, p. 127.

9 Heraclitus. *The Fragments,* No. 80. In Milton C. Nahm, ed. *Selections from Early Greek Philosophy.* 3rd ed. New York: Appleton, Century, Crafts, Inc., 1947, p. 93.

22 McIlwain, Charles Howard, op. cit., p. 370.

283 8 Pattern of male dominance through the concept of God: see chapter XIII, §1.

8 Luecke, Jane Marie. "The Dominance Syndrome." *Christian Century,* April 27, 1977, p. 407.

284 3 Religion: What is it? The literature on this question is enormous.

43 Baumer, F. L., op. cit., chap. 1.

285 12 Peterson, Merrill D. *Thomas Jefferson and the New Nation: A Biography.* New York: Oxford University Press, 1970, pp. 7, 12.

CHAPTER 18

THE WAY LEADS ON

288 25 Santayana, George. *Poems.* London: Constable & Co., Ltd., 1922, p. 5.

289 5 Newton, Isaac. Quoted in H. McLachlan. *Religious Opinions of Milton, Locke and Newton,* p. 217.

13 Popkin, Richard H. *History of Scepticism,* p. ix.

1. In Search of the Beautiful

290 9 Clark, Kenneth M. "An Art Historian's Apology." Address before the Cosmos Club, Washington, D.C., April 12, 1971, p. 12.

26 MacLeish, Archibald. *Poetry and Experience.* Boston: Houghton Mifflin Co., 1961.

37 Leroi-Gourham, André. *Treasures of Prehistoric Art.* Trans. by Norbert Guterman. New York: Harry N. Abrams, 1967.

291 5 Solzhenitsyn, Aleksandr I. "Art for Man's Sake." Nobel Prize Lecture, *New York Times,* Dec. 30, 1972.

15 Jowett, B., op. cit., vol. I, *Symposium,* p. 335.

292 26 Campbell, Joseph. *The Mythic Image.* Princeton: Princeton University Press, 1974.

293 2 Fromm, Erich. *Psychoanalysis and Religion.* New Haven: Yale University Press, 1950, p. 76.

13 Unity of all religions: many writers in many disciplines assert this. A few samples:

Agar, Herbert, et al. *The City of Man.* New York: The Viking Press, 1941, pp. 46 ff.

Dewey, John. *A Common Faith.* New Haven: Yale University Press, 1934, p. 87.

Smith, Huston. *The Forgotten Truth.* New York: Harper & Row, 1976.

Page Line

2. VALUE

294 43 Perman, Dagmar. "The Girard Street Project." Washington: All Souls Church, Unitarian, 1964.

295 5 FAF, pp. 169.

30 Anshen, R. N., ed. *The Moral Principles of Action: Man's Ethical Imperative.* New York: Harper & Bros., 1953.

31 Values: as with so many of these topics, the literature is enormous. The following are a few recent typical examples:

Fried, Charles. *An Anatomy of Values.* Cambridge: Harvard University Press, 1970.

Maslow, Abraham. *Motivation and Personality.* 2nd ed. New York: Harper & Row, 1970, p. ix.

Stern, Alfred. *The Search for Meaning, Philosophical Vistas.* Memphis: Memphis State University Press, 1971.

Taylor, Richard. *Good and Evil.* London: The Macmillan Company, 1970.

296 24 "In Memory of Edwin Silas Wells Kerr." 1976. Privately published by the Phillips Exeter Academy Press, Exeter, N.H.

31 Swain, Joseph Ward. *The Ancient World.* New York: Harper and Bros., 1950, vol. I, p. 121.

297 10 Dewey, John, op. cit., p. 87.

10 Cauthen, Kenneth, op. cit., pp. 195–6.

17 Einstein, Albert. In Philip Frank, op. cit., p. vii.

29 *New York Times,* April 30, 1975.

29 *New York Times,* May 25, 1975.

299 27 Clough, Shepard B. *Basic Values of Western Civilization.* New York: Columbia University Press, 1961.

3. THE ULTIMATE

300 37 Hartshorn, Charles. *Creative Synthesis and Philosophical Method.* London: SCM Press, 1970.

302 6 Howlett, Duncan. "The Devil." Pamphlet Sermon, Boston: First Church in Boston, May 2, 1954.

303 3 Exodus 80:7.

7 Arberry, A. J., op. cit., pp. 1, 2, 45 ff.

9 Simonson, Conrad. *In Search of God.* Boston: Pilgrim Press, 1974.

15 Lippmann, Walter, op. cit., p. 27.

20 Huxley, Julian. "Knowledge, Morality & Destiny." *Psychiatry,* May, 1951, p. 4, makes the common mistake of supposing that "God" means for everyone what it means for him.

21 The following books express in various ways the view of the nature of the ultimate I am proposing. The list is arranged chronologically:

Feuerbach, Ludwig. *The Essence of Christianity.* Trans. by George Eliot, New York: Harper & Bros., 1957, pp. 270–1.

Schleiermacher, Friedrich. *On Religion: Speeches to Its Cultured Despisers.* Trans. by John Oman, introduction by Rudolf Otto. New York: Harper & Bros., 1958, pp. xviii–xix.

Balfour, A. J. *Foundations of Belief.* New York: Longmans Green & Co., 1895.

Page	Line	
		Randall, J. H. and J. H., Jr., *Religion and the Modern World.* New York: Frederick A. Stokes Co., 1929, pp. 237, 245, 247.
		Montague, William P. *Belief Unbound.* New Haven: Yale University Press, 1930.
		Bixler, Julius Seelye. *Religion for Free Minds.* New York: Harper & Bros., pp. 157 and 172.
		Anshen, Ruth Nanda, ed. *Moral Principles of Action: Man's Ethical Imperative.* New York: Harper & Bros., 1953.
		Goodenough, E. R. *Toward a Mature Faith.* New York: Prentice-Hall, Inc., 1955, p. 1.
		Randall, J. H., Jr. *The Role of Knowledge in Western Religion.* Boston: Starr King Press, 1958, pp. 140–142.
		Wieman, Henry Nelson. *Man's Ultimate Commitment.* Carbondale: Southern Illinois University Press, 1958.
		Maslow, Abraham. *Motivation and Personality.* 2nd ed. New York: Harper & Row, 1970, p. xi.
		Eiseley, Loren. *Invisible Pyramid.* New York: Charles Scribner's Sons, 1970, pp. 154–5.
305	14	Psalms 139:7–10.
	28	Dewey, John, op. cit., p. 20.
	33	Taylor, Francis. *Good and Evil.* London: The Macmillan Co., 1970, p. 268.
306	6	Thompson, Francis. "The Hound of Heaven." In W. H. Auden and Norman Holmes Pearson, eds., op. cit., p. 564.
	8	Isaiah 52:7.
307	19	Geballe, Thomas R. "The Central Parsec of the Galaxy." *Scientific American,* July, 1979, pp. 60 ff.
308	38	Genesis 31:24–32.
309	7	Genesis 28:10–17.
	21	Wieman, Henry Nelson, op. cit., p. 305.
310	1	Cather, Willa. *Not Under Forty.* New York: Alfred A. Knopf, 1922, p. 99. At several points in her writings, Willa Cather observes: "The end is nothing. The road is all."

INDEX OF NAMES

INDEX OF SUBJECTS